First published in 2022 by PRESS DIONYSUS LTD in
London 127 Putham Road, SW156 London

www.pressdionysus.com

# PRESS DIONYSUS
## 2022

PRESS DIONYSUS

First published in 2022 by PRESS DIONYSUS LTD in the UK, 167, Portland Road, N15 4SZ, London.

www.pressdionysus.com

Paperback

ISBN: 978-1-913961-18-3

# Making of Elements
# The Collector's Offer

## By Joseph Doliczny

PRESS DIONYSUS

Press Dionysus •
ISBN- 978-1-913961-18-3
© 2022 Press Dionysus
First Edition, August 2022, London


Cover art: MiblArt


Press Dionysus LTD, 167, Portland Road, N15 4SZ,
London
• e-mail: info@pressdionysus.com
• web: www.pressdionysus.com

## About the Author

Joseph Doliczny was born in West Germany into a forces family. When his parents split he moved to South West England to the countryside. Without much to do, Joseph spent a lot of his time reading and writing short stories. His primary school teacher wrote 'most likely to be the next Philip Pullman' on his certificate when he graduated.

Although maintaining a keen interest in creative writing, Joseph went on to study Sociology at University. His desire to better understand different societies and their make-up, drove him to throw himself into his academic work. When he left university, he then travelled the world, visiting over 4 continents to see his studies in practice. Since then he has had a goal to visit every country in Europe, which he is now 65% through.

His wife Georgina has always accompanied him on his travels and is also a keen reader. When Joseph started writing *Making of Elements*, she both encouraged and helped him develop his writing (especially with his grammar). Joseph is also supported by his mother, an established author amongst many other things. She has helped give him the belief that he can follow in her footsteps.

Joseph has always had interests in many different genres, but fantasy has always been his true love in the literature world. As a teenager, he developed a rare brain condition named Dystonia. At one point it was thought to be terminal. It took all the support of his family to get him through, but also his passion for reading. Being able to pick up a book in the waiting room or hospital bed and disappear to another world is why he loves writing. He now looks to create that escapism for others through his first book. Also with the introduction of his first daughter, Olivia, he wants to be able to make her proud and show her anything is possible.

# A Special Thank You

To Olivia, for being the eternal sunshine in my heart.

To Georgie, for making my life so much more.

To Mum, for guiding me every single day.

To Alex, Daniel, Laura, Kate & Rob, for filling my life with so much laughter and love.

To Grandpa, for always being there and all the French adventures.

To Nana, for always showing me kindness.

To my aunties & uncles, for all the love from afar.

To my loyal degenerates, brothers until the end of time.

To Dad, for all your faults you always encouraged me to read.

## Disabled Readers

I have generalised Dystonia. It is a movement disorder which causes part of my body to spasm. For many years my condition consumed me. It was all I thought about every day. It became so bad I eventually withdrew from 'normal' life completely, until I didn't leave the house.

Through spending a long time on my mind set, plus tons of support from friends and family, I became more than my condition.

I set myself realistic goals to work towards. The first was to walk to the end of my drive, until it became to publish my first novel. Now I am not saying you have to publish a book, but try to focus on the things that make you happy. Do not let your disability define you, as you are so much more.

**The kingdom of Eldertude is dying.**

Thangrath's curse continues to eat away at the people, turning them into something far more sinister. All attempts of containment have failed. Alliances have broken down to the point where war now looms on the horizon.

Faith in King Vidal's reign has dwindled. Even his council is plotting against him. The Collector, the richest man in the Borrowed Lands, delivers a message. A promise of salvation, but it comes with a heavy price. The king sends his only son, Prince Zander, in a search for answers.

Others in the kingdom are merely trying to survive. Famine and poverty are rife. Many have the added burden of hiding their sick, because if discovered, they are sent beyond the gates of Hellrous, into the zones.

Alone in the desert, the Yellow Templar continue their rituals. They worship the tomb of a demon, whilst gathering more slaves. If the seal is broken, the world will fall into a new nightmare.

# Character List

## Eldertude Kingdom

Considered one of the last great kingdoms of the Borrowed Lands, Eldertude is often referred to as the Green Kingdom. Founded by the great elders, they summoned the very trees of Red Claw Jungle to twist and turn to form the castle, which still stands today. The roots and grasses however never grew back.

King Vidal, the Bloodline to the Founder and Ruler of Eldertude

- Queen Hermenize, the Second Crown
- Prince Zander, heir to the throne

General Balder, the commander of the Eldertude Army and Hammers

- Hector, the last child

Hammers, the specialist military unit of elite warriors

- the Lead, team leader of Hammers
- the Lead's Hand, second in command
- Latch, member of the Hammers

Castle Workers

- Luca, personal assistant to Prince Zander
- Moorwell, teacher of Linking, keeper to the Panthers

Kantra, resident of Eldertude far outside the castle walls

- Maxen, her half brother
- Harlow, grandmother to Maxen

## Hellrous

In a bid to contain the disease, the Kingdom of Eldertude built Hellrous. Anyone considered touched with the black mark is relocated here by law. Their families too must follow if they wish to have any type of contact. Based on how far turned an individual is, they are moved through the different zones of Hellrous, with the worst being sent to the centre. Every day, Healers travel into Hellrous to administer treatment and try to maintain some type of order.

Erica, novice Healer and resident of Eldertude

- Darian, team leader of Erica's Healer unit
- Mills, novice Healer and friend of Erica
- Otto, brother of Mills
- Dace, mother to Mills and Otto
- Leo, resident of Hellrous and friend of Erica

The Black Hand, rebel group and unofficial representatives of Hellrous

- Carmen, leader of the Black Hand
- Lensa, member of the Black Hand

The Masked Healers, the only unit allowed to the centre of Hellrous

## Neptulus

Known as the floating city, Neptulus has drifted away from the great kingdom it once was. During the breakup of the union, its sailors took to the ocean to escape the black mark. A city made up of nothing but ships and platforms all connected together. Many years at sea has taken its toll on the proud Tulus people.

Captain Holston, the captain to the entire Tulus fleet

## Yellow Templar

Alone in the desert, away from the eyes of the world is the Yellow Templar. They spend each day and night worshiping the tomb of the infamous, preforming rituals in a belief that one day the seal will break. In the meantime, they grow their numbers through a steady stream of slaves pickpocketed from the world. This is done via their fragile partnership with the Nkye, who are another race looking to return to a former glory.

Thangrath, that who turns the sky and souls black

Malum, leader of the Yellow Templar and voice of the Followers

Rexis, slave

   - Terra, younger sister and slave

# Contents

# *Chapter 1*

"The cancer can no longer be controlled, not in our cities and our hearts. Hellrous is at its breaking point. Soon the people will turn; their rage is already ravaging the foundations of this great kingdom. If we do not find a cure soon, there will be no kingdom, no world left to salvage from the darkness."

Each word echoed around Sanctuary Chamber, as the advisor held up his frail hands, draped in white. Heads around the chamber dropped. Slumping in near defeat and desperation, King Vidal quickly straightened himself.

"Fear is the biggest disease of them all. If we start to let it fester among the leadership, it was spread as surely as the cancerous dead. Get a hold of yourself, all of you!" King Vidal roared, thumping the exquisitely crafted tree trunk, which was the ancient throne of the Kingdom of Eldertude.

Sullen faces stared back at the king, who chose not to see

them. Rather, he focused on the last of the flames, dwindling in the fireplace.

"How are we doing on supplies for the castle?" King Vidal inquired.

"New livestock arrives today. We will be well fed for the days to come, but it is becoming increasingly difficult to get anything through Red Claw Jungle. The skirmishes and traps laid by the Waro are now a daily occurrence. We risk being cut off entirely. Even the stock from Darnspur is at risk."

"I thought we had an agreement with the savages?"

"The Waro do not act as one. You can shake a thousand hands and make a smile with each, but the next day you will still wake up with thorns in your kneecaps," replied the advisor.

Frustrated again, King Vidal demanded, "Do the people outside these castle walls do nothing to sustain themselves? Must they always be spoon fed?"

"Crops will not grow as the land continues to offer little. People have nothing to sell, and now, nothing to eat. Even if they did, who could they trade with?"

King Vidal leapt up and started to march down the Sanctuary Chamber. The chamber was centred around the long, polished banquet table at which the advisors sat. Hands behind his back, the king assumed his position as the master impatiently waiting for his pupils to impress him. There were only mutterings, no eye contact, and much fidgeting of feet.

Dominating the chamber was an ancient Acacia, with all its leaves stripped off. Attached to its many branches were life sized portraits of the former rulers of the Kingdom of Eldertude. From above, some of the leaves which formed the ceiling of the chamber had loosened. The moonlight shone down through the gaps, directly onto the portrait of the king, giving the painting a silver glow.

A man at his peak, the king stood tall and strong, his fine structure cast a shadow over all who stared up at it. Long hair with rough features under a well-kept beard, the face of King Vidal was one of both obligation and gloom. On his left cheek, a spiral had been scorched into the skin; the everlasting symbol represented a long-lasting leadership. He was dressed in the official Eldertude's colours of yellow and red, with a cape bearing the symbolic Eldertude tree of valour.

King Vidal had his hand firmly around the Staff of Luntive. Crafted from the original bark, its gaps were filled in with gold, with glorious gemstone embedded at the top of the staff. A dark and faded emerald held in place by branches, it looked to be harbouring energy that bubbled on its surface.

In only one portrait did the gemstone shine bright, with a magnificent and encapsulating glow that would act as a beacon for an entire race. Rightfully, it had been given the name of the heart of the kingdom. The well-lit stone was not in the hands of the king, but in the hands of the founder of Eldertude.

They had been the only person to ever unleash the power of the stone. It had pulled up a huge part of the jungle from the ground. Trees, bushes and flowers all had been summoned and bound together to form the castle, to which Eldertude had grown from.

King Vidal snarled at all before him. "That which lies beyond the black gates of Hellrous continues to pollute our streets. We cannot turn on each other like the others before us. The sooner we can rid ourselves of this cancerous affliction the better."

A deep voice joined the conversation.

"With all our focus on ourselves, we forget that our 'friend', the Captain, continues to grow his fleet. The last of the alliances have dissolved to nothing but dust. My question of war is not the likelihood of when, but who would become the first to bite."

From afar, it would be easy to mistake the general for a bear, as he had the same frame and the amount of hair to match. Unlike the groomed style of the king, the beard of General Balder was overgrown like a long-forgotten garden. His face was worn, a veritable road map of scars, pits, and lines, damaged all over, but none more so than on the left side of his head. A scar going from front to back. It was an injury that would have ended most men. His thick black hair had never fully grown back.

To add to the marks across his body, a cross had been dug into the general's forehead, the reward for letting everyone know that this was the leader of Hammers. Even in his military uniform, he always looked scruffy, his grubby shirt barely stretching over his large belly.

"The Captain does not have the bottle to challenge our great castle."

"When was the last time you two last spoke?" General Balder asked. King Vidal turned away and sighed. "Maybe the Queen could reach out."

There was a shuffle in the chairs from those seated around these two giants of men, as the king turned to glare at General Balder, who boldly held his gaze.

"There is one more point for you to consider. The Day of Dontés is fast approaching. My soldiers are starting to look like animals trapped in a cage, biding their time until they are free to cause devastation and ruin. They train hard every day, unlike the one who is the main event."

"He is simply lazy," King Vidal muttered, whilst inwardly sighing at the reluctance of his own son to show up as the warrior everyone needed and expected him to be.

General Balder did not hold back to save the king's fatherly feelings, "Maybe he is, I am not directly involved in the boy's training. From what I have been told, he rarely turns up, and when he does, it is with half a heart. I believe though he is scared; you must give him the courage to ready himself."

Snarling, the king replied, "Do not start lecturing me on my parenting; he has a weakness inside of him weighing down all his potential. I have tried to drag him up to a standard to be proud of, yet I am starting to believe it is out of my control."

"He cannot fail; you know as the heir to the throne he is expected to win. If the vote goes the wrong way, somebody else could be sitting on that tree stump. Failure in front of the people could mean a grizzly death," the general said.

"If the prince embarrasses the royal bloodline on the Day of Dontés, I will execute him myself."

Both men fell silent. Even after all these years, the general still struggled to know when the king was joking.

"Go get him."

"The Prince, sir?"

"Yes, right away," King Vidal ordered. One of the servant workers slid out of the room. The king stood arms crossed as everyone remained silent yet alert. Eventually, in shuffled the young, thin Prince Zander. Patchy brown hair hid most of his pale face. Yet it was not long enough to cover the scar on his on cheek.

"You asked for me, Father."

"This is Sanctuary Chamber. Here, I am not your father, but the king and you shall refer to me accordingly," boomed King Vidal. "Why have you been avoiding combat training?"

Zander let out a cough. Some of the advisors pulled up cloth over their mouths. King Vidal asked the question again as the prince anxiously searched for an explanation.

General Balder simply poked at the fire, which caused shadows to dance across the walls, like jesters supporting the main act, the hanging of a prince.

"I have been training alone, my king," Zander offered in a shaky voice.

The general grunted.

"Is that so. What in, duel sabers, long sword, archery?" King Vidal questioned.

"All of them," Zander snapped. King Vidal narrowed his eyes.

"Not to speak the truth in this chamber can be considered treason."

Zander spluttered again, a pain now throbbing in his chest. He could feel the advisors circling like wolves, making him shrink further into the ground. He dared not tell the true stories of where most days were spent.

Another pair of beady eyes watched from afar. They tilted sideways as the moonlight revealed a pink tinge to the otherwise white feathers. They came from a bird, resting on a branch just outside the chamber. Tired from the long journey, it could not shake off the gold tassels and bells attached to both feet.

"Look."

There were shouts from Sanctuary Chamber, every man and woman was now on their feet.

"It's a Snow Pelican" yelled one of the guards.

"Catch it, now" King Vidal demanded.

Sensing the sudden animation, it opened both wings ready to return to the sky. During its rest though, soldiers had slyly moved onto the walkway ahead. Ropes and netting were duly cast, and the Snow Pelican was trapped.

It took several men to drag the bird into the chamber, kicking and squawking as it went. All present gathered around intently as the king looked to the general. Causally, Balder opened the bird's large beak and fished around with his hand. Inside was a lump of blue wax, coated in saliva and scales. The bird was then released, and frantically retreated to the highest branch on the acacia tree.

"There's only one person left in the Borrowed Lands who would deliver a message like that," said the general, breaking open the wax which had been protecting the scroll. He handed it to King Vidal, who wiped both hands before clearing his throat.

*"The Collector has uncovered the way to stop the infliction, to live disease free surrounded by life's luxuries. Send only the pure, the most cherished of all. For we all can become queens and kings, safe from disease, cured of the world's darkness.*

*Whatever the price may be, it is worth double."*

## *Chapter 2*

"They give you a part of history. No price could ever amount to what it is worth. With it holds the power to stand with the royal bloodline, one that needs you right now. Otherwise death might be upon them, or worse. How many times have I found it tucked away in a sock?" Luca thought as he rushed back inside.

The large clay room was practically empty— an open circular space curved upwards to the chimney that nested above. The style of the house was common and referred to as a Pilpot. In the centre was a large fire basket, which hung off hooks from the ceiling. It could only be reached by one of the rings that ran around the edge. The single bed was on the highest platform; it overlooked a small dining table covered in trinkets.

Digging into a pile of clothes, Luca started to launch items through the air. A boot landed on the table and collided with a teapot. As it split in two, it snapped Luca out of his destructive spell. Picking up a broken piece in a state of mourning, a smile erupted. Inside the teapot was a leaf infused in glass and studded with tiny diamonds. Giving it a clean Luca then pinned the leaf to the centre of his chest.

Outside, it was now morning. The two suns soared into the newborn sky, breaking the humble silence of the night. An everlasting sea of blue, soft and gentle, was now simply a backdrop to these newly arisen rulers of the sky. Both suns were powerful enough to carry the responsibility of light on their own. This much was proven when there had only been one. Rather than existing in constant rivalry, they worked in a complementary partnership. As one was a red slumbering giant, the other a smaller blue vortex.

Dust clouds floated past. Parents beckoned their children back inside, pleading for them to stay put. Luca joined the steady stream of workers. There was little conversation during the morning march. Each footprint caused the path to sink a little deeper in the mud. Sat underneath the makeshift cover, elderly residents silently drew heavily on the pipes fixed in their teeth, whilst slowly fanning themselves. Sprawled out in front of them was a collection of tools or boots for sale.

The workers' progress was stopped; a large Pilpot now blocked the path. Formed from the clay and mud of the barren landscape, these Pilpots would fit into any free space and sprout up overnight. After the formation of the evergreen castle, this neighbourhood was a real contrast with all its caverns and drops. The landscape had been uprooted, all the trees and bushes gone, replaced by nothing but mud and dust.

There was not a hint of greenery left amongst the Pilpots. Luca and the other workers were forced to clamber over a mound and slide down. It was much steeper than many had bargained for. Luca could no longer concentrate on keeping his uniform tidy as he joined the others forced to attack the slope. With no real control and picking up pace, Luca ran straight into a wall of mud.

With a heavy thud, Luca rebounded off it and collapsed in a heap. Sitting squarely on the dry mud, with gusts of dust surrounding him, the dirt was finding a place to settle on his uniform. Too many days ended up this way. Not only would he turn up late and filthy for work, but today he had the added burden, of the life of someone he cared for dearly being in jeopardy.

Others hit the same Pilpot wall. From behind it appeared the Pilpot's fuming resident, angrily waving his stick at those who simply shrugged and walked on. Pointing to the inside of the hut, parts of the ceiling were now on the floor. Luca knew that there was no time to help with repairs, as the life of the Prince was at stake. Searching in his pocket for a much quicker solution, Luca's fingers rang along the rough edges of a silver coin.

"That will do, give it here."

"Look, I am sorry about your home, but I cannot just give you this. Do you have any other smaller pieces?"

The old man shook his head.

"How about you take one of the items I am selling. The rest will be for the damages. I want that coin."

People stopped and stared at Luca, their eyes following the silver. The sizing up of the silver piece carrier had begun. On a dusty blanket, there was not much to offer other than tobacco. Most matched the standard itinerary, a pile of beads and necklaces that had missing pieces, pocketknives, and a used handkerchief.

Yet, in amongst it all, a square face caught Luca's eye. Lying on its side was a little tin figure with a square body and two stubby arms that were rectangular. The arms stood stiff at the side as if standing to attention. Its head was square except for the forehead that had been rounded. There were little markings on the figure; on the chest was the symbol of life. It was the expression on the face that had caught Luca's attention. One that said save me, I do not know where I belong, but I know it is not here.

"It will act as a beacon when you are drowning in the black sea," the old man's tone was deadly serious.

The tin man was now in Luca's hand; as he fiddled with it, there seemed to be spring at the back.

"Only once! It works only once."

"Fine, okay, here is your money."

The coin was devoured.

"So, what about my change?"

There was the faintest hint of a smile. Luca tilted his head and sighed. Whilst he walked away, he could feel the old man searing two holes into the back of his head. The incident had cost him precious time. There was no more of a brutal reminder of this fact, than the landmark which lay ahead.

The black gates of Hellrous, monstrously tall, hung in the distance like an approaching thunderstorm. Built into rock, the gates blocked any entrance to the largest cavern at the bottom of the valley.

In faded white paint, the bold words of the three famous HHH were printed:

*Here is Held the Heroes*

Underneath it read.

*They tell you that Homes, Help, and Honour is inside. Any*

*Hope has been strangled out of the residents. They have been Hanged in darkness.*

The scribbled words in red stood out on the faded black. No attempt had been made to hide them. The message was fitting for what lay beyond the gates. Every time Luca passed Hellrous on the way to the castle, the mere sight of it caused his soul to shudder. Eventually, he came over the last ridge to the wide road leading up to the castle. Although the view never changed, without fail, the air from Luca's chest would react in shock.

Piercing the clouds were the mighty forest walls. Linked by the many arms of their branches, they clung to each other to create an unbreakable circle of protection. Grand Sequoia trees, which were as old as time itself, offered security to whoever was lucky enough to stand behind them.

Their roots were huge living tentacles, which dived in so deep that they were wrapped around the world's core. From the ground up, they already had many inhabitants to protect. Hundreds of thin branches rang across the face of the walls. In amongst the vibrant plants and flowers was a network of burrows and nests.

The top of the trees was dotted with thousands upon thousands of rich green leaves. Each leaf looked as if had been the lifetime achievement of a stonemason, crafting the plants from an emerald gemstone and then carefully placing them into position. The healthy stature of each leaf meant that they were magnets to the golden rays of the suns. As the rays hit the surface, it created a radiant glow all around the castle.

Behind the mighty walls was a castle built completely from nature's greatest gardens. All flora which would usually be found in a rich forest, had come together to form the courtyards and towers. There were buildings made entirely from flowers and bushes that had been shaped and trained to make stairwells.

The huge roots of the trees ran around the outer circle of the castle. Immense in size, far taller and wider than a crowd of people, the biggest, most magnificent tree had been hollowed out. The result was a living space. Doorways and windows had been cleverly formed in the earth homes, creating more life in the walls of the castle.

Luca caught his breath and hurried down the hill. He joined the circus parade that waited outside the castle gates. Each morning, an array of noise and colour would assemble outside, waiting to be admitted; it would bring both bedlam and service.

A large group huddled together in their matching, golden robes. They were all well-groomed and thin individuals, who moved elegantly and very much kept to themselves. They murmured to one other, pointing out everyone else's faults and apportioning blame to all the other castle workers. Few looked at Luca as he made his way through the crowd. None of them had the diamond leaf badge.

Separating the golden group, much to their distaste, was a herd of Ballistic cows. A local herder and his three young children were making a poor attempt to control them. The cows were the natural food source of choice. Easily bred, with their distinctive two heads, they ate two-fold, resulting in them becoming larger than most animals. The problem was that double the heads meant twice the personality. Like siblings, they constantly nipped and squealed at one other, often breaking into fights. With good food becoming a rarity, the cow's worth increased every day. Mercenaries were never far away; ready to protect the herd with their lives as long as the gold kept coming.

Hidden amongst the visitors' parade for the castle were the beggars. Slowly, they joined the long line of gardeners, merging in with those in their work overalls. The castle guards were waiting, ready to drag out any of these unwelcome invaders. Those who slipped through would spill over the castle, searching for any valuables that they could lay their hands on.

A boom in the form of a trumpet echoed through the streets. All the fidgeting and shoving stopped as everyone focused their attention on the gate. The huge doorway to the castle was gradually being opened. Castle guards watched in anticipation of the flood of noise and disorder heading inwards. Each guard was smartly dressed in highly polished, sleek emerald and silver armour. Through the pointed helmets, the sentinels narrowed their vision, suspecting everyone and everything that entered the castle.

Meanwhile, Prince Zander stood staring out of the moon shaped opening. The kingdom had started to thrive under the morning suns. With the buildings being as much alive as a dense forest, there was always an army of gardeners needed to tend to the castle's wellbeing. Seeing the movement below him, reminded him that there was still life in the world, which had seemed to become a faded memory in the dull hours he was forced to spend in the classroom.

Orchestrating the stuffy classroom atmosphere Zander so detested, was the young but dull lecturer, Loomis. He was smartly dressed and a true product of the castle teachings. By sucking up to the castle elites, he had been given the privilege of teaching their children. Zander despised him and was sure that the feeling was mutual. For starters, Loomis let all the other students sit two desks away from Zander, as encouraged by their parents.

Water ran down onto the lecturer's desk, pushing rocks that had been piling up on one of the many levels. It was a waterfall that was used to tell the time, made of leaves; the twigs held up rocks which fell once the water had built up, showing the change in the hour. Only when the time trickled onto the part of the day reserved for history, did Loomis become animated.

"So where was I, ah I remember. The day the sweltering fire dropped from the sky to both unite the Borrowed Lands and divide it. The impact sent shockwaves through the four pillars. Earth, Water, Fire and Wind all represented around the crater, as the people peered into the huge balls of dust, waiting for what mystery to reveal itself."

"That is not where we are," interrupted one of the students.

"Ah, are we not," Loomis stumbled. "Was it the outbreak we were talking about, the last days of the union, or the rise of..."

Before anyone could answer, the classroom burst open. Covered in dust and out of breath, Luca had appeared.

"What is the meaning of this intrusion?" Loomis demanded.

Luca spluttered out, "The prince, your treatment... I was late, if you do not take your dose."

The others in the class jumped out of their desk, backing against the furthest away wall.

"He is going to make us all cursed."

"We have got a monster in here."

"I do not want to die in Hellrous."

The students continued to protest as the lecturer tried to

calm them down. Zander rolled his eyes and walked toward Luca.

"Do you honestly think mother would not have a backup? I am fine, Luca."

Insults were still being thrown, the other pupils confirming their parents' fears that he should never be left with them.

"Do not worry, we are leaving," Zander retorted. Loomis did not stop him.

"I am sorry, Zander; I should have known you would be okay. There has never really been anyone else to treat you," Luca said.

"They are already terrified of me; do not give them more of a reason. I cannot always be reliant on you."

Luca began to apologise again.

"Do not repeat yourself; you know I hate that."

Luca could only open and close his mouth like a fish. The hallway was formed by hundreds of thin trees curved upwards to create a ring.

"My responsibilities are to ensure you are in the best health possible."

"One day, I will be king, and it will be my job to lead the whole of Eldertude. How am I supposed to do that when I cannot even look after myself?" Zander said with a gloomy look on his face.

The pair bundled into Zander's room, letting out a sigh of relief. Orange leaves kept in a permanent state of autumn built the walls, giving the chambers a warm and welcoming glow. It was an enormous room which reeked of royalty and privilege, with many different types of furniture in an attempt to tackle some of the open space. Sofas, chairs, tables, wardrobes and dressers, all of the highest quality— handcrafted and completely immaculate.

Before either of them could speak, the door opened again and in walked the Queen of Eldertude. A mixture of beauty and wisdom, she glided elegantly into the room, wearing a long, black dress. It was the same colour as her knee length hair. Her slim body wore as much jewellery as it could carry. Around her neck was a golden chain that held a huge purple gem. Each finger had unique rings, diamonds or sapphires, all magnificent pieces of art in their own right.

"You are not in class," Queen Hermenize spoke softly.

"Mother, how did you know we were here so quickly?" Zander asked.

"The plants which shape this castle always whisper to me where you are," Queen Hermenize smiled.

"I left class because I was feeling ill; Luca came and escorted me back to my room."

Luca's face lifted.

"They were happy to get rid of me though; the rest of the class still sits one desk away from me."

"You should have demanded they sit closer. Do not let yourself be pushed around anymore," Queen Hermenize replied. The prince's head dropped.

"It is not your fault; the teacher should be taking charge. I will talk to him again."

"Do not get involved," Zander snapped. The two of them fell silent; Luca attempted to break the frosty atmosphere.

"At least you do not have to go back to the class today, although there is defence training..." he trailed off seeing Zander's face.

"Luca, what is the schedule for the rest of your day?" Queen Hermenize asked.

"My lady, Queen Hermenize, I am still required to help with the cleaning of the stables. Some repairs are going on with the main tower I may need to assist with, and then preparing the evening treatment chamber for Zander."

The queen stood up.

"Go clean the stables and meet us on the training ground but not for combat. We will make the call; see if we can wake the Circle Dragon."

## *Chapter 3*

Sweat poured down the back of Rexis' neck, back, and legs. Strong rays of light were darting through the cracks in the side of the cart where he lay. His mind was racing as he desperately tried to piece together broken memories. How quickly this wooden box had turned into an oven in the heat. All around Rexis, others were clinging to each other, struggling to hold consciousness. Each shared the same tough skin and weathered features. Along with another similarity, whether it could be seen or not, was the newly found blackness.

Curled up in a corner was a young girl, her blonde hair stiff from the salt air. Rexis was nearly double the age of his sleeping sister and even more so in size. He was tall and athletic, as were most of the young men from his homeland, with thick brown hair and deep yellow eyes.

All around them, people swayed, coughed, and occasionally threw up. It had been night when they had been herded into the back of the dank, heat-ridden cart. The small supply of drinking water had disappeared fast. Rexis was struggling to rouse his sister; the girl had not moved for some time.

"Terra," he whispered. The cart remained silent, with the groaning wheels rumbling in the background. Rexis went to open his mouth again but stopped. There was a silent alertness passing through everyone around him. An electric fear stemming from the same memory they all shared.

The experience had been traumatic from the start—dragged out of their boats by masked kidnappers. Shoved, snarled at, threatened, and hurled into the stinking cart. Complaints about the lack of water and the conditions had riled up the kidnappers. Further threats and curses had brought every one of them to a nervous silence.

The cart came to a stop, heavy feet jumped from the roof. Light came pouring in, blinding those inside.

"Get out, get out."

People whimpered as everyone hastily and clumsily surged out of the wooden cell. Rexis held onto his sister in the rush.

"Get in a line, file up."

Jeers, taunts, and more threats were hurled like balls of hot air, from the vile mouths of the restless kidnappers. They were a sight for sore eyes with no set uniform or matching appearance. Hairstyles ranged from long braided hair to shaven heads. The only thing they had in common was the sinister streak running through them. Half of them were bare chested, wearing nothing but muscle. Their skin was a light shade of orange with brighter marks running in a pattern across their bodies. Some had leather straps running across their chests, with various tools of pain hanging from them.

The kidnappers stood and watched the crowd for a while.

Rexis counted; there were nearly three times as many of them than their captives. One of the prisoners approached demanding answers. He was met with the shake of the head by the one with the scruffy mohawk, going by the name of Kog.

Before the prisoner could repeat himself, Kog snarled and smashed an elbow in his face. The prisoner's nose split and splattered like a ripe melon, all across his sorry face. Kog pointed a sword into the man's chest as he fell painfully to his knees.

"Did we say you could speak? Get back in line."

The bleeding man froze on the spot, his nose gushing red.

"Now," Kog screamed.

The man crawled backwards as others pulled him to his feet. Quickly, the crowd organised themselves. In the middle, Rexis made sure he was next to his sister. The line stood silent, heads down and hands clenched in fear. Before them, lay a vast emptiness with only hot sand and the burning suns for company. Their cart was part of a large convoy of the same make up. The other captives pressed their faces up against the cracks.

Kog strolled down the line.

"It is like you all don't understand."

The sword was waved inches away from the faces.

"We say keep quiet and you are too stupid to obey." He stopped abruptly, a woman in the line burst into tears. Kog leaned closer to her face, only causing her to sob more uncontrollably.

"Did you not hear me?" The tip of his blade was pressed into the young woman's cheek; she let out a yelp.

"See, there you go again."

Kog moved the sword to brush away long black hair.

"Then maybe I should cut off your ears."

A voice suddenly rang out, "Leave her alone."

Everyone held their breath, not wanting to be found to be the one guilty. Kog marched down to inspect the source. It was one of the men with the loudest voices of protest in the cart. He was standing tall and had puffed out his chest. Kog met the eyes of the newborn maverick.

"So our noisy passenger reveals himself."

"You want to scare your prisoners, well pick on one that is up to the challenge," responded Milton.

"Prisoners?" Kog stepped back. "You are not our prisoners, no; something must have given you all the wrong idea."

The other members of his gang chuckled.

Milton came back again saying, "You took me in the middle of the night, grabbed me, threw me…"

"Shut up." Kog raised his sword. "As I was saying, you are not prisoners but passengers. The girl with snot trails running down her face, over here, now."

The young woman, Keti— previously Kog's target— was now so hunched over she was almost crawling. "Don't be scared. There is really no need to fear us."

He put his sword back in the holder.

"You can even leave if you like, being a passenger and all."

Keti and Milton exchanged glances.

"Yes, the both of you, go run off into the sunset together."

"Just like that?" Milton asked.

"The girl too, off you go."

More frowns followed.

"Go!" Kog screamed. The pair saw their opportunity and began to run into the vast open desert. The rest almost could not believe what they were seeing. They felt a hint of the dream of escape creep in.

Milton had no idea what his plan was. In the intense heat, they would not last long. With no refuge in sight, it seemed like suicide. Still better to die in the desert a free man, than to end up meeting the fate their captors had in store for them. He wished though he had not pulled anyone else into it.

With one arm, he was dragging Keti along— now so dehydrated from the sweat and tears; she could barely move her legs. They had not gotten far before Milton allowed himself to take a look back.

"Here we go."

Kog unclipped the straps attached to the belt across his chest. There was a thick leather handle, with thin pieces of rope hanging from either side. Attached to the ropes were iron balls not much bigger than a clenched fist. He held the handle out in front of him, the crowd watching intently. Then with his thumb, Kog flicked a switch, causing thin black spikes to burst out.

Taking a deep breath, Kog gripped both hands around the handle. He began swinging the device from side to side. Back from the left to the right, the whirling became faster and faster. Each of the balls was spinning around Kog's head so fast that they became a blur. Taking one step forward Kog then twisted his entire body, in one movement he let go of the device. Rexis had seen Milton look back just before Kog had started the ritual. Milton and Keti were running in a straight line. Desperate to yell out a warning, Rexis took another look at his sister.

Struggling to believe they were free from any pursuit by their previous captors, Milton strained his ears, but all he heard were his and Keti's feet hitting the sand. They were now struggling determinedly up a steep dune; with the two suns beating down, the suffocating heat made it an even bigger obstacle. A gap had opened up between them, so Milton waited at the top of the dune for Keti to catch up.

"We will take a breath, okay?"

Keti nodded with both hands on her knees. Milton looked back at the crowd in the distance, who were all facing in their direction. All he could pick up was a strange sound fast approaching them. He half closed his eyes and strained to identify it; meanwhile, Keti had regained her breath.

"What is it, Milton?" she whispered

Milton stared directly into the sunlight; the glare was so bad he had to turn away. Just at that moment, the whirling metal blades slammed into Keti's face. Blood, shards of skin, and teeth split, shattered and sprayed everywhere. It was the last image Milton saw, before the other ball hit him square in the temple. A scream came from the crowd. Whilst Kog triumphantly cheered, the rest of his motley crew shouted approval and heaped praise on his fine display of deadly accuracy.

"Now that is how you throw a chain spin!"

"Get back in your carts, NOW. Any more noise out of you, we kill you, and another person we don't like the look of with you. This is a new world in which the dogs obey their masters. We are the Nyke and our word is law."

Rexis could see the people in the cart once more stricken with a terrible fear. He resisted the urge to shout out to rouse the sleeping Terra; he would have to find another way to wake her soon. His train of thought was broken by the sound of loud, screeching wheels. Peering through the cracks, a horrifying realisation dawned on him— they had finally reached the home of their new world.

Pools of vomit washed over Rexis's feet as the prison cart rolled to a halt. The long journey in the heat, mixed in with the fear of the unknown, had twisted the passengers into a wretched state. As the door to the cart slammed down, menacing faces appeared on either side.

"It reeks in here, bloody stinkers," Kog said. "Right, all of you out."

Those inside froze; no one wanted to be the first to move.

"Now," Kog said louder, banging his fist on the side. "They want you to be bound and led in as soon as possible; there is work to be done."

He put a hand on the chain spin hanging from his belt. Fear and revulsion ran through everyone as they simultaneously recalled the brutal attack on Milton and Keti. Reluctantly, they all began to stagger and tumble out of the carriage. Rexis grabbed his sister.

Somehow, the temperature had soared; it felt as if they were walking onto the surface of a sun. Straight away, Rexis was finding it hard to breathe. The heat was so thick it coiled itself around his body; every breath felt like his lungs had inhaled boiling water.

They were in a completely different world to the one they knew; blue waters had been replaced with endless baking sand. The two suns were close to the surface, half hidden by the horizon. If anyone walked far enough, it looked like they would be able to touch them. Other carts were pulling up, all equally packed full of people. As they came out of their wooden prisons, all looked equally traumatised.

The dunes ended at the entrance of the valley; rich orange rocks acted as walls trailing off in both directions. Centre stage was the daunting stone gate. High and mighty, it looked impenetrable. In its centre were two hollowed out circles, home to brightly burning fires. Smoke billowed up into the sky from these fierce burning eyes. Scripture had been carved into the stone surface, giving an overall look of a fierce, livid face, which was deeply offended by the inferior beings about to enter. All the captives were truly stunned by the gates, which peered and burned into their very souls, looking for what it may wish to take from each one of them

A sharp cry of, "Right, stop gawping and get into line," had the prisoners quickly shuffling into position. From behind the group of Nkye appeared a smaller version of them. Rather than orange, they had a dark blue base with stripes of turquoise across their skin. None carried the swagger or threat of the Nkye, as all of them were mute with a blank expression. Wearing only black trousers and thick black boots, they spread out and went about their tasks in a mechanical way.

"Hurry up, Fiddlers," Kog yelled.

In their hands, the Fiddlers were holding long metal poles, with spiked collars which were soon roughly fitted around each of the new prisoners' necks. Tight and uncomfortable, no one was spared from the gnawing discomfort. Rexis' collar felt as if hands had clamped down around his windpipe. All the collars were connected through one long chain, and one thing Rexis could be thankful for was feeling Terra tug at his hand.

"They look like monsters," she whispered; her fragile young face was full of dread.

"Make sure you stay close to me," Rexis gently replied.

Terra almost smiled. Before they could say any more, the chain was yanked hard, pulling both of them forward.

"Get on with it, all of you," Kog yelled. "It is time for the royal greeting."

The globes on the gate began to glow a darker, menacing red. All along the top of valley ridge, Nkye and others could be seen gathering. There was a loud crash as rocks slammed against one other, followed by the sounds of wheels turning. Vibrations shot through everyone and everything as the huge stone gate slowly disappeared underground.

The prisoners' chain began to pull and chafe; rust ground together as they started to trundle towards the entrance. Heavy, doom ridden silence hung in the air. As they were led into the valley, it narrowed quickly; the orange rocks formed around them like a cage, rising high above them and blocking out the sun.

The further they walked, the tighter it got. Soon enough, they had to squeeze themselves through the rock formation. Finally, they reached the end of the path. Those in front of Rexis began to exit the concealed pathway. Gasps followed. The rock laden alley broke out into a huge opening, one massive circle. Its ground dipped like a crater hidden by the valley of rocks that surrounded it.

There was much activity in the open space, and an assortment of makeshift buildings surrounded by tents, were all crammed into a corner. Mining and digging equipment littered the ground. At the opposite end, it was much more organised and well kept. An inner circle area that had been flattened was being used as a courtyard; it ran up into the mouth of the cave. Above the cave entrance carved out of the valley rock, were three balconies that shrunk in size as they ascended. The top was small and hidden from view and even though it was day, many torches burned brightly.

To match the theme, there were fire pits dotted across the crater. Smoke billowed out and the air tasted metallic on Rexis' tongue. The Fiddlers moved around the area like worker ants, whilst the Nyke hung about in groups ostensibly to supervise the others, but mostly looking bored and restless. Many took turns to spit into the open well.

In the centre, with all the inside world orbiting around it, was a sight that captivated all the corners of Rexis's mind. An image he had once seen in perspective drawings and read about in the restricted history books, something people only dared to whisper about. The oval structure before Rexis stood high and firm as the community continued to orbit around it. Its surface was a mix of dark colours, mainly purple and black. Even from where he stood, Rexis could see the symbol of the old union printed across it. There was another scripture on the tomb which mostly read *"the forgotten"*.

The chain was pulled hard, and the march resumed. To see an image that was such a landmark of history exorcised Rexis' mind of all other thoughts. As his feet shuffled through the dirt, he could feel himself physically drawn toward it. The prisoners were led into the smooth circle that stood beneath the balconies. Fiddlers dispersed into the clay houses, dropping the chains as they went. From the edges, Nkye appeared to block all entrances.

The group stood there for a while in silence. It was not long before the murmurs started within the crowd. Their whispers were drowned out by loud drums. A circle around them ignited with bright flames that shot up into the air. The three balconies now became fluid with life. The lowest was filled with young faces; Rexis guessed they were the same age as him. Both sexes had shaven hair and wore the same style of robe— sleeveless with a turtleneck. The colour was a powerful red with a cream border. Their faces had been smeared with a bright red powder. There were no welcoming smiles; all bore the same vicious look.

The second balcony provided the source of the noise. Huge drums wider than the family table, with thick animal skin, pulled tight creating a slick surface. Each instrument had its own keeper; stick in either hand, the line of drummers was split into two groups. They worked in harmony as one would beat the drums while the others would wait, in rhythm. There would be a pause and then the other group would kick in. The continued surge of the tempo sent shockwaves down Rexis' spine; it played devil with his very core.

In between the drummers stood large men, who went through the same motion of raising both arms. In their hands was some sort of rattle, combining with their loud cries to produce a noise to rival the drums. Each man wore little and was covered in black spirals across his body. Their faces were hidden by animal skulls.

Another surge of the fire and the female counterparts were all around them, who roared at the newcomers. As they did, a free hand reached into a leather pouch hanging by their side. Powder was thrown into the fire, causing a flash of different colours; blue and purple flames spat in the direction of the prisoners. Terra hugged her brother's waist.

With the same speed that the drums and dancing had appeared, it ended. Hands raised in anticipation towards the third balcony. Cloaked figures could be seen, the central one much larger than the others. The young ones in red reached up in an impossible hope to be touched by the hand of their revered and adored leader. The leader slowly lowered his hand and with it, a hush descended.

"Followers, Journeymen and the cattle which pull the ropes. Together we thank the suns for providing us with the passion, and fire that clears our minds."

The voice boomed out as it rang in their ears.

"As we receive this glorious gift from the suns, it brings us ever closer to the return. That which will drag down the walls of our enemies, leaving us to sit by his side as the true leaders of the world, the power which shocked the land, one that will flow through us as an extension of the sleeping god we look to awaken. I am Leader Malum; this is the will of the Yellow Templar."

The words were met with roars.

"I see a lot of proud faces and a group of confused ones. How heavy are your chains, the collars around your neck? You have been living with the weight of the mistakes made before you, all bound to follow the same path as a result of those choices. Well, today, that changes. Society did not want you; we have collected you from the outcast pit you had been thrown into. Remember, we have given you the opportunity to become something greater than ever seen before."

Fiddlers had reappeared and were already back to work. With a sharp twist, the bolts in the prisoner's collars came free and fell to the ground.

"We release the chains from your body and your life. Do not believe you are a prisoner here but a follower; prove your worth by hard labour and dedication. It is your greatest chance to become something greater than your current exist-ence. Work to unlock the prison our god has been restricted to and we will all become kings."

The leader gave one final gesture to the crowd before

disappearing into the cave. With his departure, the drums started again, but this time there was no harmony, no rhythm— just frantic noise. Nkye screamed orders into the faces of the prisoners. The sound of drums with the blast of the heat had riled Rexis' senses. Quickly, a fuse burnt short and Rexis was struck hard straight in the face.

# *Chapter 4*

"To really be at one with the beast's movements, they must become an extension of your own, rather than a demand of action."

Luca and the prince both listened intently, leaning forward as if not to let any of the information escape.

"Many think that blind obedience is the key, that a servant is the best soldier. Give your animals freedom; let them roam within the world you create. And why is it we are following the path of the gardener and not the master?"

The question came without expecting much of an answer; the pair was still in a trance. Their trainer, Moorwell, was a short, elderly aged man with a long nose and a thin face to match. His turquoise eyes seemed to peer into the young minds around him. The small man's persona was boosted by the amount of white hair growing from both sides of his head. It had been left to grow wild, causing him to double in size.

His other common attribute was his robe. It was of simple design, a deep, dark purple with a golden pattern boarding the edge. Far too big on him, it hung past his small thin legs and completely over his hands, which were always kept behind his back.

"Because when the master's status is established, it remains throughout the life of the relationship. Although obedience may be achieved, the presence of ownership will always exist throughout any interaction between them. In the heat of battle, that condition can cause a restriction, a coil around the actions. The difference between instinct and direction can be the cause of delay; those few moments are often the difference between life and death."

"I had forgotten that each lesson is more riddles than practice," Luca whispered.

"He blows out more smoke than a Pilpot, but you know it is worth it in the end," Zander replied.

The three stood in the largest training ground placed in the castle's courtyard— a stone circle surrounded by a wooden fence with a single entry gate. It would often draw an audience when the great warriors were practising.

Sat intently was the queen; she fiddled with a rich green leaf plucked from the walls of the castle. The courtyard shared residence with a large stable, a food hall for the workers, a log barn used to store equipment, and some other small buildings. With everyone so busy around the sparing ground, they were hidden in plain sight.

The trainer had two items of importance on either side of him. One was a huge chest, beaten and old. It looked as if it had been dragged from one side of the world to the other. Hidden under a velvet cloak on the other side was a cage. The students were torn between looking into the teacher's eyes and trying to catch a glimpse. Moorwell noticed the wavering battle of attention and smiled.

"But the gardener takes a completely different approach to the relationship. It begins with the seed, the birth. The gardener keeps his plants healthy, lets them grow as it should be with the animal. Grow together, live together, and die together."

The two were only half listing.

"As always, actions say more than words when it comes to the young. Luca, will you do the honours?"

He did not need to be told twice. Grabbing the sheet with both hands, Luca pulled it off with one huge sweep.

The light caused the cage to quite literally roaring to life. As the door came open, a bundle of black fur went charging out. The junior panthers flooded over the sparring ground. Zander and Luca got washed away in the excitement, choosing to chase and run around with them.

The animals were only a few weeks old and still unsteady; they tumbled over both their own feet and each other. Although they all had the same coloured fur that was as dark as the night sky, each had a coloured streak running from one of their eyes to the end of their body. The most common was a powder blue, followed by dark purple and red.

"Come back, stop!" Zander shouted. All the panthers paused and stared at him. Luca gleamed at him in admiration. Zander went to give them another order when they broke the moment of stillness.

Moorwell felt as if he had seen enough. "Resign all of you." Automatically, the animals all stood still.

"It is time for some first-hand guidance."

The trainer brought his hands forward. From the sleeves oozed a long snout littered with whiskers. It flew upwards, spinning around Moorwell's head; sluggish at first, it became more fluid with each stride. The creature was a wild green, with two spike ended tails. Its scales glistened in the sun, arms spread out wide to let the wings breathe. All across its face were tiny white rings, giving it its name of the Circle Dragon.

All the panthers seemed to look up in awe at the creature, as it hung in the sky like a newborn cloud. Moorwell opened up the large chest. "Luca, grab a training sword." He did as instructed, the weapon made from soft steel.

"No glove?" Luca asked.

"Only for the prince."

The two of them looked confused.

"But we have always had one sword and one glove. How are we meant to practice?"

"That is right, and so far all you have beaten is each other whilst I have kept the animals in check. Today will be different; the prince will have the control of the panthers; Luca will have the sword. If he gets overrun, my creature will assist. Pick up a shield though, if you want, Zander."

None of them looked convinced. Luca held up the sword to Zander. Zander slid on the long glove made from leather; it had white patterns stitched into the palm. Hanging from the bottom was a line of bells and charms, used to attract the attention of the panthers. Or as some would believe, dictate their thoughts if used correctly.

Luca and the prince both stood there. Moorwell then nodded in their direction. In swooped the Circle Dragon, putting Luca on his back.

"Get started or face further punishment."

Luca did not need to be told twice and started to swing at Zander. The sword pounded against the face of the shield as Luca chased the ever-dogging prince.

"The advantage is with you, Zander; you just need to use it," Moorwell bellowed. Zander nodded and began to shake the glove.

"Panthers," Zander yelled and got no response; the panthers were locked in a sibling rivalry. Luca swung hard and almost took the prince's head off.

"To the bout."

One of the larger panthers turned to the prince; it had a bouncing orange streak trailing from its face to the tip of its tail.

"Contest, contest," Zander was in desperate need of back-up. With the glove, he tried to direct the animal.

The orange streak panther let out a youthful roar and charged. Accelerating quickly, the animal leapt upwards, but not towards Luca. Zander dived out the way as the animal went straight onto the top of another cat. The panther dug its claws into the black fur of its rival, who spun around, ready for a scrap. With no backup arriving for the prince, he was caught on the arm by the sword.

"Luca, that strike could have broken a bone," Zander yelped. Luca lowered his weapon.

"It is not the time for a break!" Moorwell shouted, and the dragon swooped in again. It picked up Luca, lifting him several feet into the sky before dropping him. Luca brushed himself off then came again.

The orange streak panther was back. Zander cried

frantically as the animal came to his side. He gave another command, this time with more conviction, "Shadow." The panther began to mimic the prince's actions, weaving in between the legs as it dodged the oncoming attacks.

A seed of confidence appeared in Zander, and he tried a move, but it swiftly failed. The animal misjudged the jump and went over Luca's shoulder. Zander reacted and pulled the glove back towards him in a fist; with it the panther jumped into the hip of Luca. He stumbled forward and Zander pounced, grabbing Luca and throwing him to the ground.

"I finally got you Luca. I have the link."

No sooner than the words had left the prince's mouth did the pain hit him. Blood appeared from the shoulder as Zander collapsed, opposite the dragon. It growled as Moorwell repeated the safety command. At full steam, it went for the defenceless prince. Before the dragon could pounce again, it was driven off its path. At the last moment, the large panther had thrown itself into the side of the aggressor.

The Circle Dragon retreated back to the air; it circled the courtyard as Moorwell continued to yell. Luca was helping the prince off the floor, who looked uneasy on his feet. Queen Hermenize burst onto the training ground.

"Zander, my sweet, are you okay? You're bleeding."

The concerned mother rushed to his side. Around them, sniggers could be heard. During the training, a casual audience had gathered. Interest had only increased further, when the next in line to the throne, was now semi-conscious and bleeding.

"Son, speak to me."

The queen's words seemed to snap the prince out of his daze, but rather than answer, he walked over to the orange streak panther. Spikes from the Circle Dragon had left deep wounds on the young animal. Zander cradled the panther in his arms.

"It will survive just about, like you always do," Moorwell whispered.

The crowd around the training ground had quickly grown bored; there was no entertainment to be had watching a concerned mother. Just as the courtyard had settled, the doors of the main gate crashed against the sides.

In marched a parade of guards, advisors, heads, and directors led by the most powerful man in the kingdom. Hermenize pushed the injured animal out of Zander's hands and pulled him to his feet. The Circle Dragon glided back into Moorwell's sleeves.

"Of course, I knew you would be here!" King Vidal shouted.

"Father, sorry," mumbled Zander.

"I am the king, which you know to call me. Why are you here playing with these cats? Linking is all but outlawed; it is a dead art. There is no need to side with animals when you own them."

King Vidal was now in the centre. The measure of his escort gathered around the training ground. With the other castle workers who had already been watching, it was quite a crowd.

"I have to hear about your disappearance from combat training. With all my duties, this is what I am informed about, the king. To top it all off, I come down to find you out of class, playing with animals and sticks. What possibly could cause you to make these choices?"

The king towered over the prince.

"What, you have no words for me?"

"It was my idea," Queen Hermenize said.

"That is strange, your voice sounds even more feminine today."

There was an exchange of looks; the queen repeated herself.

"I brought him down here to practice his link. Zander is actually making real progress."

"All this does is encourage him to hide from responsibility."

"He is learning an invaluable skill, something to use in life and that you have to train hard for."

"Boy, there is a pig pen waiting for you, if you enjoy playing with animals so much."

"Vidal, do we not have more pressing matters?"

Leaning over the fence was General Balder.

"How many must defy me, especially when it comes to how I teach my son?"

King Vidal was turning red. Hermenize went to open her mouth but stopped.

"So, your mother tries to defend your choices, whilst you try to train a cat to fight battles. Let's see how you fare up when you have no one else to hide behind."

"Father, king, honestly, I have been practising in combat."

"Quit whining. Someone fetch a real sword."

The request was fulfilled instantly.

"Are we going to spar?" Zander asked the question that the entire crowd was thinking. The king reading the minds of the crowd stood for a minute longer.

"You will face a real challenge. Bring me Hector."

Shock spread like wildfire; the murmurs and gasps came as if orchestrated by a singing choir. Without hesitation, Hector leapt over the fence to take centre stage. Blond hair with a long fringe to cover his devilish eyes, it still did not hide his smirk. On his forehead was a single line branded into his skin. He wore a sand-coloured shirt with tight trousers and a sword hung from a brown leather belt. Hector's most catching feature was the pink handkerchief poking out of his chest pocket.

"Have you two met?" King Vidal asked.

"I am a hot topic with your class, but believe me, Zander, there is not a person alive who can truly comprehend. I am a man of many wonders and even more talent." Hector laughed. "I am only joking, imagine that."

"Yes, well, I want a good display. You should be up to date with your disarming techniques, both of you. So I want to see what you have learned. The first man to dismount the opponent three times will receive a participation invite to Sanctuary Chamber. So you can get a real understanding of what it takes to run a kingdom."

Both looked momentarily stunned.

"And the defeated will sleep in the stables," the king said as he handed over the sword. Begrudgingly, Zander took the weapon, giving it a few swings to find the weight.

There was nothing more to say; King Vidal left the training ground. General Balder was waiting for him.

"You really fancy your boy against mine?"

"As much as I would like to, I do not think beating him in front of everyone would help. So I am going to get yours to do it for me," the king replied and the general nodded.

With nowhere to hide now, the prince thought as he stared at the floor, hoping it would swallow him up. He gave one last attempt for a lifeline, a path to refuge through his mother. He knew it was in vain, there were many situations she could save him from, but as he looked at her, eyes full of sorrow and melancholy, this was not one of them.

"Best be ready Zander because I never hold back," Hector gloated.

"First to the ground three times, I got it."

"When was the last time we sparred, prince? Refresh my memory."

"It was a long time ago."

"Tell me, prince, what happened?"

"Does it matter?"

"It matters, prince, because I want to see if I can almost break another arm."

"Quit talking and let us get this over with."

"Gladly," Hector said with a wink before drawing his sword. Long and thin with a circular hilt, it was of superb design.

The prince readied himself for the attack, but Hector hesitated. Carefully, he pulled out the handkerchief from his shirt pocket, pressed it up to his nose and took a deep breath.

"Get on with it," the general yelled. Hector seemed to remember where he was and wrapped the pink cloth through his fingers.

"Here I come."

No sooner had the words left his tongue did Hector commence the bombardment. Immediately on the back foot, the strikes came high and fast. Dust clouds hid the frantic feet. With each blow, Hector put more behind the attack. Zander's sword was being pushed further to the side. Eventually, one hit caused him to jolt to the right. Hector then rammed his left shoulder into Zander, who already off balance, went hard to the ground.

"That's one," Hector said loud enough that the crowd could hear. Zander tried to steady himself, picking up the sword. The worst thing about the first round was not the speed in which he had lost, but the fact Hector had not broken a sweat.

"Let us see if you can last a little longer this time."

Zander gave a weary nod of acknowledgement, but this time led the duel. He swiped at the side of Hector. He blocked, holding his sword with one arm, whilst grabbing the handkerchief with the other. The prince tried at the other flank, but Hector was quicker. He twisted his body and using the power in the turn, struck away the prince, throwing him forward. Zander stumbled but did not fall. Hector did not turn, but stood with his back to his opponent, taking another deep breath of the pink handkerchief.

The prince saw his opportunity and charged. Just before Zander went to strike, Hector moved sideways. As the prince went past, Hector struck at the back of his legs. Zander went straight into the dirt; the fall was met with laughter as Hector put his foot on top of the prince. The latest sign of disrespect caused the prince's blood to boil. He looked up and saw that Hector was no longer paying attention to him, but rather waving to the fans. A new surge of energy washed over Zander's body. It cleared away his fatigue, causing him to jump up and launch himself into a new attack. Hector only realised it late and brought his sword across his body.

Zander was in frenzy and kept striking; the rage had blinded his decision making. Hector could not plan his next move. Caught off guard, the handkerchief slipped momentarily from Hector's fingers. Quickly, he reached for it. The prince struck the butt of his sword hard down onto the shoulder. Hector seemed not to notice the strike, as all his concentration was focused on retaining the pink cloth.

Before the final blow was landed, Hector's instincts kicked in. He swung himself around, almost cutting Zander in two. Hector could just about cope, but his attention was not on the duel, an eye stayed firmly on the handkerchief, which was now almost covered in dust. The dancing feet were kicking up more dirt.

Hector was now countering so powerfully, it was changing the momentum. An overhead strike came down hard onto the raised sword of the prince. It caused Zander to stagger backwards, inviting the knockout blow. Hector turned and grabbed the handkerchief. Taking his chance, Zander kicked out at his opponent, sending him downwards.

A collective gasp could be heard. The general threw up his arms and screamed blasphemy. King Vidal, although not as animated, shared in the cursing.

"There is no weakness within me; stop saying that!" Hector roared, as he franticly cleaned the handkerchief. Everyone just stared at Hector. "Nobody said anything" General Balder yelled. "Get your head straight."

The next round was approached with caution, both lashing out at each other with no real purpose. Zander was tiring and knew the superior skill of Hector would soon take over. He made a move. Faking a shot to the chest, Zander then spun his whole body around, trying to hit Hector in the face.

Hector may have been out of rhythm, but he dodged with ease. One handed gripped the oncoming sword, and the other punched the prince's jaw. He jolted with the impact but kept his sword up straight and gave another half swipe back. It was no real danger to Hector, but it let him know the prince's last fall would not come easy.

There was then a sweep made at Zander knees. Rather than make a block, Zander smashed his blood-stained face in his opponents. Hector reeled back his head, disgusted by the move. With his free hand, he tried to wipe away the foreign blood. It gave the opportunity for Zander to smash his sword into the ribs. Hector keeled over, gasping for air. Zander then slammed all his weight into his back. Before Hector fell, he hooked his leg around the prince's, causing the pair to go tumbling to the ground.

"That is three, you have lost," Hector quickly announced as he scrambled to his feet. "Everyone saw it happen; I have won that three to one."

"That isn't what happened. Give me one more round, and I will beat you."

"I do not know what match you were watching, but I have put you on the floor three times. My supporters will back me up on that."

Hector raised his arms and looked at the crowd. He was met with half cheers and stares. King Vidal then stormed into the ground. Hands on his hips, he said nothing, watching as Zander readied himself for the next round.

"The match goes to Hector; that is three falls by the prince."

The king was the only one not to look to Prince Zander.

Even the panthers stood still. There was a deep sigh let out by Hector. He then held up an arm and gazed over to General Balder.

"Father, another victory under my belt; did you ever have any doubt?"

"What in the curses are you celebrating about? You lost one and got lucky on the other. Stop smiling; you are a disgrace."

Hector's face dropped. Zander finally gathered back the ability to speak and mustered some words of protest.

"How could you go against me like that?"

"The battlefield is not built on what is fair. There is only cruelty and pain. Learn to make your own fate," King Vidal replied. Each word caused Zander to slump further back down to the floor.

"You hear me, boy?" King Vidal picked up the sword; the young man did not even flinch, already lost. He went to strike when the gate flew open.

"Get out of the way."

"No, that is too much. He is bleeding; let him be," Queen Hermenize cried.

"I said move. Stop protecting him and let him fight his own battles."

The king raised his sword again, only slightly. Hermenize continued to cradle her son; the king threw down the weapon and stormed off.

"Get back to work, all of you!" he shouted at anyone who was still gawking.

"Does this still mean I get an invitation to the next meeting?" Hector asked.

"Shut your hole, boy; now is not the time." Balder grabbed his son by the back of the head.

Zander looked inside his shirt; he could see the searing black pain trying to burst out of his chest. He wanted to cry, but before he could, there was a familiar hand on his shoulder.

"Looks like I am going to have to clean you up for the second time today," Luca chuckled.

# *Chapter 5*

"Never forget you are about to pass through the gates of Hell-rous, into the zone of destitute. Around every corner, your demise is lurking. If you do not want the place to become your new home, make sure you suit up correctly."

The words rang out around the preparation room, as the team started their ritual. It was full of people changing from normality into their new identities. Made from thick white material and chainmail, the suits were oversized and clunky. It was like putting on a suit of armour. Each symbol on the chest varied depending on the rank, but all had the same much larger sign on the reverse— the palm of a hand drawn in green, from it rays of life flowed out. Tying up her black hair, Erica's face was pretty but with deep lines under her eyes.

"You forgot your gloves again."

Light blue gloves were thrown onto the bench. Mills was of the same young age but with long red hair.

"Thanks, Darian would have had my head if I lost them again."

Mills then beckoned Erica to stand, tightening the straps of her uniform.

"I hope you are ready for another day in paradise city."

As they exited, the black gates loomed as they organised themselves into teams. None of the healers looked up. Along the top of the gates, rows of silver rings were attached to grey rope. At the other end, it was tied around large oxen. A signal was given and the Eldertude soldiers slapped their backs. As the animals grumbled, slowly the gates were dragged open in the thick, dry mud. Erica felt a twinge of panic, her legs resisting the command to move forward.

"Get out of the way."

Sage pushed past, barking at the others dragging the cart full of the giant urns.

"We will go together."

Mills linked arms with Erica. Slopping downward, the manmade valley was almost invisible beyond the gates. The zone was surrounded by rising cliff faces and rock. Any possible escape points had been filled in with stone. As the gates started to close, so did the only route out of Hellrous.

"My team, we are in a different sector today, further down the valley," Darian shouted. He was younger than most but had already started turning grey. "The new place is closer to the centre of Hellrous, so you all know what that means. The risk of infection is much greater, which makes the people more desperate. It is going to be dangerous, well more than normal. I want extra protection on the supply cart and everyone's head on a swivel. Sage, no disappearing acts to see your wife; we need all the muscle we have today. You are not the only one with family in here."

Sage just scowled back.

"Also, it is going to be a lot bigger area to cover than normal, so we will be going to each duty visit alone."

Erica and Mills gave each other a glance; Darian choose not to see it. An early morning start meant that the suns had only begun to peek out from the horizon. Mist still hung in the air. It could be seen all the way down the valley where it accumulated at the drop. Through the fog, Erica could hear the shouts, *'Into the other world'*.

Out of the shadows, appeared a sea of small hands grabbing at the air. Hopeful faces yelled at the group.

"They're here; they're here!"

Children surrounded those in white, separating the healers from each other. From all angles, their cries, pleads, and demands were lost in the background of noise. Erica felt a hand grip around her wrist.

"Erica! Erica! How are you? I missed you. You need to come see my goat; it has gotten so big."

The child could not get the words out fast enough but had casually joined hands. Although it would be best to, Erica did not resist.

"That is not the way. It has been forever since you visited. My home is sad without you. Goat is so fat," Leo pleaded.

"I am sorry, Leo, we have been so busy," Erica replied.

"Can I have just a little bit of food then? My sister she is so hungry."

Erica smiled and put her hand deep into a pocket. Mills was also surrounded by children, all receiving gifts. It was a much better option than risking a beating if caught stealing off the carts. As they ventured further down the hill, the children left as quickly as they had appeared.

The streets in the Hellrous were like none other in the kingdom. Most of the shacks had been built many years ago, from the castle donations which had now nearly eroded. Attempts had been made to repair dislodged roofs and collapsed walls, but resources were hard to come by. Attached to nearly all of the shelters was a black hand made from rags. Below, on the porches, people lay sprawled out with an eerie stillness.

Erica felt a chill across her body; the atmosphere was hindering her spirit in a way it had not done before. The people here were much thinner than those in the last sector. With their arrival, the residents had gathered at the doorways and along the street.

"Have you seen how many Black Hand flags are here? They look like they control this whole area," one of the healers said quietly.

"Great just what we need, another rebellion" one of the unit muttered back.

Darian raised his hand, bringing the convoy to a halt.

"Remember, be on guard but make a good impression. We are going to be in this sector for a while. Although you're making visits alone, you each have a watch assigned. Sage, Amos, and Tylor will be checking in. Go now and do your duty."

Everyone started to prepare themselves for the day's work. Erica and Mills filled up flasks at the back of the cart.

"See you on the other side."

The two touched foreheads before turning towards the first houses. Both had black hands flags but only Mills encountered the resident outside. The woman was a shadow of a person, her body a tight ball of anxiety. She stared at Mills during the brief introduction.

"Are you waiting for trumpet and drums for a grand entrance?" Darian shouted at Erica, who nodded back. Long cloth hung over the doorway. Moving it to one side, the rays of sunlight cut through the thick dust in the air. Inside, all the windows had been boarded up.

"Is anyone there?" Erica called out. "It is one of the healers; I am here to treat…" She paused, looking for the list handed to her that morning.

Rather than the stench of rot, Erica was met with a strong herbal smell. Grey smoke billowed out from around the corner; the incense was so strong it almost made her head spin. Erica froze as she locked eyes with a pair full of disillusion. Sat at a circular table was a man, silently alerted to the new presence.

"Sorry, I didn't realise anyone was in. I am here to treat Jade."

The man said nothing but continued to stare; it was then Erica realised he was not looking at her but through her. She moved out the line of sight and he remained still, an unnerving presence in the shadows. There was a faint sound from across the room, like a rustling. As Erica went to investigate, the man shot out of the chair like an attack dog.

"Stop it; she's fine Galton," a weak voice powered itself to command.

Galton settled again. Huddled on a bed, only the woman's face could be seen. Jade's black hair had almost fallen out. A collection of blankets and mouldy rags had been piled on top of her. Gathered at the end of the bed were all the house had to offer. Candles, more incense sticks, sweet rolls, and small offerings of fruit, all untouched and now rotten.

"There is no need to fight; she is just here to drop off the Improx. We have some Red Drops leftover," Jade paused to let out a nasty cough. "Do not worry, dear, he is just being protective. You are new, are you not?"

The woman's voice was gentle, a mixture of zapped strength and age.

"Yes, well new to this section. I have been committed to healing duties since last winter," Erica answered.

"Ah, so you are still new to it then."

Erica chose to ignore the tone. Kneeling down, she got to work. Reaching into a leather backpack, Erica pulled out a number of items, placing them carefully on the floor. Firstly, a mixture of plants and herbs was broken down by a worn pestle and mortar. Next to be added were Red Drop flowers, which had been wrapped separately in white cloth. Long stems and a small black bud, the ruby petals were plucked and placed in the bowl. A fire stick was then set alight. Erica held it above her head in both hands and whispered.

"May this body be free from affliction."

The stick was dropped into the bowl; it caused the contents to sparkle. It was followed by a pop, as a cork came out of an hourglass shaped bottle, a thick silver liquid inside known as Improx. With it, the eyes of all the people in the room lit up.

"You can leave now; my husband knows what to do," Jade ordered.

"I do not mind doing it; after all, it is what I am here for. Plus, it needs to be applied directly to the skin."

Erica had a rag in hand.

"But my curse, it is on part of my body that only a husband should see. The other healers before have always left it."

Galton was out of his chair again and had homed in on the bottle.

"I have to administer the treatment; it is the rules."

Pulling back the covers, Erica covered her mouth. The woman's thin body had been feasted on. Her skin was black and broken; the veins turned grey, throbbing on the surface. The patient could see the diagnosis on the face of Erica.

"It is not as bad as you think; it is manageable," Jade pleaded. "Do not take me to the centre."

Erica reached for her whistle, but the pain came first. The first strike to the head caused a stumble; the second sent her off balance. As Erica fell, she knocked over all the candles placed at the end of Jade's bed. The man came to strike again, but Erica instinctively threw what she had in reach.

Surprisingly accurate, the potion landed on Galton's face; hot liquid began burning his eyes. He screamed, going into a blind rage. Tearing the home apart, it gave Erica a valuable minute to try and recover. On all fours, she went to yell but her voice was timid. Erica drew a dagger, but it slipped from her hand.

The whirlwind of anger found Erica again. This time, it was in the form of a sharp kick to the chest. Now with his gaze returning, Erica was in real trouble, as another blow came her way. Galton's attention became diverted as smoke started to billow around the room. The spilt candles had set alight one of the sheets hanging over the window, which had now reached the bed. Galton desperately tried to save his wife but was consumed by panic; his attempts to put out the fire only seemed to spread it further.

Erica was battling to stay conscious as the smoke filled her head. Galton could not stop the fire; it burnt through his home with as much destruction as the curse itself. There was only one choice left. He charged across the room, both smoke and flames encircling him. Erica had nothing left; she curled up in a ball, ready for the fatal blow. Galton had commandeered the dagger. It was raised in two hands, ready to be stuck down into her skull.

There was a crunch, but Erica felt no pain. Darian smashed a bucket onto Galton's head before kicking him across the room; he had arrived with back up.

"Stay down or you will be resting for eternity," Darian shouted.

Galton had collided with a bookshelf and ended on the floor, but the words had caused a reaction in him. Using the wall as a support, Galton hauled himself up, shaking off the injury.

"That blow to the head should have ended him; how is he getting back up?" the healer yelled.

"He has probably been infected a long time; you know what that can do to them— it can go either way. I am warning you to stay down now." Darian raised his sword.

The command only seemed to trigger more defiance. Galton stepped forward and flung an arm at the two men. Both jumped back. Like a wounded animal, Galton was vicious but lacked direction. With one smooth action, Darian stepped forward and skilfully tackled the oncoming predator, straight down the centre of the neck to the torso. Galton tried to scream but blood filled his windpipe. Purple mixed with red came gushing out; the other healer just stared as Darian went over to Erica.

"Where is your watch?"

Erica mumbled some attempt at a reply. Across the room, Galton was still twitching.

"Come on let's go, we are all going to need to leave."

Darian helped Erica to her feet, leading her out like a parent with a sleepy child. Outside, a crowd had gathered. All the other healers had also congregated, sensing the trouble brewing. Darian tried to ignore the suspicious eyes whilst whispering orders.

"Another upset again?" the woman from across the street said, who had appeared on the doorstep.

"Nothing of the sort; go back to your homes," Darian said, trying to sound casual.

"Do you think I am both blind and simple; we can smell smoke. Tell me what is happening, or I am going to have to find out for myself."

Darian said nothing, still blocking the entrance.

"Fine then, get out of the way."

The neighbour pushed past both Darian and the other healer, who made no real attempt to stop her. Erica was now sitting on the cart amongst the clutter. Slowly, she made a blind attempt to examine the back of her head.

"Look at the state of you."

Mills concerned voice came from the crowd; Erica almost instinctually put out her arms, wanting to be swept up.

"I got caught out."

"That is ridiculous, who was meant to be your watcher? Was it Sage? I bet he snuck away from his duties to go see his sick horse of a wife. I am going to tear his elbows off when he gets back."

Mills continued to rant as she tried her best to tend to Erica's wound, when a scream came from within the house. Everyone turned to watch the neighbour come running out; dramatically she announced:

"The family has been murdered."

A collective gasp and a theatrically pause.

"By that man."

A bony figure pointed at Darian, all eyes turned to the suspect. Covered in fresh blood stains, the trial did not last long. The crowd started to roar. Like a tidal wave, destruction was fast approaching the healers.

"Let's move!" Darian shouted at his people who did not need to be told twice. They grouped together, using one hand to drag the cart uphill and the other hand resting on their swords. Around them, people edged closer, screaming profanities. Others slowly were arming themselves with sticks, rocks, and anything else which could be turned into a tool of pain.

A large man pushed his way forward, both neck and chin black from the curse like it were slowly choking him. His eyes were yellow, seized up by the hatred of everything he saw. As he leaned over the side of the cart, Erica could smell his unwashed body.

"I may be sick, but you are the filth. You lock us away here and only take us one by one. It is time we gave out some of the punishment." The large man held up a hand and bellowed, "A soul for a soul."

Straight away, the crowd took the words and turned them into a slogan, repeating the chant. It riled them, helping the mob focus their anger. The wheels of the cart were struggling with mud. One of the younger members of the crowd shouted, "Get out murderers," then launched a stone. It hit the target; the healer took it straight to the side of the head.

The act unleashed a bombardment. Darian grabbed the man who had taken the first rock and pulled him up. Erica had tried her best to shield herself, but the barrage was relentless. The front line of the crowd, weapons in hand, threatened to surge forward. Others were already tearing at the cart; Erica was desperately trying to fight against the swarm of cursed hands.

"Draw and run!" Darian bellowed. "Leave the cart; it is already gone."

All the healers simultaneously grabbed their swords and waved them at those closest.

"Erica, we have to go, now!" Mills shouted as her friend tried to act. One of the mob jumped into the back of the cart and came at Erica; she kicked out, threatening with a dagger to slice off a finger. He kept coming. The two of them wrestled as he tried to throw her to the circling sharks. In a move of desperation, Erica plunged the dagger into the belly. Howling in pain, the man fell forwards, and both of them toppled over the side of the cart.

Erica hung onto the knife as the light above her was quickly blocked out. Before she could be consumed by the pit, Mills came bounding over. With other healers in support, they forced the crowd back. Grabbing Erica, they all now raced back towards the gate.

The rest of their unit had already lined up at the entrance to the Hellrous— now in a large number and poised for the oncoming attack. The legs of the mob slowed up the valley but did not stop. Each of the healers braced for impact. There was a long thunderous note. It rang out through every corner of Hellrous. The horn Ebb had been sounded, used only in an emergency. All the other healers stopped what they were doing and started running for the gates.

"I demand a full account; we just lost a week's supply," the overwatch said, hands on hips.

"It is the same thing as always; one of our groups was assaulted and then it escalated" Darian replied, a sullen look on his face.

"Damn right it did. A small incident is meant to be just that, not an excuse to gather the anger of everyone around you. We had to pull out every last healer just to avoid a full-blown riot. The relationship between the kingdom and zone is bad enough. What with the Black Hand rebels gaining power and the rumours circling the centre of Hellrous, people are already terrified as it is."

The overwatch continued his dressing down of Darian, mainly just repeating himself. In silence, the others changed out of their uniforms. Erica had stopped listening; her mind was drifting as she still felt hazy from the blows to her head.

Outside the window, it had begun to rain— a miserable end to a dejected day. The rain was coming down hard, the cracks in the ground becoming full of water, then washing away. It did not rain in the kingdom often, but it was not rare enough to cause alarm. Passing through the shower and heading towards their own private assembly room, were the masked healers.

Their faces were hidden, the eye holes covered in netting

as the horn shaped masks sloped upwards. With each step, it was as if the mountains were parting for them. Powerful and tall, they moved with much force and presence. Erica struggled to imagine that there were mere people inside of those suits. Nobody spoke about their duties in the centre of Hellrous. As their coats trailed in the mud, the rain was washing out the blood.

"Don't even pretend that you have been listening to me." Mills was now next to Erica, causing her to snap out of her daydream. "Let's go before the rain gets worse."

Arriving at home, it felt to Erica as if a warm blanket had been placed around her. Both the smell of food and burning candles brought such comfort. The family sized Pilpot had many rings, like the inside of a tree. In the lowest and central circle was the source of the heat. A bonfire was slowly cooking various black pots, carefully tended to by a woman humming to herself.

"It appears that it has been quite a day. Change out of those wet clothes before your bones freeze over. Dinner will be ready soon," Dace said without turning round, otherwise known as Grandmom.

Both instinctively nodded and headed up to their own individual circle. Stepping behind the long hanging cloth, Erica peeled off her clothes. Leaning into the mirror, she examined the gashes on her head; a nasty bruise was already forming across her forehead.

"How is the face looking?" Mills whispered through the cloth.

"No worse than normal; the bruising is beginning to show. I will be okay though. Please do not tell Dace; she worries enough. I cannot be dealing with any lectures today."

Erica brushed out her fringe as straight as she could.

"You really think her third hidden eye did not spot that the moment you entered, wishful thinking. Come on, let's go eat."

The three of them sat down at the table. As the food came out, eyes widened with the look of a starved animal. Each with a bowl in front of them, Dace called out. Out from a pile of blankets appeared a small boy. From a deep sleep, he was quickly alerted to the prospect of supper. His body was small and thin; he was on the edge of double figures but was a lot smaller than he should be. Almost with a grumpy expression on his face as he climbed up onto the chair, it quickly changed. A huge smile appeared; it was contagious for everyone at the table.

Looking back into the innocent eyes of the boy, Erica was reminded of the growing danger. Running across the left side of his face was an angry purple vein, surrounded by black decaying skin. Often, she wondered of her own fate, had Dace not taken her in from the streets.

"How are you, Otto?" Erica said.

"Hungry," he replied and started to dig into his food. Only the sound of spoons hitting bowls then followed.

"Such a starved table we have today. Try and take some breaths in between those mouthfuls."

"It has been a busy day for all of us, I am guessing. You been made to study hard again?" Mills asked Otto. He gave Dace a glance and then nodded anyway at his sister.

"We learnt about how to write, counting, the history of the kingdom but then I got tired," Otto's voice trailed off.

"Tell us about your day, both of you. Was it fruitful?"

Dace said. Erica looked at the boy and then started into her food; Mills answered.

"Things got a bit crazy today, Grandmom. We did not have a chance."

Dace dropped her knife and then scrambled to pick it up again. "We are running low."

"It's my fault. I will ask to be put on the stock count again," Erica said.

"No, don't, it will only raise suspicion. We cannot have you sent to the castle prisons. Otto would miss you." Dace gave a smile. "I am sure I have a stash somewhere; he will be okay for a few more days. So, Erica, when are you going to tell us exactly how you got those marks on your head?"

"When was the last time he had treatment?" Erica asked.

"It does not matter; I will never let him be taken."

# *Chapter 6*

"Are you going to strike me down too?" Queen Hermenize cried.

"Do not push me," King Vidal snarled.

"You think humiliation is the key to building a leader."

"What other option is there? I give him the opportunity to prove himself and he ends up in the dirt."

"Because you put him there. He fought hard against an opponent you knew he was no match for. Why rule against your only son, throwing him into the cold like that?"

"The world can be a cruel place. The only way he will learn is by totally dominating his rivals. He has to fight his own battles and not always look for a hand to hold. The weaker the boy looks, so do I."

"Because no one gave you a help up the chain, especially not your father, everything you have is down to your own merit alone?"

The queen did not need to turn to know that King Vidal was scowling at her. She chose to focus on her own reflection. Picking up a jewel studded hairbrush, she moved it through her long black hair in a smooth, fluid motion.

The mirror was held up by grape vines, which were littered with ripe fruit. Within the glass, the sleek riches of the royal sleeping chambers could be seen. The bed was on a raised platform in the centre of the room. It was made from luxurious material, and the velvet bed sheets were covered in pillows the size of grain sacks.

Next to the bed was a long clothes rack, full of many fine garments that had dazzling designs. Each cost more than a year's salary for the average castle worker. Stood opposite was the king's royal armour, the sword and shield both polished to perfection. Mounted to the wall above was the Staff of Luntive, the bark faded and some of the branches now withered. Its gemstone though, still mesmerised those who were lucky enough to set eyes upon it.

Vidal sat in a white chair overlooking a map of the Borrowed Lands. Made from green marble, the surface of the land had been carved down to fine detail. Each bump and turn of the road from the Red Claw Jungle to the Draygo Mountain range, even the Everlast Ocean had waves rising up and crashing down. The king pushed over the figurine of a ship.

"Any updates from Hellrous? I take it you have it all under control." The rhythm of the brush faltered. "Of course you do. After all, they are just primitive beings without the strength to clean their own bodies, let alone separate the curse from their souls," Vidal said with real venom. He glanced up from the map. The hairbrush came slamming down. "Once the curse touches them death is the only option, like a wounded animal, there is no better outcome."

"Is that the fate you would wish upon your own son? No real parent would say that," Hermenize snapped.

"Yes, my only child, another question that will always leave me awake at night, is that only child," the king roused.

"I could never bring another to live through such cruelty," Queen Hermenize snapped back.

"How dare you. I have you swimming up to the neck in gold and fur and you call me cruel."

"There is more to a relationship than how many riches you can provide."

The king went to the rack and began to throw off the items.

"You have everything you ever wanted— clothes, diamonds, and status. Why do you defy me and throw it all back in my face?"

Queen Hermenize laughed.

"You shower me in these gifts so I look like a polished trophy; do not act like you care about me or my child. You keep trying to argue with me when I am already lost, do not cast out your son as well."

"How dare you throw accusations."

The king stormed over to Hermenize, who spun around off her chair and stood to face him.

"So are you going to humiliate me like you do your own son? Go on then, I am not afraid of you."

The queen rose up and stood to face Vidal.

"Maybe you could do with your own line of discipline."

The standoff was broken by a loud knock at the door; another look passed between them. Vidal called out for the visitor to enter, and the chamber door swung open. Knocking at the door was a young castle server.

"Boy, what do you want?" the king spat out.

"Sorry to disturb you my king, highness," he said, nodding to them both respectively.

"Yes, yes, the message, what is it?" King Vidal had turned around now. The young man eyed up the many dresses across the floor.

"My king, my apologies, the message is not for you but rather the queen."

He winced as King Vidal looked set to banish him. Hermenize stood forward gently placing her hand on Vidal's wrist.

"Thank you, what is the message?"

"There has been an incident at the zone. It was only one unit, but they were ambushed by a large number."

"Why are you bothering the queen with this? Healers are assaulted all the time."

"My apologies again, but it was quite a serious incident. There were causalities as the whole street turned on them. It resulted in the Ebb horn being sounded. The queen has requested that any reports be fed back to her immediately."

"Yes, I did; thank you for informing me."

"Now leave us."

The boy nodded with relief, closing the door behind him.

"You need to know every little matter of your project, to keep up the appearance that you have some importance around here," the king snapped.

"Hellrous is on a knife's edge; the people are closer to the truth than ever before," Queen Hermenize replied.

"It is under control; I have my own watchmen. Do you really think I would just leave you to it? Plus, I have more pressing matters to attend to on the other side of the zone, the side that matters. If it is truly at boiling point, then let it erupt. Hopefully then they can all melt away."

"You cannot mean that; those are still your people too."

"They're all gone already; you cannot save them. We have tried for years with no result."

Hermenize's face dropped.

"What I say may be harsh but true. Do not pretend to believe they will get better. With what they are given, if death comes quicker, it is a blessing. As the world's resources begin to evaporate, the vultures' eyes will turn to our kingdom. It will not be long before they are at our gates, our beaches, old grudges and flames."

The queen chose to ignore the comment.

"We are being consumed from within. It is blindness to ignore that which eats at our core; it will bring us to our knees. The plague cannot be ignored." The king went back to his chair. "So what we need is a way to stop the spread of the disease, to treat it in a new way. Well, yesterday I received information from a credible source, that a cure may have finally been discovered."

The queen's eyes bulged.

"Do not lie to me; there have been so many false hopes before."

Vidal went to a drawer and returned with a damp scroll. "We took it from the mouth of a Snowtip Pelican; there is only one person who would send a message that way."

"The Collector," Queen Hermenize said, her face stunned.

"We did not even know he was still alive, but his message is simple."

*The Collector has uncovered the way to stop the infliction, to live disease free surrounded by life's luxuries. Send only the pure, the most cherished of all. For we all can become kings, safe from disease, cured from the world's darkness. Whatever the price may be, it is worth double.*

"What could he possibly want? Most of the Borrowed Lands is stashed away in his palace."

"Eldertude will have to offer its heart," King Vidal announced.

"That is a huge bill. How can we trust that the cure is even real, it is not just more smoke and mirrors?"

"There is only one way to truly know. We will have to send Zander."

# *Chapter 7*

"That is some serious punishment you're dealing out."

The pickaxe came down hard, splitting the rock like a bird sailing through a cloud. As the rich orange mineral fell apart, it revealed shining gifts. Using the head of the pickaxe, Rexis pushed the debris away. It fell down a chute into the cage opposite. Sat cross-legged and sifting through the rock was a young man of similar age to Rexis. His rough skin was covered in scars.

"Not big on conversation are you?"

Rexis broke another rock.

"Not even a single question?"

"That's because you do enough talking for both of us."

Rexis paused to wipe the sweat from his brow. The sorter gave a scowl then broke out into a smile.

"I guess I do; no wonder my tongue always feels tired. My name is Tilbet."

Another rock was demolished.

"Now is the space in time when you tell me your name."

Rexis sighed and gave in, "Rexis."

"Well, it is lovely to meet you Rexis. You give as a warm an embrace as you treat those rocks."

The two of them were in a long line of paired cages. Outside, Nkye patrolled back and forth, making sure that the work never stopped. Rexis recognised those chosen from their journey. Well, most of the faces anyway. To Rexis's horror, a somewhat random separation had occurred; Rexis's sister had gone with them. Seeing the panic in Rexis face, one of the women had put a caring arm around Terra. The Nkye had set them on another task, different but just as mundane and physical.

"What is this place? I never even heard of a whisper of it before," Rexis asked.

"Now we start with the questions, finally. Well let me be the first to welcome you to paradise."

"Do not play games with me or it is back to silence."

"This is paradise, just not our version of it. Rather that of those red-faced darlings known as the Yellow Templar, living in a cave."

"Why us?"

"Apart from that black spot you got growing somewhere? It is so you can do their donkey work. Also on the menu is slavery, torture, starvation, and making us fight each other for their amusement. On very rare occasions, they make us join them."

"Join them?"

"They always need more heads to nod in agreement to their bizarre rituals. No one really knows what happens if you get accepted into the cave. A lot of us seem to think that once you get in there, it ends up just being another cruel trick. I do know one thing, their creepy faces and shaven heads keep on growing in numbers. Although I wouldn't worry; you are far too hostile to get invited even for them."

Tilbet sniggered at his own joke.

"I recognise people here," Rexis said.

"Be worried if you didn't; your captain is the number one customer. Not me though; I was taken from a farm outside Darnspur. Been here six summers now."

"The captain knows about this?"

"Could not really tell you, never had the pleasure. The number of seamen here though, I'd be surprised he was not pushing you into the carts himself."

"How do you survive here?"

"It's not all bad; I recently got a promotion from breaking rocks to sorting them. They make us do this nearly every day; the supply is endless. From the conversations I hear, it is the only place in the world where these rocks have something of worth inside. The larger, light blue and the green rocks are the most common. I have seen them being carted out, guessing to be sold."

Tilbet had several buckets in front of him, each full to various levels. As he spoke, he held up a rock to back up the presentation.

"These yellow ones, the Nkye are always hounding us for more, which is a pain because they camouflage in with the rock. The Nkye seem to horde them all to themselves, not that the red faces seem to care. There is only one thing they're looking for— the purple gemstone. I have been here for a while and have only seen one discovered. Everyone came charging over and grabbed the girl. We all thought she was going to be executed. The next day, she was allowed to spend it lying in sun, accompanied by plenty of food and water."

"I will keep my eyes open then."

"So you can watch me enjoy my day off. Remember it is your job to smash the rocks, leave the technical stuff up to me."

There was more laughter from Tilbet, and Rexis shared a smile.

"Tell me how to escape."

A Nyke patrolling down the line passed them, running a stick across the face of the cage. The prisoners picked up the pace as the wave of terror swept past.

"Don't be loose with words like that here. They may look like they're not paying attention but believe me; each one is much more clued up than you would think. Life here is nothing. The Nyke's boredom stems from all situations that do not involve bodies being ripped apart. Do not give them a reason to be entertained."

"This is not the life for my sister."

"She is pretty. Girls like her do not go unnoticed."

The pickaxe came down hard. Pieces of rock sprayed against the side of the cage.

"All the more reason for my need to escape." Rexis almost shouted; the closet Nkye turned his head.

"Stop trying to get us both executed. The only way to leave this place is by the cost of your life, or to sacrifice your sanity by joining them; otherwise, forget about it."

Tilbet's bleak outlook ended the conversation. Rexis looked to punish the rocks even further. As he did, the pick-axe got caught in the griddle underneath him. Now blocking the shoot, Rexis used his foot to try and unhinge the tool. Amongst the sand and rock, there was a sparkle. Glimmering in the sun, the purple stone's rich surface seemed to absorb the sunlight, reflecting it back to give the image it was glowing.

Tilbet pressed his face against the cage. Rexis bent down and casually slipped the rock into his boot.

"Are you for real? You just stole from me a day of rest. Look at me; I need it."

Tilbet jumped up and pulled up his shirt; there was a darkness sneaking out of the waistband. Both the workers next to them stopped sorting through the rocks.

"Now who is the one that needs to sit down and shut up?"

Tilbet obeyed, slowly resuming his position on the floor.

"I have been doing this for as long as the birds own the sky. The guy in front of me doing this for what, a day and a half, uncovers the golden egg. Just the luck I am used to. Why haven't you shouted to the cliff tops about the find?"

"If they want this lump of rock so bad, I am not just going to hand it over."

"They find out it has been kept a secret from them, all the world's trouble will be brought down on you and your sister."

A cry came from one of the cages and immediately the Nkye descended on it. Throwing open the door inside was an elderly man slumped over his bucket. Opposite, a young boy pleaded with the man to rise up. Nkye hands grabbed the old man by the neck and dragged him out.

"Please, he just needs water or his Necro. He has not had any Necro today," the boy cried.

"Something to drink, yes?"

A Nkye with a long black ponytail and a look of spite about him lead the group.

"Who wants to see what happens when work stops?"

He carried the old man like a dusty rag, pulling him by the arm. Other Nkye followed, bending down to curse in the victim's face. The crowd was heading down towards the small oasis where the other group were washing clothes. Everyone watched in silence as the old man was thrown in.

"You want water? Well there you go; drink."

The old man just lay there looking confused; Nkye surrounded him, "Drink."

Louder and this time pointing towards the source, the old man span onto his hands and knees, crawling further in. Frail hands dipped into the water. The more he drank the liquid, the more it seemed to ease his suffering. Finally, the ponytailed Nkye stepped forward; a fist came down hard onto the back of the elderly man, forcing his head underwater.

"Have all that you can."

Bubbles rose up as the man struggled aimlessly; still the Nkye held him under. His body was kicking out its last signs of life. The Nkye brought him to the surface gasping for air, mouth wide open like a fish out of water.

"When will you understand, that ownership of your lives remains in our grasp. We want workers, not deadweight."

Back under the surface he went; it took little time for his

body to become limp. The Nyke let go. Face down, he began to float out towards those who stood holding dirty clothes and baskets.

"Back to work."

The show was over; Tilbet came up close to Rexis and whispered "Get caught with that gem and you will be begging that they just drown you."

**** 

Overcooked vegetables circled around in the bowl; Rexis forced down another mouthful. Crammed inside the feeding hall, as bad as the food was, no one hesitated against a hot meal. With barely enough food for everyone, it was a frenzy inside the grey walls. Due to the suffocating atmosphere, the Nkye kept outside; this was one of the few places they were unsupervised.

Many choose this time to try and bend the ear of familiar faces. The only time Rexis had engaged in conversation was when he had talked his way into the kitchen. Overworked and only offering the benefits of extra scraps, it was easy to get a tour as another potential volunteer. Amongst the bed-lam, Rexis had slipped a knife under his shirt.

"Pick up your fork and stop scratching."

Terra had been gnawing away at the black mark on her wrist.

"I hate this weird drink they gave us."

With each meal came a warm mug. It was full of a thick dark liquid. Despite its rancid taste, everyone else did not hesitate to wash it down.

"Try and eat; the food's not that bad," Rexis lied to his younger sister, who scrunched up her face in reply. Her blond hair had become frazzled in the heat and was thick with dust and sand. The sun was bringing out the freckles across the centre of her face; her complexion was of sorrow masked by innocence.

"They cook worse than you do."

Terra had still not given into the bowl in front of her.

"Maybe, but still you have to eat to keep up your strength."

"Why, so I can wash more smelly cloths?"

"The girl does have a point."

Both of them looked up to see the small space on the bench now occupied. Terra greeted the women with a smile.

"Is this the brother that you talk about?" the woman said.

"I have been meaning to thank you," Rexis mumbled.

"Pia helps when we go to do the stupid washing," Terra explained.

"It's no bother; Terra makes as much a contribution to the task as the next. Plus, she has a sympathetic ear for when one needs to unwind."

"Do not burden a child with more than she already has to carry," Rexis said in a cold voice.

The woman's face dropped.

"The real reason I cared for her is that I recognise one of my own and you for that matter. As much as you try to keep a low profile, everyone remembers a High Sea Roller drop out. Drink your Necro if you don't want the black mark to get any bigger."

Pia pushed the food away and marched off. Terra froze and watched as her brother stuck his fork into the table.

"That was mean."

"I do not care what they think. None of it will matter when we are away from here."

"One day, I hope we get to see the sea again," Terra said.

The statement was followed by a heavy sigh.

"Believe my words when I promise you will; I just cannot say yet when it will happen. All I need you to do is keep your head down, and not to tell anyone that we have a plan," Rexis whispered.

"There is a plan?"

"Soon there will be, but do not say anything, not a word to anyone. It could be very bad for both of us if we are caught plotting. We need to build up our strength. That includes drinking whatever this Necro is. We do not want to raise suspicion right now."

Terra nodded and then forced down some more dinner. Rexis smiled; his sister was willing to do her part and now he had to do his. Ever since he had entered the lair of the Yellow Templar, he had been looking for a way out of it.

The options were limited, as the enclosure was so secluded; nearly all entrances had been cut off. His first instinct had been to try and climb out with Terra on his back, but it provided more problems than just the practicality. There were guards everywhere that patrolled day and night. The open space provided little cover; Rexis did not believe that he could scale the cliff face unseen.

The only clear entrance was the narrow and busy pathway between the rocks. He had thought about trying to hide both of them in a cart and pray that no one looked inside. The thought of their fate being completely out of his control put him off the idea. Rexis did feel that there could be an answer hidden within the cave, a route protected by the madness of its dwellers. Still, it also offered nothing short of a huge gamble of what waited for him inside. As it was, no real opportunity had presented itself; Rexis was far from having any type of fixed plan.

His thoughts were interrupted as a group of Nkye marched into the dining hall. "Outside, all of you."

No one hesitated. Whilst they had been inside, night had fallen, and the place had become alight with torches. The entire crater looked ablaze, as if they had stepped inside the centre of a sun. Each prisoner was led to an open space and told to wait as most of the Nkye left; the normal guard positions had vanished. No one said anything, too scared to speak as they waited.

A loud clanging echoed around the valley; the cave burst to life. Out appeared a horde of dancers; the Yellow Templar were dressed up in uniform and brought with them a surge of energy. Many were holding torches and long poles that had both ends lit. The flames left golden streaks through the air as the members twisted and turned. Their dance was one of random bursts of excitement as they spun and jumped, moving in rhythm to the huge gongs which had been rolled out. Each time one of the gold circles was struck, it sent out powerful sound waves magnified by the cave's tunnels.

Close behind the dancers came moving platforms, pulled along by the Fiddlers. On it stood a Rave; his face was painted light blue with black lines across the chest. He was surrounded by the same figures seen on arrival. Wearing animal skulls and beaded robes, they chanted and shook rattles. Leader Malum sat on a chair raised above the others.

The parade was an army of light and colour. As it reached

the base of the runway which spiralled around the tomb, the red faces galloped up the walkway. In a race upwards, they halted just before the main platform and lined the edges. Facing outward, the arbitrariness stopped, and order arrived. In harmony, each member lifted a burning flame above their head, then side to side in a swirling motion.

As they chanted, the gongs changed tune, letting out small chimes. Noise built up the anticipation as Malum and his selected few made it to the top. Behind him there were smaller shapes. The prisoners all strained their necks to catch a glimpse; the whole valley was transfixed on the bizarre display. Once at the top, the leader raised his arms, and the members simultaneously dropped their fire sticks. A flame appeared at the front of the spiralling platform all the way to the top.

"Tonight, we come together on our journey towards the ultimate goal, the return of all existence and power. Let this be a reminder, when combined, we have assets but for us to take this world by the force, the almighty needs to be beside us. Never a day goes by that the struggles and pains of our ruler are forgotten. Even the waste we drink empowers us. As we come closer to breaking the tomb's seal, a gift is offered. To remind him we are together in spirit and in mind."

Malum's words were met with cheers as he gestured to those behind him. Stood in a line was a group of seven; they were dressed in the same buttercup yellow robe and all wore blindfolds. When the wind passed, the thin cloth pressed against their bodies; it was clear they were women, all with blonde hair. Each one was shaking as they shuffled forward. Malum then ordered for the women to be forced on their knees, in the direction of the tomb. With that, the Nkye became agitated, moving closer for a better look.

"Our lives are dedicated to re-opening, the return of the true holder of power. We all must do our part, give ourselves to the cause and make sacrifices. We give thanks to you for your dedication; the cost you have paid will not be forgotten; the blood will be honoured."

The seven said nothing but let out a whimper. Without hesitation, daggers appeared across their throats. Gargled cries as blood poured out of the fresh wounds, the yellow robes turned red as all seven fell forward onto the tip of the tomb. As the life drained from the sacrifices, the red liquid ran down the sandy surface. Below the platform, dark blood trickled into the curves and gaps formed by the ancient inscriptions. As it did, it was met with demented faces and eager tongues of the Followers, who pressed their skin against it whilst others licked up the gore, yelling their appreciation.

The ceremony was both enticing and completely terrifying; Rexis had never come across such madness before. He had understood the everyday dangers of the Nkye but could not have imagined the nightmares which surfaced from within the cave. The emphasis to escape could not be greater, and only now did he have a plan

## *Chapter 8*

Kantra landed with the impact of an earthquake. With a curved sword in either hand, she spun her body, launching a series of frantic strikes. Her opponent shuffled backwards as he blocked the attacks. Steel cried out as the blows kept coming. Kantra showed no signs of letting up but also not breaking through.

Frustrated, Kantra changed her strategy and went for the quick kill, thrusting at the throat with both swords. Her opponent tilted his body. With one hand, he grabbed both wrists and threw Kantra over his shoulder. Kantra came crashing down onto the floor. Letting go of the Dual Sabers, with the opponent's weapon to her throat, she accepted the defeat.

"There was no control in your approach. Without a plan, you make mistakes, leaving you exposed."

"Have we not met before? Help me up."

Kantra's face was covered in mud and sweat, but it did

not hide her exotic features. With fair skin and strong cheek bones, she was eye catching. Nothing turned heads more than the feature of her hair. Shaved short at the sides, in the middle it was thick and wavy with white beads randomly woven in. Most of the time, she painted her sockets with charcoal; it was in an attempt to hide those inviting purple eyes.

"Throwing everything into your attacks is bold. It also means your weaknesses are exposed at the same time. Being more aggressive in a fight does not always equal having more strength; it is important to be patient when using Dual Sabers," Latch said.

Almost three times the size of Kantra, he was abnormally large. Skin as thick as an ox and hands big enough to crush skulls. Contrary to his magnitude, his overall appearance was neat and organised. Short brown hair kept tidy; his square jaw was cleanly shaved. The clothes he wore were the under layers of his regiment's uniform. They did not have a speck of dirt upon them. Even the symbol of the regiment scorched into both his wrists was kept clean and presentable.

"Last time we practised, you were slightly more reserved in your approach; this is a step backwards," Latch said.

"I have had a bad day," Kantra sighed.

"They keep piling up."

Now approaching dusk, the two of them were tucked down an alleyway. It was buried between the many wooden storehouses just outside the castle walls. They had made their own space and hidden weapons to practice with.

"Don't think I will be welcome back in the kitchen. I finally lost it with the old lady crab that ran the place. I was ordered to do double shifts again to cover for the seniors. She wanted me to serve the leering castle guards again, saying some of them had asked for me. So I decided the stew looked more appetising thrown over her," Kantra said with pride.

"That is a lot of extra food you are missing out on," Latch calculated.

"I could not stomach any more of that burnt taste everything had. Plus, there isn't much worth stealing," Kantra replied.

The head kitchen was at the base of the centre tower of the castle, the tallest tree in the land. The staff worked hard at the bottom to provide banquets for everyone above; due to the place the food was cooked, it all had an oak smoked taste to it.

"Some of us would rather have something to eat than nothing at all," Harlow muttered.

Positioning herself on a crate behind them was an elderly lady accompanied by a child. Harlow, the child's grandmother, wore a light purple robe covered in a thick layer of dust; it was baggy and far too big. Her face was stern and full of complexion; with dark blue eyes which could cut through the strongest of opponents.

Maxen, the child and half-brother of Kantra, was nearing double figures in age. He wore faded trousers that were held up by rope and a brown hood. With an army of freckles and black curly hair down to his shoulders, he was the emblem of purity. In contrast to the burns to his face.

"I thought it would be a good idea to stop some of the treats. Maxen is starting to look more like a potbelly pig than a boy," Kantra teased as the boy pretended to ignore her, picking up one of the Sabers.

"Soon, the only job left for you will be the ruler of Eldertude," the elderly lady said.

"I would predict that Kantra would still find a way to fight with authority and get herself dismissed, even if it was with her own rules," Latch said who looked on as all the others laughed.

"Where does all your energy come from, Latch? You still have time to spar with Kantra, even with all the work the Hammers are assigned to?" Harlow asked.

"From my creation to the very end of my existence, I will act as a tool in whatever way is required to better kingdom. There is no rest for me, nor am I entitled to any. Once the Hammers' daily work is over, we must go out into the Borrowed Lands and find ways to improve it. Kantra wants to improve her combat skills; one day she may be required to defend the castle. So I will teach her to fight whilst practising my skills. You already know this information though, so why ask again?" Latch said in his monition voice.

"I was just trying to see if you were okay, Latch, to make conversation," Harlow replied.

"I do not understand; you can see I am in health. The role of a Hammer is well known; this exchange has no point. You have raised Hammers before."

Harlow sighed; Kantra cut in.

"Don't be annoyed, you of all people know why he is like this."

Maxen had been swinging one of the swords around his head.

"Do you reckon you'll ever have a real pair of Duel Sabers? These ones are wonky."

Kantra winced, but rather than snap, she took a deep breath.

"I will one day; they will be handed to me rather than stolen."

The little boy stopped.

"Why do you even care though? None of the soldiers have ever been nice to us."

"I just want some, okay?"

Harlow chirped up. "Come on you two, we need to leave before the suns set. Otherwise, I have no light to prepare supper."

"Grandma, this hood makes me hot. How much longer do I have to wear it?" Maxen asked already knowing the answer.

"Until that scar on your forehead fades."

"It is not fading."

"Or when your face stops scaring people," Kantra added.


The three of them moved swiftly. Both the boy and the old lady had their hoods up. Kantra wore a loose vest and was showing a lot of skin. Those around her were well-groomed in smart dresses and expensive coats. They could all be the same person.

"Why do we always walk through here?" It was Kantra's turn to ask a rhetorical question.

"Because the route we are taking cuts off about half our journey time. Also, this part of the kingdom is beautiful. I will not be condemned to a life in the Pilpots."

Harlow was right; it was a special part of the Eldertude. With the historical transformation of the landscape, the roots of the tree walls had become the anchor of the castle. They wrapped themselves to the core of the world deep underground. All were seemingly invisible, except for those on Elm Grove. The deep black roots had been forced to the surface. Gigantic in size, they were the same colour as the night sky, only to be mixed in with streaks of golden coloured vines that ran across the surface.

The vines held rich minerals that shone in the sun. Most had been twisted and arranged to border little windows and green doorways. Each root, where it was possible, had been hollowed out and converted into homes. Running by the castle walls and next to a supply of fresh water, they were very desirable. Inhabited by those wealthy enough to afford them, Elm Grove was a popular alternative to the constant hustle and bustle of the castle. With the many important faces came substantial protection. Patrolling in pairs, the smartly dressed guards nodded politely to the residents.

"Why do people keep looking at us, Grandma?" Maxen asked. "I smile back at them, but they don't smile. They just stare."

Neither Harlow nor Kantra answered; they both sensed the frosty atmosphere that surrounded them. Doors quickly closed, faces shuffled behind windows, people stopped what they were doing.

"Maybe I have misjudged the value of a shortcut," Harlow said. The boy was struggling to keep up with the increasing pace. Both adults grabbed the hand of the child.

"Fleeing from the scene of the crime, are we?"

Two patrolling guards had jumped out at them.

"Do not be ridiculous," Harlow snapped.

"Why are you running then?"

"We are on our way home. The child is feeling unwell, so we are trying to get him to bed as soon as possible," Harlow replied, holding the suspicious gaze of the guards. They were both in royal armour. It was mostly hidden with a long green overcoat, which dropped round their necks and hung over their trousers.

"Not from around here?" the guard asked.

"Well, not exactly. Although you could say I belonged here once. Many years ago, when the castle was a much different place," Harlow said in a distant voice.

"So none of these houses is yours," the other guard, who was fiercely ugly, interrupted Harlow. Both of them were now standing close to the trio.

"Acting strange, dressed as thieves in a place you do not belong, I believe that is enough evidence for an arrest."

"This is ridiculous; we have done nothing wrong," Harlow said.

"Nothing but bullies," Kantra growled.

"How about I plough my fists into that loose mouth of yours, to get a real taste of a bully?"

The ugly guard's face barked. Kantra went to bite back, but Harlow grabbed her wrist. Around them, a small crowd had gathered of nosy onlookers, enjoying the show.

"We have had reports of attempted break-ins."

The guards would start talking as soon as the other finished, as if they had rehearsed it.

"People have noticed that you walk the same path on the same days. It makes the residents nervous, strangers walking around their homes. You could be deciding the place you want to rob."

"Do not be obscene, an elderly lady and young child can hardly be the prime suspects of a heist," Harlow said without hiding her smirk. One of the guards pointed at Kantra.

"You saying I look like a thief or now it is a crime to be out walking? Kantra cried.

"Both, when it's the Pilpots you belong in," the guard said, still holding out his finger out.

Harlow could see where the situation was heading. Kantra was turning red, boiling over.

"Look gentlemen, I apologise. We did not mean to cause any distress to the people here. Let us leave and we will find a new route home for tomorrow, no harm done."

Harlow gave a smile but was returned with only blank stares. Gripping Maxen's shoulder, she went to lead them away. The guards did not move.

"You said the child was sick."

"I did."

"Has he been marked with the curse?"

"Not a chance, no. He has a tummy bug."

"What is the need for such baggy hoods then?"

"Well, we try and protect ourselves from the sun."

"Remove your hoods now. Actually, take off the whole robe; prove you are not cursed."

"How dare you ask that in the open, how can her word not be enough?"

"Kantra, it's fine; we can easily prove there is no disease on our bodies."

Harlow dropped her purple robes from her head. It revealed her short white hair and a face, although aged was still shining with life. Then she rolled up the sleeves revealing nothing but pale skin.

"The child as well."

The boy looked up at Harlow who nodded. He did as instructed. Maxen's long hair became open, blowing in the wind. The two guards peered at the child and then back to the elderly lady. As they stared at the mark on the boy's head, the gears of the guard's mind could be seen moving.

There was a movement towards their swords, but Kantra reacted first. With both fists, she stuck hard into the chest of one of the guards. The other went to draw his sword. Kantra grabbed his hands, forcing the weapon back into its sheath, followed by a head butt straight into the nose.

Now recovered, the guard grabbed Kantra from behind. Being almost twice her size, he managed to hold on, letting the ugly guard have a free punch in Kantra's gut. She clenched, trying to absorb the impact. Harlow screamed as the guard went to go for another punch. Kantra stamped down hard and broke free, rolling away.

Kantra then ran and jumped at the first guard, spinning her body to hit him square in the face with a round house kick. The guard toppled backwards. Now with a sword drawn, the other swiped at Kantra, missing by inches. More swings came at her; ducking under one, Kantra hit the guard in the belly. As he hunched over, Kantra grabbed his neck with one hand and the sword with another.

In one powerful motion, she leapt forward, throwing her knee into his face and ripping the sword away. The other guard still in a daze sat up, only to have Kantra clobber him on the side of his head. She struck with such a force it caused him to go completely limp. The remaining guard was now at her mercy. Thinking back the dressing down and disrespect made her hand tighten around the sword. Kantra grabbed a fist full of hair belonging to the ugly guard.

"Do not be talking about what you've seen today, the boy you think you have seen. If not, I will be back to administer a much worse pain than this."

Holding up the sword high so everyone could see it; Kantra slammed the handle into his forehead, blood appearing on impact. Both the guards had been indisposed, a breeze for Kantra who now stood shaking.

The lady and boy were gone. Amongst the gasps and screams, a sharp whistle could be heard. Kantra took one depth breath.

"Get to your knees."

More guards had now arrived heavily armed and ready for revenge. Kantra hesitated, even though she was surrounded and outnumbered, the sword was still in her hand.

"Drop it."

The sword was raised at the guard closest; he jumped back. Kantra then let it drop from her hand as she got to her knees, waiting for the rope to be tangled around her body.

## Chapter 9

"You took a real beating by Hector, but I got to say I really think you were going to win. I have never seen you fight like that," Luca said.

"Still, it ended in a lost and now the whole of Eldertude will be laughing at me," Zander replied in a dreary voice.

"I'm not though."

The two of them were back in the main tower. Across the hallway from Zander's chamber was a small hexagon shaped room with a single window. The wooden walls were varnished red and slopped inwards at the top like a funnel.

"My body and soul hurt, Luca." The words were spoken like they had a weight to them. "The impossible is expected of me all the time; I sometimes feel I would be better off far away from these green walls."

"There will always be challenges; my guess is that the king is testing you to make sure you will be a great leader."

"Tests, Luca, that is what you call it. Well to me, it feels like torture; you have no idea."

Zander threw himself into the only chair in the centre of the room.

"Really, who has been at your side for years, picking up the pieces. There are people in Eldertude who do not have the means to eat. When it is your job to figure out how to do right by them, you have to be ready."

The prince sighed. "You're right, Luca, I am sorry. When I am angry, I guess you're all I have. The people though will have to wait; I have to get myself together first."

On a small table was a velvet cloth tied around a black box. Luca delicately untied the cloth and took a key from the chain on his neckless. Inside were three exotic purple plants, known as the Cosmo flower. Each stem had been dried out and there were only a few remaining petals. Picking them up, Luca then made his way around the room. Zander's chair was sat on a walkway in the centre of the cross. Underneath was a hollow pit only a few feet deep, the red varnish wood was covered in silver stains. As Luca walked, he threw the flowers into the pit.

"How are you feeling?" Luca asked, but he did not need a reply. Zander was grey, slumped in his chair, sweat appearing across his face.

"It is getting worse, Luca, I swear. My whole body feels like it is trying to rip itself apart and that is not even the worst thing about it. The only thing that seems to help is setting me on fire."

"It is not quite as bad as that."

"As I said earlier, Luca, there are some things you do not understand."

Both stared at each other; Luca could not work out if it was callous in Zander's eyes or just desperation. Luca then pushed over a huge urn full of Improx which poured out into the pit.

"It's ready."

Zander shifted in his chair and then began unbuttoning his shirt. In the centre of his chest was a throbbing nightmare of infection. It was spreading across his body like a spider web. The skin was black and broken, as the angry purple veins pulsated across the surface of the skin.

"Do you need the buckles?"

A timid nod was the only reply. The buckles on each armrest were tight around the wrists. Luca lit a match and the prince jumped. Pity washed over Luca's face as he looked down at the sinking boy in front of him.

"Now might not be the time, but we need to think about the day of Dontés. Today you showed that can really fight when needed. There is a winner inside of you; I can feel it. The king would not let the bloodline of your entire family rest on your shoulders if he did not think you could handle it. There may have been families before who have lost the throne but not you— curse or no curse."

Zander leaned back to stare into oblivion. Luca hesitated, letting the match burn down to almost nothing, before throwing it into the silver pool. It made a loud fizzle, a sound which was Luca's cue to leave. The flame caught alight and sparkled to life. Across the surface, the liquid started to boil. Smoke rose up under the prince's chair, wrapping itself around his body. The heat was intense, and the smell was overpowering. Zander's head started to turn as the sweat poured down him. All across his chest, the black mark shimmered. A toxic glow formed as it took on more heat.

It was not long before Zander jolted in the chair, grabbing both arms. Below him, the pit was now roaring, the flames tickling the walkway. It became too much for Zander, who lifted his head and let out a painful moan. The heat roared and smothered its victim. It turned his skin red and black. Amongst the screams of pain, Zander begged for the fire to be stopped.

## *Chapter 10*

It was another muggy day in Hellrous; the stuffy air caused the healers to fry within their uniforms. It was playing havoc with the residents. Tensions were boiling over. Erica paused to open her water bottle and took a long sip. Her current patient was a middle-aged man that lived alone in a tiny makeshift shack. For someone who had so little in his life, it did nothing to dampen his spirit for conversation.

"So how am I doing? It's been a while now since I have been on the end of your visits."

"You are showing signs of steadying, I think. It does not look too bad since the last time I saw you," Erica lied.

"If you say so. I have been feeling weaker each day. Lately, I am getting out less and less. It is good to see a friendly face."

"I am sure you will be able to be out and about in no time. You are probably just feeling the heat; it has been worse lately."

"Just what the people of the zone need, another spell of misfortune. It is like the whole of the Borrowed Lands are against us. I know you healers get a lot of stick, mainly because you tell us things will be alright. Residents in the zone are frustrated that the Eldertude has banished them. They are expected to be thankful for the zone. To be kept in arm's length of the castle, rather than meet the fate of how the other kingdoms have treated their sick. But what kind of lives do people here live? Is it any better?"

Erica was unsure if it needed a reply.

"Ah, I'm sorry. Once my tongue starts, it's harder to reel in than a whale on the end of a stick. None of this is your fault. You have always been a friendly face, and I appreciate that, even if you might be killing me with kindness."

Erica turned to gaze into the man's eyes.

"Something I said? Oh about you lot being about okay, yes I suppose you often don't hear it enough. I am not surprised you want to hear it again."

"Am I killing you with kindness?"

"There I go again. Don't really matter when you get to this age. Do you healers not ask yourself, does anyone return ever return from the centre of Hellrous?"

Erica went to answer but was interrupted.

"Almost done in here?"

The Eldertude soldier appeared at the doorway, hot and irritated. Erica was almost done and started to pack up her equipment, giving the man a smile.

"Thank you."

Erica walked to the doorway and the soldier glared at her as she passed. Outside, the looks were just as frosty despite the temperature. Since the increased outbreaks of attacks, soldiers had been allocated to each of the units. It was easy to say they were far from pleased with the assignment.

"Got caught chatting him up again," Mills said as she came bouncing over. Her energetic glow shone brightly in the despondency of the soldiers, causing them to be more irritated.

"Yes, in full form as always. I am not sure even death would stop him talking."

"Really, because he barely said two words to me. I think he likes you," Mills teased as they walked down the street to their next job. As they did, they passed more soldiers.

"They have never cared about us before," Erica said.

"Who doesn't?"

"The castle, the guards. We have been attacked countless times before; they have never bothered trying to protect us. Do you not think it's strange we now have an armed escort?"

The healers' presence had a common effect on Hellrous, bringing more life and animation to the streets. Although the people were lining up, their actions were subdued. None came to greet or question the healers, or to try their luck at extra supplies. Even the beggars kept their hands by their sides.

"Something is different today; it doesn't feel normal," Erica said, scanning the area.

"There is a normal day in the zone?" Mills replied.

"You know what I mean. I am serious; things are different."

"Look, you're probably still on edge after the attack, how it got out of control so quickly," Mills trailed off. "Maybe the people are behaving off. Where is your other boyfriend, Leo? Maybe he can tell us what is going on."

The pair stopped in their tracks as the soldiers charged past them. Moments later, a door burst open, and a young man went flying out. Instinctively, the soldiers surrounded him. As he tried to climb to his feet, the soldiers pushed him back down.

"It's just another dead end," one of the soldiers yelled.

The soldiers showed no signs of becoming bored of toying with their captive. A sharp punch to the face caused the young man to spin around, only to be caught by another soldier who struck him in the gut.

"Stop this now," Darian announced, bringing the attack to a halt. The ringleader of the pack stepped up.

"This boy wasted our time, another decoy no wonder. There is only so long you can hide," the soldier cried out.

"Are you trying to start another riot?" Darian hissed back. The two men held each other's stare; the soldier drew his sword.

"They can try and riot if they want, but they will be cut down to size."

The other soldiers roared in agreement. Their display was drawing a crowd; Erica could see the storm brewing. Her thoughts were interrupted as she caught sight of a familiar face.

"Come on."

Erica darted through the crowd; Mills was just keeping up with her as she picked out Leo. She grabbed him by the hand and pulled him out before he could answer.

"Leo, you should not be here; it is dangerous."

"Erica, it's so good to see you. Why are you beating that man?" the boy said in a voice that already seemed to know the answer.

"Come on, let's get out of here. I want to see how big that goat has gotten."

They arrived at Leo's home only a short distance away. Built at the entrance of the wall, the square block was tucked into the corner of the valley. Leo's house was larger than the others; the first buildings of the zone were designed to house groups of families.

Leo eagerly pushed open the door; Erica and Mills almost turned back the other way. The stench of decay mixed in with the mess in the hallway was almost too much. Leo did not seem phased, so the pair held their breath and followed. They were led into a large room full of people who froze at the sign of the healers. An excited Leo started to sound off names. There were nearly a dozen women and men, mostly young and able bodied. Mills looked at Erica; those in the room understood the silent conversation.

"You're intruding," one of the older girls said sharply. Tall and with dark hair, she was poised for action.

"We're here to deliver treatment," Mills tried to say cheerfully.

"There is not meant to be a healing unit in this district today, so again you're intruding."

Everyone in the room looked to be thinking the same thing. Leo answered.

"I brought them here; they are my friends and so are you. I wanted everyone to meet up because I know some of us are really sick here; I thought they could help."

The boy was right; with the reception from those on their feet taking all the attention, Erica and Mills had not noticed those close to death wrapped in blankets.

"So it is just the two of them?"

"They are good people, Lensa." The girl stared at them.

"Fine, they can stay and help some of the people in this room only. We will do introductions later."

"We will all be friends, I promise; Erica always has sweets in her pockets," Leo beamed. Lensa did not smile but looked away; Erica and Mills took that as the signal to get started.

"These people do not look like they have been treated in weeks. I'm not even sure if some of those lying over there are alive," Erica said under her breath.

"We shouldn't be here; I know we are doing our jobs, but we have left our unit. The others will be looking for us soon," Mills whispered back.

"Well, do you want to tell Lensa we are leaving?"

"I would think she would be happy to have us gone. Let's go; I feel uneasy being here without backup. I will give Leo some excuse." Erica agreed, and they went to leave. As they had been working, all the able bodied had left, even Leo had been taken away for a private word.

Out in the hallway, there were still a number of people all gathered around the room at the end, blocking the entrance.

"You shouldn't be out of the room," one of the young men said.

"We are leaving."

"Wait, I will have to check with Lensa."

Before they could protest, there was a roar of noise from

outside. A member of the house came running in.

"The soldiers are here, and they are letting everyone know about it."

"There probably looking for you," the man hissed at Erica before darting back outside with the others.

"We should go; maybe it will clam things," Mills said, but Erica was not listening.

There were dozens of muddy footprints leading down the hallway. At the end was a sheet hanging where the door should be. Mills protested but Erica crept forward. The noise from outside was coming closer as the soldiers swarmed the area. Erica lifted up the cover and looked inside; her eyes widened.

"We are in control here; don't be telling us where we can go." In walked a group of Eldertude soldiers with Lensa firmly in their ear.

"Look what we have found already, two healers astray from the pack. Out you two; we need to search the place for weapons."

Erica did not move.

"Have you moulded to the ground. Get out of the way."

"There is nothing inside." The soldiers stopped as Erica spoke, "Only a lot of the sick and dying which do not need to be disturbed, unless you are looking to catch the curse yourself."

Lensa looked stunned as the rest of the soldiers jumped back.

"There are a lot of them inside?"

Erica nodded.

"Well then why are only two of you trying to heal them all. Get back to wherever the rest of your unit is."

All of them left. Erica and Mills walked out; the soldier watched them leave before looking inside the first room.

"They're not wrong," Erica heard them say.

Mills leaned in. "What was in the room?"

Erica waited to reply as the soldiers exited with them.

"They have been making a tunnel through the wall into Eldertude."

It was a similar scene to the one they had escaped from earlier. The soldiers were inside nearly every home on the street, with the residents outside letting them know how they felt.

"Quit your moaning; it would be much easier if you had just brought us all the kids as we told you," the commander said.

"Never would we bring you our children."

"We don't want all of them; we are only after ones with scars on their faces," the commander stopped. "Soldiers, regroup now."

There was a crowd approaching, men and women dressed head to toe in black. Most had rags tied around their face, the others held up makeshift flags. All though wore the symbol of a black hand.

At the front of the group was a woman marching the line. Wearing a black shirt full of holes, the infection glared through. Her eyes were full of deviance; she held up a hand and the assembly came to a halt.

"Someone having a funeral?" the commander muttered.

"We are the resistance group of the zone. We gather to-gether to create the united front for all those in Hellrous," Carmen announced.

"United against what?"

"The kingdom, the suppression, and the mistreatment. We are finally organised in our own way to resist and reform."

"More moaning and complaining about the hand that feeds you," the commander dismissed.

"The same hand which strikes down onto those which are in need. Today already, you drag a young man in the street and beat him like a dog, whilst terrorising people in their own homes," Carmen yelled.

"People don't follow the rules, they get punished. What is hard to understand about that? I should remind you, any type of organised rebellion carries a heavy sentence in the dungeon, no matter how many there are of you."

There were howls of support from the Eldertude soldiers.

"You do not seem to have grasped what is happening. We will no longer allow ourselves to be suppressed; the fight back begins now."

The crowd roared behind her.

"We are the Black Hand, and we are going to force the change so desperately needed. I, Carmen, will see to that. It starts with no more healers, no more soldiers. Bring the sup-plies to the gate and let us treat ourselves."

More cheers from the people but the commander looked unmoved.

"That's been tried before, and it didn't work. Some stole the medicine and then charged the rest for it. You lot cannot be trusted to be left alone."

"Things are different now; the zone has been driven to unite against the greater enemy. We will no longer live in fear. All have trained to fight our repressors," Carmen replied.

"If it is a bloodbath you're asking for, my soldiers will be happy to get the rivers flowing."

The commander unsheathed his sword, which had a ripple effect on all the soldiers around him.

"If death is the only way to have freedom from the castle, then I will be the first to jump on the sword."

Another roar from the resistance, doors closed as the street cleared. The healers were slowly arming themselves too. Erica grabbed Mills wrist and backed against the wall. They had no escape as the exits were blocked by people. All they could do was ready themselves to fight.

Screams came from an alleyway. Black Hand and residents flocked out as if the place was on fire. Even on its hands and knees, everyone else backed away. The suit was ripped apart, showing the heavy bleeding inside. A trail of blood and silver ran thick behind the masked healer. Its mask had a huge amount of damage, with one of the white spikes ripped clean off. Exposed was the face and neck, covered in scratches; bloodshot eye darted side to side. It edged towards the commander who could do nothing but stare, along with the rest of the soldiers. The masked healer continued to crawl until it came within a few meters, raised a hand, then collapsed. No longer was anyone looking at the masked healer, but rather in distance towards the centre of Hellrous.

****

"I cannot believe that the inner gates have been breached. Never in the history of the zone has there been an unauthorised opening before. Also, the brutal attacks on the masked healers; they have always been the silent rulers of the zone, the top rank of all the healers. Eldertude soldiers have tried to regain control with an iron fist, which has done nothing but rally a black hand to strike back. Would they really unleash the horrors from the centre of Hellrous?" the overwatch said in a dejected voice.

In a small room next to where the healers changed, the relevant heads had gathered.

"We need to show our force and strike against all those who defy us. It will not take that many bodies before the message becomes clear, and the others step back into line. We can force the gates shut," the commander said, foaming at the mouth.

"More violence, more deaths. Do we really want to give any more reason to hate us; there has to be a new strategy. Maybe we could come to an agreement with the resistance group. If the centre zone gates are open, then the people of Hellrous will be looking for our help," one of the team leaders said.

More arguments and cunning filled the air like a dark cloud. On the other side of the wall, Erica and Mills sat with the other healers. Although spoken in whispers, the rumour mill was spinning. There had been no sign of the other masked healers. The door to their changing rooms had been chained together.

"Each day gets stranger by the next. I never have really known what goes on in the centre or wanted to find out," Mills said out loud.

"I have never seen a masked healer without their suit on before."

Back in the meeting room, there was only one who had

not pushed the line between a discussion and an argument. Dressed in all blue with slick grey hair, Puros held up a hand.

"I have been listening to your contributions and insight into the current situation. As the queen's head and as the overseer of Hellrous, the decision I speak is final. The first objective should be to regulate the centre. That is the core of the kingdom's control; word gets out that the castle cannot even keep the inner gate closed, which is when the foundations start falling apart. Hold off supplies, food, water, and treatment; they get nothing. Once they've torn themselves apart, they will be begging for us to restore order. Then we close the centre, it is our first and only priority; to get it done no matter the cost."

Puros looked to the only healer still in uniform. Darian marched back into the changing room.

"Everyone, it is no secret that the masked healers are missing; they are our brothers and sisters in the zone. To be blunt, we do not exactly know what has happened to them. The result is that the centre gates looked to have been breached. We need to find them and close the doors; we need volunteers."

No one said anything.

"Now I know it seems dangerous; well it is. We are in a corner and need everyone to work for our people out there. Also, I have been given the nod to reward you all with double wages. As for the supplies, we will not be counting every last drop of the Improx taken with us, you understand. So who is with me?"

One of the healers stepped forward then another, each stared daring the other to go next. A few more volunteered but not nearly enough. Erica took a deep breath and stepped forward. Mills grabbed her wrist, leaning into her ear.

"Are you crazy?"

"Did you not hear what they said, more treatment up for grabs. Your brother is only getting worse. I am already risking my life in Hellrous. How much worse can the centre be?"

## *Chapter 11*

"Do not make us cut those hands off; put the plates down and get moving," the Nyke yelled. Terra went to put down her knife.

"Keep hold of it. You might have to use it later," Rexis whispered.

Outside of the food hall, the cavern was on fire. Screams could be heard as the red faces came charging out of the cave. It had been a long wait; word had spread about how it had been the longest break in the tradition. Now though was the night as the tomb was set ablaze; Rexis readied himself. The ceremony started, as the menacing red faces made up the carnival. Those wearing skulls danced around the flames with energy and excitement. Malum leads the sacrifices up to their destiny. Like before, the prisoners were led up to the same spot.

Rexis checked himself; the kitchen knife stolen from the kitchen was still hidden in his belt. The purple rock, still in his boot, had rubbed and rubbed. Terra had her pockets full of scraps and water tied in a bag. Two of the Nkye were staring at her; Rexis pulled her close. There was another roar; the women dressed in yellow were pulled forward. It was the height of the show, drawing in all the eyes around it. As the audience held its breath, the two began to drift away from the circle, like a cloud moving overhead in the night's sky.

Sticking to the shadows, they moved shiftily towards the main entrance into the valley. There was only enough room for about two people to stand shoulder to shoulder. Through the cracks between the gorge's break, there was nowhere to hide if they met someone head on. Rexis held out the kitchen knife in anticipation. Reaching the clearing by the gate, they were now exposed. Quickly, they had to dive behind a rock.

A single Nkye strode past them; he looked more miserable than the normal weighted complexation. Straining his ears, Rexis could no longer hear the drums off in the distance. A frustrating amount of time had been spent watching the Nyke trudge back and forth. They would have to take their chances. As soon as he turned, the pair sprinted out from their hiding place. There were no hic ups as they made it to the small tunnel. It was underneath the stone gate which sealed them off from the rest of the world. Heading in deeper, Rexis caught a mere glimpse of the mechanics used to control the gate. Endless amounts of perfectly rounded boulders all sliding along man made tunnels. As they walked further into the caves, Rexis could feel the breeze above him, fresh air in the otherwise stuffy caverns.

Terra pulled at his arm, getting lost in trying to figure out a plan; Rexis had not been focused. A fatal error as now they had walked right into the path of another Nyke. Both of them froze, waiting for the alarm to be raised. It did not; rather nothing happened as the Nyke continued to sit in his chair, feet up, arms still. As the candlelight flickered, Rexis breathed a sigh of relief; even with their eyes open, the Nyke was asleep.

From the tunnel behind shadows crept towards them; Terra's eyes widened. Holding up a hand, Rexis let his fingers become wrapped around the strong breeze. Climbing up on the boulders, Rexis could see the end goal. There was a gap between more rocks and mechanisms; it was tight but the night stars were within reach. Rexis looked to his sister; she shook her head.

"You can fit through there fine; we have to move," Rexis whispered.

Crouching down to make his hands a step, Terra used the foot up to force herself into the crack. Dust fell as gradually Terra began to disappear. A small stone became dislodged, falling to the ground. The sound echoed through the cave; the Nyke twitched in his chair. Terra seemed to be making her way up but her accent was slow. The footsteps of the patrolling guard were now so close they were ringing in Rexis's ear. He pulled himself up, forcing his body into the tight squeeze. In a desperate scramble, more debris fell.

"There's something there." The Nyke was out of his chair to investigate.

"Chicken." A huge hand came slamming down on the table. "It's gone; you ate all the chicken."

The patrolling Nyke was eye balling the other who was in no mood to back down. Meanwhile, Rexis made his final push. Covered in dust, the two prisoners were now on the other side of the wall outside the valley.

The desert was vast and empty, like a golden sea stretching out to the splits of all land. Around them, the sand glowed as it was illuminated by strong stars above. The gate's flames were gone, as if the horrors of the hidden realm had evaporated from reality. With the Templar contained, the closest signs of life were the prison carts scatted around a ring of horses.

All the animals were settled for the night. They were guarded by a handful of Nyke, who were slowly cooking a stew of desert rodents. As the escapees edged closer, Rexis moved towards the straggler. There was one Nyke standing alone with the horses. Rexis and his sister waited for him to be enticed away by the smell of the dinner. Seconds felt like hours as the discovery of their escape became ever closer.

"Wait here."

Rexis began to slither through the sand. As he closed in, the horses stared at him. One shook its head in alarm. Rexis did not give the Nyke the chance to turn. In one motion, he plunged the kitchen knife into its neck. His other hand was placed across the mouth, dragging the Nyke to the ground. Rexis wrestled to keep the blade deep in the wound. Only the weight of his responsibilities kept the Nyke restrained. Rexis glanced back; the others around the campfire had not been disturbed, until now.

"Look who's trying to escape?"

The Nkye around the fire stood up.

"There is nothing out there but sand, you idiot."

All of them watched as the slouched rider charged off into the desert. Kicking his heels into his own horse, Rexis and his sister set off. They had no compass, but it did not matter, as long as they took the opposite direction of the Templar.

Passing over a huge sand dune, they were now out of the direct line of sight. Rexis wanted to push on, but the horse was slowing.

"Get it moving again," Terra pleaded.

Rexis kicked his heels, but the protests were ignored. All around them there was a tremor, as the sand began to move. It was slight at first but rapidly picked up speed; it was as if a tornado was rising up from the ground. Terra squeezed Rexis' waste. The horse kicked up and both of them were thrown to the floor.

"Run!" yelled Rexis as they both scrambled to their feet. The horse retreated one way as they went the other. It ran up the bank, the sand seemed to jump up and sallow it. Huge tentacles appeared from the ground. Long and dirty, they wrapped around the horse. It was squeezed so hard, that the powerful muscles were crushed without any tangible resistance. All the steed could do was let out one final cry, before it was dragged into a sandy grave.

Terra froze as she watched the horse disappear. All around her, the tentacles could be seen on the surface, readying themselves to take another soul.

"Terra, we have to run."

Rexis had turned back around and grabbed his sister by the shoulders; her body was a statue cemented by panic. The young girl tried to say something. All around them, the tentacles circled, waiting for the best moment to strike. Rexis tried to move his sister again but stopped, realising it was pointless.

In the distance, voices could be heard; the flames on the gates had been lit. Soon, they would be back in the hands of the Templar and sentenced to death, if the tentacles did not tear them apart first. He wanted to at least give his sister a few seconds of peace, to feel something other than fear for just a moment. Holding her close, he whispered.

"I'm sorry."

A retched tentacle bound itself around his throat. Rexis was pulled backwards as his windpipe was crushed. Just before he lost total consciousness, Rexis could see the figures of the Nkye.

Quickly they surrounded the pit, the bodies of Rexis and Terra now barely visible. One of the Nkye took out a long silver flute and blew a high note. All the tentacles stiffened and then shot in his direction. The Nkye jumped back, inches away from being grabbed. He held out a finger and shook it slowly. The tentacles became still but poised, following the finger. Cautiously the other Nkye crept into the pit and retrieved the pair. Once safe, the flute was blown again and a bag of cinnamon was thrown into the pit, sending the tentacles into a frenzy.

The two of them were dragged back to the valley. With the ritual happening that night, everyone was already gathered, and the taste of blood was in the air. The Nkye crowded them and cheered. Most prisoners hung back, making sure to avoid any eye contact. As Terra was held, Rexis was thrown into the middle of the ring. Ignoring the insults, Rexis looked to his sister, tears filling up his eyes.

"These two would have escaped if it was not for a Wormas."

A finger was aimed at Rexis. He recognised the owner instantly, the one with a mohawk. Kog smiled as he slowly drew a jagged knife from his belt. The smug look across his face incited a hidden rage inside of Rexis. As the Templar began to make their way to the front of the circle, Rexis screamed out and spat in the direction of Leader Malum. Kog charged at Rexis, which was exactly what he wanted. Rexis threw the force of his body at the legs of the oncoming attacker. The both of them went to the floor and sniggers could be heard from the other Nkye. As Kog got to his feet, the smile was gone.

Rexis went on the front foot this time, throwing himself again at the Nkye. Kog was not about to be caught out twice and lashed out. Rexis took the kick to the face. As his jaw went back, he wrapped his arms around the outstretched leg. Using his body weight, Rexis spun the Nkye off balance onto his back. In their eagerness to take them to their punishment, the Nkye had not searched them. Rexis still had the kitchen knife, which he slammed into the stomach of Kog.

The other Nkye were in no mood to host more acts of defiance; they came armed with swords and axes. Rexis was now unarmed and with his fate already bound, he fought without fear. More Nkye looked to cut him down; they had power but no precision and kept getting in the way of each other. Each handed Rexis the opportunity to duck and roll out of trouble. Frustration grew amongst the attackers; one came forward with a lazy, unplanned attack. Rexis let the axe fall, then grabbed the Nyke's arm and turned the weapon on the owner.

Blood pored as the body dropped to the ground; the other Nyke looked confused and backed off. Rexis waited for the next attack as he grew in confidence, swearing to himself that he was going to take as many as he could with him.

Kog pushed past, now recovered and out for revenge; he came at Rexis with a newfound furry. As he desperately blocked the attack, another Nyke stepped forward with a chain spin. It struck his chest, spinning his entire body. As he struggled for breath on the ground, Kog struck him in the temple. Rexis tried to collapse, but the Nyke held him up with a fist full of hair.

With the escapee now truly beaten, Kog could give his speech. Rexis did not need to listen to know what was being said. Regurgitated talk of how the prisoner should never disobey the rulers; punishment will always find them no matter how far they ran. Well, that may be right, but at least Rexis could muster one last act of defiance. As everyone was concentrated on the speech, Rexis fetched the purple stone from his shoe and swallowed it.

"Halt." Malum stood up out of his throne.

"This is my kill."

"Are you going to make me ask twice?"

Kog threw Rexis to the ground and pushed past the other Nkye.

"Stand up, boy," Malum ordered.

Rexis did as told; the voice seemed to echo through his mind.

"You do not know it, but you are more a member of this Templar than many of its founders. The journey to the reawakening will need many brothers and sisters' lives, but none is more important than the one who can think like our master. All our bodies may have the mark, but you now share the same space of mind."

Rexis started to dribble. His head was pounding as the tingle sensation in his stomach grew rapidly. The pain soon took over; Rexis could no longer stand. Before he hit the ground, the hands of the Yellow Templar were upon him.

"Begin the transformation."

# *Chapter 12*

"The Day of Dontés is almost upon us," the prison guard announced.

"With the king's neck on the line, the odds have never been tastier," the other guard replied.

"That weed of a prince looks like he is about to snap."

"That dirt stain has no chance. I almost feel sorry for him."

"He is still the favourite though."

There was a chuckle from the first guard.

"The betting house has to, that's why; they have a duty. Also, we all know he will have the easiest path, the best weapons, even the tamest Grey Tails to fight."

"My money is on Hector. That brat will not be able to stop himself from finishing top."

"So you don't fancy any of the army's best?"

"Well, let's look at the competition's best two…."

The two prison guards continued their debate, each offering expertise and strategy in an event they have never participated in. The conversation soon drifted out of focus for Kantra, not that she cared. Her day had already hit its peak. She had found the only place on the wall to lean against, which was not completely damp. There was no natural light in the single cell or the entire jail itself. It was built deep underground with the river running almost overhead. The result was a permanent state of both darkness and dampness, married with the threat of the whole place caving in.

Kantra though was used to the musky smell and all that came with it. This was not her first time visiting the cells. Even still, she had never been arrested before for assaulting two guards. No one yet had told her the punishment, but experience told her not to ask. By keeping her head down, there was always the chance that the guards would forget why she was there. Eventually, they would clear the cell for a more recent law breaker.

Whatever happened, Kantra was not getting out soon. That would mean that Harlow and the boy would have to fend for themselves. The only hope that Kantra had, was that she'd beaten the vision of the mark out of the guard's head.

"Girl," her thoughts were interrupted. "Oi, girl."

There was just enough light to see into the cell opposite. Pressed against the bars was a huge stature of a man. Dressed only in tattered clothes, the face of the brute showed many years of punishment. Large, bruised lips slapped together, causing Kantra to turn her head in disgust.

"I know you can hear me, girl."

"Never speak to me."

"We are locked in here together, just me and you."

"Thanks for pointing that out. This place already stinks, don't add to it."

"Don't normally get girls in here, especially pretty ones like you."

The brute grabbed his crotch; Kantra jumped up.

"Keep talking and I will cut that ugly tongue out of your fat head."

Kantra let out a scream of rage. With it, she launched her waste bucket at the cell opposite. Its contents splashed against the bars, quickly followed by immense cursing.

"You will pay for that." A threat spat across the floor.

"What's all the noise, you to making friends?" the voice of a guard echoed around the cells. "No hassle from either of you; it is feeding time."

The guard then appeared at the cell doors.

"Hands."

Kantra put both her hands between the bars. The guard placed a wooden infinite circle over her wrists, pulling it tight.

"I told you not to add to the smell," Kantra said in the direction of the fuming and soaked brute.

Kidnappers, thieves, and thugs— just some of the many types jam-packed into the dining hall. All now causally lined up waiting to receive their dinner. Kantra stood with them; being one of the few women in jail, she was subject to leers and stares. Silently, she collected the foul-smelling meal. Finding a small refuge, Kantra sat alone and with a fork, picking at her food. It was only until she made eye contact did she slam the cutlery down. The brute from the cell opposite came striding over, accompanied by two equally as thuggish types.

"Don't worry, we are just here to say hello."

All three of the men sat around Kantra.

"I said we would be meeting again," the brute said with a grin.

"And I told you, I would cut your tongue out if you talked to me again."

"It's your tongue were interested in."

They all gave the same nauseating deep belly laugh. Kantra slammed her elbow into the throat of the thug next to her, causing him to go flying backwards. The brute stood up and gave an instinctive jab. Kantra dodged by leaning back. In the same motion, she kicked him under the table. He keeled over and Kantra grabbed his head, slamming it onto the table. With the other hand, Kantra rammed her fork into the left eye of the brute. He screamed and rolled away in agony.

The remaining thug backed off but not fast enough. With a fork still in hand, she launched herself. Others cheered as the canteen was in an uproar. Kantra filled her latest victim full of fork shaped holes. Well behind the action, the prison guards came running over and began wrestling with Kantra. It took several of them to restrain her.

"Is it really that hard to keep a few ne'er-do-wells in check?"

The commotion stopped at the voice of General Balder.

"General, we were not expecting you to be down here."

"So what, you normally expect the unexpected, does that not just make it routine?"

The guard looked dumbfounded.

"So these are the lot been causing trouble?"

"Yes general, that is correct; they have been quite disruptive."

"Well, that is the reason I am down here, for troublemakers; the worst the better. I am sure you are all aware it is the tournament soon. I need some hardened fighters for the pit, those who will put on a show before they are eventually cut up. What about you then, sure looks like you know to handle yourself," the general nodded to Kantra who looked uninterested.

"Screw me, right? I'm the man who built this place. Guess what, I can also be the one to give you an official pardon. Participate in the Day of Dontés or stay here; it's your choice."

The pit was dangerous, almost a certain death. Odds piled against them in the hunt for spilt blood. On the other side of the canteen, the remaining thug was talking to a large group. Kantra gave a nod.

"That is settled then; show me some others." Balder moved on. The guards went to take Kantra back to her cell.

Passing the one-eyed brute, she whispered, "Don't think I have forgotten about your tongue."

## *Chapter 13*

"Keep up the pace, Hammers, and know this— history may only remember the sword, but it is a hammer that can craft a thousand weapons. You are the most important tool. The kingdom relies on us, no slowing down. We do not want any more bodies in the street."

The Hammers jogged side by side, making no noise except for the dry leaves crunching under foot. All were gigantic beasts, with the muscle to break boulders with their bare hands. None had distinctive features; all were clean shaven and mirrored the same box trimmed haircut. Their uniform was a plain grey, except at the bottom of the leg, where it had become thick with mud. At both ends of the unit were Eldertude soldiers on horseback. Three younger scouts lead the troop. The Lead, a stocky man who had long turned grey, took the rear. He was accompanied by his Hand, a stern faced slightly younger man, also known as the soldier who never smiled.

For all the hard work that it came with, Latch always felt

privileged to venture deep into Red Claw Jungle. It surrounded the kingdom like an outstretched hand, with a reputation to crush those who entered. The result was few got to see its marvel. Thin trees intertwined and twisted amongst each other, like an eruption of dancers paired together. No single plant was the same, each curved in a new direction as they battled for space in the crowded wilderness. None stood out more than the lone tree in the distance. Situated on the side of the clifftop, it hung over the edge, as if only to illuminate its superiority over the other trees. The landmark confirmed what Latch already expected, that they were forced to go much deeper into the jungle.

"Halt. Here will do for a start. There will be no putting your feet up; we are going to get collecting right away. There are thousands of sick back at the zone, depending on their Hammers to get to work."

All of them dropped their bags. There was a loud thud as the trowels and spades spilt out onto the grass. Large maroon-coloured flowers hung off the trees like rain drops. They spread down the trunk to the roots and bushes.

"Get as many of the Red Drops you can."

The Hammers worked like a ravenous plague, stripping the land of all the nutrients that it had to offer. As quickly as they cleared the area, they moved on to the next, edging deeper and deeper into the jungle. The further they went, the thicker the vegetation became. Often, they used their swords and machetes to cut through tangles of vines. The light had begun to vanish as the trees above were slowly suffocating the outsiders. With more places to retreat to, the wildlife became more confident. Furry faces had appeared to investigate. Scales glided past looking for dinner. Smitten Apes hooted a call to the rest of the jungle.

One of the younger Eldertude soldiers tried to clear away the animals, by yelling at them. Both the Lead and his Hand momentarily froze. The Lead's Hand then galloped up to the scouts. As the three of them argued with each other; the Lead was focused on another direction. A loud crack came from the bushes. The trees began to vibrate as the birds took to the skies.

"There is something out there!" one of the scouts yelled.

"Shut your hole," the Lead's Hand replied. As the scout did as ordered, it was just in time to hear the booming echo. The jungle had roared. Over and over, it came; Latch recognised the sound and readied his weapon. Thin wooden missiles fired like thunderbolts from all directions. Those quick enough blocked and dogged, whilst others felt the needle-sharp darts penetrate their skin. Following the bombardment, a rush of aggressors came out of hiding; it was as if the jungle itself had pounced on the Hammers.

Tall and ridged, the ambushers were animals fused with the undergrowth. Running upright, they had tough black skin, enforced further by bark fused into flesh. Around it, small plants and flowers grew, creating a powerful camouflage. At the end of their lanky arms, razor sharp claws poised to tear their opponents apart. Their faces were hidden behind more wood, leaving only a menacing long snout in view.

"Hognails!" the Hand cried as the beasts charged into the Hammers. A furious battle broke out as the outsiders were caught off guard. Desperately, they tried to organise themselves into a liable defence. Long swords and hammers hurdled back at the frantic charge. Latch was set upon by two Hognails with a dire thirst to inflict pain. They swung their bodies left to right, letting their loose arms strike at random, claws trying to slice open Latch. He jumped backwards holding up his broad sword to block the shots. The weapon itself was huge, wide, and strong enough to counteract the strikes. One of the Hognails became frustrated. Pushing itself with powerful hind legs, it flew at Latch.

He replied with expert timing and precision. Splitters flew everywhere as he drove the sword deep into its chest. The Hognail cried out in pain; momentum drove it forwards as it fell on top of Latch. Jaws continued to snap as they slid down the sword. He was forced to use the body to shield him from the other Hognail. As it concentrated on Latch, another Hammer snuck up behind. Using all their might, the other Hammer brought down a huge double headed axe, straight into the spine of the animal.

Back on his feet, there was no time for Latch to recover. More spears came whizzing through the air, narrowly missing his face. Hognails continued to pour out of the jungle; the unit had already lost its shape and was in real danger of being overrun.

"Get back to a circle."

The Hammers tried to organise themselves, but the speed at which the Hognails came was causing major problems. Around Latch, more skirmishes broke out as the Hognails began to surround them. He quickly sided with his saviour holding the axe. Back to back, the pairs fought hard just to keep themselves breathing. As the axe made powerful swings, Latch would use the space to dart forward, jabbing his sword into the torso and knees of the Hognails. As they began to get the upper hand, a surprise attack split them apart.

From the trees above, a Hognail pounced, coming full force onto the Hammer holding the axe. The deadly claws plunged into his skull like a knife into wet cabbage. Latch grabbed the Hognail from behind, wrapping an arm around the neck. It tried to throw him off. Latch used his immense strength to bring his hunter's knife across the throat. Purple blood spilt out as the Hognails thrashed around with its last moments, before being tossed aside.

The Hammer that had been ambushed lay face down; they had huge gashes in the back of their head. As Latch turned him over, he could not make out the expression of the victim, their face covered in red. Not that it mattered to Latch; he pushed the body away. Now with an axe and broad sword in either hand, Latch finally took the fight to the ambushers. Targeting those already in a duel, Latch used the full force of both weapons. Cutting them down with powerful swings, he would block with the sword and then devastate his opponent with the axe. As the Hognail bodies began to pile up, the Hammers could reorganise themselves into a real force.

Sensing the shift in control of the battlefield, the Hognails rallied into a final charge. All the Hammers braced for the impact. The Lead came galloping past with the other horsemen just behind, meeting the Hognails head on. Such the velocity of them both coming together threw horse and Hognails apart. The Hammers came as the second wave, picking off the Hognails who had shifted their focus. Engrossed by the presence of another animal, they seemed determined to massacre the beasts. With one of the younger soldiers already down, the Hognail turned to the Lead's Hand. His horse had become isolated by the Hognails; the pair desperately trying to avoid the snapping jaws all around them. The retreat failed as teeth massacred the horse's skin, ripping chunks out of the animal. Howling in pain, the horse threw the Hand from the saddle.

Scrambling to his feet in a bid to defend himself, he lashed out at the approaching Hognail. The sword bounced off the wood around its wrists. The Hognail lifted its snout up and cackled. The Hand drove his sword into the eye socket of the monster. Howling in pain, it threw back its head, taking the sword with it. Fumbling through his pockets, the Hand produced a dagger. Its blade was barely the same length as one of the Hognail's claws.

It roared and looked to seek immediate revenge, sinking its teeth into the arm of the Hand. He stabbed back at the fiend, barely breaking the skin. On cue, the Lead appeared, his white horse showing no fear. Knocking over the Hognail, it kicked up and then slammed down both powerful legs. Attached to the horse's hooves were curved points; they sliced open their foe. The Lead finished off the Hognail, his sword removing the head from the neck with one strike. Latch finally had a moment to catch his breath. The once peaceful woodland was now a mix of snapped branches and broken bones.

"That was no coincidence we came against such a force. When coming of age, the females look to prove themselves to the rest of the tribe. They go out to hunt for a foe to prove their command to one another. They are the fiercest of all the Hognails; my wife would fit right in."

The Lead's joke was met with blank faces; the Hammers had many casualties with even more injured. Marching over to his second in command, the Lead barked, "Well, how many have we lost?"

His Hand was still licking his wounds. Gingerly, he tried to wrap a cloth around the huge bite mark.

"I'm not sure, I have been injured."

"You think that was bad, wait till we get back to the kingdom empty handed. I would have rather tried to fight that lot off with a stick. I did not save you so you can just lie around."

The Lead's Hand let out a sigh then switched back into his role. He started to count and briefly spoke to the Hammers. Most were tending to the wounded or collecting supplies from the dead.

"From a first look, I would say we have lost about a third of the unit. With injuries, it puts us up to half, maybe even more."

"That large a hunting party will mean the tribe will be nearby. Eventually they will come looking for them. Each Hammer is meant to bring back four sacks each; it will take double the time to get that now."

"We will need to tend to the injured as well."

"I suppose so; make camp for now. There might be a way to save us from being thrown into the dungeons. A haul of quality rather than mass is the best we can hope for now. There is still a golden crop at the edge of danger."

## *Chapter 14*

Rexis sat bolt up and gasped for air. As he tried to swing his body out of the bed, it was slow to react. He could not feel his feet as they pressed against the cold floor. Letting his body catch up, Rexis's mind fought through the haze it had been locked in. The only memory he had was swallowing the purple rock. There were endless rows of single beds, all neatly made up. On a small table was a gold tray with grapes and a generous slap of meat. Although Rexis was starved, he left the food.

Standing up, he had been dressed in the red robe of the Yellow Templar. There was a strong light coming from one of the hallways; Rexis stumbled towards it like a drunk to his bed. To keep himself upright, he ran his hand across the cave wall.

Protecting himself from the rays, Rexis stepped out into a small circular courtyard which was concealed in the rock. Lined up were seven others wearing the same robe. All had their hands behind their back. Rexis felt very out of place; as he walked towards the line, he felt himself being drawn in.

"Do you feel it yet?" Leader Malum's voice boomed as he stepped out of the shadows.

"We practice here to give over our pride. To have any worth when our great leader walks with us again, we must better ourselves. Stand close to the sky, hold your hands to the flame and remember. To have a place within the journey, amongst your brother and sisters, is the true strength."

The words oozed out of the leader like a thick fog, slowly wrapping itself around the audience. Standing close to Malum was a looming figure. Head to toe in a thick blue paste, his yellow flaming eyes bugged out of his skull. Wearing nothing but a leather belt and shorts, as Rexis made eye contact, Rave spat at him.

"There will always be a need for warriors; even when we are lead back to power, we must be ready to grasp it. Some of you will follow closer, and go further on the reawakening. If you can prove your worth, then you will be rewarded by standing by the side, rather than at the feet of our leader."

Pearlsa stood tall in her knee-high boots. She wore the same turtleneck robe as the rest, but with a gold line running down the middle. There was a loud crack as she lashed the three headed whip to the floor, flicking her long black platted hair as she did. The rest of her head was shaven and covered in scars.

"On your knees, Followers."

Her tone was sharp and direct. The seven did as instructed.

"Do not move."

Pearlsa launched the whip, bending it to lash inches past

the face. Nearly all of them flinched but one held up his hands. Pearlsa was on him like a flash. The beating was brutal, the victim defenceless as the whip cut into his scalp. As the rope went back and forth, it flicked out parts of the skull.

"That's the first lesson for the day."

Those with authority left; Rexis did not move. The other Followers got to their feet and surrounded Rexis.

"There is mess on your robe."

Flesh from the broken skull had splattered across Rexis' chest.

"You have to get it cleaned."

There was a gesture to the only balcony overlooking the small courtyard. Slowly, Rexis made his way back into the cave. His shaky hand ran along the rock as he climbed upwards. Eventually, he met a huge wooden door, the brass key already in the lock. Pushing it open, the room was like stepping into a blizzard. Its walls, furniture, and drapes hanging from the ceiling were all white. All the vases, bowls, and plates had the same theme, although there were hints of the original colour, where the white had not been fully painted over. Sprawled on a bed of cushions was a young woman in a silk yellow dress. She paid no attention to the door opening; neither did the other women dotted around.

"Rexis, you have woken up then, lazy bones."

Terra appeared holding a tray plated with an array of succulent fruit. Rexis grabbed her, holding her tight.

"Careful, I almost dropped it."

"I feared the worst."

The woman on the sofa snapped her fingers. Terra went to pull away, but Rexis held onto her.

"There will still be a way for us to get out of here."

Terra pinched her brother.

"They can't be left waiting." She took the tray over. It was only then that Rexis noticed one of the Followers at the door.

"There is no time to get your cleaning done. It is already time for another lesson."

## Chapter 15

The dust had begun to settle after the ambush on the Hammers. They had suffered heavy losses with many injured or dead. A makeshift camp had been created, but there had been no time for rest. The jungle was reading its next move.

"Do not think about sitting around to lick your wounds, Hammers; there is work to be done," the Lead's Hand barked. One of the scouts had still not left the tent. The other two sat with them, holding onto their hand.

"That goes for you as well, soldiers; there is not much you can do for him now."

The words fell on deaf ears.

"The Hammers need assistance collecting the Red Drops. We are hardly going to get half our orders done at this rate."

Still no movement, the Hand marched in and grabbed one of the scout's shoulders. The young man jumped out of his chair and squared right up.

"I do not remember saying it was time for a break." The Lead had now appeared at the entrance of the tent.

"The men were in here, not working and worst, disobeying an order."

"It could be argued so are you, failing to control a couple of young soldiers who are having a wobble. You are supposed to be my hand. Maybe you have become too accustomed to the passive management of the Hammers."

There was a drop of the head.

"And you two, how dare you to confront the authority. His orders are law, not something to be questioned. The work we do out here keeps countless numbers alive in the zone. You want to mope around over the life of one?"

"We have known him since we were little boys; he does not deserve to die like this."

"No, he should have died on the battlefield," the Lead replied. "He is a solder; death is part of the job to keep the main objective going. We are all pawns in the kingdom's army. Shedding a tear when one is sacrificed, is as pointless as hiring a duck to manage a tavern. You want to know why the Hammers are such an effective unit, because they cannot dwell on the consequences of war, only on the victory. Look, I will show you."

The Lead called for a Hammer; he had to duck to fit in the tent.

"Tell me about this soldier's wounds."

The Hammer inspected the bedbound soldier. "He will not recover."

The words caused the two other younger soldiers to wince.

"So any attempts to help him would be in vain?"

"Time taken away from our work."

"So finish him; put him out of his misery."

There was no hesitation; the Hammer's massive hands clasped around the mouth of the patient. The two other scouts tried to stop him. The Lead and his Hand restrained them, as they watched the life being squeezed out of their friend.

"Monster!" screamed one of the young men; the Hammer just looked at him. Frustrated, he twisted out of the hold and went for the Hammer. The Lead reacted faster, pushing him to the ground.

"Have you learnt nothing? Your friend was in pain; keeping him alive is a selfish act. The reason why the Hammers are the most valuable tool to Eldertude, is because they are only concerned about getting the job done. Go now and think about what you have seen."

The two younger scouts were thrown from the tent; the Lead watched them sulk away.

"Think that was a bit much for them," the Hand said without thinking.

"Looks like you are still as stupid as them. Well, you have made my next decision simple; fetch me the Hammer which was our edge over the Hognails."

"You asked for just me, Lead, not the rest of the unit?"

Latch had attached his broad sword to his back. Amongst the relentless work, he had still found the time to clean his uniform.

"There is no point trying to move the unit. More than likely, we are going to get attacked again. If we stretch them thin, we are in danger of being wiped out. Rather than quantity, we might be able to bring back some of the rarest fruits of the forests. Ones that only get fed to royalty."

****

The pair stood at the base of the cliff; it had looked high from afar but now it seemed goliath. Its jagged surface looked determined to throw people off. It would not be long before the fall would shatter every bone in their bodies.

"Least the recent heatwave has dried the rock," the Lead said, reading Latch's mind. He had removed his uniform and now was in a simple vest top. He was still in impressive shape, for a man with many winters under his belt.

"Leave your sword here, as you are going to need the extra strength for the return journey."

Latch did as instructed, slamming the broad sword into the ground, leaving him only with a hunting dagger.

"Ready."

There was no wait for a reply; the Lead started the climb at a blistering pace. Latch could just about keep up, his massive hands ripping out chunks of mud as he ascended up the cliff. Amongst the dirt there were clumps of twigs and leaves nested together. Soon, they reached the halfway point, treetops were becoming a distant memory. Latch could now see across the jungle, all the way back to Eldertude.

There was something else in the distance. Heading towards them in a neat formation were Hawgales. With a wingspan of over the size of two fully grown men, these animals blocked out one of the suns. The feathers of the adults were an ivory white, with clusters of orange in different patterns across their bodies. The younger Hawgales, known as Betas, were born completely orange. It helped them to blend into the cliffs' surface. Only when they took to the skies, to mix in with clouds, did the white feathers appear.

With his concentration misplaced, Latch put a hand into fresh droppings and lost his grip. Immediately, he slipped down the cliff face, desperately grabbing to stop the free fall. Fingers clasped a rock that was sticking out, which seemed to offer a lifeline. It ripped from the cliff and left Latch with mere seconds before the inevitable death. In a last ditch attempt, Latch slammed his knife into the surface of the cliff, plunging the blade deep into a patch of mud. The action stopped the momentum for a second, just long enough for Latch to grab a chunk of grass.

"That was close." The words came from the Lead above. "Now, hurry up."

The last stretch of the hike was complete without any further incidents. Both stood at the summit, momentarily enjoying the view of their achievement. The dynamic change in the landscape was truly visible from above. Eldertude castle absorbed all that green around it, leaving the surrounding area dry and earth exposed. Eventually, the trees dared to start growing again, breaking out into the jungle outskirts.

"I think I underestimated how big a climb that was. You cannot afford any mistakes on the way back down. You will not get lucky twice."

Latch said nothing.

"Come on, let's get this over with".

The lone tree was decorated in vibrant purple flowers, which danced in the gentle breeze. There were dozens of Cosmo, all in full bloom and ripe for the picking. With thin outstretched branches, it would make it difficult for the two heavy set men, but not impossible. The rest of the forest had formed a distant circle around it, as if the individual tree had been cast out. What was almost a perfect border; one section had been ripped apart. Branches had been broken and the roots ripped out.

"We need to strip every twig before sunset" the Lead grunted.

Systematically, the pair began removing each flower from top to bottom. Its lower branches were simple enough, but for the ones above, both of the men had to climb into the tree. The collection was slow as the pair moved with caution. Fragile outstretched branches threatened to break under their weight. The Lead stopped moving; Latch thought he might have spotted a Hawgale that had broken from the pack. The Lead nodded and Latch followed the direction of his gaze, just in time for the smaller animals to come scurrying out of the forest. The trees were vibrating; there was a thunderous noise ripping apart everything in its pathway.

Out of the wildness bounded out an enormous Rognith. Riding on all fours, the beast had thick dark brown skin, almost the colour of leather. The long tail was made from a build-up of sharp scales that swayed side to side. It raised its large head to show off ivory rounded tusks. There was another in the middle of its head; it faced the other way and dug into the end of its long snout. It gave a loud growl and kicked up on its hind legs. Latch crouched even though the plant offered little to no cover. The Lead did nothing of the sort; he held a finger to his lips and then pointed at the beast.

The Rognith roared and violently struck its head about, seeming intent to destroy more trees. Latch did not wait for instructions. He made a move to exit the tree; the branches creaked, and the Lead grabbed Latch's shoulder. The faint noise caused the ears of the animal to perk up; straight away, it charged at the lone tree. It clattered the bark, almost pushing the entire tree over the cliff. The two of them hung on for their lives. They could do nothing as the animal pushed again with its front legs. Roots started to appear as the tree leaned even further over the edge.

More roars and loud snorting covered Latch in snot. The assault on the lone tree eased. Delicately, the Rognith opened its mouth and swallowed the flowers whole. Both watched in silence; the Lead looked to have almost a faint hint of a smile. Its chewing became slower, the breathing heavier as the Rognith brought its front legs down. Letting out a loud moan, it then collapsed in a heap, resting against the base of the tree.

"Let it get into a deep sleep first," the Lead said quietly, holding up a hand.

All the men could do was watch and wait. On the horizon, the suns had finished crossing in the sky. The end of the day meant that the Hawgales would soon be upon them. With the beast now snoring, each deep breath caused the lone tree to vibrate. That was the signal for each of them to make their escape.

The Lead made it to the ground first, only feet away from the snoring beast. Latch did not take his eyes off the animal, so much that he misplaced his footing. A large boot went through a branch, causing Latch to slide down the tree and land clumsily on the floor. The Rognith's ears perked up; both men froze just starting at the animal. The head dropped and the deep slumbers returned. Finally, they continued their sulk towards the edge of the mountain. Latch went to start the decent, but the Lead stopped him. The sky above was a swirling white swarm of feathers and claws.

"There is no time to try and make the climb down; we will be picked off before we have broken a sweat. We are stuck between a rock and hard place to fall," the Lead sighed.

"There is only one thing that might get out of this."

Latch acted before the Lead could reply. He drew his hunting knife and using the butt, slammed it into the head of the sleeping animal. It awoke with a roar and spun round in a blind search for the culprit. The move acted as a signal for the birds to make their assault. Taking up the formation of a spearhead, they struck like a thunderbolt. Both the men jumped to the ground as the hunters rushed past them.

The beast was in no mood for retreat. Even with all the squawking and movement around the Rognith, it struck hard. Both of its front feet slammed a Hawgale down to the floor; white feathers filled the air. Others came to the aid, clawing at the back of the beast. Deep scratches appeared as the Hawgales focused their attack on the main threat. In danger of being overrun, the Rognith kicked out its hind legs and sent another Hawgale trailing. Latch was there to pounce on the straggler; jumping on its back he was almost thrown straight back off. The strength of the bird was only overcome by the knife to its throat; it still wrestled with Latch as the blood poured out.

Another came at Latch; he managed to use the momentum to push it into the path of the lone tree. It became entangled in the branches; thrashing around it did more damage to the already suffering plant. Using its power, the Rognith crushed the bones of another bird, throwing it over the cliff edge. Half a dozen then swarmed the beast. The attacks were coming from all angles and for the first time, Rognith needed backup. As the animal beat back the birds, Latch did his best to cut down the number. Those that were dazed had a dagger speared into the exposed bellies. More dead Hawgales piled up, but it was still not enough to drive them away.

One last push and a Hawgale came right for him. Catching Latch off guard, he was disarmed with the strike of a powerful wing. With the knife gone, he was forced to use his hands to battle with the claws. Latch's fists were bleeding as the Hawgale's furious eyes were ablaze. It tried to rip apart Latch's face. To his surprise, the Rognith came to the rescue again. It clamped down on the back, teeth penetrating the spine. The Rognith lifted up the helpless bird as if a message to the other, then spat it out. The injuries were too severe for it even to cry out in pain.

This time, the other Hawgales did back off. As Latch picked himself up, he was covered in feathers and scratches but relatively unharmed. The beast had its own set of injuries, but still had the energy to let out another loud call of power from the clifftop. It was enough to send the rest of the Hawgales retreating back to the safety of the skies. The Rognith then sniffed the air and turned its head. Both of the men were drained; the Rognith bounded over still full of fight. The beast was an oncoming volcano ready to erupt. It stopped inches away from the pair. The nostrils flared up again and there was a low growl. Latch slowly unclipped one of the bags of flowers from his chest. Holding them out, the jaws grasped around his hand. Quickly, it pulled away, leaving nothing but a ball of slobber in his palm. The Rognith then trotted away back into the trees.

"I am not sure how much more of this bloody jungle I can take. My praise to the elder kings for their commitment to deforestation," the Lead said wearily, and then gave a laugh. Latch said nothing but nodded.

"You need to lighten up by the time we get back."

"We are leaving right away?"

"Of course, it is essential I am back as soon as possible."

"To make sure the Cosmo flowers are delivered fresh?"

"No, something far more important; tomorrow is the Day of Dontés. I do not want to miss the slaughterhouse."

# *Chapter 16*

An air of expectation had gripped Eldertude by the throat. It was the day of the Dontés. Electricity was in the footsteps of everyone involved. Pens hovered in anticipation to write the day's events into the history books. Legends would be born and broken; the light in which they were remembered would be decided by the fighters alone. Tensions were high throughout. With Hellrous out of control, the kingdom was losing faith in the leadership, both current and future. If the vultures were about to make their move on the throne, it would be now.

It also was the only day on which the castle doors were thrown open. No checks or hassle as anyone could flow freely in and out. All around the stronghold, decorations in the form of banners and flags had been brought out in force. Flowers had been timed to bloom, creating a mosaic of colour. Armour had been polished and uniforms pressed, as every member of the castle looked at their smartest. Stands for the audience had been brought into the main courtyard, long benches jam packed with expectancy. Many talked about different strategies whilst tucking into their free meal.

The gauntlet was shaping up to be the deadly spectacle that was promised. Its first stage was simply known as the pit. Built to be a greater size than ever before, it was wide enough for over fifty men to move freely. Painted with dark colours and layered with black sands, within it were wooden pillars wrapped in chains. There were several exits to the pit sealed with iron gates. Each escape had its own runway, the wooden corridors had many obstacles all put together in a mix of twists and turns, traps and falls— all leading the final circle. All around the pit there were walkways and viewing platforms. They were positioned to corner off all angles, making sure it was impossible to hide. The contestants were well aware that all eyes of the kingdom would be on them, none so more than the prince.

Sat alone in the main tower, Zander stared out of the window. It overlooked the courtyard, which was now the temporary home of all the people of Eldertude. So many faces, all were waiting to cast judgement. He knew this day had been coming, but now that it was finally here, it seemed even more of a nightmare than years of dreaming could conjure up.

Hermenize came to the doorway then hesitated, resting herself on the edge as she watched her son. Dressed in white and green, the colours were the traditional scheme of the heir to the throne. It represented the journey of the prince, before he could take the royal colours reserved for the king. The amount of pressure was gigantic on small shoulders; the kingdom demanded a physical and mentally powerful leader, one who could strike down anyone who dared to oppose him.

All she could see was her sick boy, one about to be thrown into a world of blood thirsty warriors. Luca walked past her;

the queen shot out an arm blocking the doorway. He opened his mouth in confusion but followed her gaze. Luca then understood the need for just a little more time. Both watched as the prince became illuminated by the sunlight. Zander sensed their presence and turned; the glow was broken. Luca entered carrying an armour chest plate and a small, brown sack.

"I have got something readymade that should settle your stomach. Wildflowers mixed with a Tableside Mushroom. It is meant to bring the storm in your stomach to rest."

"At this point, I can only hope that a storm appears in here, so I do not have to face the thunder outside."

"Come on, with those suns out, there is no chance of rain," Queen Hermenize said, joining them.

The prince looked even gloomier with his mother's arrival, knowing that it meant it was almost time. He let his body go limp as the queen and Luca attached the rest of the armour to him.

"I know you are scared but you can do this. The tournament is there for the taking. I will be watching to help support you," Hermenize tried to sound as inspiring as possible, as she hid daggers behind the prince's chest plate.

Luca's back stiffened; the king entered the room. Hands on hips, the others seemed to melt away into the background.

"Stand up." Zander stared at him blankly. Vidal sighed and let his arms fall, then gestured again. "Come on, rise up to your feet. I want to see you in the uniform."

His son rose, trying to look as tall as he could while King Vidal inspected him. "You're almost done," he snapped his figures and the missing shoulder plate appeared from the hands of a servant.

"So you look the part; now you just have to play it. No excuses and using the sickness saying it affects your skills. Make your own fate."

"It does affect him, though and you have never chosen to understand that," the queen cut in.

"All her mothering has made you weak; that is why I went against you with the sparring match. You understand?"

Zander gave a timid nod.

"I have been trying to balance out that softness. You will become the next king, so go out there and show them that. I need you today; the questions against me are mounting. Keep our bloodline on the throne; make me proud."

****

Far from the main tower, in a hall next to the courtyard, many of the other fighters were going through their own rituals. Blades were sharpened and war paint was applied. Next to Kantra, a brute was rubbing out the stains across his double headed axe. Her hands were shaking; the only way to help stem it was to tie them in white cloth. A plain uniform was thrown at her.

"Put that on," the castle guard shouted.

"I haven't got a sword yet," Kantra replied. The brute next to her snorted.

"You cattle do not get weapons, one of the perks of being out of the jail cell. There might be some spare armour. There is though one thing all cattle get."

The helmet was heavy and clunky. It covered her eyes and the face guard made it difficult to breathe. For the rest of her body, she could not scavenge much else to protect her. Shin plates and chest plates, the best find was metal gloves with blades across the knuckles. A huge bell rang out throughout the hall, over and over again as the doors to the hall flew open.

"Get ready; it's time to die," the castle guard yelled.

The crowd stamped their feet; others banged their hands against the wood. Kantra felt a surge of energy flow through her, as she was funnelled into one of the corridors connecting to the main pit, shoulder to shoulder with brutes and thugs who carried axes and long swords. There were many other unarmed cattle around her, all wearing the same plain uniform and bulky helmets.

Spectators roared with exhilaration. In their own tunnel, the professionals had arrived. Military faces that looked to make a name for themselves. Men and women of all sizes and builds, wearing newly crafted chainmail and carrying elegantly formed swords. Leading the marvel was Hector; he had no shield but wore a grin so full of arrogance, that it would carry its own protection. Trumpets sounded the arrival of King Vidal, with Zander trailing just behind him. As they headed to the centre circle, the pair was met with both cheers and boos, mostly though it was just noise.

"Noblemen, ladies, Heads, staff, and the people of the Eldertude, it is the day of Dontés. Our parents before us would have passed on the stories of this day. When legends are born and made before your very eyes. The day when great warriors and soon to be leaders show this kingdom why it is them you believe in. Sit back, enjoy the performance, and remember that when you vote, the castle commodities all its people."

The king made his speech and nodded to the prince, who made his way into the pit alone. Up above on the highest balcony, a smartly dressed man with a large gut cleared his throat.

"As the official gauntlet speaker," his voice was like the

wind; it carried itself across the courtyard. "It will be the word of the king, but my voice that will deliver the instructions. Each member of the kingdom will have a voting slip under their seat. At the end of the tournament, you must decide on your confidence in the current ruling and its future, no matter where they finish. Alongside this, there are great prizes for our other contestants, to win their freedoms from the shackles of a former life, to gain entry into the army of Eldertude, or even to help govern it. As a sign of gratitude from the king, the amount of gold promised to each competitor has been doubled." There was a cheer. "Paid to all those who survive. May your battle be glorious; enter the pit."

"Now chuck in the cattle," one of the guards yelled.

Kantra did not have time to curse as the stampede forced her in.

"Position yourselves," the speaker instructed.

Everyone fanned out, weapons raised. Kantra made sure she had the wall behind her. The fighter closet kicked dirt at her; she went to lunge at him.

"Steady."

Everyone looked puzzled by the hold up; another door opened up, one hidden in the pit wall. Castle guards appeared wrestling with a number of ropes. They dragged along a large cage, full of Timber Vexes, also known as Grey Tails. Each creature stood on all fours; their claws were long with teeth like broken glass. Across their brown fur were zigzags. The patterns all lead up to the tip of their tails, turning them grey. There was something unnatural about the animals, each one had a yellow ribbon tied around a leg. Overcrowded in their cells, the animals were fighting amongst themselves.

"Only five participants who collect five ribbons each will

progress to the next stage. Release the cage," The speaker explained.

The guards pulled the bolt and the animals burst out like a fuse had been lit.

"Let the fight begin!"

The pit erupted, as all strategies seemed to go out the window in an instance. Some of the fighters struck out at the person next to them, whilst others tried to find an impossible place to hide. After the initial explosion of anarchy, some went on the offence at the Grey Tails. The animals moved with incredible speed—frantically darting in between those in the pit, randomly choosing to attack whoever they passed. Amongst the desperate victims with little combat experience, two types of fighters emerged. There was the agile, which weaved in and out of the chaos, picking out targets with bows and daggers into the backs of their foes. The much larger brutes rampaged through the broken limbs. Monstrous battle axes and hammers caused devastation to flesh and bone, as they cut through the air with a loud swoop.

Kantra ducked just in time; there was no sparring as the brute went straight for the kill. Another swing and another miss; if the axe hit her, she would have been split in two. She kept moving, sensing the frustration as the kill was proving more difficult than those before her. The hindrance was making the brute sloppier and more predictable. Looking to crush Kantra's head from the top, she side stepped the swing and stabbed her spiked knuckles into their elbow. He yelled and the brute shifted all the power to his other arm, swinging the axe to the side. Kantra had thrown herself to the floor. She rolled behind the brute and struck into the back of his legs. Falling to his knees, Kantra then leapt up and slammed both her knuckles into the eyes. There was a muffed cry, as Kantra then dislodged the spikes from the brute's skull. As the man clutched aimlessly at his face, Kantra took two ribbons from his belt.

****

Hector smiled as he could smell the fresh blood running across the sand. He would pick a target and stalk them around the pit. The cattle annoyed him; he could not understand why but killing as many as possible made sense; he could gather ribbons later. As he crossed the battlefield, Hector came across the path of the prince, almost surprised that he was not yet amongst all the dead. Zander met his gaze, the fear inside of him rose as he could see the calmness in Hector's eyes.

A Grey Tail came darting over, its direction focused solely on the prince. There was no option but for him to meet it head on. A nervous swing missed its target as the beast crashed into his chest plate, pinning him to the ground. It went for Zander's throat so quickly that he dropped his sword to grab it. The beast's jaws locked around his wrist guard, with a mouth so big it almost swallowed his whole hand. Zander held the throat; he could smell the foul smelling breath as the jaws snapped at him. Reaching inside his chest plate, Zander took out one of the daggers and rammed deep into the belly of the animal. Over and over again, he stabbed until it eventually stopped moving.

He threw the limp vixen off before taking the ribbon from its leg. As he stuffed it into his pocket, he quickly pulled his hand out again. In his palm were three other ribbons. There was a sting of guilt inside of him. Around Zander there were so many putting their lives in danger, just for one of these. He went to throw the extra ribbons away when another fighter came bounding past him.

The emerald armour had already lost its shine; holding

her side, the military woman leaned against the pillar. Panting heavily, she stared at the prince, before inspecting the arrow lodged deep inside her waste. Zander yelled to the woman but she took a swipe at him; he shouted again but it was too late. A blade plunged into her neck, a sword followed into the stomach. Weaving like a serpent from behind the pillar was Hector.

"They didn't even have a ribbon," Zander blurted out. Hector just winked and left to find his next target. The three extra ribbons all went back into Zander's pocket. Two lean thugs came rampaging. Swords in all available hands, they descended on the prince with a calculated madness. Each block was a reflex by Zander, in a last-ditch attempt to keep himself alive. Shuffling backwards, he was struggling under the pressure. Eventually, he became pinned against one of the blood stained pillars. Ducking out of the way, one of the swords came crashing into the wood, sending splinters flying.

The thug was about to come again but stopped mid swing. Zander was thrown forward. The pillar behind him exploded as shards of wood flew everywhere. Out from the shackles it roared, tearing up the ground around; it was a Colossus. Made from a dark green gem rock, it was easily the size of ten men with the same structure as a stone wall. All the different blocks that made the body would slide and turn, constantly rearranging themselves. As the Colossus moved, the stones never stopped turning. Its heads would rotate relentlessly, changing the direction of attack. The individual clashes paused, as the Colossus swept a blanket of mayhem over the pit. As many ran for cover, simultaneously the other pillars exploded as four more Colossus emerged.

"Colossus have now been let loose in the pit. They have a red ribbon around the arm; one of those ribbons gets you automatically through to the next round," the speaker announced. His words sent ripples through the crowd.

On the high balcony, Hermenize slammed back her chair and left. The king watched her walk away then leaned into Balder, "I thought we had decided against the Colossus."

"We had to throw them in there. To distract away from the fact that none of those representing Hellrous was invited. Do not worry, though; there is a technique to defeat them. It was covered in the training sessions; I am sure that was one your son did not miss."

The Colossus were on a rampage; they steamrolled the pit, crushing both Grey Tails and fighters. For many, it had become too much. The reward was not worth the desolation they were bound to, so they made an attempt to escape. For all their rotation, the Colossus could sense the attempted escapes and sentenced them all to death. Those climbing out were smashed into the pit walls, bones became flat as the bodies covered the edges. With the fatalities pilling up, it meant easy picking for those fast enough to collect discarded ribbons. Spaces were disappearing fast. A Colossus made a swipe at a fighter, which narrowly missed. Diving into one of the corridors out of the pit, the fighter desperately shook a handful of ribbons. The castle guards let go of the rope and the doorway came crashing down.

Only three spaces left; those still alive knew they had to make a stand. Hector eyed three of the brutes that had teamed together. They were trying to tackle one of the Colossus. The hammer strikes and axes rang out as they hit the stone. One of the blows was so hard to the knee of the Colossus, it caused the stone to come flying out.

More thugs pounced and repeated the action on the other leg. The Colossus was now on its knees, swinging around in circles. Hector watched as the brutes struggled, waiting for the chance to strike. Taking the stage, he leapt forward through the air, heading straight for the Colossus. In a flash, the rock changed its direction; Hector had misjudged the jump and was caught with a stone fist. Hector flipped over. Tasting blood, the Colossus tried to finish him. Rolling away, he could feel the tremors caused by the strike. One of the cattle jumped onto the arm of the Colossus. They ripped off the red ribbon before leaping back to safety.

There was just enough time to see the helmet come off, to give air to the beaded mohawk. The purples eyes found Hector in the crowd and winked. Hector quickly got back to his feet and spat the blood from his mouth. There was a limping thug close by; he grabbed them by the neck and rammed a dagger into his waist. Whilst the thug tried to break free, Hector held him, staring back at Kantra.

The slaughter continued. Hector cut down anyone in his path before making it to one of the corridors. He scowled at the guards on the platforms above him. One of the Colossus was heading towards Hector.

"We need to see them, and you have to throw your weapon."

Hector sighed and then emptied his pockets; there were at least a dozen of the yellow ribbons. Far more than needed to pass the round.

"Only one position left."

The words of the speaker rang in the prince's ears. He stepped over another body, the floor around him riddled with death. Two of the Colossus had begun to fight each other, with everyone else trying not to get caught in the crossfire. Another thunder block of a Colossus' fist, smashed through the last of the standing pillars. Zander had to leap out into one of the corridors to avoid being swept away. As he lay there panting, Zander started to count his ribbons, he still only had four.

The guards above him were in deep discussion. It was interrupted by another fighter, who came charging in looking to escape the mayhem outside. With others now looking to seek refuge, the guards slammed down the barrier to the pits. Trapped in a confined space, the two men backed off into the opposite corner, savouring the moments of safety.

Back inside the pit, one of the Colossus was pounding a corpse into dust. The remaining fighters were climbing up the bodies to scramble out of the tournament. Around the edges, the guards were appearing in pairs; they dragged bubbling cauldrons behind them.

"Clear the pits," the speaker bellowed out.

The guards obeyed and tipped over the cauldrons. Dead and wounded became caked in the hot tar, burning them to a crisp. The boiling liquid quickly ate away at the Colossus. It finally drowned out their destructive rampage. Black tar started to seep through the cracks of the pit. It spilt out into the corridors that the remaining contestants were trapped in. The toxic smell was causing Zander's head to spin.

"Prince, only one of you will go forward; the other four spaces are taken. The other needs to disappear," one of the guards whispered standing above the walkway.

Sensing the danger first, the fighter leapt across brandishing a switchblade. The price was slammed back into the wall, holding off the dagger inches from his face. A dollop of tar dropped onto the fighter's shoulder. Hollowing in pain, the blade slide across the box, both then scrambled to get it.

Zander won the race, plunging the switchblade deep into the other's chest. The fighter though still had life in them and kept clawing at the prince. There was no choice but to push the head into the hot tar. It was followed by a piercing scream. Zander stuck the knife in again. The fighter did not even seem to notice the stab wounds. They desperately tried to wipe away the burning tar from their eyes. Eventually, the screaming stopped; Zander crawled away and huddled in a corner. A trap door opened on all the boxes.

"The next stage is open. A race to the upper circle has begun. Those who make it there first, will reap the most fitting of rewards."

Five identical runways sloped upwards, filled with gaps and obstacles. The vines of the castle walls had been intertwined into the gauntlet. One slip and it was a sheer drop to the hard ground. Inching in front of the race was Kantra, who had Hector close on her tail. The large thug was finding it hard to drag himself up but was struggling less than Zander. He was soon to be overtaken by an agile warrior, her silver and gold armour now stained from the red of her opponents.

Still ahead, Kantra was now faced with a vertical climb. The vines on her runway had been mostly ripped off. She had to dig her fingers in between the cracks of the wooden slates. The faster she mastered the climb, the louder boos rang out from the crowd. Guards started to throw rocks. As she tried to protect herself, Kantra lost grip and fell. Plummeting to her death, she rammed one leg into the side of the climbing wall and pushed her back into the other side. Holding steady by using the splits, she screamed profanity as another stone hit her on the forehead.

There were no rocks thrown at Hector. Pulling himself onto the final circle, he had the first choice of the weapons. Sprinting to the sword, he gave it a swing; the weight suited him perfectly. More had been spread out across the platform;

he had just enough time to reach another, before chucking it off the side. The others were arriving; the warrior and thug went to run to the closest weapon but paused. The pair exchanged a look, but as Kantra hoisted herself up, they both made a grab. The thug picked a set of throwing knives whilst the warrior grinned, claiming the battle axe. There was one contestant still missing. Zander was drenched in sweat; his chest was on fire as he desperately tried to pull himself up. As he looked up to the summit, it might have been on a cloud. The crowd was getting restless and was adding to the unyielding fatigue weighing him down. Trying to be suitable, a guard sent a helping hand in form of a rope, with a sword attached.

****

"Are you kidding me?" yelled Kantra as she picked up the last weapon, a table knife.

"Against the might of the Colossus, the fierce jaws of the Timber Vexes, and the blades of the other contestants, these five have made it to the final circle. Now there can only be one champion but until that final duel happens, you must work together in order to survive," the speaker announced.

On cue, one of the floor panels gave way, crashing to the floor below.

"If one of you dies, then you all fall, until the command changes. Now fight."

The wooden tower became alive with new challengers. They were dressed in plain black and armed to the teeth. Each had a spring in their step as they launched themselves off the platforms, motivated by the payment on delivery with blood. Hector met them head on; the brute burned through the daggers. Barely hitting a target, he looked to the warrior next to him. She managed to lift the axe in a lazy swing. Zander had drifted towards Kantra.

"You're the one with a sword," she barked but Zander kept hold of his weapon. A fighter came between them. Kantra dodged and hit them in the back, before throwing them into the path of Zander. He raised his sword, but the panel dropped in front of him, the fighter disappearing with it. A shoulder came into Zander's spine; Hector laughed as he stumbled into the gap. Kantra just managed to catch the prince before he fell. The warrior screamed as she let go of the battle axe, spinning into the chest of one of the fighters. Their body had not even landed, as the thug ripped the weapon away and started on the assault.

Hector, the thug, and warrior, who had now each collected a weapon more suited, spearheaded the slaughter of the other fighters. They tiptoed around the holes in the floor, before dispensing their opponents with ease. The thug went for the theatrical and jumped with the axe raised. As he smashed it down, he missed the target. A fighter then rammed a sword into the exposed gut. The thug groaned; Kantra arrived and stabbed the fighter in the back of the head.

"Stay on your feet."

The thug gave a limp nod. One of the taller masked fighters pushed past the others and came straight for Kantra.

"Prince, you need to make sure he does not pass out."

Zander put his head under the arm of the thug. Still only armed with a table knife, Kantra did not shy away from the challenge. The aggressor was armed with an axe. Even with her determination, Kantra was forced back. As she dodged and ducked, the force of the aggression caused her to lose sight of her footing. Kantra stepped onto air and went backwards. The fighter stood over her and took off the mask. It was the face of the brute she had encountered in jail, minus an eye.

179

"Think I'd forgotten about you, love? I told you I wouldn't. I'm here to split you in half."

The brute went to strike down his revenge. Moving just in time, the blade came inches away from Kantra's face. The only retaliation she could muster was to run the knife across his wrist. It did not do much damage but was enough to cause the brute to pull back, leaving the axe. Kantra slammed down on the panel the brute stood on. As it buckled, the brute tripped in the direction of Kantra. Leaping back to her feet, Kantra grabbed the axe. Blood poured out of his neck, eyeball expanded, as his head went flying off his shoulders.

"And I told you I would take your tongue. I guess that is close enough."

The circle was full of corpses. The thug with the gut wound was pale and threatening to join them.

"Halt," the speaker yelled. Hector kept fighting. "I said halt."

Hector pushed the last of the fighters off the platform, but then lowered his sword.

"Congratulations, you have all made it to the finals alive, well for the most part. As you know, there can be only one winner. I will make this quick for you all," Hector said, followed by a smirk.

There was a murmur from the crowd. Quickly, the speaker repeated something similar. Zander pushed himself away from the thug, who almost bowed straight away without the support.

"Fight."

The warrior reacted first, coming at Kantra. Spear met sword as the two became locked in a duel. Using her free hand, Kantra punched the other woman in the face. The warrior took the blow well and landed her own strike. It caused Kantra to pull back but the warrior came again, right into a trap. Kantra pounced and with a clean strike, sliced off a hand. There was a deafening scream. Backing away, the warrior was staring at the bleeding stump where her hand used to be. The crowd, high off the bloodthirst, roared as Kantra peeled back the fingers from the spear. With both weapons in hand, Kantra moved closer.

"Jump, you might have a chance of still surviving."

The warrior was not listening; the look of sheer terror was transfixed on her missing limb. With chants of encouragement from all angles, Kantra sighed. Both spear and sword were driven into the warrior's chest.

Hector was circling the thug. Occasionally, he would slice another chunk before moving back.

"Just me, you, and the girl left now, prince. I didn't even know cattle were allowed to get this far."

The thug made another swing at Hector.

"How do you fancy your chances?"

Like a vulture, Hector swooped in at the thug, ripping out his insides before pushing away the carcass. Taking a deep breath, Zander made the first move. Charging at Hector, he tried to catch him by surprise. The jab was blocked. Zander swung again and Hector stumbled. Lurking in the background was Kantra. Now armed with two swords, she was waiting for her time to strike. The two men seemed to have forgotten about her, or even worse they were not that concerned. A big mistake as she picked her moment; both swords went straight for the back of Hector. Spinning out of the way of danger, Kantra missed. Both blades almost went into the prince.

"I was going to wait but looks like you are eager to die."

Hector now turned his attention; Kantra cursed herself for not landing the first blow. As they duelled, it was clear that Hector had the technique and training over Kantra, but not the power. He would try to disarm her by knocking one sword down, then aiming for the wrist. Kantra would swing the other sword with such a might, that it would almost shatter his weapon. Zander joined the assault, with two verses one, Hector could do nothing but defend.

Boos were starting to ring out. Kantra beat away the sword, then with her own, went for the heart. Hector moved out of the path, but the blade caught him across the chest, drawing blood. There was a collection of gasps. Hector snarled then retaliated. In a single move, he stuck both of Kantra's swords in the opposite direction of each other. With her body open, Hector locked the arms of Kantra and spun her round, into the path of Zander's sword. Catching Kantra on the shoulder, Hector then pushed her into the prince and both of them when tumbling to the floor.

Holding up his hands, Hector soaked in the praise now orbiting him. Kantra kicked Zander and then readied herself for the next round. The evening was settling in; the light was fading, and on cue, the outer circle of the platform became alight. There was a type of squeal from Hector. Transfixed on the flames, his body looked to be in a state of confusion. He would reach forward but then pull himself back, stuck in a trance.

"I won't be burnt again; I don't care what you want. There will be no more of you" Hector was screaming now whilst continuing to fight an invisible enemy. All around him the crowd watched in shock, as Hector appeared to argue only with himself.

There was no hesitation from Kantra; taking a long run up, she leapt through the air. Both feet landed square into the back of Hector. There was no resistance as he was thrown through the flames and out of the tournament.

The courtyard fell into a deafening silence, only to be broken by Hector hitting the ground. With that, the protests started; betting slips were torn up as members of the crowd stormed off. General Balder jumped out of his chair, letting it fall backwards as he too made his exit.

It had become very lonely in the circle for the last two. Zander was holding up his sword in between coughing. Kantra was pacing up and down like a cadged animal.

"There can only be one winner," the speaker bellowed.

The words forced Zander to start another assault. Like a drunken boxer, he staggered around, landing little punches. Kantra was only using one arm to block; the wound to her other shoulder was bleeding heavily. Taunts were starting to mount up. The promised clash of the titans was not living up to the spectacle. Zander went for all or nothing; aiming for Kantra's shoulder he put all his weight behind the attack. Kantra sidestepped the move, her opponent stumbling forward was left total exposed, but rather than taking her chance, Kantra fell to the floor. The prince stood over her, blocking the view for the rest of the crowd; Kantra took out a dagger and stabbed it into her leg.

"Remember this when your king." Kantra held up her hands; Zander looked confused.

"You caught me with your sword, that's what happened."

The penny dropped as Zander slowly raised his sword into the air. Putting the truth to the back of his mind, Zander started his victory lap of the circle. The speaker was resisting his prepared speech, encouraging people to vote in their confidence in the King, in the spirit of the Day of Dontés. The tournament was over, but no cheers came, no celebrations or praise from the crowd, just noise, a defining noise.

## *Chapter 17*

Another loud roar could be heard in the distance. It came across the walls that surrounded the zone, through the black smoke that bellowed all around. Hellrous was burning; the residents had torn down houses as the streets had been ripped apart. The last of the soldiers that were not at the tournament, were walking alongside the masked healers. Each had a weapon drawn as they tried to search for signs through the smoke. Their progress was slow, as around each corner, they came across bonfires and roadblocks.

The masked healers were sluggish themselves as those inside were still adapting. Inside her suit, Erica was already hot and sweaty. The mask felt like a brick had been put on her shoulders. It was tight to her face, which was restricting the amount of air she was getting. Through the sockets, she could see some of her former patients watching the group pass. They looked smaller now as she towered above them. Erica gave out a wave; there was none back.

Iron bars had been bent backwards, the chains in pieces. The barrier to the centre of Hellrous had been ripped open. Soldiers lined up on either side as Darian started to inspect the breach.

"Don't be long because we won't wait," the commander said.

The horn of Darian's masked nodded slightly, before he headed into the unknown. There was a burst of flame; the masked healers held up long golden poles with torches on top. Others ignited golden balls hanging on chains; a burst of orange then purple smoke flowed out.

Normally met with demands and frantic energy, they were left standing alone. The central zone was derelict. Erica could feel the drop in temperature even through the suit. There was no natural light. It was so deep in the valley, that it was always cast in shadow, no matter which directions each of the suns were facing. It resulted in little to no vegetation being able to grow and the ground drying up. The centre of Hellrous was a tribute to the darkness it was engulfed in.

The theme continued as the group walked. Vacant streets matched the cold stone buildings. Square with no windows or doors, the buildings were as soulless as the rest of the land. Although deadly quiet, they would still need to be searched; the missing healers could be anywhere. As Erica and the others walked through the entrance, the flames from the masked healer's torches caused shadows to dance across the stone surface. Inside, it was deserted, only the sense of a deadly secret being hidden in the black.

Onto the next building, an elderly man appeared wearing nothing except a rag. The man had long white hair and eyes jet black, just like the rest of his body. Disease was everywhere; toes and fingers were curled and decayed. His heart could be seen beating on the surface of his skin. Both hands went up; down his arms were thick stains of a dark and menacing red. There were no visible wounds to the man. He kept his hands up and then walked forward; the masked healers moved out of his way, and the man strolled off into the nothingness.

Inside, it was almost empty except for a blanket and a few bits of rubbish. Propped in the corner were the remains of a person. Their sex was unidentifiable, as the injuries were so severe to the face and the chest. They had been ripped apart, exposing the insides that had turned rotten.

The search continued. More buildings turned up nothing. They were moving too slowly, creeping round every corner expecting something to jump out at them, until something did. The masked healers were gathered around a deep pit. As the light from the candles crept further down to each crevasse, more bones were uncovered.

Darian leaned down. "This isn't what we are looking for."

There was now a clear sign; it came in the form of a long and thick blood stain, dragged across the floor. The trail led into the largest of the buildings, with red all around the doorway. Everyone hesitated; no one wanted to follow the path of horrors.

Inside, it was one long rectangular hallway, made to seem endless as the far side was hidden in the dark. Running parallel to each other were three pools, also running off into the distance. Each one was drained, with silver and red stains up the side of each pool, but still empty. The blood was still thick across the floor, too much for one person. It had split up and ran in three separate trails, just as the masked healers did.

Nothing in the centre made sense to Erica. Her time in Hellrous had been spent giving false hope and promises to its patients. There was no special treatment here or chance for a better life, only desolation and abandonment. Everyone stopped as the light uncovered that of revulsion from the darkness. Feet appeared then arms and hands, countless bodies rotting at the bottom of the pools. They had become plagued by the curse eating through to the bone. With the stench of death nauseating, horror hung in the air. For the first time, Erica was thankful for the mask.

Back at the entrance of the central zone, the crowd around the soldiers was now blocking all the exits. None of them wore the markings of the Black Hand but looked just as threatening. The commander was itchy, as was his unit.

"How much longer are we going to wait?" one of Eldertude soldiers asked.

Only half of the agreed time has passed.

"If the real masked healers could not stomach in the centre, there is not much chance of those coin grabbers surviving," the commander replied.

All around them, torches were being set alight, rags tied around stones. There seemed to be a plan, but others could not wait. The flaming missiles started to rain down on the soldiers as they held up their shields. The commander gave the order, "They are on their own now."

****

Erica and the others had found the sources of the blood, more bodies at the end of the building. The open surface was covered in corpses. Some were naked, the others wearing the masked healers' uniform which had been shredded. Only one was lying face up; it was a middle aged woman stained in red. The woman gave a dry cough and shifted slightly. Most of her hair had fallen out; the clothes she wore were nothing

Erica

more than a few rags. Next to her was an empty Improx bottle. Darian and Erica bent down to the side of her.

"She is still alive; get me some water."

Erica produced a canteen and lifted it gently to the woman's dry lips. She coughed again and opened her eyes. Dust had settled upon the blood-stained face. The injury must have drained all her strength, the last of it spent keeping herself breathing. A dose of water seemed to give her a few drops of life; she gave a grisly, haunting cough then gestured for Darian to lean forward.

"What happened here?" Darian asked.

"The disease happened; it came and took our people, killing them without mercy. It took the lives of the innocent, hiding itself amongst us."

The woman coughed again and took another sip.

"I have seen so much death, so many lives lost. There is only one way to stop a disease that cannot be treated. All stems of it have to be removed and destroyed."

As the injured woman spoke, her voice became clearer, louder. It absorbed those around it, as if it had crawled under the skin and was gnawing at the bone.

"We have seen so many bodies on the way in," Darian said.

"And that seems to surprise you?" the woman replied. Time was running out. Erica could feel another danger closing in on them, unsure what exactly but certain it was waiting in the darkness.

"Why are the masked healers being slain?" Darian's patience was running thin.

"The riots on the other side of the zone have stopped

189

supplies. No more pools, no more treatments. Our bodies changed again and again. For the first time, the blackness which appeared touched our souls."

Her voice had changed; the timid, broken woman was gone.

"It was strange; we kept on living. Our souls had been consumed but not broken, reinvented."

"This is getting us nowhere; the woman has been driven mad. We are going to have to move on."

Darian went to leave. The woman grabbed his arm and sat up bolt upright.

"We had a curse all around us. Inside, making us weak, putting those to death."

There was a stir in the bodies around them. Something was wrong. A scream could be heard far off in the distance. It echoed from outside. The bony hand around Darian's wrist only tightened.

"You are the disease, and you must be destroyed."

The woman jammed a dagger straight into the stomach of Darian. All of the bodies reacted at once, jumping into life. They pounced on the unsuspecting masked healers in a joint attack. Everyone was caught off guard, quickly leading to a slaughter as the numbers were overwhelming. Some tried to fight back, only to have the darkness consume them.

Erica had reacted well enough to block a lunge, only to be thrown into one of the empty baths full of dried blood. A masked healer with slash marks all across the chest came crashing down next to her. *Run*, the only thought in her mind as she crawled to her feet. A few others had escaped, running down the pathways as the sound of death chased them. Erica was in a blind panic; she forgot about the pile of rotting corpses. Unable to stop herself, she landed on top of them.

Even with the mask, the smell of decomposition could not be hidden; it rose up her nostrils and gripped Erica by the lungs. As she pushed herself up, her hands slid through the rotten flesh of the victims. Dragging herself out of the pool, she joined the healers exploding out of the doorway, running back towards the gates for their lives. It was then Erica truly realised how far away she was from safety. The warm home and caring family seemed a lifetime away, separated by a twisted blizzard of a living disaster.

Sprinting fast enough just to make it out alive from the centre of Hellrous, Erica had stepped out of one nightmare into another. The armed escort for the healers was long gone. All that remained were the bodies of both soldiers and residents. Homes were on fire as Hellrous had again descended into anarchy. There was a clear path of desolation as the soldiers had battled their way back towards the zone's entrance. Where Erica stood now was relatively empty. She guessed most of those must have chosen to chase out the remaining soldiers.

There were still people though, prowling the streets. They held chains and iron bars, ready to deal out punishment where they saw fit. Erica had no real experience with fighting and had no interest in gaining any today. Quickly, she ducked into a narrow alleyway; pressing her body up against the wall, she squeezed under a fallen roof panel. Surrounded by vehemence, Erica wanted just to crawl up into a ball and disappear from the world. One of the houses she was pressed against was on fire, the roof slowly burning. Erica shut her eyes, enjoying the few moments before the violence found her.

An arm grabbed her shoulder. Erica almost jumped out of her skin; gleaming back at her was Leo.

"You are in great danger; they are hurting everyone."

"Have you seen any of the others?"

"The healers have been chased; I don't know where to though. The soldiers are still here, I think, but they are surrounded."

The cries and screams were getting closer.

"I need to get you out of here, Erica."

"Leo, if they know you are helping one of the healers, they will kill you as well."

"You spent every day in here, risking your life to help the people, my family and me. You didn't even say anything when you saw the tunnel. Erica, I am going to try and lead you to safety. First though, you are going to have to take off your uniform."

Sinister figures still roomed the street. As much as Erica and Leo tried to use the shadows as cover, it was not long before they ran straight into company. The topless man had one eye ripped out. Its remains were smeared down his face and chest. In his hand, he held a pipe covered in blood. Erica and Leo both crouched down almost to their knees. He held up the pipe and began to yell at them. The words were indistinguishable. Erica wrapped her figures around the handle of her dagger. Before either one could move, one of the masked healers came charging past. The man yelled again and then charged off in the direction of the healer.

Elsewhere, the commander dragged up one of the soldiers from the mud. Missiles rained down onto their shields that were held above their heads. Slowly, the Eldertude soldiers made their way to the entrance gate. Trying their best to group together, eventually gaps would appear. Attackers would run up and try and inflict damage, but the soldiers would cut them down or get dragged out. Even with the trail of bodies, the soldiers were almost at the line of safety. The walls to Hellrous were now lined with archers. With the backup arriving, the mob received reinforcements of their own, coming in the form of the Black Hand.

"Stop, stop, stop!" the commander bellowed. His words brought a halt to the missiles. Carmen was waiting for him.

"Your deals are dirty, as are your streets and the people in them. I knew we would be turned on." The commander spat at the feet of the Black Hand leader.

"The agreement was broken by the castle first; the centre gates were meant to be closed hours ago. Now the poison flows into our streets and what do you do, run, leaving us to deal with it."

"Our hand, ironically, was forced by your people attacking us."

On the edge of the crowd were Erica and Leo. They blended in as best they could but were on the other side of the street from the soldiers.

"Erica, look."

It was the women and the other ambushers who had slaughtered the masked healers. They were recognisable by their lean muscular bodies which were all jet black. Disease had spread across every vein in their entire body. None of the previous colour could be distinguished. Some still wore the stolen masks and uniforms used for the trap earlier.

"Friends of yours?" the commander asked sarcastically.

"You have let them out— the Soldiers of the Infamous, the Demons Disciples."

The commander turned his head on cue. SIDD charged at the soldiers, breaking the line with ease. It took all by surprise. The Black Hand reacted first, but they did not take advantage of the Eldertude soldier's weakened position. Rather, they pushed past them to tackle the Soldiers of the Infamous.

## *Chapter 18*

As the suns beamed down on the courtyard, Rexis was surrounded. Pearlsa spurred them on, demanding blood as she cracked the whip. Each recruit was armed with an iron pole and charged. Backing away, Rexis put up his arms in a futile attempt to defend himself. He managed to dodge the first few swings before one of the blows finally landed, causing an avalanche to follow.

The hits came to his abdomen first, driving him to his knees. One of the Followers leaned back and brought the pole down hard onto the back of Rexis's head, sending him to the floor. The blows did not stop as he lay face down; the Followers were relentless. Rexis could feel the battering to his body but still his mind worked. Before the next strike, he flipped over and grabbed the iron bar.

He took out the legs of the Followers he had just disarmed and spun himself up. The others were on him again, but now Rexis had a way of defending himself. Blocking shots as best he could, he shuffled backwards, until his back was against the wall. With nowhere else to go, Rexis had only one option. He jumped back, launching himself off the rock into his aggressors. They fell backwards, and Rexis took the advantage, swinging his pole into the face of a Follower. Blood and teeth sprayed everywhere.

"Halt!" Pearlsa yelled but Rexis ignored her. He went to strike again but the pole was ripped out of his hands. The whip had ripped away the weapon and was now at the feet of Pearlsa. The other Followers were trying to tend to the worst injured, but he was struggling to keep consciousness. Still panting, Rexis did his own assessment; there were cuts and scuffs but no real damage. The only real pain was coming from his stomach.

"Stop helping him," Pearlsa said, marching over. The others backed off as the injured Follower could now just about stand.

"Collect your teeth."

There was a weak nod from the Follower who leaned down. With his back turned, Pearlsa then bound the whip around the throat of the unsuspecting victim. Without the strength left to resist, all the Follower could do was grasp at air. Pearlsa held him up, so all could witness the terror in his eyes before the pupils finally dilated.

"There is no weakness of body or mind, to those who can truly reach out and touch our leader. They will not bleed; they will not be allowed to die. If there are any more imposters amongst us, leave now; you can still walk away."

The five Followers looked at each other with one glancing to the courtyard's exit. Pearlsa snatched out the pole from her hands and threw it to Rexis.

"Looks like it's your turn."

****

Rexis watched the candle flicker next to his bed. The draft was almost enough to blow out the flame, as the breeze whistled through the cave. It crept up onto the shoulders of Rexis, sending a shiver through his body.

"I get now why they decided on red." Terra picked up the discarded robe; it was covered in bloodstains. "This is worse than the washing at home. I do not want to stay here much longer."

Rexis just stared at her.

"Are you okay?"

The young girl edged towards the bed and pointed. His stomach was glowing all across his abdomen. Pressed up under the skin was a small round block; it was radiating a violent string across the body. Terra pulled away and grabbed her own wrist. As she rolled up her sleeve, the black rot on her arm had changed colour. Moving it back to Rexis' stomach, it began to glow.

More light entered the chamber; the Followers carried candles in their hands. Terra pulled her sleeve back down and hurried off with the sack. As the four approached Rexis, he jumped up from the bed. One of them held up a hand.

"This is not an ambush."

Rexis slowly sat back down; the others joined him. Terra melted away.

"Too much time is being wasted. We are not helping ourselves or the Templar. Many others wait to take their place in the journey. As trainer Pearlsa says, we will be found out eventually. Now, we get to decide to go further, or our lies get cut open just like our bellies. Now some of us may think we are ready for this, others might be just chancing their luck. Reading every page written on the history of our great leader does not make you a part of him. All of us have been touched, but only a few remain in his grasp."

There were nods all around; a blade was produced.

"We decide now which path to take, everyone hold out a hand."

Rexis was handed a candle.

"Our leader will protect us."

The Followers all put the candles inches below their palms and stared at each other. Rexis could feel the flame tickling his skin. No one flinched as the seconds slowly passed. There was a stir inside of Rexis' stomach. As he watched, the other Followers had the same glow seeping out of their robes. As he could smell the flesh starting to cook, nearly all the hands were steady. One pulled away. All the other recruits, including Rexis, surrounded the one holding his wrist.

"The last one to drag us down reveals themselves."

"I didn't know."

"There are no excuses. You have disgraced yourself, taking the place when there is another more valuable journeyman, fighting for your place."

The Follower pleaded their innocence again, louder this time.

"There is still time to repair some of the damage. You can make this choice now and be thankful it is not at the hand of our trainer."

Everyone looked at the blade. The burnt hand gripped around the handle; he held it up to his own throat. There was a tremble as it pressed deep into the neck; blood began to trickle. It came away and was swung at the Follower closest. The others pounced. As they piled on top, the weapon was wrestled away. There was little resistance as the blade went over and over again into the belly. Guts spilt out over the chamber floor.

"That is it; there are no more imposters. Only those who get to walk with him."

## *Chapter 19*

"I had rather you boy had died than the tournament ending like that," King Vidal snarled.

"You do not mean that," Queen Hermenize snapped.

"Honours of the kingdom before all. Protect the name of the castle, my name," the king muttered to himself, turning to face the window.

Back in the central tower, Hermenize, Vidal, and Zander all had been watching the courtyard. Slowly, the crowds were filtering out. The closing ceremony had been cut short; the results of the vote had still not been announced. One of the most senior castle's servants had arrived, envelope in hand.

"My king, the count is ready."

"He was victorious on the day of Dontés, no matter the method. The vote is irrelevant," King Vidal said, not turning to look at the servant.

"Those who did not spoil their slips were keen for their choices to be heard."

Zander slumped further on the bench. So far, he only managed to remove the gloves from his blood-stained armour. Vidal snatched the envelope.

"Never have the people still voted after there was a standing winner," the king yelled.

"Did they not witness that whirlwind of death? So many lives taken in the name of pride and entertainment. Those trying to survive amongst better fighters, who would not honestly take any type of a helping hand. Even with support, he still had a disease inside of him, taking his strength," Hermenize said.

"Enough!" the prince yelled. "I am sick of having to spend every day drowning in criticism. This castle is suffocating me."

King Vidal reacted first. "Then leave; maybe time away from the castle will help toughen you up. It may provide an opportunity to actually help the people outside of these walls. Not to mention repair some of the reputational damage."

The queen went to protest but the king held up his hand.

"If he is going to sit on the throne one day, it is time he became involved in its operations. We need you to travel across the Borrowed Lands, to where the land meets the ice, to see Odell the Collector. It is a mission of the utmost importance to the kingdom. It is a chance to prove to yourself, that you are of use to the people. Forget the tournament; this is a real chance to be a hero."

An arm came over Zander's shoulder. "Do not worry, I will make sure nothing happens. Things will stay the way they are," Hermenize said as the prince stared into oblivion.

"Maybe father is right. If it will bring me some respect and a chance to help people, I should take it."

The embrace stopped.

"Sorry to interpret," General Balder had appeared who did not look sorry at all. "I am here to tell you that Hellrous is now under military control. The rebels have broken off negations after a tactical ambush on more of my soldiers. The masked healers are gone, and the zone is in ruins. I have taken authority to restore some order."

"So the plan is to have the army slaughter everyone," the queen replied.

"You have such little opinion of my tactics, Your Highness. Now that the centre is open, we will not be sending any more of our people into that cesspit. No, we are simply going to wait it out."

"Then they have been condemned to a death far worse."

"It makes no difference to me," Balder replied.

Hermenize jumped up. "Then you won't mind when my son brings this kingdom a cure. Then the same people, who have spent so much time at the end of your soldier's swords, will be back on the streets. Come Zander."

As the pair left, the general looked to Vidal for answers.

"The Collector's message, from the snow pelican. It said there is a chance of salvation," King Vidal stated.

"So we trust the riddles of a madman now. There have been tails of a cure before, in a faraway land so far away that it can never be found," the general replied.

"The kingdom is rotting. The Collector would not make this claim without something to show for it."

General Balder stroked his messy beard. "Why now though?"

"There is only one reason I can imagine in his greed. Really though, the motive is unimportant. The reality is that we have few other options; soon others in the world will force our hand."

"His palace is on the other side of this realm; the Borrowed Lands have become treacherous. Armies have been swallowed up by the darkness. Not to mention that Eldertude is almost bankrupt. It will take over a hundred carts of gold just to get the door open."

"Or one stone," Vidal snorted.

"That stone is the reason the castle exists; take away its heart and the place turns to nothing."

The king turned to the window.

"Have you not walked the streets in the while, listened to the people? I thought the events in the Hellrous would have awoken you. Eldertude has been rotting to its core for years; at least this is the chance to stop that. The stone is one of the only things left in the world that the Collector has not been offered."

Balder joined Vidal at the window.

"Sending your boy is risky; if he does not make it back..." Balder trailed off.

Vidal turned to face him. "Finish the sentence."

"The council could turn."

"And what? You would support them, outvote me?"

"I am just saying. You have no other bloodline. Without another child, your position can be challenged."

"Or my child comes back free of the curse and with the ability to heal others. He would be a true hero, one that the kingdom would worship, unlike yours."

The men squared up to each other.

"How did he do with the vote of confidence?" Balder asked.

The result remained unopened, in the hands of the king. He looked down at the envelope and then held it above a nearby candle, the paper catching alight.

"He won."

# *Chapter 20*

The safety of Eldertude was creeping into the horizon. Its castle disappeared behind a ball of faded smoke. Above, the knot of trees was slowly binding the soldiers deeper into Red Claw Jungle. As they did their best to march down the overgrown path, there was a murmur in the shadows.

"Have you ever been this deep into the jungle before? I don't think I have," Zander asked.

"If you haven't been, then I wouldn't have," Luca muttered.

"It is a shame we could not take one of the panthers. I had grown quite fond of the orange one. Still think how big it will be when we get back from our mission."

Zander glanced back from his horse. The heart of Eldertude was tucked safely in his satchel.

"Does it not feel good to know that we finally are helping, to make a difference?"

"I need to go to see if the healers have all the supplies I asked for."

Luca rode off before Zander could say another word. He only got a few meters before he hit a wall of soldiers. Luca edged the horse forward as they glared back at him. One of the soldiers did not move. The horse let out a loud snort as it almost jumped onto the back of the unsuspecting. Kantra leapt out the way, almost falling into a bush.

All the other soldiers laughed as she straightened up her helmet. The plate of steel across her chest felt as if it was dragging her down. A brand of her newfound rank was imprinted on the armour. The symbol was worn by all those around her, also trudging through the mud. Kantra was already furious about having to wear the crest. So much of her life had been spent resenting the castle; now, she was a part of it. The choices however had been between paid work, or facing those who had bet on Hector to win the day of Dontés.

"Should there not be a huge sack of Red Drops dragging along behind us?" one of the healers asked to no one in particular. There was a small group of them, who spent most of their time fighting off branches or battling away the flies.

"Apparently, the prince does not need it, has some special method us peasants are not allowed to know about," another healer replied.

"Then why are we here?"

"As spares, I guess. In case the prince's main servant finally decides to take his chance and run. Who knows really, the only thing certain is that before we left, my family got paid a huge bag of coin, and there is more on the way. Is that not the reason why we are all here? I mean, with the zone now gone, how else fare our families meant to eat?"

"Hey you, put a top on your head if you are feeling the heat."

One of the healers threw the material. Erica grabbed it and spun around.

"Nothing goes on my face, nothing," Erica snapped.

"Are you okay?"

Erica was now staring into a pair of flaring hairy nostrils. Upon the horse was a concerned looking Luca, who asked the question again.

"Is there something you wanted?" Erica replied coldly.

"No, well, yes, actually. I wanted to make sure that you all have everything you need," Luca stuttered.

"We think so; there is plenty of Improx loaded up."

"Even the purple flowers?" Luca asked.

"Red Drops are, well, red."

There were blank looks all around. Slowly, Erica raised her hand to the horse's face. It shook its head, but Erica did not pull away; eventually her hand sunk into the black fur.

"This is Two Step. I already think he likes you more than me," Luca said. Erica gave a half smile.

"The Cosmo flower though. If you haven't seen it before, I would be happy to show you. All of you, I mean," Luca blundered. There was an outbreak of smiles; Luca then bid them all a good day.

Latch's hand had not left the handle of his weapon; his eyes darted around the wilderness. There were so many different arrays of green life, all had to fight for a spot amongst the dense plantation. Even the vibrant flowers looked as if they could devour each other given the chance. The further they walked, the more wildlife appeared. Colourful birds chirped away, as twigs and leaves crunched away as others slithered to safety. Occasionally, a swarm of Smitten Apes would gallop through the trees. They would stop overhead, point and natter away, then return to the hidden corners of the jungle.

For years, the main road out of the kingdom had been preserved. Over time, when the world's relationships had eroded, so had the desire to protect it. Now, only braved by travellers and merchants, the vines and bushes had taken back the pathway. There were yells from partway down the convoy. The Lead went galloping down the line to investigate. One of the carts had gotten itself entangled with a large tree root. The soldiers were mostly shouting and arguing, rather than putting any hands to work.

"We cannot be sitting around like this," the Lead muttered as he scanned the jungle. There was so much greenery, that it was hard for the eyes not to get lost in nature. The blend of colour was a constant trick on the senses. Straining his ears, the huffing and puffing masked the sounds, which were circling the Eldertude troop.

Then it came, a single cry— animalistic in a tone— which seemed to come from all directions. Kantra heard the shout from afar; she drew her sword just in time to see the wilderness swarm towards them. The Hammer next to Latch went to charge; the Lead held up a hand.

"So our stalker reveals itself," the Lead said.

The numbers kept growing by the second; it was as if the trees were transforming into clenched fists and plated hair. Flesh was only covered by small parts of leaves and wood. From head to toe, their skin was a mixture of yellow and blue patches. All the Waro carried the same two weapons, either in both hands or tucked into belts. Half-moon swords, curling up past the back of the arms. The deadly tips stood just above the shoulder blades, like the heads of cobras.

"Do not tell me this is not expected, Pontiac."

The Lead seemed to be addressing one in particular, a short but powerful looking Waro. There was a response but not in the same language. Nearly all of those around the Lead started murmuring in the same quick tongue. The horse kicked up, the Eldertude soldiers started to close in on the Waro. Both parties squared up to each other.

"Do I need to remind you, Waro, of the agreement?" the Lead shouted. This time, Pontiac looked up.

"We want more." Her words were sharp. Tilting her head, the beads in her hair rattled against the bark.

"The negations have already been done."

Before the words had left his month, one of the circular blades spiralled through the air. It slammed into the tree closest to the prince. The Lead was now off his horse, the Hammers were at his side, and the Eldertude soldiers were ready to pounce. A long and ragged scroll appeared in the hands of the Lead.

"The Waro are the true beings of the jungle, are they not?"

Around him there were the faintest of nods.

"Their dedication to what grows and exists around them, makes them the most natural of all. Then why would they lie on such a grand scale?"

The Lead threw the papers at the feet of Pontiac; she took out one of her blades and picked up the scroll with the tip. As she held it up, there were various symbols and handprints at the bottom of the long lines of text. Pontiac grunted then started to shout again in her foreign tongue; immediately the

Waro ascended onto the marooned supply cart.

"That's more like it," the Lead muttered.

The royal escort for the prince now had an escort of their own. Waro walked in between any of the gaps of the soldiers. All the Hammers had now surrounded Zander. It had bunched all of the other non-combatants together. The language of the leaves was a constant sound, drifting up to the Smitten Apes waiting above. The Eldertude soldiers taking point halted. Their boots sunk into the dirt as the road melted away. They had reached the edge of the Ethereal River. Zander climbed down and put his foot in the water.

"This river runs all the way back to the kingdom," one of the soldiers said.

"Maybe we could follow it home," Erica meant to whisper.

"Only if you fancy your chances against the rapids." The soldier was right. It may be easy enough to conquer the river directly in front of them, but it soon took a terrifying turn. A hazardous drop followed by a raging current, quickly followed by a minefield of rocks.

"They're still surrounding us," Latch said and looked up; the waterfall above them was lined with Waro. The entire Eldertude troop was now at the riverside; the Waro continued to push them forward. The Lead went to protest but Pontiac already had an answer. Around them, busy hands of the Waro were at work; long planks of bark were placed on the steppingstones. Slowly, a zig zagging bridge was forming across the water's surface. Evening was on the horizon; the Eldertude soldiers were thinking about making camp and had started to unpack. In preparation for the night, one of the Hammers lit a torch; the Waro swarmed around it.

The Hammer gripped the burning torch, holding it up to

the sky; the flames sparked a rage in the eyes of those around it. Hands grabbed at the Hammers; all pushed back as neither wanted to give up an inch of their line.

"Put it out," Pontiac demanded.

"There is nothing in that deal that says we have to be blind, when being led to oblivion," the Lead hissed.

"So the invisible line through our jungle moves further north. This is nothing to us. The Waro want the jungle to heal, that is all. If you must scald the plants, then you must move quickly; otherwise, I will not be able to stop those around us from violence."

The suns had not yet set but the Eldertude soldiers had lit more torches. The Lead made his assessment quickly, as the Waro started to unhinge their weapons.

"We will cross if you take us there."

Pontiac stepped onto the wooden board, with the entourage around her following suit. Begrudgingly, the Lead started to make his way across the stepping stones. As the rest of the soldiers began to make their way across the river, Kantra was hesitant; she glanced back to the jungle. There was no break in the line of the Waro. One of the other soldiers pushed into her and she stepped up onto the plank. It bent under the weight as her boots became totally submerged.

The creaking of the wood was the only sound that could be heard. Smitten Apes were now lining the trees across the riverbed. Kantra started to push forward toward the prince. Nearly everyone from Eldertude was now in the middle of the river.

"Get in line, soldier."

Kantra ignored the order and instead called to Latch. He

was part of the tight ring around the prince and the healers. Latch's head turned, but he barely acknowledged Kantra. Instead, he moved a little bit closer to the Hammers next to him.

"We are not moving any further. I'm not having my soldiers trip and drown in the night. Light more torches," the Lead shouted.

Waro started to protest, but it was overlooked. Pontiac gave a whistle. Red Claw Jungle started to hum; turquoise light illuminated the trees as the ground looked to open up. Fireflies swarmed the river, bathing all in a warm blue glow. They spread themselves out but mostly circled Pontiac, giving her a halo.

"Got an answer for everything, haven't you?"

"Fire brings nothing but destruction. Put out your torches."

"We are not going completely blind to rely on some bugs."

"Then just those closest to the trees."

The Lead thought it over, but without finding another reason to argue, he passed on the message. Those still close to the jungle started to drop their torches into the water. One of the younger soldiers paused, his gaze set on the trees. There were more howls and laughter as the branches shook all across the riverbed. Taking a long swing, the soldier launched the flame. His aim was true; it whistled through the air and struck one of the Smitten Apes.

The animal cried out; its companions grabbed their heads as others were knocked off the branch. A whisper of smoke started to creep out from amongst the bushes. The eyes of Pontiac became alight.

"Do not overreact."

The cobra headed blades went spinning into the soldier next to the Lead. There were splashes as more bodies fell into the river. Blood started to pollute the clear water. The Eldertude soldiers kept losing their footing and were struggling with the surge of the Waro. More were arriving from the jungle. In an attempt to stem the tide, more torches were flung into the greenery. It only spurred on the Waro as the fighting became more intense. Kantra slashed at those approaching, her blade ripping off chunks of bamboo. One of the Waro leapt forward, swinging a rusty machete at her. Kantra beat away the sword, but the Waro landed on the plank.

The wood snapped on impact. As both of them plunged into the river, a brawl then broke out in the water. Kantra stuck the sword into the gut of the Waro. Twisting its body, Kantra then stabbed again. The Waro started to sink; Kantra went up for air, but another body landed on top of her. It was a Hammer. Their huge frame pushed Kantra back down towards the bottom of the river. The lack of air was zapping her strength. It took all her might to shove the Hammer aside.

Her chest let out a silent, crippling scream. Arms then locked themselves around Kantra. The Waro she had sentenced to a watery grave was determined not to go alone. Panic kicked in; Kantra tried to twist free, but the Waro's deadly grip only tightened. With only a few more seconds left of air, Kantra dug her hand into the Waro's wound. The deeper she went, the lesser the hold. It was only when she could feel the warmth of the first organ that Kantra was set free. The surface of the river looked to be in another world. Kantra shut her eyes and dreamt of being there, as her body clawed its way back to survival.

Above the water, the jungle was imploding. The fireflies

were now a deep red and swarmed the battlefield. Waro hacked out the innards; Eldertude soldiers drowned the injured enemy. Balls of smoke swept over the floating corpses. A massive hand dipped into the water and dragged out Kantra.

"Join the circle; protect the mission," Latch yelled.

The remaining Hammers were shuffling the prince and others across the river. Waro would swing in on vines, launching themselves at the ring. Most would be swept away by the powerful strikes of axes. Being grouped together, they were a constant target of the spinning blades. The Hammers would act as a shield for as long as they could.

"They are everywhere!" Zander cried.

"Do you still have the stone?" Luca replied.

"Who cares? We aren't going to survive much longer."

"Just stay close."

Luca held out a hand; Erica took it.

The Lead was panting; blood ran down his arm and sword. Pontiac swayed on the plank; one of her blades was missing.

"Call off the attack," the Lead yelled.

"These are the people of the jungle. They will only stop once the threat to it is gone," Pontiac snapped.

"We learnt our lesson."

"Do not insult us. Your kingdom continues to destroy the world which has given you so much."

"Then let's not disappoint."

The Lead took out a small flask and poured it all over a torch. The flame roared as did Pontiac. One of the discarded carts had the Improx seeping out into the grass. The Lead took aim.

"The jungle has suffered enough." Pontiac let out a loud, animalistic cry. It rang out above the sounds of anguish, carrying itself across the river and up to the top of the river waterfall. There was no hesitation from the Waro above, as they disappeared upstream.

"Do not stop moving," Latch said to the other Hammers.

"Do you think I plan to hang around?" Kantra replied.

"We are almost there."

"This is not what we signed up for."

"It is no different to the zone," Erica whispered.

The healers linked arms; Luca and Zander bunched in between them. Their progress was slowing; the water had been steadily rising for some time now. The current of the river picked up. It went from a steady stream to grabbing them without mercy. Most of the Waro had stopped fighting and started to cheer.

"Pontiac, what have you done?"

The head of the waterfall opened up. An endless tidal wave was unloaded. It swept through the trees and overloaded the river. There was no escape. Luca grabbed Zander as their cries were drowned out. The water hit them like a raging bull. There were flashes of desperate faces, as the troop from Eldertude was banished to the mercy of the rapids.

## Chapter 21

Alone in the kitchen, Terra crushed up the black seeds into dust. In front of her was a tray lined with golden cups. Putting down the mortar, Terra glanced back to the other room, then started to pour in the content, except for one. Using a spoon, she then stirred each cup already filled with Necro.

It was the early afternoon and that meant it was time for the fog, as Terra called it. The yellow room became full of a hazy mist as a thick smoke slowly trickled in. Terra spent as much time possible outside as she could get away with. The fumes left a foul taste in her mouth, and the more she breathed, the less connected Terra felt to her body. She took a little respite as the smell hung to drapes and furniture. Each time a Templar would look the other way, she would venture as far into the cave as she dared.

Holding the tray, Terra started to make her rounds. Each woman watched as a cup was placed down in front of them. Nobody touched their drink. Terra was almost done handing them out; she only had one cup left. The last girl had herself tucked away in the corner, legs up on the chair. A boat wheel tattoo was visible on her shin. As Terra approached, she put her head between her knees. With stringy chestnut hair, it hid most of her mouse like face. A cup was presented to her. The girl glared at Terra.

"It's okay," Terra said as she gestured again with the drink. "I made it just for you."

In her hand, the girl fiddled with a knot tied with a small piece of rope. A shadow appeared over them.

"It is time," the Follower said, looking down her nose at the girl.

Next to them was a headshot portrait of a young blonde woman. Through the flowers and the cloth lined up to the sides of the picture, her bright smile beamed out. The woman had olive skin and mesmerising eyes, one red and the other white.

"Drink up," the Follower said again, this time holding up the cup. The girl held it up to her mouth, and then threw it in the direction of the portrait. Grabbing a fist full of hair, the girl tried her best to wriggle free as she was dragged across the room. An arm came around Terra as she was also pulled away. In the kitchen, a bony finger went to a mouth, as the pair watched the girl be taken to her punishment.

"That could have easily been you," Nola said, taking the tray off Terra and slamming it down.

Bone thin, the woman was not much taller than Terra. There were thick rings around her eyes, married with a long scar running across her neck.

"I did as I was told," Terra said.

"Do not lie not to me; I saw the colour on the portrait. Run out of seeds, did we?" Nola replied, hands on hips.

Terra blushed.

"If you get attached, you will be dragged down with them."

"I know her from home," Terra pleaded.

Nola ran a hand over her bald head.

"That is not something you want to be sharing, with anyone."

Terra scratched at her wrist; Nola opened her mouth.

"I know, if I don't stop it will bleed," Terra said before Nola could speak.

"You have been here long enough; it should not be bothering you."

Nola inspected the black mark slowly crawling up her arm.

"It is spreading," Terra muffled.

"Have you been drinking Necro regularly?"

Terra looked away.

"You need to every day. Also being close to the tomb helps. It will not spread or get any worse, but it does stay with you."

Nola lifted up her top to demonstrate. The wrinkled skin was a faded purple and black.

"What happens if I leave?" Terra asked, scared of the answer.

"Then you have a choice; stay here and be ruled by monsters, or wonder the desert and become one."

Terra scrunched up her face and then went to wash the dishes. Nola grabbed her by the shoulders. "Get out of here though, any way you can— even if it means death."

Nola pulled at Terra's hair.

"You need to get rid of this or you be dressed in yellow soon enough."

"Let go of me," Terra cried.

The grip tightened. "Do you think I am lying? Women who are deemed to match the founder, that woman in the portrait, become nothing but livestock. I was one of those kept fed and floaty. The monsters seem to believe that our blood will help break the seal. In order to release that curse back on the world again. They took a knife to the neck without hesitation. Like I was nothing."

Terra was in tears now as the roots were being pulled out.

"As I was bleeding, one of the others tried to escape. It caused a scene, which meant less time spent with a blade to my throat. Her death meant I survived. Now though, I know what she was really doing to me. She was always jealous. That is why she condemned me to this."

Nola was shouting now. "Do not you think I am a coward, that I do not have the guts to do it? I am more than any of those monsters. I keep on going each day just to see their faces. The day when that tomb cracks open and the true evil consumes them all."

There was a cry from the courtyard; Rave knocked down another one of the Followers with a fist like a sledgehammer. It gave him enough time to pick up the chain spin and slam it into the face of Rexis. On the ground, Rexis tried to scramble up but was caught with a sharp kick to the chest. Through the sea of legs, he could see the other three Followers, also taking the blows.

The same chain spin was now wrapped around Rexis' throat. As much as he tried to resist, he was hauled outside. The prisoners put down their tools; the Nkye let them drift over to the entrance of the cave. It was not just the crowd that gathered; there were now four gigantic black cauldrons. They sat upon a bed of burning sticks and wood.

"There can be no decisions with your brothers and sisters. You have not earned the right to choose."

The whip came down hard on the back of Rexis.

"We were only trying to help the journey," one of the Followers on their knees yelled.

"Nobody cares about the motivation. The training is there for a reason. You think that because you can survive a few beatings, you have the right to take into your own hands, who gets to move forward. The Templar moves as one. We have no time for outsiders," Pearlsa shouted back.

The argument continued; Rexis looked up to the balconies and could see Malum peering down.

"There is blood on all your hands. The Follower you cut down had not been proven a failure in eyes of those who matter. Now in front of everyone, you will be punished; there is no coming back for you. There may be protection from the flames, but nothing can save you when that is drowned out."

There were more shouts of protest, but they were quickly snuffed out. More chains were placed around him. As he was pulled towards the cauldrons, Rave leaned into his ear.

"I started each fire myself. The water will melt the skin from your bones. However the training went, this was always your density."

The water was spitting out over the top. A final chain was

placed around his neck, on it a stone.

"May this drag you down, just like your actions have the Yellow Templar," Rave announced.

With the signal, each of the four recruits was dumped into the water. Rexis wanted to scream but the fire ripped through his body and took over. As he thrashed against the chains, he could not stop himself from sinking to the bottom. Trying to look at the surface, he could not keep his eyes open long enough.

Hair began to slide down his face; his skin was turning to a deep red. Rexis had already lost count of how much time he had spent in the cauldron. Each second felt like another lifetime in a noose as he choked, desperate for air. Flashbacks of being dragged down to the seabed were causing him to panic. It was not his first experience of being chucked into the water with weights upon him. Training as a High Sea Roller had been almost as brutal as with the Templar. This time, the shark had been replaced with boiling water.

There was not much time left; Rexis had forgotten how to truly deal with pain. All he could do now was close his eyes and accept his fate. His stomach began to rumble; he thought the skin around his belly had split out. Reaching down, he could feel the chains now loose. His skin felt surprisingly cooler. There was a surge through his body. With both hands, he managed to free himself some more but he was still rooted to the ground. There was only one option left. He started to pound the cauldron. It struck out but to little effect. The choking became worst as he could feel his eyes rolling back in his skull.

Now there was a beaming light in the water. It washed away the pain and before he knew it, both hands were striking out. Over and over again, the water melted the chains away. He kept on punching until his knuckles bled. The wall of the cauldron finally broke; its content spilling out into the daylight. Water spread across the circle until it made its way to the feet of the Yellow Templar. Steam bellowed off the naked body of Rexis. He put both hands to his scalp and enjoyed the fresh air, accompanied by the smell coming from the other cauldrons.

As he stepped forward, the crowd went backwards. All were staring at the white and red marks across his body. The whip bolted through the air towards Rexis; before it could land, he grabbed the end of it. Pearlsa's arm went to the floor, as did the whip. Rave pulled out a sword and headed towards Rexis.

"No more," the words rang out from the top balcony. "This is not how we treat a brother, a true Follower. Finally, we see you. Welcome to your place in the journey."

## *Chapter 22*

The rapids were relentless as the water turned its captives inside out. If it did not drown them, they were smashed against the rocks. Amongst the butchery, two had locked hands together. Other Eldertude soldiers floated past, whilst the Waro remained underneath the surface. The river then took a sharp turn; most of the water flooded out as did the people. Its riverbed was a spluttering graveyard. Victims were spread across the mud, frantically trying to clear the water from their lungs, Waro and Eldertude alike. Zander gave Luca a hard slap. He rolled over into a coughing fit.

"I can't believe we survived that," Zander said as Luca kept on coughing.

They were not the only ones. Next to them was a group of the healers, face down and stirring. A dripping wet Erica was already on her feet.

"How much water did you swallow?" Zander asked.

"In what way am I supposed to know that?" Luca replied in between coughing. "Did you manage to hold onto it?"

"Is that all you care about? Yes, I have the stupid stone."

Zander picked up the bag. One of the Eldertude soldiers then immediately jumped up and staggered towards them. They went to open their mouth, but nothing came out. There was the bleeding tip of a blade sticking out of her stomach. The Waro then yanked out the sword, taking the innards of the soldier with it.

That was the only signal needed. Zander as ran as fast as he could. Luca and those still alive were fleeing with him. They could hear blood curdling cries from the last of the kingdom's soldiers. In a panic, they were heading deeper into the jungle, entangling them further in a web of peril. Erica was struggling to keep up, but the fear of being left alone was driving her onwards.

It was not long until Red Claw Jungle consumed them. Each direction they turned only offered a path leading further into confusion. The jungle sensed their vulnerability; it rustled and hummed all around them, ready to pounce. Luca grabbed Zander's arm. A long yellow tongue dripping in a white drool tasted the air. It was quickly followed by another, then another. They watched in silence, mesmerised by the three-pronged Viper. Its heads were a tangle of yellow and red scaly skin, not much thicker than rope. The body had a hard shell, pointed downwards as it clung to the branch.

Luca backed off; as he did, he stepped on a twig. The Viper's head turned towards him, letting out a ball of the white fluid. It caught Luca square in the face; he sneezed and then collapsed. It jumped to the tree directly above. Erica dropped to his side and started to shake both of Luca's shoulders. Zander had not moved, still transfixed on the yellow and red stripes. Ever so slightly, they vibrated across the long scally skin. Each tongue was circling the prince's head. Quietly, he mouthed the same words over and over.

"To the bout."

A ball of black fur erupted from the leaves. A panther leapt onto Viper; its jaws locked around the flailing heads. Both of them fell from trees. The Viper did its best to wrap itself around the beast's body, as the panther tucked into the exposed underbelly.

"Is he awake yet?" Zander demanded. "Wake up! I did it; I linked a real grown panther."

"It will wear off soon; Vipers only stun you before they eat you, apparently."

Erica was now helping Luca to his feet. A young, fair haired healer named Alumn burst out from the trees. The look on his face told the others they needed to run.

\*\*\*\*

"Take my hand. I cannot wait here forever," Kantra yelled.

"Leave me here," Latch replied, not looking away from the rock he was holding onto. Kantra was battling against the current. She screamed at him again and he did as ordered. The two of them went under, the water throwing them in all directions. Kantra took control and fought herself back to the riverbank, dragging a helpless Latch with her.

"No wonder you were so bloody heavy. You were still holding onto your hammer. I have lost everything," Kantra said in between breaths.

"You should never let go of your weapon," Latch replied.

"Rich coming from you: I thought you could not feel fear."

"I cannot swim, and I cannot leave my hammer."

"So what was your plan?"

"To wait to see how it pans out."

"You are an idiot."

"I am back out of the river alive, with my hammer."

Kantra scowled.

"We need to follow the prince and continue the mission," Latch concluded.

"What mission? It is already over," Kantra went to continue her protest, but Latch was already gone.

**\*\*\*\***

The night was creeping in, transforming the jungle and setting the senses alight. Every echo and rustle caused Zander and Luca to freeze. There were footsteps racing towards them. Both of them crouched down in some hope they might disappear. The sound was now upon them. Appearing from the bushes were Erica and Alumn. Luca went to speak but Erica stopped him.

"There is one coming."

Hot on their trail a Waro appeared. Drawing out the long, curved blade, it charged at Zander. In the thirst for more blood, they had ignored the warning signs. From the bushes, Latch threw himself into the back of the Waro. Kantra wrestled away the blade and stuck it into their waist. It kicked and twisted away, but Kantra held onto the weapon. The wound opened up further; the pain spread across the face of the Waro. They backed themselves into the base of a tree, as the Eldertude group now surrounded them.

"Where are the others?" Latch asked.

"Which way is it out of the jungle?" Kantra said followed by a sharp kick. The Waro gritted its teeth and glared back. Erica stepped forward, putting herself in between them.

"More violence will solve nothing. There is no need to carry on this destruction of each other. The fight is over. Why keep chasing us? We can let you go back to your people, and us ours."

The Waro gave a pitiful laugh.

"You want to talk to us about destruction. You wonder why we attack you. The leaves of the trees layer our skin, the vines running the blood up to our blossoming heart. Years ago, when the elders could control the Paraforce, one of your leaders took full advantage. He ripped out the living plants from the ground, bent by the power of one man's self-indulgence to build your castle. Now you go to march the same stone through our hands, out to the nothingness to be lost into more pits of greed."

The story had kept them stationary for too long. There was a thrashing heading their way. The Waro took a deep breath. Drawing on the last of their strength, they let out a tribal cry, before their throat was slit. It was long enough for the cries to be answered. Latch led the retreat further into the green maze. The howls continued to chase them. Bushes seemed to claw at Zander, trying to hold him back. Alumn tripped up; Erica ran back to help him. Kantra grabbed the pair and shoved them forward. As they pushed on, there was a break in the trees.

The group hesitated; through the darkness there were shapes drifting across the opening. Latch ushered them to crouch down and then began to crawl forward. The rest slowly mimicked him, trying their best to avoid the sticks and branches across the ground. Latch then paused as they reached the first nest. Leaning over the wall of foliage, he quickly ducked back down. Piled upon each other in a cluster of still bodies were the Hognail. There was a chorus of humming, echoing out into the night.

One of the patrolling Hognails headed straight for them. The ears of the Hognail were twitching. It paused and stared out into the darkness, quickly followed by a deafening scream.

"Now!" Latch shouted.

The group leapt up and fled into the nest. All around them, there was a ripple of an awaking. The cries of alert rang out. All the Hognail were now on their feet and looking for blood. There were plenty of sources available appearing from the trees. Driven by the chase, the Waro steamed into the territory.

Another almighty clash broke out. Caught in the eye of the hurricane, the group ducked and swerved the claws of the Hognails. Hurdling over the nest wall, a Hognail threw itself into their path. Kantra took a swipe, her sword cutting through the bark. It was not enough to stop the animal. It landed on Alumn, digging its claws deep into his shoulders. Kantra went to fight it off, but Latch stopped her. Under the cloak of the chaos, they made their retreat into the jungle.

**** 

"If I keep walking, I am going to collapse," Zander moaned. The others chose to ignore him. "I'm serious; we need to stop."

"We have been walking for hours," Erica added.

Latch brought the group to a halt.

"So are we all just walking sacks of Hognail bait then? Ready to be left behind to feast on," Kantra hissed in Latch's ear.

"Potentially, except for the prince," Latch re[

"I have already saved you once today; you o

"It would be beneficial to keep you alive for
sible. None of the others have the same combat

"Charming, any more words of wisdom on getting back to
Eldertude?"

"We are going to leave the jungle soon, then continue on
with the mission."

All of the others, sodden in dirt and scratches, turned and
stared at Latch.

"That is mad. How are we expected to? I am defenceless, we
have lost all my guards, we do not even know where we are,"
Zander said.

"No, you do not know where we are, my prince. I do
though; we have been heading towards Acrux star. It hangs
over the road to the north, the path towards the Millside hill-
tops," Latch replied.

"This is ridiculous. I am the prince; take me back."

"That is not an option. Eventually, I will be bound by code
to follow the orders you give until my death. That will be from
the day you become the king and ruler of Eldertude, inheriting
a certain level of control over all military rule. Until then, you
have no authority over the mission I am assigned to. My orders
can only be changed by a commander or higher. Otherwise, I
must continue with whatever resources are available. The stone
must be delivered to the Collector. Who delivers it is optional,
according to the general" Latch said without blinking

"I am optional?" Zander yelled.

"The preferred option but not compulsory, obtaining the
cure is paramount."

"Luca, is this true? I thought the Hammers are meant to be compliant. Let's just find our own way home."

"You fancy our chances of navigating back through the jungle?" Luca replied.

There was another break in the trees, then nothing. No more trees or bushes, just the light from the stars and endless fields on the hillside.

"We are further than ever from home now," Zander said.

"You would rather be back in the Hognail's nest?" Kantra snapped.

"Where is everyone else? We cannot have been the only survivors," Erica's voice trailed off as she sat on the ground. "More will come it will just take time."

No one argued, all in need of a rest, slowly they slumped to the floor. Latch was the only one who stayed on his feet.

"If reinforcements do not arrive soon, we will have to leave."

Time moved slowly as they waited, listening intently for any signs of life. Occasionally, there would be a noise heading towards them. Everyone would tense up, readying themselves for another fight. It would pass and they would continue to hold out hope.

"No one is coming," Kantra said.

"Just a little longer," Erica said in almost a whisper.

The rain started with a few drops which turned quickly into a heavy downpour. Kantra put an arm on Erica's shoulder. "Latch thinks there is a town up ahead. Come on."

As the group marched through the rain and mud toward the glow in the distance, Latch was indeed right.

"I have heard stories about this place," Luca said. "I was always told never to trust a single word spoken here. I could not imagine a time I would actually be here."

Walking into Darnspur, those from Eldertude were stepping into another world. The city had been made famous by its reputation, as a gathering point of swords for hire. Those available ranged from big time thieves to small armies. As the last of the kingdoms had shrunk, the demand for muscle had skyrocketed. The last resources of the Borrow Lands were mainly being taken by force, with many willing to help for a price.

Gangs had not only been the only reason for the town's existence. Darnspur was placed on the world's largest remaining natural source of fuel. It was dangerous and exhausting, but the mines offered stable work for those with little else to choose from. Most of the profits were taken by the criminal who owned the mines. With only a tiny amount of the money making it to the workers, it was just enough to keep their families fed. Many though were thankful not to be prisoners of the mines already.

The function of the city dictated its aesthetic design. Huge spiralling towers and roaring furnaces bellowed out smog and black soot. Its roads were a constant flow of huge carts stuffed to the brim, whilst skeleton like figures helped wheel them out. Run down factories dominated the landscape. Attempting to find space in between the factories were the makeshift homes of the workers. Built from scraps taken from the mines, the other buildings in Darnspur were nothing more than a slum.

As the group wandered the streets, the air seemed to absorb the light. There were plenty of fires, lanterns, and torches hung up in force, but it was all in vain. Its black smoke was everywhere, darkening every corner and forcing the city to exist in a shadow.

The further they walked, keys turned in locks and windows slammed shut. Workers and residents gave scowls, then would clear around them. One of those on the street did not walk away— a rough looking heavily armed brute leaning against a wall. The others met his gaze, all focusing on the distinct feature of the man; he was watching through one eye.

Kantra went to challenge him, but Luca stopped her, "Look at us." He was right; although soaked through and covered in dirt, they still were all in the official uniform of the Eldertude. Not only was the son of royalty within the party, but also the heart of the kingdom. A priceless stone loose in a plain leather satchel, brought into the den of the Borrowed Lands' most notorious thieves.

"We have to get off the streets," Luca mumbled. No one contested, still in a state of shock. After turning another corner, their hearts lifted. In all the gloom and smog, tucked in between two factories was the Rat Bag tavern. The paint was peeling off; there were holes in the roof and the windows looked like they had never been cleaned. The group saw none of that. To their starved minds, the inn only offered a hot meal and a warm bed.

The inside of the tavern was just as rundown as the outside. It was haggard and made filthy by the soot which layered the tables. Mostly, it was occupied by men who sat alone, each sipping foamy beer which became soaked in their poorly kept beards. The new arrivals caused heads to turn; all watched closely as they shuffled in. Waiting for them was a large, bald woman. She spat into a bucket as they approach the bar.

"I am after five beds and hot meals to match," Kantra ordered.

The barwoman shook their head; as she did one of her eyes span freely in the socket. It took a meaty finger to stop it.

"No beds left and kitchen closed."

Kantra sighed then looked at Luca.

"We need coin," she told him. He looked shifty then dug around in a bag. From it appeared several purple sacks. Kantra took one and threw it at the barwoman; the coins clinking together as she caught it. Testing out the weight of the bag, the barwoman's eyebrow rose slightly.

"There is one big bed we can give you; the others will have to sleep on the floor. Meat we got left is Ox."

"Will there be any veg with that?" Erica asked. The barwoman gave a toothless smile and went to leave.

"Hey," Kantra banged her hand down. "You're forgetting our beers."

Squeezing around a table, each had a huge brown tankard in front of them. Kantra was first to take a long swig of the warm beer. Erica was still trying to work out how she was going to tackle hers, as it was almost the size of her.

"I have never had a beer this large before." She lifted the tanker with both hands, the liquid running down her chin as she sipped. Putting it back down on the table, she let out a small burp; everyone began to giggle.

"This is the first beer I have ever been given," Latch said.

"Why's that, are you more of a wine man?" Erica giggled. Latch looked back at her with a blank expression.

"He is probably right; being a part of the Hammer unit, alcohol is forbidden. From what I understand about Hammers, they rarely go against a rule," Luca explained.

"One of the many ways the castle puts controls on people, trying its best to turn them into a possession," Kantra said, glaring back.

"As you rigorously explained earlier, Latch, I may not have much military authority, but I still have a place in the castle. Take this commandment with the note that one day I will be king. Therefore, I order you to drink that beer," Zander instructed in a tipsy voice.

Latch picked up the tankard with one hand and began to drink. It did not take long for him to finish it off, before slamming it back down. As he did, Latch let out an enormous belch; the table again erupted in laughter. The smiles continued as the hot food arrived. Quickly, they had become absorbed in themselves, forgetting where they were. All around them, the faces on the tables had been changing. Those who originally sat there needed but a look from the one-eyed thugs.

The doors to the inn went flying open; all the heads turned. Dressed in a tattered camel jacket, dozens of satchels, ribbons, and bracelets hung off him. Strolling up to the bar, he nodded and gave a smile to every scowl. The man's good looks were hidden by the many lines on his face. He lifted a bowler hat to the barwoman.

"Always the warmest of receptions here."

"You never showed up for our date."

The group had also noticed the new arrival, especially Erica and Kantra.

"Who is that?"

"Well, we are about to find out."

"Can I tell you all a story?" he said to his dumbfounded audience around the table.

"Now I remember being in the woods. I was sat down by the river to be exact, spending most of my time observing a lone, grey rabbit. It was the end of winter and the snow had begun to melt. The rabbit was starved as food had been scarce throughout the season. Then it spotted it, growing out of the hard ground was a single green shrub. It wanted to leap over but hesitated, knowing it should not. The shrub was growing at the entrance to a dark hole, covered in carefully arranged branches. Hunger outweighed all the other animal's instincts, as it hopped toward the shrub. Today again, I am seeing a rabbit, five in fact. You have all jumped into the den of the fox. If I were you, I would follow me for well, some sort of a chance of safety. We won't really know till we go really."

Colton reached into one of the many satchels. Before the first thug could grab him, he threw a handful of powder into the table candle. A huge burst of green light filled the room. Colton kicked over a table. Food and drinks went flying as he shoved one of the stunned thugs into another. They started to fight each other, and Colton threw another load of the powder. Rat Bag tavern erupted into a brawl. Colton grabbed those from Eldertude and pushed them out the door. The chase was on as Colton took the lead. Darting down an alleyway, he leapt over a market stall, narrowly missing a group of miners. As the others scrambled past, Latch went straight into the table. There were roars of protest as the cauldron of soup went all over him.

The gang was closing in. All entrances to the busy market were now flooded with one-eyed brutes. Colton darted behind a cart full to the brim with coal. Gesturing to Kantra, the pair of them charged. The force was enough to move it off course towards a wall; both of the horses panicked and ran in opposite directions. Their reins snapped, and it caused the cart to topple over. Its contents pored over the street, blocking one of the alleyways. Kantra kicked open a door to one of the factories and they all darted inside. Colton held a finger to his lips as they watched the pursuers rush past.

"It is a pretty quick tour, but you do get to cover a lot of the city." Colton laughed at his own joke. "Come on, lighten up. You could all be handing over one of those lovely eyes right now."

"That was some welcoming party," Erica replied.

"Those were members of the Prime Oko Gang; their boss controls the largest mine in Darnspur. They really do believe an eye for an eye, funnily enough."

"So why would you want to help us? Now surely you are in as much danger as we are?" Luca asked.

"Well, I cannot remember the last time I was not in trouble. Really though, I hate seeing rabbits get hurt."

"Do you really think we have time for games?" Kantra said.

"I have all the time in the world for you. I will be straight though, there is a rumour going around that Eldertude has let its heart wander. I wanted to see if it was true. Didn't think they would let it go hand in hand with the green king's son."

"Tell me which kingdom do you hail from?" Zander asked.

"It would be easier to tell those from which I am banned, not that there are many left. We could become allies though, if I were to be compensated."

"There it is; here is the real reason for the helping hand, looking for more of our gold," Kantra said.

"One that you were all in dire need of, might I add, and I never said anything about money."

There was a loud shout which echoed across the empty storeroom. All of the six turned to see a thin man wearing scruffy overalls.

"Oh, this is Nod. How are you doing? How are the family?" Colton said.

"Is there anyone you don't know here?" Erica added.

"What are you doing here? Wait, you're one of the brothers, are you not. Which one, I forget?" Nod blurted.

"I'm disappointed; normally, I tend to leave an impression."

"Let me remember, did something not happen to them, there is one left. Yes, that's right, you are the crooked one."

"Why does that not surprise me?" Kantra muttered.

"Yes, a brother of the Blossom Clan. It was either you, or all the brothers, who not only conned the last owner of this factory into a sale, but then the criminals who brought it next" Nod was shaking his head.

"No, not me; this is mistaken identity."

"I reckon you are the reason the Oko's are tearing up the street. There is one of our carts turned over in the streets. We now have to work twice as hard for half the pay," Nod had gone bright red. "They're in here; get in here now."


The captives were marched deep underground into the largest mine in the city. The walk took them into the gigantic caverns of the Diavik mines; the foundations of the land had been devoured. Lining the walkways, skinny figures were clawing at the coal. With tattered rags tied around their faces, the look of hopelessness could not be seen, but instead hung over them.

Now deep underground, the group were pushed into the

pitch black. For a while, they stood in silence, as one of the Prime Oko fumbled in the darkness. Striking a match, Erica let out a squeal. The room could loosely be described as an office. There were piles of tattered scrolls and old contracts, some overflowing from the various dusty filing cabinets. Also scattered around, and mainly being used as paperweights, were rare stones and coin sacks.

Sat behind an ivory desk was an ominous presence. It rose out of the chair and slammed two fists into the surface. Lucid filled the room more than the shadows. As more candles were lit, it revealed grey and faded skin starved of sunlight. Lucid leant over the desk, slowly his long black greasy hair fell to the sides. Two black sockets stared back at them.

"We caught outsiders; they have something valuable," the tallest gang member announced.

The heart of Eldertude was emptied out onto the dirty floor. Lucid walked straight past it. In the centre of the room was a stone bowl. Picking up an animal skull, Lucid dipped it into the murky liquid.

"We will stick it with the others then. Any orders on the prisoners, they are from the Green Kingdom. There's been talk they were attacked in the jungle. I know we wouldn't want to upset a customer but if the Waro has had most of them, a few more gone missing won't hurt."

"Take their eyes first," the voice of Lucid was low, like the growl of a dog.

"How insulting, you have overlooked the fact you are in the company of royalty. The younger, scared, and rather unwell looking boy is the son of Vidal, the king of Eldertude. As you all will be aware, he is not known for his willingness to let things go. His son is now a guest of your cosy but dreadful underworld," Colton announced.

"A prince will be expensive to buy back," another one of the gang said. Lucid stood up and leaned in, sniffing Zander all over.

"My father will not pay a penny. He sent me clearly knowing I could die. That was probably his plan."

Lucid grabbed Zander by the neck and dragged him to the stone bowl. Pushing his face down, Zander started to choke. It was the smell which came first, a rotting stench which burnt the senses. Thick and sticky mucus embedded with an array of coloured eyeballs. They floated at the top, some slowly turning to stare right at Zander.

"Double, that is what the Green King will pay you," Colton shouted.

"We haven't said how much yet."

"Name a price and it will be doubled; I can assure that. The prince is trying to save his treasury another bag of gold. Believe me, there is plenty."

Lucid pushed the face of Zander closer to the bowl.

"Come on, you owe me, sort of. I also owe you. Take the ransom and we will call it both our debts cleared," Colton pleaded.

"Put them in the hanging pit."

\*\*\*\*

The world had been turned upside down, at least for the six. All had their feet tightly bound. Rope from the ceiling dangled each one several feet from the floor. The guards had long gone, leaving them only with the rats for company.

"I believe that went rather well," Colton said.

"Maybe for a snake amongst the chickens, you planned to

sell us out the moment you saw us. If I had my hands free, I would rip off that smirk from your face," Kantra replied.

"That is a little harsh. You still have all of your eyes, don't you?"

"How could they want to collect our eyes?" Erica asked but Colton was not listening. He had pulled himself up towards the ceiling. With some cursing and a lot of wriggling, Colton twisted his whole body and landed on the floor, catching his bowl hat. The others looked on, trying to hide the fact they were impressed.

"You all did not think my whole plan was to stay in this cell with you. Plus, I hear princes are not worth much on the open market nowadays."

"Get us down and then we will see about your stupid plan."

Kantra was yanking hard at the ropes. Colton had been slowly taking off one of the many buckles of his footwear. Sliding neatly out was a thin, brown knife.

"Now that I think about it, the entire part you had to play has finished. Your job was to get me inside of this cage."

Colton had turned over the waste bucket. By climbing on top, he was able to reach up to the rope attached to the ceiling. He had to balance on tip toes. Leaning into Kantra, she scowled as he smiled.

"You can follow me or just leave yourself, on your own."

"Boo." Colton went backwards off the bucket. Kantra was already laughing as the rope came loose, sending all of them to the ground.

"How do we know you are not going to trick us again?" Luca asked as he helped Zander back up.

"The plan needs to remain hidden; it affects too many for it to be jeopardised. Also it is very long to explain, and I cannot be bothered frankly. Trust me though, it is important. I will walk you to the light if you let me. First though, I can say being in this prison cell gives us a rather particular advantage. In their arrogance, Lucid has little to no guards in the holding cells. Those who are about are, well, blind."

He pushed himself up at the bars of the cell. Zander asked the question everyone was thinking.

"Right, what is with the bowl of the eyes?" Erica said.

"Funny you would ask; Lucid believes that it can be used to make a magic soup or something," Colton replied.

There was a loud click; Colton grinned as he pushed open the jail door. He left and the others followed.

"We still need to get the stone back; work that into your plan," Kantra said.

Colton was busy fiddling with another one of the prison doors. Slowly, the other prisoners were coming up to the bars.

"I am setting the people free. No longer will the captives of Oko have to be locked away, in fear of when the gift of sight will be snatched away from them. I might be a bit late for some, sorry. For the most though, freedom," Colton announced to the cell of prisoners.

"Isn't that voice of the drunk? The one who is always getting thrown out of the Rat Bag."

"No, no, well, not always. Anyway, I am here now to free everyone."

The prisoners just stood there, remaining inside the cells. They were mainly full of Meral Folk. Not much bigger than a child, they huddled together. It was hard to tell the men from the women, or even their age. Nearly all Meral Folk had the same long hook nose and droopy ears. Rarely, did they concern themselves with any type of grooming; the result was frizzy hair hid most of their faces. The only feature which could not be concealed was the large eyeball in the centre of their head. Other prisoners who mixed amongst them also had one eye; for them though, it was less natural.

"Well, what's the holdup?" Kantra asked.

"So we just follow you all out of the cells to what, an uprising? Take the hold of the mines ourselves?" one of the Meral Folk replied.

It was almost laughter that followed.

Colton shrugged. "Yes, that was kind of the idea."

"What is with the racket in here?" A voice echoed down the tunnel leading to the cells; everyone froze. Light from a torch began to home in.

"The doors are bloody open; it's not time for work, is it?" One of the Prime Oko gang appeared at the entrance of the large cell. The prisoners had gathered to the back of it; the guard went in, further straining his one eye. Everyone had gathered at the back; all were mostly small and thin, blending into one.

"Look at the size of you," the guard blurted.

There was no hiding Latch. Before the guard could say anymore he leapt on him. Latch wrapped both of his huge hands around the neck of the Oko. Kantra reacted just as fast, grabbing the knife from his belt and ramming it into the belly of the victim. Gutting him, Kantra then smeared the blood onto the Meral Folk closest to her.

"Now, we are all in it together," Kantra said, and Colton

smiled at the stunned faces. There were more voices coming toward them.

"What is the plan?" Latch asked.

"Well, you've put me on the spot now," Colton replied.

Kantra sighed and started to swing the knife at the other Meral Folk. They jumped back as she came for them. Colton followed suit by picking up the flame and waving it at the rest of those in the cells. The guards were not expecting it; the fleeing crowd came crashing into them.

"This way."

Colton disappeared down one of the tunnels, letting the other Meral Folk spill out into the mines.

"I can't imagine they will put up much of a fight," Erica said.

"No, it's a fact they will be herded up pretty quickly," Colton replied.

"Then we need to escape as soon as possible," Luca said.

"We should not leave the heart of the kingdom here," Zander mumbled.

"There is only one way I can think of."

Colton turned another corner into the vast cavern of the Diavik Mine. It was impossible to tell how deep it went. The place had barely any light at all. Faded green gems amongst the rock offered no reflections from the few burning flames. What could be seen was the death trap of a place it was to work. There were shear drops everywhere. The bridges and wooden walkways looked as if they could come apart at any moment. Piles of rocks held up with a few iron pipes threatened an avalanche of death.

"It is pitch black in here. Are the gang hoping that we just fall off the sides rather than having to catch us?" Erica asked.

"The rock they are mining for is highly flammable and burns longer than any forest wood. It is used to keep the factories running," Colton replied.

"Okay, it is starting to make a little sense now why Lucid takes the eyes, so they do not need light to work."

"You would think so but no."

There were shouts echoing around the mine, followed by the squeals of the Meral Folk.

"Time to move," Colton said as the group charged across a rope bridge. It strained under the weight and with Latch at the rear, the bridge gave out. With the ground disappearing under their feet, some reacted better than others. Erica, Kantra, and Colton who were the closest to the other side scrambled to make it. Latch, Luca, and Zander did not.

The three of them plummeted into nothing. Luca snatched at anything he could, desperate not to plunge into the bottomless cavern. He was rewarded with the rope from the dismantled bride. Luca managed to stop himself and instinctively he grabbed out. The two of them touched but Luca could not hold on. Zander dug his nails in, and the weight dragged Luca back down.

"They have disappeared!" Erica cried.

"Is the prince alright?" Colton yelled. Kantra and Erica both gave him a look. "Well, he is the most important one, after all."

Down below, there was a murmur of noise echoing back towards them. A huge mound of dirt left over from a recent dig had broken Zander and Luca's fall, that and the fact they had landed on top of Latch. As they crawled to their feet, they were not the only thing to be discarded away. The broken bodies of Meral Folk and other prisoners lay around them. Huge stones had been chucked upon them.

"I cannot see a way out," Zander said.

"There is nothing to see, that's why" Luca replied.

The pit was deep, made with walls which were nothing but thick mud. Above, the Oko gang could be heard rallying themselves. Kantra, Erica, and Colton were again fleeing for their lives. The twists and turns would only provide a temporary place to keep running, before it led straight into their hunters.

"Now I know it does not seem like it, but we have the advantage," Colton said through pants of breath. He kicked one of the support beams in front of them. Down came rock and wood. The boardwalk collapsed and dragged everything with it, landing on some of the Oko gang below. Those caught in the rubble cried as they drowned in dirt and stone.

"This place is really falling apart. As I said, now we have our lead on the rest of them."

"If you count running around in circles waiting to get caught, while the other half of us is stuck in that pit below," Kantra said, looking into the same place the others had fallen earlier.

"Not quite." Colton pushed Kantra and Erica at the same time, before jumping in after them. They all landed in a heap; Erica was winded whilst Kantra scrambled in the mud trying to throttle Colton.

"Your face, I thought you were a lightning warrior ready for anything," Colton chuckled.

"I'll rip your throat out then see how you can keep laughing. Why would you chuck us down here with the corpses? We're stuck now."

"Don't yell, it will let the others know we are down here."

"So what, they can leave us here to rot; I would rather be back in the cell."

Colton had stopped listening as he examined a pile of rocks in the corner.

"Can you help me with this?"

Latch rolled away the largest of the rocks which revealed a tunnel. Colton clapped his hands as Kantra almost looked annoyed. As they all squeezed through it, there was a voice on the other side.

"Intruders, intruders," the alert rang out through the small cave and with it they were surrounded.

"Pickle!" Colton shouted out, holding up his hands. "Where is Pickle?"

Pushing through the crowd of Meral Folk was Pickle.

"I never thought you would actually show up. My brother said there was no way you could walk down a street you would be so drunk, let alone make here to this mine."

"Why does everyone keep saying that about you?" Erica asked.

"Well, Pickle, the brother was more than happy to sell the secret," Colton smirked.

"Did you tell anyone else about our safe haven?" Pickle said in a timid voice.

Despite the fire, it was freezing in the small cove buried at the bottom of the mine. There were a few makeshift beds in which most of the Meral Folk were huddled in. Even with the new arrivals, there were few who turned their heads. Amongst the bleak survival, there were many still with their eye intact.

"Not much of an existence," Zander muttered.

"I understand it must be risky letting anyone know about this place. We are just as fearful of the gang; a moment's respite is invaluable to us. Thank you," Erica said.

"We might not have much, but we still have our sight."

"Lovely as this is, I am guessing we are not starting a new life here," Kantra added.

"As much as it would be a joy to stay in this confident space until you murdered us all, it is my understanding that there is a way out of here?" Colton asked.

"It is very dangerous; we only use it when we absolutely have to. It may be possible to make it to the surface, but we have to pass Lucid's office first." Pickle explained.

"Sounds delightful; point us in the right direction," Colton said.

"We need a promise, a seal of a bond. If you lead them here, we are all done for."

"I won't tell a soul."

As expected, the tunnel was narrow and stuffy. Mixed with impeding rocks and no light, it was a task to clamber down. The Meral Folk provided an escort, who was constantly turning around to tell them to quieten down. Although there was a certain danger on the other side of the tunnel, Luca was almost relieved to meet it. One by one, they slowly crept onto a bed of coal. Above them was a thin sheet. Poking out a head, the coast was clear. As they climbed down from the cart, both of the front wheels were missing.

"Right, this is where we split up. Don't worry though; some of you will still be with me. It is just we need to get the stone back whilst the Oko look the other way, ironically. That path to the left, from what I have been told is the road to freedom. If we do not come back, run that way." Colton instructed.

"Who are you talking to?" Erica asked.

"Latch is not best at sneaking nor is Kantra at remaining still. So I think it would make sense if we go one way, whilst the rest go the other. The distraction we will conger up, the stone should be free to take."

Erica went to hide at the tunnel entrance to the Meral Folk retreat; Colton stopped her.

"They're in here," he yelled down the corridor; his voice echoed down the tunnels of the mine. Erica's jaw dropped.

"They will thank me soon enough," Colton said before heading off with Kantra and Latch.

The Prime Oko gang was fast approaching; there was no time to argue as Luca pulled Erica away.

"He is crazy absolutely crazy; I do not trust him in the slightest."

Erica was still fussing; Luca and Zander had darted away.

"Those folk let him into their home, and then he sold them out without a second thought," Erica cried.

"It was a low move, even if it is to give us some cover," Luca said, looking at the floor as he spoke.

"I think we are here."

Zander was right; they were right outside the room which

they had first been dragged into. It was the last place they had seen the heart of Eldertude. Poking her head around, Erica whispered, "I cannot see anyone in there."

"Are we really going to do this?" Luca asked.

Erica did not answer as she crept inside; Luca gave Zander a look as they followed. The dank cove attempting to pass as a type of office was almost pitch back. A single flame burned in the corner, the light giving off just enough to cause the stone to sparkle.

"There it is."

The three of them could not believe their luck; sitting between gold coins and a pile of papers was the heart of Eldertude. Edging over, Zander slipped the stone back into the tattered satchel. Erica stood by the dish of Lucid's potion, watching as the occasional eyeball floated to the surface.

"How many people have been thrown into a world of confusion? Just so they can be mixed together in some mad poison. I always dreamed of leaving the kingdom. It cannot all be like this; we have barely climbed over the first hill but already I want to go back." Erica said with a heavy heart.

"Just because there are monsters out there, does not mean we have to become one," Luca replied

With that, Luca pushed over the centrepiece, the stone smashing as the body parts spilt out. With it came a roar; emerging from the darkness was Lucid.

****

"Surely, we cannot be the first people to think about this" Kantra asked.

"Many have fantasised about it, but none have had the guts to. Imagine my shock when I was hired, by Meral Folk of all people," Colton said with a chuckle.

"Because you are the only one stupid enough to go through with this plan," Kantra replied.

"There are invested interests for me. At least though, I am being paid to do this, rather than for free because a stranger told me to. Brother Pickle has been arranging things with the other prisoners. Well, the ones that he likes, considering the reaction in the cells earlier."

They were heading up to the top of the largest cavern in the mine; all around them, huge carts of the Orelit were being moved to the edge. Orelit was the main resource of the mine. A turquoise rock that could easily be broken like clay, it was mostly stored in long vials to stop it from crumbling. The three had now cloaked themselves in rags, which if anything made them stand out more. Closely, a Meral Folk with a red and yellow dotted hat watched their climb.

"This had best work, because the Folk below will be being made to suffer."

Kantra was right; there were screams coming from the pit below.

"We are almost in position," Colton gave a salute.

****

The three of them froze; the retched potion was running past their boots. Lucid towered over them, blocking the only route to escape, Zander clutched to the bag waiting to be swept aside.

"Who goes there?" Lucid cried. "I can smell you."

Lucid moved over and the three of them nearly all dived on the floor.

"The others are going to hear him," Erica whispered.

254

"There has been an accident," Luca said. A deadly stillness followed.

"Tell me what one of the idiots has done now?" Lucid replied.

Luca did not answer. Lucid stamped down, demanding an account. As they did, the eyeballs near their feet squished under the impact. It sent Lucid into a rage, picking up the cracked stone ball and throwing it across the room. Lucid unleashed an avalanche of mayhem, pushing over the cabinets and kicking up the pile of golds. In a blind rage, Lucid smashed a pile of the Orelit, the green content spilling everywhere.

"That is our cue to leave," Erica and the others began to back out of the room.

"You smell different."

"What, what's that boss?" Luca stuttered. Lucid took another deep long breath.

"That is not the normal stench…and nobody calls me boss."

Lucid spun round and with his full force caught Zander, sending him spinning across the room. Luca yelled and without thinking stabbed a dagger into Lucid's knee. He was rewarded with the same treatment and was launched into the desk. Erica, rather than follow the same fate, stood completely still, not even daring to blink. Lucid sniffed the air.

"There is a third."

Erica stifled a cry; she took a step backwards. Lucid came straight for her.

****

"Every time I go visit the hole, all the bloody work stops.

Get back to it," one of the gang shouted.

Meral Folk started to head back to carts.

"Not now, don't sell us out yet. Just keep spreading the Orelit," Colton mumbled. All around them shattered vials stained the walkways and trailed down the tunnels. Below, the Prime Oko gang were surrounding the stalling workers. As they yelled more abuse, the Meral Folk huddled together; those at the back were now fighting to stay on the ledge.

"Not quick enough."

One of the gang kicked a Folk in the chest. The force sent those at the back tumbling into the pit below.

"They're up there, the intruders, just stop kicking us."

Colton sighed.

"It is another race to the top."

Latch, Kantra, and Colton threw off the rags. Kantra grabbed the swords from her side; Latch had recovered his hammer from outside the cells. As they charged up the mine, the gang appeared from the tunnels around them. Kantra leapt upon the Oko, slicing down her enemies. Latch sent many flying the same way as the Meral Folk moments ago, straight into the mouth of the pit. Colton led the way with the gang on their heels. Quickly, they reached the top of the mine. As they did, a red and yellow hat was flung in the air.

"Now, now."

"We cannot hold them back forever" Kantra shouted.

"Don't worry; it is finally time for action," Colton replied with a grin.

\*\*\*\*

Lucid was almost upon Erica. The fear turned her to a

statue as danger loomed. Before danger could reach her, there was a clang, the echo hanging in the air. Lucid stopped; the sound came again, as if the walls were calling out. Crouching down, Lucid put both hands to the floor.

Holding the only lit torch in the room, Zander beckoned for Erica. Her legs were cemented to the ground as she stared at him. Frustrated, he waved the torch to try and break the spell. It fell from his hands and landed in the patch of the Orelit. There was an instant reaction as the rock burst into flames. Zander desperately stamped on the fire before diving out the way of the Lucid.

"You are in my world now."

Lucid grinned in the darkness. Zander was on all fours crawling to anywhere he could hide. There was so much on the floor— coins, glass, rocks— it all was singing out under his weight. Zander squealed as the huge hand of Lucid grabbed his leg. As much as he kicked out, there was no wriggling free. The vibrations then came again as the clanging was louder this time. With it, his grip on Zander's leg loosened. Luca smashed more wood across the line of iron poles, louder and harder until it drowned out all the other noise.

Lucid pounced; Luca let out a cry as the hands grabbed him by the throat. Zander tried to pull Lucid off but was brushed away. He came again smashing one of the Orelit vials over Lucid's head. The action managed to pull the mighty hands off Luca, for an instance. Lucid picked up Zander and launched him across the room.

"Erica, you have to find a light."

The feeble voice of Zander came from a heap of filing cabinets. Erica emptied the content of her rucksack, as the life was being squeezed out of Luca. A serpent had coiled itself around his neck, powerful and unforgiving there was no resisting, just a horrifying wait for the end. Over the heavy breaths and the sinister laughs, Luca could make out another sound. It was something to focus on, over the pain and the fear which was consuming him; it was the sound of a match striking a box.

Erica's hand was shaking uncontrollably as she broke another stick. Luca made a small gargle; he was seconds away from death. One match left. Taking a deep, long breath, Erica tried to focus herself. The last match struck once, twice, and then caught alight.

****

"Now!" Colton yelled, his voice echoing around the mines. The Meral Folk still standing, pushed all the Orelit carts they could off the sides. They came crashing down onto the paths below the rock, flying everywhere.

"Where is it?" Colton muttered to himself.

"They're still coming!" Kantra roared as she and Latch fought off the first wave of the Prime Oko. Colton lifted up a sheet; hidden away was a long bow with a single arrow. A rag had been wrapped around the head and was dipping in oil. Holding it over a torch near him it became alight. Pulling back the bow, Colton took aim. The arrow cut through the air like a thunderbolt, leaving hot streaks behind it. As it flew, everyone around it seemed to stand still. All watched and waited for the mine to erupt. Closing in on its target, the arrow hit the side and landed in the soft mud.

"Oh, that wasn't meant to happen," Colton muttered to himself.

Kantra and Latch did not need to hear the words, as they had seen the look on Colton's face. The Prime Oko gang had seen it too; they blocked all exits as the numbers were piling up. Even with the mighty hammer and the deadly Duel Sabers aimed at the gang, each thug was smiling.

There was an almighty roar. Below, the main tunnel into the mine began to glow. Out came Zander and Erica, running at full pace. Behind them, there was a fireball in the shape of Lucid. Flames danced off the arms like the burning wings of a Phoenix. Zander and Erica dived in opposite directions; Lucid went tumbling into the pits' mouth.

As if a firework had been lit inside of the mine, the place exploded in a surge of light. The pit roared into a manic firestorm, its embers sparking the rest of the fuses. Trails of the broken Orelit vials ran up and down all the walkways. The reaction was instant, the blaze of fire running all the way to the top. Each of the Prime Oko gang did not know where to turn; everywhere was blocked off by the bedlam around them.

"It is spreading faster than I thought," Colton said. "It will not be long now till the finale."

Kantra went to yell back but instead Latch shoved her out the way. A running flame darted past them, caught on a trail to the top.

"A lot sooner, jump!" Colton shouted and leapt off the top of the side; Kantra and Latch followed with no other choice. The fuse had run straight up to a huge stash of the Orelit. As the fire hit, there was another blast; that time, it was as if the sky had broken into two. The furious reactions ripped through the mine, tearing down the foundations like wet paper.

Hanging onto one of the winches running through the central cavern, they spiralled down trying to outrun the devastation. The Oko pushed past each other, as they tried to flee the inevitable burning tomb the mine had become. Colton and Kantra hit the ground but quickly rolled out of the way;

Latch landed with a thud. The others had gathered around them, but there was no time for words. A huge part of the ceiling came crashing down. More rocks and flaming pieces of wood caused them to scatter.

"Follow the Folk," Colton ordered as the Meral Folk were the only ones showing any real sense of collection; they flocked for the exit in numbers. The group from Eldertude let themselves get washed away, back to the streets of Darnspur.

# Chapter 23

The world tilted again; sprays of the ocean jumped up over the side. A floating home sat as a circular stage, which rocked on the blanket of endless blue. Stroking his well-kept beard and narrowing his jaded green eyes, more water sprayed up onto his long navy coat.

"My captain, I know you value your time with the ocean, but decisions have to be made. It will not be long till our kingdom collapses." Alden said.

"When I sit here and look out to the sea, I feel like I am making bad jokes. That any choices I make could affect the creation we exist in," Holsten replied.

"It does to the kingdom of Neptulus."

Holsten sighed.

"I hear you and your right, as always, Alden. With all that sea and yet still there is nowhere for me to hide. Please though, do not ruin this spot for me; it is one of the few places I have left."

The captain and first officer stepped off the floating platform onto a rope bridge. It connected to a long, wide boat. As they stepped onto the deck, the wood underneath their feet screamed back at them. Making their way to the other end, an elderly lady opened the curtains of her cabin window. A young man then let the pair cross the plank onto his boat, tilting his hat as they passed.

Hundreds of small floating podiums were mixed in with an array of different sized ships. All efforts had been made to join them together. Makeshift bridges, planks, rope, stepping stones, and anything else which could be drafted to connect the sea dwellers together. The tangle of small ships filled up most of the bay, which was sealed off by huge white cliffs. Standalone military ships guarded the entrance, creating a protective ring. The kingdom was a constant flow of activity. Fishing boats were constantly on the lookout for the next catch. Cages were set up all along the rocks of the Infinitros waterfall. Fishing rods lay hopeful next the One Point Island, a spiralling rock in the middle of the bay.

Using a handrail to steady himself after a wave, the wood snapped. The captain cursed as it broke off in his hand.

"That rot is the last of our worries. We have been in their waters too long; the fish are drying up and the lands around have been scavenged to the bone," Alden said reading the captain's mind.

"Have the scouts found anywhere close to suitable?" Holston asked.

"Potentially there are some further bays down the coast. None though with the same size we are accustomed to. There is less protection from the open waves and no grantee of the same fishing sources. After that, we leave the Borrowed Lands. Moving the sea dwellers will not be easy. We need to be certain. If I am honest, the best places are near Eldertude."

"They cannot be relied on. If we moved with any reasonable size, it could be seen as an act of war."

"Could we not just explain the situation to the king?" Alden said gingerly.

"Believe me, there is no reasoning with that man, especially by me. Also, officially our kingdoms have not communicated since we chose our stances on the plague" Holsten's voice trailed off as he spoke.

Tulus soldiers had surrounded a family boat. With gloved hands, they dragged all the belongings from the cabin onto the deck. Chairs, clothes, and a dolly were some of the items which made up the pile. Alden handed a handkerchief to the captain; he held the cloth up to his mouth. Oil was poured on the deck and then set alight. As the soldiers jumped from the ship, the guide ropes were cut. Quickly, the current took a hold of the burning boat.

"The whirlpools will deal with it," Alden stated.

"Another sign the bay wants us gone," Holsten replied, the reflection of the flames dancing in his eyes.

"Do you think it was the right decision, to take the stance we have?"

Holsten let out another sigh. "Every night, I think of those vermin we let into our kingdom. Smug faces behind the mask. It pains to me think I must send those away who are a part of us. It is for the greater good of the fleet though. We cannot help them here. Eldertude tried a different approach; all it has done is subject them to chaos and ruined their economy. Nobody wants to go near that place to trade."

"Things are not much better here. People are getting wise.

It is not hard to make the connection between the black marks on their bodies. As much as we contest, the snatchers are less than subtle. Do we even know what really happens to them?" Alden said looking directly into the captain's eyes.

"They are given a job; they contribute in a way their body lets them. Also, they receive some type of therapy for their condition. What that looks like, I do not really know. Nobody tends to ask questions," Holston said holding Alden's gaze.

"I cannot believe we can even have any type of dialogue with them, given the history."

"Desperate times."

Up ahead, there were shouts. Half a dozen guards were grappling with a young man. Dressed in blue overalls, Crookie was then pushed to the decking. As they went to restrain him, he clawed away and scrambled back to his feet.

"Don't put that on her door," Crookie yelled.

One of the larger guards just stared at him, thick bags under her eyes. In her hand was a brush dripping with red paint. Crookie went to grab at it but was shoved straight into another navy uniform. He was bounced around some more again, until eventually he went overboard. The ripples of laughter soon stopped as the captain leaned down to fish Crookie out.

"What is the meaning of this?" Holsten demanded, pulling seaweed from Crookie's short black hair.

"We should leave," Alden hissed.

"He was resisting, captain" a guard reported.

"Damn right, I was. They were about to mark my mother's door with a red stamp. In the next few days, she and the boat are gone," Crookie said.

Alden pulled the arm of Holsten; all the guards saw the tug.

"Is this true, was the boat deemed worthy of the stamp?" Holsten asked.

"That's our orders."

Running a hand through his thick black beard, Holsten peered through one of the port holes.

"Where is she now?"

Crookie turned away. Drifting past was a small rowing boat within arm's length of the pier.

"Come on boy, I am the Captain of Neptulus; you can tell me."

"My mum raised me; I don't want her sent away to some death camp."

"It is not a death camp," Holsten said dismissively.

"Then why the bandanas?" Crookie asked.

None of the guards made any attempt to pull back their material. All had it firmly tied around their mouths. More boats were now circling. Other faces were slowly drifting out the doors and windows. A cry rang out from across the decking. A short woman with high boots and a yellow raincoat was sobbing. Crookie yelled out her name and then went straight to the crying woman.

"This is not going to be good," Alden muttered.

Wiping away snot and tears, Nora started to yell in the direction of Holsten.

"I have been docked here my whole life, and now you want to cast me out. No curse has touched my skin," Nora had pulled both sleeves and was waving her arms to the crowd.

"There has clearly been some mistake," Holsten said.

"Yes, the captain is right. We do need more people to help build the new fleet. Everyone of all ages and abilities can contribute. But it doesn't seem to be from here. These are volunteers who give themselves to the cause. Stand down, all of you" Alden announced.

The soldiers slowly moved away from the boat, Holsten with them. Crookie took hold of his mother, as if the words were some type of trick.

"Nobody believes the lies about the new fleet. We know why people are really being taken away," Crookie hissed at the officials as they passed.

"I thought you said your mother wasn't sick," Holsten muttered.

Once the group had a fair distance between them and the crowd, Alden dismissed the soldiers.

"It will not be long before that story is in every tavern and porthole," Holsten said.

"Rarely is the information wrong about which doors to mark" Alden replied.

"Send the guards back out tomorrow. No risks can be taken with the spread of this blasted curse."

"Are you sure; should the sources not be checked?"

"Of course I am. Either way, it does not matter. The message cannot be that tears will get you out of your duty to this kingdom, no matter what that really means. We have our own accountabilities too; it is time to find out what the snatchers really do with our people."

# Chapter 24

"Alert the castle."

The cries rang out through the Pilpots. People dropped their bags and tools. Others stopped and starred as the Elder-tude soldiers came out of Red Claw Jungle, at least what was left of them. Most supported each other, covered in wounds and blood; they stumbled back into the outskirts of Elder-tude. Castle guards appeared, led by a red-faced commander. As her soldiers went to tend to those limping out from the trees, she started to bark orders.

"Pull yourselves together. Where is the unit's shape?"

The stern eyes of the short haired commander were met with glares. Gaunt faces said nothing as they made their way up the hill. The news was travelling faster than the tired legs. Queen Hermenize had appeared at the castle walls, King Vidal with her.

"I cannot see him, where is Zander?"

Vidal did not reply to Hermenize but rather counted the number of wounded soldiers.

"They have only been gone a few days. I thought you had a deal in place with the Waro?"

"We did; clearly those savages cannot be trusted," the king muttered.

A castle guard appeared beside them. Before he could open his mouth, Vidal snapped. "Yes, I know. Find out what happened and bring me the prince."

There were more shouts from below. The soldiers were gathering in the courtyard. Hermenize was gone. Vidal sighed and went to follow her.

"Where are the rest of you then?" the commander asked to the small group.

"We need help."

Food, water, and bandages appeared as the courtyard turned into a treatment room.

"I want a report, now."

"Tell us what happened," Hermenize said, marching right past the commander. Trailing behind her was the king. More of the castle had gathered across the walkways. Surrounded by guards was General Balder, who watched intensely.

"Who is the highest rank; make themselves known," the commander shouted. One of the soldiers shuffled forward; they had their arm in a sling.

"Well, give it to us straight; do not mince your words, soldier."

"The prince and the heart of Eldertude are gone."

\*\*\*\*

The heads of Eldertude fiddled with their hands; next to them, the highest ranking military figures sat crossed armed. Reciting the full story again was the soldier from the courtyard. The words describing the bloodshed of the Waro echoed around the Sanctuary Chamber.

Queen Hermenize winced as the soldier described the collapse of the river and the obliteration it caused. Each survivor and their footsteps all the way back to the kingdom had been featured in the tail, minus the prince. None had seen Zander or the stone. From his throne, King Vidal dismissed the soldier, who despite their injuries quickly departed.

"This is a disaster," Queen Hermenize said, head in hand.

"I must agree with the lady," General Balder said stone faced. Vidal shot him daggers.

"How did your soldiers let this happen? I thought the Hammers were meant to be the greatest warriors in all the land."

"The Waro command the jungle; nobody can deal with that might."

"Then why send my boy out there then?" Hermenize was almost in tears now. The heads looked at each other. Vidal placed a hand on her shoulder, but it was pushed away.

"We need to think of the next step," Darius, the head of treasury, said.

Everyone turned to the short stocky man.

"The heart of the kingdom is gone; we now must think of our next most valuable resource."

Others nodded in agreement.

"We must continue the mission; it is of the utmost importance. There must be something more we can offer," another one of the council added.

"It must be presented in a different means," Darius replied.

"Agreed we must create a new path and means of transport."

Individual decisions broke out; plans and strategies were being decided. Amongst it sat Vidal, alone in the conversation.

"My son is missing," Queen Hermenize cried. Silence engulfed Sanctuary Chambers once again.

"I shall call for the most experienced scouts to recover him," General Balder said.

"This is my kingdom," King Vidal jumped out from his throne.

"With all due respect, if there is a cure out there, we must seek it," the head of craft said, a tall and gaunt woman.

"I know that," Vidal snapped.

"Marching out our soldiers with a target on their backs failed. We need a new plan; one more fool proof," Darius said.

Vidal almost leapt on him. "So you call me a fool, do you? Make a joke of my son!"

"With all due respect."

"Silence."

There was a pause then Darius started again. "The prince, in his condition…"

"Who was victorious on the day of Dontés."

Darius coughed. "As I was saying, it is no wonder he did not survive. The Borrowed Lands are treacherous. Shame, him being the last of the generation's bloodline."

Vidal grabbed the collar of Darius with both hands. He dragged the short man across the chambers to the nearest window.

"Say it again."

Far below, the courtyard beckoned, with Darius dangling above it. The head of treasury had turned as white as his shirt. Vidal screamed the words for a second time and loosened his grip. Balder and other military figures were now pulling both the men back. As much as he tried to fight against it, Vidal was restrained. Darius hugged the floor as he was brought back in from the window.

"My son is alive. Nothing happens until he is found. Hellrous and the rest can boil over for all I care."

## *Chapter 25*

By the skin of their teeth, they had escaped from the depths of the Diavik mine. In the process, they had left an already troubled city hanging by the seams. The streets were tearing themselves apart as the last of the Prime Oko Gang tried to restore order. Amongst the turmoil, Colton's last contact had come through. All six had managed to pick up supplies and a horse for each. The heart of the Eldertude was also back in their possession; spirits were the highest they had been since leaving the soil of the kingdom. All of them were in full voice about the recent events. From the clutches of Lucid to making their way on the hillside overlooking Darnspur, with both eyes intact.

The only one who was not a part of the conversation was Colton, who rode behind quietly. Kantra turned her horse to ride alongside him.

"That could not have been the plan to escape like that."

Colton smiled, still not turning away from the view of the city.

"I definitely need to work on my bow skills."

"Seriously though, now you are just tagging along. Waiting to get us into more trouble?"

"So you rather I leave?"

"I didn't say that," Kantra said.

"So you are coming with us?" Erica now asked.

"For the time being, I thought I might join your adventure. Seeing as I cannot go back to Darnspur for a while. A prince can make a very good ally, if we can keep him alive."

"Are you not owed some type of reward for helping blow up the mine?"

"Meral Folk do not pay well; seeing the Oko squirm was reward enough. I am however in need of entertainment, like trying to watch that large man get onto a horse."

Colton was right; there was a battle going on with the animal. Latch was huge and the horse was not impressed. Worst still, he had very little experience riding. Currently, he was flapping around trying not to be thrown off the back. Out of nowhere, Zander came charging up to the disobedient pair. He shrieked then slapped the animal round the head. It shook even harder, kicking up its legs; Zander did not budge and yelled again. This time, he jumped up and grabbed the reigns. With the other hand, he went to punch the stallion in the face. Luca tackled him and Zander let go. The horse gave a furious jerk, strong enough to throw off Latch. Then the animal was gone, galloping into the distance.

"What is wrong with you?" Luca led the inquest. Zander lay on the floor, hands on his chest.

"I don't know what happened. My body was not with me, Luca. I was just watching from the sidelines. It took on a form I have never seen."

"How long has it been since you have had treatment?" Erica said.

Luca answered first. "It has been nearly a week since a real session; I would have thought he would be too sick to walk by now."

"I am fine," Zander said, then stormed off. Erica and Luca watched as he disappeared over the hill's edge.

"How long has he gone before?" Erica asked.

"Since I have known him, never, really. I mean, he is the prince of Eldertude. If really honest, I do not know what truly happens. My mother got sick, but it was at the time Hellrous was first forming. My father was a gardener at the castle. He had befriended the queen and asked if I could stay whilst mother got better. They went and I never saw them again."

"I have worked in many different zones, even the centre."

"What was it like?"

A cold look crossed Erica's face. "Let's find some treatment soon."

"There are bound to be some Red Drops around here."

A puzzled face came across Colton's face. "I was under the impression those made you sick."

****

Darnspur had now faded into the horizon, another mark on their memories. The smog and filth of the city could only reach so far. Fields of golden flowers, trees which sang out nature's call, and streams of clear rivers, made the bleakness of Darnspur seem also a dream.

"It is actually beautiful out here. Who would have thought?" Kantra said.

"The castle greenery is far more impressive," Luca replied.

"Well, it is hard to tell when you are barely allowed to visit. Latch, you have been inside the castle walls many a time, even if it is to clean up after the horses. Tell us which compares better?" Kantra asked.

"They are the same," Latch replied.

"No there not," Zander added.

"Come on, help decide," Kantra pressed.

"I have no view, except the castle structuring can provide shelter and act as a fortress if required."

"There you have it, the castle wins. I might even be able to sneak you all a tour when we are back." Luca hesitated and looked at Colton. "Well, maybe not all of you."

"How come I would be left out; it is not like I would steal or anything." Colton laughed at the expression on Luca's face. "You should be more welcoming to me; I am the only one who knows which way we are heading."

Nobody could argue.

"So I have figured why most of you are here— slave, servant, and hired by the prince. You though do not strike me as the regular serve-the-kingdom type. Even if it does mean you get to be paid for violence."

"I have my reasons." Kantra looked to Zander "Sometimes it is easier to bury your secrets, until it is time to pay for them. Mainly though, it is to save my brother and his grandmother, once I am rewarded."

"Don't you mean your grandmother?"

"No."

****

The campfire was slowly burning. A gentle breeze was dictating the rhythm of the flames. Everyone was sound asleep; they had raided the last of their supplies and were now well fed and watered. Luca began to stir; he could hear Latch snoring and wondered how any of them had got to sleep.

Eyeing up the nearest tree, he gently stepped over the body of Zander. As he wandered through the night, there was something in the air. It was a metallic, harsh smell which clung to the inside of Luca's throat like a cobweb. It was too much of a grab for Luca to ignore. The stars above were giving just enough light to see each footstep, as the scent was providing a trail for him to follow.

Sat crossed legged was Colton, holding a shell. It was bulky enough that it took two hands to hold. The circular base had a break in it, just big enough for a creature to crawl into. Two spikes twisted themselves from the centre; they spiralled up until one had snapped off. Colton cradled the shell carefully as you would a young child; the rancid smell oozed around him. Putting the broken spike to his mouth, Colton took a deep breath. There was crackle; he did it again and again in a silent symphony. Smoke crept out of the shell; it caught the breeze and began to swirl around Colton's head. Luca climbed up onto the rock; it took a while before Colton even turned to look at him.

"I thought everyone was asleep."

"Well, I am not. I didn't know you smoked."

Colton was grey; he looked as if he had aged many winters.

"I thought I was alone."

"Yes, you already said. Would it not be a good idea to get some sleep?" Luca asked.

"This is what I do, what I have to do. I take it you have not seen one of these before," Colton replied.

Luca shook his head.

"What is the purpose of it?"

"That is a good question; I have never really put it in words before. The best way to describe it is to imagine you are all alone on a stage. Its audience is made up of everyone you know, everyone you have wronged. At first, they are quiet, it is only a murmur you can hear. Throughout the day, the voices get louder, the audience more agitated. There is nowhere to hide as all the anger, all the shouting it as you, and only you are on that stage. It becomes deafening, until the shell. One drag and smoke fills the mind, another and it is spinning around. A tornado appears and the audience runs for cover. No more voices can be heard; it all stops, until…" Colton's eyes were now transfixed on the shell, Luca prompted him. "The winds die down, the audience slowly returns to their seats and the muttering can be heard again."

"I do not know what insults I could hear to drive me to that."

"They're simply reminding me of what I have done."

"If you live in the past, how are you supposed to make a future?"

"Some of us do not deserve a second chance."

# Chapter 26

"We will not wait any longer. If it cannot be done, we will take it ourselves, no matter who has to be cut down. The agreement has failed. There is only so much time we spend with our hands in the dirt. The gems are drying up whilst the tomb's seal remains locked. You must find another way to pay us."

Trogon, the Nyke leader, held up his hands. Around him other Nyke roared, waving axes and swords. They crowded the floor, spilling out onto the largest balcony of the Yellow Templar's cave. Sat on his throne, surrounded by the Followers, was Leader Malum.

"So rallying yourself up for a fight is the answer? This will produce more of what you want? No is the truth. The soil will give back what is searched for. It is simply out of season," Leader Malum dismissed.

"Lies! What seasons do you talk of? I have seen nothing but the blasted heat from the retched cloudless skies," Trogon cried.

"Do not talk ill of that which provides. You want gems then thank the suns, for what they have already given us."

Trogon spat; around him, Rexis could feel the other Followers ready to pounce. Rave was in the ear of the Templar closest to him. There were shouts outside, heading towards the balcony.

Malum stood up, "Outsiders."

A group of Nyke appeared, wrestling with the intruders.

"There were more but we cut them down as they tried to escape."

Rave marched over to one of the men. He had a scruffy beard and a blue uniform. As Rave picked him up by his throat, the man groaned, holding his side.

"How did you find this place?" Rave shouted. The man tried to answer back but could not get the words out, sweat poured down his face. Rave leaned closer and started to scream further integration.

"You talk about the agreement being broken by us. This is the ultimate betrayal. We have no contact with the rest of the world. One of yours must have talked," Malum was on his feet now, in front of Trogon.

"The Nkye need this place a secret just as much as the Templar," Trogon shot back.

Rexis' leg was shaking; the new arrivals had drawn the interest of almost everyone. Passing through the crowd, he could see the face of his sister. One of the outsiders found her voice.

"There is no need for such violence. We are sailors of the Neptulus kingdom's fleet, with orders directly from Captain Holsten. Spilling more of our blood will only bring war to your walls!" Emil shouted, her navy uniform drenched in sweat.

"Will there be others?" Malum stood over the woman, who began to shrink under the shadow. "Answer me!" he yelled.

"Stop it Emil. Just stop," Teo, still holding onto his side, spoke up. "We deserve this. If this is what we have sentenced our people too, then there is no punishment severe enough."

"Is this what you are here for, answers?" Malum said.

"The Nyke showed us before the power. A Tulus man marked with the curse, he returned to the kingdom years after he should have passed. Neptulus had no way of treating it. In desperation, we decided to trade our sick. It seemed like the only solution to stop the spread and to fund the healthy. The lines of what really happened were always blurred. No one wanted to know. Now, the Nyke rub it in our faces. They have pushed us to this; the captain could no longer ignore it. The Nkye have become so arrogant, it was easy to track them," Teo announced, his face turning greyer by the second.

"So you weren't given the location?" Malum asked.

Teo nodded.

"You see, the Nyke have not broken our agreement," Trogon shouted out.

"Still though, it appears you have grown sloppy over time. There are however things we could better ourselves. Let's discuss how we settle this between us, for the better of both our journeys, back in my chambers."

Malum gave a gesture to Trogon and then started heading up the stairs.

"You can start by silencing those who wish to give us away," Trogon said.

The Nyke pulled out daggers; Rave stopped them. He called out a name; all the eyes turned to Rexis. The Followers pushed him forward as Rave placed an axe into his hands.

"Slaughter them," Rave hissed.

Rexis could barely hold the weapon up; the smile on Rave's face was drawing his strength. He looked away, only to see that Terra had made her way to the front of the crowd.

"These people cast you aside; if you truly want a place here, you have to earn it," Rave yelled for all to hear.

Emil grabbed at Rexis' legs.

"It's not our fault. There was no other way to treat the curse; we had to save the fleet. It kept you alive, didn't it?"

The Followers stared as Rexis pushed her away.

"High Sea Roller," Teo said. "Nobody forgets them, especially the failures. Could not handle it in the cold waters, so you have to cuddle up to the heat instead?"

A black cloud came across the face of Rexis. It turned him blind, blocking his ears. His mind had been left behind as his body wandered off into a dream. Everything went numb as all he could do was wait. Rexis' vision slowly returned to reveal the hot blood running up his arms. In front of him were the bodies of the Tulus; they had been opened up like a savage animal had been set upon them. The axe made a loud twang as it hit the floor.

In some act of desperation, Rexis went to his sister. "Get away from me." Terra was as pale as a ghost. Rexis tried to speak, but his throat was caught by the look of sheer terror on his sister's face. As he held up a red hand, the young girl started to back away. "You are scaring me."

Rexis kept coming; Terra was running out of space as she

climbed up onto the balcony.

"That girl needs to get back to the yellow room," one of the Followers yelled out. Terra looked to her brother; he gave a timid nod in agreement.

"I don't know who you are anymore," Terra whimpered.

There was one final cry as the girl took her last step. Rexis collapsed.

"Even though you look weak now, you have started to prove yourself," Rave hissed in his ear. Rexis could not process the words as he was paralysed by reality.

There was a ripple of movement throughout the valley. Everyone started to point and yell.

"The tomb is opening!"

Simultaneously, both the Nyke and Yellow Templar started to run from the cave. Rexis had not even looked up; all he could do was stare at the broken body of his sister.

## *Chapter 27*

Finally, the suns had settled, and dusk had fallen across Eldertude. Around the outskirts of the castle walls, the fire pits were kept alive by the patrolling guards in Elm Grove. Each Pilpot had a candle in the window. Smoke from the chimneys created a blanket over the valley. The entire kingdom tried its utmost to hide from the darkness, ever since the disappearances had begun.

Even though it was late, the streets were still busy. Castle workers made the long rush home. Making his way through the nightly crush was a young man known as Smug. He hurried through the different levels of the clay runways making up the streets of the Pilpots. The hand-me down uniform hung off his body, the white colour a distant memory. It was so badly covered in stains, that Smug could probably make a stew out of the fabric. The only part of him which always remained clean was a black leather bracelet. It was a gift from his mother; he remembered the words she had said when giving it to him.

*"This symbolises the bond between us, that we are always bound to each other. Wear it always."*

Smug picked up the pace. He had been the last one out again. It took him so much longer to finish his tasks than the others. In his mind, he pictured his mother waiting at the door, the lecture she would give about the thieves lying in wait.

Running a hand down the dry surface, Smug slid off one of the main valley paths onto a bank of corridors. The thick mud formed a narrow maze of walkways. Above the alleys, the neglected fire pits had started to fade away. Grey clouds filled the gaps of corridors; Smug's eyes started to sting. One of the reasons his mother wanted him to leave work on time, the smoke could be perilous. It was not unheard of for people to become lost and eventually collapse.

Although he knew the path well, the combination of tiredness and all his concerns was fogging his mind. Others pushed past him without a word of apology. A hand gently rested on his back. Smug spun round; there was nothing but shadows following him. Walking backwards, he tripped on the uneven surface.

Lying on the ground, the smoke pounced on him. It acted as a chain across his body; with each cough, more energy left his body. Smug could feel himself curling up into a ball. He knew he should not, but his withered mind begged him to rest. Gradually, his eyes were closing.

"Come with me."

Two hands grabbed Smug's wrists, pulling him to his feet. With his body in a trance, he could do nothing but obey. Through the corridor, they twisted and turned. They passed through a huge ball of smoke, much more than he had ever seen before.

Smug took a moment to recover. He had been led out of the maze into a small opening by his saviour. The cloaked figure in red was much taller than Smug, their identity hidden by the shadows. Silently, they watched as Smug tried to recover his breath.

"It was really smoky in there."

Smug blushed at his own statement.

"The smoke is horrible."

They were alone in the clearing.

"Sorry, I meant thank you for saving me."

Still no reply.

"Well, time to be going now; mother will be waiting."

Smug rubbed his bracelet.

"I need you to come with me."

There was a firm tone in the well-spoken voice.

"Will we have to go far? My mother will be scared if I don't arrive home."

"It is to save your mother. Follow me now."

Smug was given no time to comprehend what has been said. He was already struggling to keep up. The cloaked figure moved through the Pilpots with ease, occasionally they would pause to let the guards walk past. It was not long until they were outside the castle. They stood by two enormous roots which had collided with each other.

"Are we allowed this close to the castle at night?" Smug whispered.

The cloaked figure was running a hand across the rough surface of the wooden wall. Smug watched inquisitively as the search continued. Eventually, the fingers struck success; slowly the bark was pulled away and with it revealed an entrance. The eyes of Smug almost popped out of his skull.

"In you go."

Smug did not move. Staring into the black venture, there was only the hint of light in the otherwise dark vortex.

"Do you not trust me? I saved you. Now your mother is in need. Will you not step up to save her?"

"Why though, why would mother be down there?"

The cloak came back.

"Dare to call me a liar?"

Shaking with each step Smug descended into the unknown. As they ventured down deeper, Smug was pushed down the stairs. He could feel himself welling up; he wanted to be brave, but he felt like the world had swallowed him whole. Smug let out a hopeless squeal but there was no answer, only a burst of light.

A spark was lit, causing a circle of fire to light up around the edge of the room. Smug was in the centre, around him were four, rectangular, edgeless mirrors. They were much larger than Smug, and placed at four angles around him. Although the rest of the cove was filthy, the glass had been polished to perfection. That however was not what had drawn Smug's attention; it was the stains all across the floor.

"Do you know why I have brought you here? Of course, you don't." It was the same stern voice but was now morphed by menace. "I have been watching you."

The voice seemed to come from all angles, bouncing off the walls.

"It was how I rescued you from suffocation. Remember

how I was the hero, the saviour. Now I need you to help me, help both of us."

With every word, the flames danced.

"You think I am lying?"

The presence startled Smug; he had forgotten how much taller the man was than him. In one hand, he held a sharply curved dagger and in the other, he dragged a body. Dressed in simple grey cloth, the captive had a puffy chest and static arms tied behind the back.

Where the body was stiff, the head hidden by a sack was the opposite. Thrashing around, it was close to exploding out of the material, violently throwing itself in all directions. Smug could hear the tiny yelps for help. The dagger was forced into Smug's trembling hand.

"I don't understand. Where is mother?"

"Let me make it easier."

A handkerchief was wrapped around Smug's eyes. It was soft on his skin; the expensive silk offered a strange comfort in a world of intense fear.

"One strike, then it is all over. Save them both."

Tears were leaking through the cloth.

"They are all burning. You have to stop them, not again. Do it and kill them all now."

A hand dug into the shoulder of Smug; he yelled and lashed out. The dagger went into the side of the bag. There was a squeal then silence. The tight clench on his shoulder released itself, the flames dampened. Plucking up the courage to take off the blindfold, he almost threw up. Despite the dagger still being firmly lodged, the sack was still moving.

Smug pulled off the bag and screamed. The body of a rat fell onto his feet, others landed on their backs; they scurried away for safety. A wave of relief washed over Smug; he had not harmed anyone. The moment was short lived, as the confusion piled upon him. As he turned left and right, the blaze around him flared up. Screams and yells shot in all directions before a long, rattling hiss.

"They always burn; they cannot be saved."

The blindfold was now around Smug's neck, being pulled from behind.

"From every angle you always see you failed them. There is no second chance; they burned and now you must be released."

The last words Smug would ever hear, the dagger plunged into his chest. There was no thought given to the pain or his last constricted breaths. Smug could only think of his mother, who would be forever at the doorway, waiting for his return.

*Chapter 28*

The strong winds lashed across their skin like the bite of a snake. With it came the relentless cold. Erica had never experienced a chill like it; there were winters in Eldertude but nothing like this. Just like the others, only her eyes were visible. The rest of Erica was wrapped in anything she could find.

Their horses battled through the snow; Erica could barely see those around her as they trudged onwards. With the odd break in the blizzards, she could take a few movements to enjoy the landscape. They had entered the mountain range of the sleeping gods. Each mountain challenged all who came close to them with its sheer existence. Hidden amongst the Draygo Mountains was the palace of the Collector, according to Colton. Erica tried her best to be heard above the wind.

"How close are we?"

The reply was lost amongst the snow, followed by a half smile. Kantra now chimed in.

"You best not have gotten us lost."

"It is here somewhere. We just have to make sure we do not get ourselves mixed up," Colton replied.

As they pushed on, the blizzard became worse. It would not be much longer before they would be consumed by the elements. Colton pointed at the foot of the mountains, towards the entrance of a cave. The others did not need to be told twice. It would be a hard push, but the idea of shelter was enough to spur them on.

Firstly, they would have to conquer two sharply rising chunks of ice in their path. It was a steep climb to the top which was tough on the horses. The task was worsened by the ice being formed into steps rather than a slope. At the top, the frost was a different colour to the snow. It was a light glimmering blue which stood out amongst the sea of white.

Colton had been the first to lead his horse. It thrashed around and tried to pull back, but slowly it made it to the peak. Eventually, the others joined them. The horses stamped their feet. A small offer of food was made in an attempt to calm them. The gesture was well received, but the threat of mutiny remained if they did not reach the cave soon.

All went to remount the horses when the floor started to shake. Luca fell, letting go of his horse's rains, giving it a chance to escape. Zander watched as Erica helped him back to his feet. Kantra threw her rains at Latch, as she went to chase the runaway horse when another wave of tremors hit them.

"It is an earthquake?" Erica shouted at anyone who could hear her. Colton was next to the floor. He was on his knees, shifting through the snow with both hands.

"How is that going to help?"

A look came across Colton's face they had never seen

before, one of fear. His mouth moved over and over again. The grounds beneath them started to open up, then shattered. All were thrown into the air. The very ice they had been standing on rose up into the sky. Zander landed on his back, sinking deep into the snow. It did not take long for the cold to awaken him. Looking up, Zander wanted to shrink back into the blizzard.

Standing tall, the Ice Golem had risen up from nothing. It was of such a huge structure, that it blended in with the other glaziers. Seemingly only made of square ice blocks and sharp icicles, the Ice Golem had dead, soulless eyes. There was nowhere for Zander to run to; all he could do was wait for the impact. Snow was thrown over him. One of the horses darted past Zander in a blind panic. The Ice Golem turned its attention, giving Zander a narrow window in which to flee.

All of them were heading in the same direction; it was the only move which made sense in the panic and the snow- storm. Even with the great threat behind them, everyone was moving too slowly through the snow. Zander stole a look back; the Ice Golem was now in hot pursuit with no traces of the horses left.

They collectively picked up the pace; arms linked, they dragged themselves into the cave. As they came out of the cold winds, even with the approaching Ice Golem, a slight relief washed over them. Holes high up in the rock ceiling let in beams of light, snowflakes drifting downwards would glisten in the air.

"We have to find a place to hide!" Luca yelled.

"What was it doing just lying there?" Erica asked.

"Sleeping and if I can remember, they are allergic to hors- es, hence the reception," Colton said whilst turning back into the cave. Moving deeper in, it quickly narrowed. As they turned the corner, the cave came to an abrupt stop.

"A dead end, how fitting," Colton joked.

As the majority looked for a place to hide, Kantra was the only one who was standing still. The wall at the end stared at her. Its surface was jet black with bright blue hexagons spread out equally. An endless black all-consuming presence was drawing Kantra in. As she ran her hand over the surface, it was smooth, polished. Kantra pulled her hand away; the wall had moved on its own.

"Not again."

The wall turned to face Kantra. Yellow eyes full of warning met her gaze, supported by razor sharp pincers. Kantra leapt back, drawing her sword, now face to face with an almighty Bliss Scorpion.

"I really need to watch where you all put your hands," Colton muttered as they turned to run, only to find the entrance had become blocked.

They had nowhere to hide, now surrounded by the gigantic force of the Ice Golem and the deadly Bliss Scorpion. Weapons drawn, the group were having the luck only experienced in a nightmare. It was a standoff. The Ice Golem had come bounding in but now halted. Both titans sized each other up; the Bliss Scorpion made a snap of the tail. The Eldertude group blended into the shadows. With a crack of its knuckles, the Ice Golem charged.

The Bliss Scorpion reacted, flying forward through the middle of the group. It came with an all-out attack, snapping with its pincers and ripping chunks out of the Ice Golem. The Bliss Scorpion would get beaten away but come straight for more. What it lacked in size in comparison, it made up for in speed and aggression. The Ice Golem was soon covered in small but plentiful wounds; made up only of ice it was easy for it to be stripped away. As the Bliss Scorpion swept over the challenger like wildfire, the Ice Golem finally connected well with a punch, sending the scorpion flying.

As the beast crashed into the wall; the impact caused it to rain deadly stalactites. Once again, the group needed shelter, or soon they were collateral damage in the clash of the titans. The Bliss Scorpion let out a cry. It was deafening, echoing off all the walls and disappearing down the tunnel. The cry came echoing back, followed by the sound of intense scurrying. Out of the shadows came an eruption of smaller Bliss Scorpions. As they poured out the tunnel, they washed over the cave floor.

Swords bounced off hardened shells. Only the real blows came from the power of the Ice Golem. Thunder strikes came crashing down; causing the bodies of the infant Bliss Scorpions to be flattered, dark blue fluid staining the snow. Those not caught by the blows leapt on the arms and legs, swarming over Ice Golem.

The group were too in danger of being overrun. Kantra was in a deadly duel, using both her swords to fight off the claws, whilst having to duck to avoid the stinger from the tail. Another joined the assault. Two stingers came in at once; Kantra had to reply with a powerful strike to beat them both away. With the motion, Kantra had left herself exposed and a claw latched onto her hand. She yelled out, dropping her sword as she tried to pull herself free. The scorpion had a good hold; blood started to pour from the wound as the other claw came to finish her off. Kantra managed to bring her other sword into the path, but this time the blade was gripped.

The two of them were now locked together. Its claw tightened on Kantra's hand; she gritted her teeth, refusing to be brought to her knees. Still, there was no amount of resilience that could defend against the deadly tail. Looking to land the stinger square in the face, Kantra had to throw her head side to side in order to stay alive.

One of her companions came to her aid. Sword raised, Erica came charging in, as she had picked her spot almost perfectly. The blade sunk into the only part which was not covered in the tough black armour. The Bliss Scorpion's face was gored, the tail frantically spun. Kantra tried to pull away, but the pincer still kept its grip.

Regaining some control, the small Bliss Scorpion came again with its tail. This time, it connected, digging the stinger into the shoulder of Kantra, causing her to drop to one knee. It was as if she had planned it. Letting go of her weapon, she then punched the handle of the other sword.

It went deeper into the scorpion; the grip on Kantra's hand finally loosened. Seeing her chance, Kantra then pulled out the sword. In a flash, she sent it straight back in, this time right between the eyes of the Bliss Scorpion. Finally, the opponent was defeated but not without casualties. Kantra was bleeding heavily.

"We cannot make it back the way we came. It's into the tunnel before we become scorpion food," Colton said.

The young Bliss Scorpions seemed to sense the retreat. As the group headed into the darkness, Latch hung back for the pursuers. The first one to reach took his hammer head on. The sound of cracking could be heard, almost splitting the scorpion in two. Another one leapt at Latch, but he did not have enough time to bring the hammer back up. Rather, he met it with a fist, powerful enough to send it flying backwards into the others.

A roar came from the other side of the tunnel; the Ice

Golem was on the brink of defeat. It could not cope with its rival, when it was supported by a militia of smaller versions. Sensing the loss was near, it entered a shambolic rage. The only resolution was to decimate as many of the scorpions as it could before the end. The Bliss Scorpion made another deafening roar. Those perusing the group turned once again, heeding the cry of its master.

It meant Latch could join the others heading into the unknown. After running for a while, there was now a gap between them; the group all paused for a breath.

"Is everyone okay?" Luca called out. Where the tunnel had narrowed, the light had almost disappeared behind them.

"Not sure okay would be the right word, but alive, yes," Kantra answered.

There was an almighty crash which echoed down the tunnels. The noise caused the walls to violently shake; ice started to break underneath them.

"Looks like we have chosen being buried rather than eaten alive," Colton said.

"Shut up for once!" Erica yelled and to her surprise, Colton did. The silence came just in time to hear the scurrying in the distance, heading straight towards them.

"Do they never ever give up?" Luca said.

Zander picked up his sword and started heading towards the Bliss Scorpion.

"That is the wrong way," Luca called to Zander.

"I will hunt them down and disembowel all those which challenge me," Zander's voice was deep and full of anger.

"There is no time for games, and that is coming from me," Colton added. Luca started to walk by him.

"You're putting us all in more danger than we are already."

Zander head-butted him; Luca fell backwards. Towering over him, Zander snarled and raised his sword. Latch grabbed his wrist before he could strike. Zander jumped, as if coming out of a trance; he went to say something but rather walked away.

The scurrying was getting louder and closer as impending doom was almost upon them. Erica helped Luca to his feet and instinctively they all began to start running again. The further they went, the darker it got. Soon they were reduced to having to run their hands along the ice wall. It was slowing them down immensely until the wall ended. They had walked out into the pitch black.

"We are completely stranded," Erica said in a desperate voice; no one replied having nothing to offer. It was as if they had been lured into an unbreakable prison, built by simply suppressing one of the bodies' key senses. Now all they could do was wait for their execution; Erica began to sob.

Luca tried to take charge. He stepped forward, tripped, and fell face first into the darkness. On the ground, cursing to himself, a breeze passed. It was faint but sharp enough to cut through the stuffy air of the underground tunnels. The cluttered pockets of Luca had scattered around him. Mother always used to say hoarding was just carried nonsense. Now he hunted for anything which could help them. Luca's palm made contact and everyone in the tunnel yelled out. He pushed down again on the small tin figure he had purchased for a street merchant. Back from one of his walks to work at the castle, a normal day in a different life. As he did, everyone cried out again; the little mouth opened and out came a beam of light. The longer it was held, the mouth would stay open, and the head would spin. Luca could hardly believe what had been nested in his pocket.

"Probably the best coin I have ever spent."

"Don't be pleased with yourself just yet; get us out of this cave," Kantra yelled and turned to run. Holding down the head's figure, it rotated in a full motion, letting out a beam of solid light. The group started to move through the narrow tunnel. All along the wall's surface were deep scratch marks.

"The scorpions are almost here," Latch said. When the beam of light travelled backwards, it revealed the endless legs and claws racing towards them. Luca stopped the tunnel split into three different paths.

"Which way, Luca?" Kantra screamed in his ear.

"I can't feel the breeze anymore."

"If we do not move now, we die."

Everyone looked to Luca.

"This way," he said and disappeared to the left. At the front of the line, he fell to his knees as the tunnel halved in size. Luca was forced to crawl with a voice now screaming inside of him. The Bliss Scorpions were closing in and now there was nowhere to run.

"Get a move on, Latch" Kantra shouted. He said nothing but instead took out his weapon. Kantra squeezed past Zander and grabbed Latch.

"We do not have time," Kantra yelled.

"That's right, you don't; I am about to buy you some," Latch replied.

"All of us need to get out of here."

"No, you do, to achieve the mission. Now leave."

"Leave you to die? If you do, we all do."

"What's going on back there?" Erica called back.

The sound of the approaching swarm boomed towards them.

"Kantra, we are not the same. You have the opportunity to craft your own fate in life. Mine is sealed the same day I made it. There is only one path, to be a tool in helping build a better castle, to keep the kingdom alive."

With that, Latch leapt forward at the oncoming attackers. Kantra went to follow, but Erica and Zander grabbed her. Kantra's screams echoed as they dragged her away.

Latch held up his hammer; he could feel the vibrations in the walls. Each time the beam of light would pass down the tunnel, it would show the hordes coming towards him. There were only a few moments left before the deadly pincers would connect with his body; Latch slammed his hammer into the wall.

"It's collapsing!" Erica screamed now, all of them scurrying for their lives. Luca could feel the ground moving all around him. He drove forward; the ground wanted to drag him down. All he could do was close his eyes, summon all his strength, and push.

Fresh air and a cool breeze, he welcomed it like lovers do a sunset. There were no more rocks or suffocating tunnels, only plains of endless white snow. Above them was a sea of blue with the two suns hanging lazily in the sky, watching on as the others emerged from out of the ground. Kantra tried to go back as the others tried to stop her, all except Zander. Although he had never seen it before, he knew it was the Collector's palace.

# *Chapter 29*

Screams circled the mob as they kicked open the doors. Inside was a feast of crates, weapons, and flasks. Busy hands tore into the supplies, turning over tables and pulling down black flags in a frantic swoop. Lensa appeared in an attempt to block the exit. Two men came charging at her, arms full of loot. With the butt of her sword, Lensa caught one of the men square on the chin. Flasks dropped to the floor, breaking on impact. Improx poured out into the dirt. The other man did not even blink. He disappeared into the balls of smoke, leaving behind a trail of silver footsteps. Lensa pulled down her bandana and cried her frustrations.

"Cowards, that will not save you!"

Other Black Hand members arrived and walked slowly into the remains of their headquarters.

"It's all gone; they have taken everything."

"Hellrous turned on us."

Lifting up a banner, there was still a box untouched. It was stacked with half full milk bottles, cloth sticking out of each one.

"We are not done yet," Lensa said.

There was an exchange of looks.

"Carmen and the rest have not returned."

Lensa leaned in close to the woman next to her.

"Then we go get them."

Slowly, everyone picked up the milk bottles.

"Lensa is right; we cannot leave our brothers and sisters alone against those creatures."

"Can they be stopped?"

"We must find a way. The centre gates must be shut."

The Black Hand armed themselves to the teeth. Outside, the zone was intent on devouring itself. Huge balls of smoke filled the broken streets. As they started their march, cries filtered their way through the fires. Lensa squinted as she tried to make out the shapes racing towards them. The others lit the rags in the bottles. Something collided with Lensa. Grabbing the young man by the throat, a sense of relief washed over both, it was only another person. Despite the smoke strangling the air around them, none had encountered the terror leaking in from the centre. Without a word, the man sprinted off towards the gates of Hellrous.

Panning out, the Black Hand moved towards Carmen's last known location. More residents came running past. A flag was thrown to Lensa's feet. Everyone stopped, horn Ebb rang out its warning, but it faded into nothing. Huddled in a ring, Soldiers of the Infamous all stood inwards. They rolled back their muscular shoulders and collided with each other.

One stamped down hard and then kicked out. The closest spun around and raised its fists.

"The demon's disciples walk amongst us once again."

All of the fidgeting stopped; collectively, the SIDD turned and faced the Black Hand. It revealed the massacre which they had been gathered around. Carmen's cold eyes stared up to the sky; her head was placed on a pile of bodies. They belonged to Eldertude soldiers.

A flaming bottle whistled through the air. It exploded onto the black flesh. More followed as fire rained down on the SIDD. All of the Black Hand charged, swords and axes raised. Their daring was crushed almost instantly. The SIDD pulled apart the Black Hand like bones from a carcass. It was not long before Lensa was running with the others.

"They cannot be stopped."

"We must regroup."

Those who could keep up darted down an alleyway.

"What are we going to do?"

The remaining Black Hand paused for breath.

"Our brothers and sisters are gone, crushed in an instant."

"There is nothing we can do; let us flee."

Lensa and the others went silent. Cries for help still followed them through the bloodied streets.

"This is our space, as much of a nightmare as it is. We must drive them back to the cesspit they crawled out of."

"It cannot be done alone. The zone must be cleared of all residents, then we will have to side with the kingdom."

"Those in their ivory castle would rather watch us burn."

"Don't be stupid; this disease is inside their home too. Once cast out to the shadows, it will now be at the doors of their loved ones. It cannot be ignored. Take everyone to the entrance gates. Then we will mount our challenge."

No one argued at the talk of further retreat, even if only temporary. Lensa and the other Black Hand members split up. Each headed for one of the large buildings, with a black and yellow flag hanging on the roof. Using a key tied around her neck, Lensa opened the chains. Inside there was a scurrying; little bodies backed into a corner. Wide eyes pierced through the darkness, only one pair bounding up to Lensa.

"Leo, it is time to leave."

"It looks scary outside."

"Yes, it is, but there is no time for that. I know you have no trouble navigating yourself around danger. Gather the other children and get ready to leave."

Leo nodded then gave some type of salute. Quickly, he informed the young and concerned faces. Each child clutched tight onto the little possessions they could carry. Lensa turned back outside to see others in hiding being given the same news.

"Tell me where is Carmen?" An elderly woman, dressed in a purple robe with a thick scarf, appeared from the shadows. In her hands were the shoulders of a young boy, also with the same attire.

"This is where the children lie; you should not be here. Also, I can't hear you with that round your mouth," Lensa replied.

With some fuss, the woman pulled down her scarf and then repeated the question.

"Carmen is gone," Lensa said bluntly.

"What do you mean gone?" Harlow spluttered.

"Her head was on a pile of corpses. So will yours if you choose to stay here. It makes no difference to me though. As she dies, so does your protection."

"Maxen, pull your hood up."

Outside, they were met with other Black Hand members leading their own groups. Both young and old, all were desperate to get away from the circling black clouds. The flames now engulfed most of the zone. Hurried legs were fuelled by the heat. A relentless pace was set but little argued. Nearly all of the children took each other's hands. Leo hung onto a young girl named Thistle. Maxen reached out but Harlow stopped him.

"Remember what I told you about touching. Stick close only to me. This is a dangerous place to hide, but hide we must. The castle guards will be looking for you for some time, until then we must try to survive here. I have nowhere left to protect you."

One of the children started to cry. Lensa looked to the rooftops. Leaping through the skies were the Soldiers of the Infamous. Everyone started to run. The black gates were waiting on the hilltop like the finishing line of a race. SIDD closed in on them fast. Dropping the last of their belongings, the residences and Black Hand sprinted alike. Waiting for them were Eldertude soldiers, an army of statues. They lined the entrance of Hellrous, each with a bow drawn. No one so much as blinked as the first of the Black Hand reached the gate.

"Open it, open it now!" Lensa screamed.

The SIDD were now at the foot of the hill and charging

into the open space. Panic swelled up to the point all residents were banging at the gate. The Eldertude soldiers were unmoved. Rather they took aim and fired. Lensa then grabbed the children. The Black Hand charged toward the SIDD. Residents fled in any direction they could. Amongst the chaos, Leo took hold of Maxen. Following the side of the wall, it trailed into the corner of Hellrous. A dozen or so of the children clung to Lensa. Reaching the building, Leo started to beam, recognising his home. He rushed inside and pulled down the cloth.

"You first, Thistle," Leo said to the young girl. Her powder blue eyes gazed into the dark gap between the wall and valley. Rock and stone had been hacked away to create a small passage.

"We can go first, if you're scared, dear," Harlow appeared and went straight past the two children. Wedging herself in between the gap, she paused and reached out for Maxen. Leo let more pass until it was only him and Thistle left.

"It's okay; it leads to the other side."

"I have never been in the kingdom before."

A chill swept over the two children. A Soldier of the Infamous entered the hallway, malice and hate radiated from its daring glare. Leo and Thistle backed into the passage. The SIDD leapt forward and grabbed out. Blood-stained fingers caught a chuck of Thistle's red hair. Leo tried to pull her away, but the girl was wedged in between the wall. Both of them started to cry.

"Hey."

The SIDD loosened its grip. Waiting at the doorway was Lensa, a burning rag and bottle in her hand.

"I banish you back to the demon's hole that you crawled out from."

Lensa let fly. Flames erupted on the black leather chest of the SIDD. It roared, throwing itself through the fire. Leo and Thistle took their chance. Scurrying their way through the gap, both burst out into the fresh air, into the blinding light.

"Which way?" Thistle asked.

On the other side of the tunnel, the three children huddled together. Harlow was already behind a rock, beckoning them to follow. Torches were appearing from all angles. Calls to contain the disease echoed in the children's ears. Around them, other escapees of Hellrous ran in all directions, soldiers followed. Amidst the confusion, Leo, Thistle, and Maxen made their escape. Now the middle of the night, the children drifted into the Pilpots. Most had locked their doors in an attempt to block out the noise from Hellrous. None bat an eyelid at the three wandering strays.

"These houses are silly. They look like giant mole hills," Thistle said.

"They are called Pilpots," Maxen replied sharply. "My grandma is back there."

"We will find her," Leo said. Looking up over the clay mound, another stampede of boots raced past. It was enough to drive them further into the Pilpots. All of the patrolling guards had been dragged away to help the containment. Nobody bumped into them in the muddy walkways. Even the smoke which normally polluted the streets was gone. The children only had the cold night for company.

"Does everyone get a Pilpot?" Leo asked.

"Pretty much" Maxen mumbled.

"There aren't any walls here," Thistle said.

"Why would we need more walls? Have you really never been outside the zone?"

Both Leo and Thistle went silent. Simultaneously, they stared into the empty fire pit.

"It's late to be out alone." A stern voice from the shadows caused the children to jump. Out appeared a cloaked figure, tall and empowering. "Where are your parents?"

Maxen looked to the floor. Thistle and Leo just stared back. Slowly, a gloved hand went deep into a pocket. It produced a small loaf of sweet bread, wrapped delicately in a leaf.

"Supper was a long time ago."

The food was held out like it was being offered to a horse. Thistle edged forward and snatched at the parcel; as she did, the gloved hand caught her. Leo helped the struggle, as both tried to pull away, the black marks could be seen on their skin. Thistle was released.

"So, you carry the disease."

All the children looked shell shocked; they backed away as far as they could.

"Do not worry, I will not report you. Now eat."

In silence, the children ate. The cloaked figure rested on a rock, watching each mouthful. Quickly, the food was gone, and everyone paused.

"Have you seen the castle?"

Leo's face lit up.

"My mother told me about the castle— its mighty tall trees and beautiful flowers."

"It is so big, it reaches the clouds," Thistle added.

Maxen started to shake his head.

"There is a special entrance."

"Can you take us there?" Leo asked.

The cloaked figure stood up and clenched both hands, the leather screeching from each glove. "Yes, I could. Should I though?" the deep voice quivered. "It's a walk."

No sign of protest.

"Follow."

It did indeed take a long time to reach the castle. The cloaked figure did not take a direct route out of the Pilpots. Rather, they climbed over mounds and avoided the main pathways. Each of the child's pace had slowed right down. But their backs straighten when their eyes feasted on the green. All their necks titled upwards as they reached the base of the woodland wall. Even Maxen had only been this close to the castle a handful of times. A door opened into the wall. It was a step into darkness. Waiting to lead them into the black was the cloaked figure, hovering by the entrance.

"I'm not going in there," Thistle announced; Leo and Maxen agreed. Above them, castle guards were making their rounds.

"Do you want to be caught? There is severe punishment for those who escaped from the zone. I must hide you."

Tiredness warped the young minds of natural thinking. Begrudgingly, they followed the steps down into the winding abyss. A single candle was burning in the middle of the room. Its flame bounced off the four mirrors positioned an equal distance apart.

"We shouldn't be in here," Maxen announced.

"The outside kingdom is scary," Thistle said.

Leo stopped them and pointed to one of the mirrors. In the reflection, the cloak came down. They faced away from the children, staring bleakly into the flame. The man then moved forward, leaving the children to search the other mirrors. All three screamed as they caught sight of a double headed axe. Turning to the stairwell, the man was blocking their escape.

"Let us go," Leo said defiantly.

"I can't do this anymore"

Thistle started to cry, Maxen soon followed suit. Leo held both their hands whilst staring up into the face of their captor. There was a quiver of the axe head. It came up high and slammed into the closet mirror. Shards of glass rained down upon the young and confused faces. The man then slumped to the floor. It took all the courage the children had to crawl past towards the exit. There was no movement behind them; the only focus seemed to be on the candle.

As the children crept up the stairs, like a switch, the man jumped up. He let out a roar and raced after them. Tired little legs climbed as fast as they could. Maxen stumbled; a hand locked around his ankle, dragging him back. Leo stopped but Thistle kept running, eventually reaching the hidden door. Maxen was pulled face to face with the man, who for the first time looked solely into his eyes. Tears streamed down Maxen's cheeks, sweat running across his scarred forehead.

"I know that mark."

The man let go and started to laugh, crawling up into a ball on the stairs. Leo helped Maxen back up as they made their escape. Retched shrieks echoed in the darkness.

"Best we burn together."

## *Chapter 30*

It was as if an artist had painted the scene ahead; the mountain range in the distance formed a near perfect circle around them. In the enclosure, the group was protected from the wind. The blizzard had been replaced by sunshine, which glimmered across the surface of the vast lake. It lit up the water, enriching the colour and giving it a blue aura. To the side of it was their final destination— the one they had left the safety of Eldertude for, ending up in more danger they could ever have imagined.

As they walked slowly through the snow, everyone was silent; it was too painful a time for mere words and much easier to be absorbed by the surroundings. Around them were gigantic statutes of commanding women and men crafted into stances of immense power. Fists clenched, mouths roared open as the frost hung from their bodies. They varied in dress and race, with each statute appearing to have come from its own world. Some tackled fierce creatures and wild beasts.

The group marvelled up at them; Colton could see the wonder on their faces.

"I take it you all have never left your home much, or at all. Well, these are the leaders from the Union of Kingdoms. All who dwelled in the mighty city of Starvogue, before the disbandment. The others are Gods."

"Gods," the word was repeated back at him.

"Yes, before it became a dirty word."

Beneath their feet, the ice and rock were fading. The pathway was now polished stone on which the snow seemed to melt away, leading up to the entrance of the grand palace. It was a diamond nestled on the landscape. From a distance, it appeared to be made entirely of glass, shimmering in the light; it was more of a piece of art than a building. Now at the doorway, the immense level of detail put into the design was clear. Shapes had been hand painted onto the surface, all across the palace. It was the most delicate shade of light blue, with swirls and patterns which were almost invisible to the naked eye.

"That must have taken years just to do these," Erica marvelled.

The gates were almost as tall as the statues. As Luca touched the surface of the door, it eased open; a confused look followed.

"Be careful, Luca; it could be a trap. The Collector hired a small army of Ruinmore Warriors to protect him. Known for both their ferocious combat and deviant ways, they will already know we are here," Colton warned.

The long, towering hallway was empty. Huge panes of glass on both sides featured similar patterns. The only real difference was that the colour had changed to a strong violet.

As the frost on the outside was slowly melted by the beams of light, it created an enriching sparkle. At the other end, was another doorway; this time, it took nearly all five of them to push it open. It appeared to be made of solid white gold. Luca went in first and straight away tripped over a thin piece of rope. It snapped and with it a weight fell, triggering a mechanism attached to a horn; it started to howl. The sound shook the walls around them. All of them covered their ears in vain. Slowly, the horn wound down to nothing.

"Get ready." Colton drew his sword as did the others, bracing for the next challenge. They waited and waited.

"I do not understand; the Collector's palace is one of the most defended places in the Borrowed Lands. We should be surrounded by now... unless," Colton paused.

"Don't say it," Luca warned.

"The curse has already made it here," Erica's words hit harder than thunder. Everyone's expressions dropped so low, that it almost pulled them to the floor.

"Latch best not have died for nothing," Kantra's voice had a tremor.

"Do we at least have the stone still?" Zander asked. The drained and burnt-out figure of Kantra was gone, replaced with a flare of rage.

"He just died getting you out of that nightmare of a tunnel. You do not even acknowledge his death. No wonder you could not win the Day of Dontés on your own."

Kantra was shaking now.

"Tell me what is there to talk about? He did his duty as a Hammer; it is always about the kingdom," Zander said then turned away.

Everyone waited for Kantra to erupt. She took the satchel and slammed it against the wall. Kantra then stormed into the nearest room and immediately started to tear it apart. Furniture and vases were demolished in an instance. Kantra picked up a chair and smashed it against a low hanging chandler. Ice and glass fell whilst the dust filled the room.

"That was very expensive." Everyone turned to look at the new voice. "It was built using a technique mastered only by a small village outside of Wonderliss Forest. When the members become of age, they are given their own personal piece of glass. For years, they had to keep it clean and polished. If the glass is cracked or broken, so is their reputation in the village; they become an outcast. Those however who keep their glass intact, are then entrusted to mould their glass into that very same chandelier. In the village, it is the highest of honours."

"Oh, I am sorry, I guess, then." Kantra had let go of the chair.

"Well, it doesn't matter; the whole village has probably died out by now."

Nearly touching the ceiling was an incredibly tall and equally as thin figure, with pale yellow skin. They had long stretched eyes and two slits for a nose. Carefully, Krooney examined the group, rubbing his hands together.

"We want to see the Collector," Erica said bluntly.

"I would imagine that would be the case. Everyone in here is very dirty," Krooney replied.

"Although our appearance may be somewhat muddied, within our party we have us a representative of the royal variety. Having travelled all the way from Eldertude, heir to the throne of one of the last surviving kingdoms, I present to you Prince Zander," Colton announced and pointed just to make sure. "He wishes to have an audience with the Collector and speak of a business proposition." Colton made a slight bow; Krooney started to rub his hands together even faster.

"The Collector has not given a meeting in almost a decade."

"We understand that a meeting with the Collect is rare, but what we offer is a once of a lifetime. For every time the world speaks about him, his ability to grasp opportunity is married with tails of hospitably."

"You sent us a message to come. We need to know how to stop the curse before it devours our kingdom," Luca said.

"Many of those were sent; never did I think anyone would actually believe it. Oh well, I shall ask him. Odell. Maybe if I shout louder, he can hear me. Odell! Nope, let me go find him; we will need his permission. You may however stay here. I can grant that, mainly because I do all the cooking around here. Follow me."

Krooney had to duck under the doorway. He then led them down another long walkway, causally pushing the golden doors shut as they passed. The others followed at a distance.

"So when did you become the ambassador for Eldertude?" Luca whispered.

"Well, you just stood there dribbling. I must say though this is not what I expected," Colton replied.

The palace was just as impressive on the inside. Its walls were coated in wealth, all following the same theme of white and elegance with hand painted decoration. Although aesthetically pleasing, there was no avoiding that the atmosphere was baron, like a graveyard of a ballroom. They were taken up a huge stairwell to a fleet of readymade rooms, which looked as though they had been waiting over a thousand years. Even though the feeling that they were being watched hung in the air, the temptation of a moment's rest was too much. Krooney bid them all a good day and left.

\*\*\*\*

The group awoke to the sound of banging. Outside their rooms was Krooney holding a silver spoon and hitting it repeatedly against a dinner bowl.

"There will be a feast prepared for the royal guests in fifteen minutes. The Collector has agreed to hear your position, not to discuss the offer but the idea of one. Is that understood?"

No one could answer before Krooney had disappeared.

"We are not to discuss the proposal? I am confused?" Erica wondered out loud.

"And I am hungry; let's go. We will figure it out," Kantra said, pushing past and heading down the hallway.

"Have you seen Colton?"

There was no reply as Kantra disappeared down the stairs. Luca shrugged and then others followed. The dining hall had the same grand theme, which left such an impression it was a scar to the memory. Above was a glass ceiling in which the snow gently landed from the sky. The dining table was made from Bristlecone Pine, long enough that it could seat over a hundred guests. Five places had cutlery already laid out. The food appeared one by one, silver platers all delivered by Krooney. It did not match the same riches as the dishes it was served on. Mainly, it was a mixture of potato and water.

"Eat up; I spent a whole morning making this."

Just as they were about the start, the doors at the other side of the room burst open.

"All rise for his praiseworthy," Krooney announced.

In strolled the Collector, wearing a fur coat, black boots, and a bright purple shirt. Although he was elderly, it was clear the spirit of youth still flowed through his body, all five feet of it. The anticipation of his arrival was immense, not to meet the man, but the information he could offer. Countless lives, the future of the Eldertude, and the answer the world was waiting for, all in the palm of such small hands. Odell seemed to be able to hear these thoughts; he smiled and nodded whilst picking a chair. It screeched as he dragged it along the floor, all the way to where Zander was sitting. He hopped up onto it and smirked as he leaned right.

"So, it is true that the son of the green king is in my abode. Hopefully though without his temper."

Zander looked a taken back; everyone else glared at him to respond.

"Yes, well, I am here on his behalf; actually, it's official business. The invite we received."

Glancing at Kantra, she gave him a look back; the satchel with the royal stone was up in her room. Odell held up his hand. There was a liver spot on the centre of his bald head, the last strands of his hair dangling on the side of his face, his skin with more lines than a rich tapestry. All of that was irrelevant though as Zander looked into his eyes. They were truly absorbing; his eyes promised adventure and excitement, which could draw out the curiosity hidden in the most guarded of onlookers.

Zander tried to speak again, but Odell stopped him.

"Was there no warning?" Odell said sharply.

Krooney came over.

"Of course they have been warned," Krooney dismissed.

"So why would this one break the rules then?"

Odell looked to Zander. Before he could say anything, Krooney said, "Or maybe they have not because I did not tell them."

He grabbed the plates of Erica and Luca.

"Wait those aren't finished," Erica cried.

Ignoring them, Krooney disappeared into the kitchen, only to return with bowls of what appeared the same dish. Odell scowled momentarily.

"Here, is where we eat; well, for most of the meal. Not for business, not for deals, but replenishment only. Everything has a place, when it is time, I will take you to my place of work. First though."

Odell placed his hands on the wrist of Zander; as he did his whole complexion began to change. Zander snatched away his arm. Odell's eyes narrowed, changing from a warm delight to drowning in spite. Colton came into the room and threw himself into a chair. He looked terrible; his skin was pale and his hair soaked with sweat. Odell jumped up and Krooney appeared.

"Your man looks awful. What's wrong with him?"

No one said anything, just as surprised.

"Does he carry the plague with him?" Krooney was behind him now. Colton made no attempt to straighten up. It looked as if it was an ordeal simply to stay in the chair.

"Check him." Krooney did as ordered. He pushed up both sleeves and moved Colton's head from one side to the other. Odell came over and did his own inspection, turning over Colton's hands.

"His palms have turned yellow; he is not cursed but rather a different type of pain. Missing your smoking shell, are we?" Odell asked. Colton perked up for a moment. "No do not get excited; there is none of that poison here," Odell added as Colton slumped back down.

"Rest will help for a start; go back to your bed." Odell went to leave. "Don't worry, I know why you are here, but for now, I must prepare. Please finish the food Krooney has cooked; it is upsetting for him if people do not enjoy it."

He smiled as the others winced, looking back down at the grim bowl in front of them. It was too much for Colton who slid out of the room.

"Do you think this is some kind of a test? If we can handle the stew, we are worthy of saving," Erica asked under her breath. Krooney slammed down the bowl. They ate in silence, the only break being Kantra leaving and returning with the satchel. Once the food was gone, they waited patiently for Odell to make his reappearance.

"Well, as fun as I am, I would imagine it is not all about me," Krooney looked sadder than ever. "Come on. I should have taken you all to the chamber hours ago."

Kantra held onto the satchel as they headed down a spiral staircase, the steps taking them deep under the palace. At the end was a set of huge iron doors, which Krooney had to force open. As he did, he let out a deep sigh, just as the others had their breath stolen from them. They were at the bottom of the lake, looking out at the wonders it hid from the surface. It was a window into the world that existed at the bottom of the sea. The glass used to make the circular chamber was crystal clear. Fish of all sizes and colours drifted past, from the playful clownfish to the tough skinned.

Odell looked even smaller in the centre of the room; he

stood with his back to them, seeming to be enjoying the view himself. He turned and smiled as he watched the newcomers' jaws drop; a two headed white whale came within inches of them. The whale moved with such grace, like a leaf caught in the wind.

"See why I like to make my negations here?" Odell was glowing.

"I did not realise so much would exist at the bottom of a frozen lake," Erica said.

"It is amazing what life can survive," Odell replied. "I imagine that is why you are here, to keep on surviving."

"Not just us but many of the people of the Eldertude. The plague continues to thrive, eating away at the kingdom. We are here for answers, for the cure of infection," Zander announced.

Odell looked unmoved. "People have been asking that question ever since the demon fell from the sky."

Luca was already prepared; he rolled open the scroll which has been handed to him at the start of their journey.

"This message was received by King Vidal himself, saying you know how to protect people from the plague. It has the Collector's official stamp."

"That it does, and before you ask, yes, I did send that." Everyone's faces lit up. "So I am guessing the thoughts are that I have the cure?"

"That is why I have been sent here," Zander said.

"By your own father, the Green King. Tell me, what did he offer for the most valuable information in the history of existence?"

"He offers the heart of the Eldertude, delivered by him by

his only son. It gives life to the castle and cannot be replaced. It is the most treasured possession in the history of our people. It is the only thing we can offer that truly expresses our desperation for a cure."

The satchel was opened.

"It's gone!" Kantra cried.

"What?" Erica grabbed the bag. As she did, the contents fell out. Rocks then scattered across the floor; Erica looked devastated.

"He has stolen it." Kantra held the bag, shaking. "We never should have trusted Colton."

"Ah that is a shame; I was really looking forward to seeing the stone," Odell said. Erica was on her knees now, searching through the rocks for some type of miracle.

"Too many lives depend on the information you have; you must give it to us," Erica pleaded.

Odell gave a smirk; he turned and sat down in the only chair in the room.

"The years ever since Thangrath brought his curse upon the world. It put everyone's lives on a different path, including mine. As the kingdoms fell, unable to cope with the infection eating into their roots, I saw opportunity. It was me that picked up the pieces, from where suspicion and conflict drove relationships apart. I helped broker the trades and supply the goods that were needed. It kept the world alive for as long as possible. Yes, I took a little each time for myself, but who wouldn't? My intuition was needed in a time when so many were lost. As but always, the more money you make, the more resentment is paid out to you. I could see it growing around me like the fog from the first days of autumn. So if you have all the money any one man could need, what do you buy next? Secrets. Some will put a higher price than any amount of gold, to make sure that the mask they live behind is never exposed. The things I learned about what really kept the suns rising each day shocked me. It also put me in grave danger. All that wealth and knowledge in one person, why not get rid of him, that's what I would do."

As if on cue, a long, thin, fierce looking fish cut through a group of smaller ones. It ripped off scales with needle sharp teeth.

"I became paranoid with fair justification. So I hired more and more guards and moved further and further away, disconnecting myself completely from the Borrowed Lands, in order to stay safe. Out here in the mountains made the most sense. With an army acting as a fence around me, it was near impossible for my enemies to get to me, as it was for most people. To me, isolation was my saviour but also my downfall. I became so off grid, my secrets became irrelevant, as did I. I kept paying my soldiers but what is the point of money if there is nowhere to spend it, so the army left, taking as much as they could carry. All that remained was me and Krooney."

"Why did he stay?" Luca asked.

"He had the same procedure done to him as the Hammers, known in your kingdom, I believe. Also, the Butrins race loves to be surrounded by wealth. I had him specially designed, extra strength and loyalty to the end."

Krooney grunted.

"Not sure how happy he was about that last one," Odell chuckled to himself.

"How does the cure come into this?" Erica said.

"Did you not see from the moment you arrived?" Odell was met with confusion.

"I don't understand; how do we stop it?" Erica asked.

"You cannot stop it, but you can separate yourself from it."

"No," Erica's voice trailed off in disbelief.

"I thought that was clear from my message; protection comes by removing yourself from the danger. It worked with my enemies, as it did from the plague itself."

"But what about all those already sick?" Luca said.

"They are gone already; the best is to get as far away from them as possible. I am sorry if this was not the answer you were looking for, but I am offering sanctuary from all diseases. A real chance at life," Odell announced with open arms.

The words came crashing down. It was as if the sky had broken in two and the pieces had fallen upon them. Luca joined Erica on the floor as Zander's whole face turned grey. Kantra looked as if she was about to blow.

"So all you do is lie and trick people into joining you in this ponce home. Is it some type of vile joke?" Kantra said.

"Rather the complete opposite. I am serious about you staying and anyone else disease free. It gets lonely here; also, I am in need of a decent cook. My solution to the cure is as honest as it could be. Everyone used to flock to the mountain Shaddai. It was always regarded to be where all the world's protectors should gather. I used to get the travellers passing by to stop in. Eventually, however, most gave up after they just found humble folk worshipping a locked door.

"Anyway my message, I would assume it would attract those from the Eldertude. Those who disagreed with the methods used already to rid the world of the plague. One your very father brought in, I believe. I am just trying to hide from the disease, not kill it off," Odell replied.

"My father may not be perfect, but at least he has always tried to help the people's suffering," Zander said with defiance in his voice.

"To end their suffering more like; he really has kept everyone in the dark, or was it the Queen? I am amazed no one has ever really questioned the use of the flowers."

"I have been using them to help people in the zone," Erica cried.

"Then there is blood on your hands too," Odell said without even looking at Erica.

"Many important people in the castle have taken them, they can't be as dangerous as you claim," Luca said glancing at Zander.

"Maybe not or maybe I do not know the whole picture. The last I heard, the zone was very much alive and kicking. Maybe things are not so black and white. As I said before, information is the key, and I had to pay a lot for the parts of the story I do know. If you want real answers, ask Queen Hermenize. Either way, I was more in favour of the captain's technique; just leave all those rotting corpses at the bottom of the ocean or banish them to the desert."

Kantra's anger hit its peak; she flung the bag at the Odell and marched over to Zander. "Think you're so safe?"

With both hands, she ripped open Zander's shirt. His chest was a searing black cesspit of infection, eating away at the skin. Underneath, the muscles had unnaturally formed, like they had been inflated overnight. Odell jumped out of his chair like a chemical reaction, pressing himself up against the glass.

"There is no room for the blasted plague here. Why would bring this filth to the last place of purity?" Odell spluttered.

"Filth. Do you know of whom you speak to, what I am?" Zander's voice was hollow, a scratch on his former self. "The deep-rooted tongue of someone beneath me is more than tiring. But to be insulted by it causes the power in my fingertips to almost burst out, in a desperate urge to rip out your throat."

"I cannot believe it is true. His reach cannot be stopped, the grey man." Odell looked to Krooney. "The plague must be removed."

Krooney's size seemed to double with the words, as if he had expanded to cover the whole room. He pushed past the others with ease and went straight for the Zander. Clasping both of his long hands around Zander's shoulders, he threw him across the room with force and precision. He hit the metal door; the sound rang out in the globe. The impact was strong enough to break the prince's back in two. Krooney went to finish him off, towering over the Zander, ready to crush the rest of his body as Odell spurred him on. There was an almighty roar. Zander grabbed the metal door and ripped it off its hinges. Krooney backed off.

"He is here; it flows through him!" Odell yelled just before the door was launched. It hit Krooney hard, smashing him into the glass; cracks instantly appeared. There was no respite as Zander leapt at Krooney.

"The glass is going to break," Kantra yelled.

The rest of the group ran to the outer door of the airlock. Its huge metal wheel had been a challenge to turn for Krooney, but for the rest of them, it was near impossible. Behind them, the duel raged on. Krooney had gotten over the shock of the challenge and was throwing his own punches back. The two juggernauts were determined to abolish each other, with no regard for the destruction they were causing around them. Kantra, Erica, and Luca all pushed down as hard as they could onto the metal wheel, but it only turned a few more inches.

"Hurry up, you need to push harder."

Collectively, they turned and glared at Odell. There was another smash. Zander was cracking Krooney's head onto the floor with such power, the vibrations were shaking the globe. Water had started to seep in from the ceiling.

"Get out of there; we need help opening the door" Luca cried. Zander picked up the loose metal door and thumped it down onto the skull of Krooney. The servant's body went loose, blood mixing with the pools of water.

"Door now or we all drown!" Kantra screamed. Above them, the two headed whale could be seen heading towards them. Zander though did not move to open the door but rather grabbed Odell. He resisted and begged but it was in vain, as the Collector was dragged into the middle of the globe. The others shouted at Zander, but he was only focused on one thing. Both powerful hands wrapped around the old man's neck.

"That's it; we are going to drown," Kantra said, defeated. Luca went to run to Zander but Erica stopped him.

"Stay here with me; we only have a few more seconds." She hugged Luca as they waited for the ice cold water to consume them.

The entrance to the globe flew open; on the other side of it was Colton. Before he could say anything, Erica pushed Luca into Kantra and the three of them fell through the doorway. Back in the globe, Odell was limp as Zander stood over him, still holding the victim by the neck.

"My prince!" Luca screeched as the whale hit the glass. The ceiling collapsed, as the full force of the lake came crashing down. Colton slammed the airlock shut.

\*\*\*\*

All of them sat around the huge table they had eaten breakfast from. Only the sound of the water dripping from their clothes could be heard. Erica stared into oblivion, the words of the Odell echoing through her mind.

"I have to go back to the kingdom. If there is something wrong with the treatment, I need to stop it. My friend, the family I am a part of, the boy he has the disease…" Erica trailed off, remembering how much of the extra treatment she had given Otto.

"I cannot believe Zander is gone. I have been looking after him ever since we were little boys. At the end, I could not recognise him. He has not been treated for weeks. Where did that power come from?" Luca asked no one in particular. They had to come to the Collector's palace for answers, but now were as far from the truth as they were from home.

"So, you decided to come back? Could not find anyone to sell the stone to out here in the mountains?" Kantra asked Colton with her hands on her hips.

"Silly me for thinking the first words out of your mouth would be thank you," Colton replied.

"When you disappear after stealing a small fortune, do not be surprised there is not a warm welcome after."

"I have never stolen anything in my life. Actually, that is not nearly close to being true, but I did not take the stone. Well, I did that also but for good reason. I was not up to shape to attend the meeting with the Collector, so I thought it would be best to delay any real exchange until I was there."

"I see there has not been any loss of arrogance with your withdrawal," Luca added.

"I thought you were sick?" Kantra asked.

"A discussion for another time. Hopefully, I can distract everyone with this." Colton opened a bag holding the heart of Eldertude. Kantra snatched it away.

"Become quite attached to it, have we?" Colton sniggered.

"Now that the prince is dead, this rock is the only thing of any value from this stupid venture. It is my ticket to save my brother from a life of slavery in the castle gutters. I am taking it and there is nothing to stop me."

## *Chapter 31*

Hector was close to suffocation. Each time he went for air, he would breathe in more of the sack. Again, he pulled each hand against the rope. He was only rewarded with more cuts to the wrists and orders to settle down. Eventually, he did, biding his time as he listened to the wheels of the cart turn.

The bag was pulled off; the sunlight stung his eyes as he was thrown into the grass. Slowly, as his vision became less blurred, Hector wished the sack had stayed on.

"The stupidity that leaks out of you turns my nose. Do you know the favours I have had to call on just to get here? The future you have destroyed?"

General Balder stood over Hector; he had a look of utter disgust upon his face. Still on the cart and facing the other way, were two of the oldest soldiers in the general's personal unit.

"I have spent years protecting the dirty secret, creating a safe outlet for the poison. All you had to do was keep it contained, to wait until that pathetic excuse for a prince died of a cold. Then we could have taken the throne together. My legacy to yours."

Eldertude was nowhere to be seen. Hector had spent much of the time unconscious, but he guessed that they must have been riding for at least a week. Now all they had were the trees and fields for company.

"I did not want it to end this way, son, but we always had a deal. That torture chamber of yours was meant to be a release. Now it is exposed; I have to face the embarrassment. You are lucky I did not leave it to the kingdom to carry out the hanging."

General Balder pulled out a sword and waved it above the head of Hector.

"Both your mother and sister would be ashamed."

The words triggered a switch inside Hector, leading to an explosion. He spat and swore at the general, desperately trying to break free of the binds around his body.

"Stop rolling around like a wet fish out of the bucket."

Hector reacted by throwing himself side to side. The back of Balder's sword went across his face. He shouted and his father hit him again.

"You have no right to even say their names."

"I have more right than you, boy. I'm not the reason they died."

His mind was forced back to a time many years ago. Even though it had been pushed into the deepest corner possible, the event was burned so badly into his memories, that it could never be ignored. All around him there were flames, the gold paint melting away as the arches above burst into yellow. Hector gripped his mother's hand; he tried to hold onto his sister, but the smoke was making his head dizzy.

"Put this across your mouth."

It was his mother's handkerchief; even amongst all the anarchy, he could still smell the scent of her perfume.

"They're coming; we must hide."

All three of them turned a corner and stopped; at the other end of the hallway, the exit was blocked. The little girl screamed, and their heads turned. Ezra spun back round, dragging her children through the nearest door and locking it behind her.

"Nola, you brought them to us," Hector hissed at his sister.

"No she didn't, do not blame her for this. The fall of the union is to blame, nothing else," his mother snapped. They had entered a simple guest bedroom.

"Where is father? Why is he not here to save us?" Nola pleaded.

"He is a soldier and meets the enemy head on. It is the only way he knows to protect us," Ezra trailed off. Voices could be heard in the hallway.

"Mother, they are coming," Hector yelled as his mother paced around the room, her mind desperately trying to work out an escape plan. She went to the window.

"It is not that far a jump. If we can lower ourselves down some of the way, we can survive."

Both the children looked confused, but Ezra made sense of it. Pulling down the long curtains, she began to tie them together; the other two helped as smoke began to creep into the room. Then the voices arrived at the door, a roaring boom which channelled waves of anger through the walls.

"Get the door."

Hector nodded and gripped the huge, black knob.

"Nola, you will go down first. Hold on tight."

The little girl looked out of the window at the shear drop.

"Mother, I am scared."

The fire was trying its best to find its way in; the doorknob was letting off steam. Hector's hands were trembling, but he held on tight.

"You must; it is the only way. I will not drop you."

There was an embrace before the little girl started to climb down. Hector let go of the knob. He was flung across the room as the door burst open.

"They are escaping. Stop them!"

Nkye charged over and shoved Ezra out of the window. They laughed as the girl and mother fell to their deaths. Hector screamed; he tried to claw at the Nyke but his hands were burnt to a crisp. As more voices arrived, he recognised one through the tears. Swords and axes cut through the room; the Nkye howled but crumbled under the sheer numbers.

"Look at me."

Hector was on the floor, the smoke burning his eyes. The words were repeated; it was the voice of his father.

"You dropped them. I don't care how much the rope burns your hands, they are your family. Whatever you accomplish in life; I will always remember for your part in their deaths, you are as much a murderer as the fallen enemy around us."

The words were seared into the mind of Hector forever.

"There was no way I could have known it went that way, son; you never told me."

"I did not know how to, or I never thought you would have believed me."

"Possibly then, the blame should be placed elsewhere. Maybe I have been too harsh."

The sword was now limp by the side of Balder. Hector tried to ignore the gloves that hid his burned and damaged hands. He wanted to savour this movement with father, one he had dreamt about for years.

"Or maybe I was not hard enough. Whoever was to blame for their blood being spilt, it is your fault for what has happened now. I will not kill you, but I not bring you back to the kingdom. Consider yourself banished from Eldertude."

General Balder drew out a large hunting dagger, walked up to the closed tree, and wedged the knife into the bark.

"No more hand-outs or cover ups; time to make your own way in life, boy. If you can get to the dagger, then you have a chance of surviving the night. Don't you dare grumble; I have to get back and deal with the aftermath of your actions. It is bad enough with the sea dogs breathing down our necks. Part of me thinks I should go the extra distance just to spy on him, now we are out this far. One day, you could have led my army into battle, to protect the kingdom and make a real name for yourself. I will have to fight our battles as always."

"I know where Maxen is," the words oozed out of Hector.

A look of confusion spread across the General's face.

"Careful now, I can easily change my mind about letting you live."

"He is still in the kingdom, mixing in with the cursed souls of Hellrous."

"Lies."

"Come to think about it, maybe the SIDD have already got to him."

Balder kicked Hector in the stomach; he did not flinch. The general kicked him again and then stormed off. Hector remained deadly still. After a lot more cursing, Balder climbed back into the cart. None of the men looked back as they headed off into the distance.

There was a part of Hector that wished his father had killed him, for it all to end with no more pain. Letting out a deep sigh, he knew that was not an option. The voice inside of him would not allow it. All the obstacles in the world would not break the drive to prove himself. Eldertude would be talking about him now but in the wrong light. Hector would change that; he just had to figure out how.

Whilst contemplating his next move, Hector stared out into the distance. His mind was starting to piece together where he had been left. The ocean dominated the horizon. Being this close to the coast, Hector was surprised his father had not just chucked him into the water. It was only then he was truly thankful for another chance at life. On the edge of the blue, was a ship with a flag held high. The symbol of Neptulus was flowing in the wind.

## *Chapter 32*

A short time ago, Zander never could have imagined he would be in control of such a beast. The Trojas ploughed through the snow. It showed no signs of protest as the prince steered it by the horns towards the giant mountain, the largest in the Draygo Mountain range. He had been able to swim from the bottom of the frozen lake with ease, to then bend a creature with so much power without any resistance. The Trojas had been found roaming the grounds of the Collector's palace— a beast famous for having the combined strength of a whole heard of horses. Its vast muscles bulged out at the joints, causing stretch marks across its red skin.

Only Zander's eyes could be seen. He had wrapped himself in any clothes he could find to try and protect himself from the brutal winds. It also hid the shadow which had a tight grip on his body. The infection had spread across his veins, like the winter ice across a pane of glass. There was little to see of his former self.

A conversation was going on in the back of his mind, driving him towards the mountain. Even in Zander's new state, he could not go back to the kingdom. Whatever had previously drawn people to the mountain was now under his skin. He may have the ability to crush his father but not to honour him. It would only be done by offering Eldertude a real chance to change. If there was a chance to help protect his part of the Borrowed Lands, he would find it amongst the summit, no matter what the test may be.

Now, as he slowly edged up the mountain of Shaddai, the world was engulfed around it. As the mountain stood firm, piercing the sky, everything else in existence would have to sit at the feet of the king. The wind had picked up, becoming sharp and intent. With each gust of wind becoming so strong, he could almost see the punches coming from all directions. Although the mountain was gigantic, the path was disappearing fast. With the size of the Trojas, it was struggling. As its feet slipped, it kicked out, causing lose rocks to drop off into the vast distance. The stone fell through the clouds into nothing. Another came loose; the animal began thrashing side to side, almost throwing Zander off. The movement just made things worse, as the whole ledge felt as if it was about to slip away. The Trojas cried out in panic, knowing what was fast approaching. Zander had no choice but to leap off into the snow. With it, he caught the look of defeat from the Trojas. It tried to twist itself back onto the path, but as the rocks fell away, the Trojas was thrown into oblivion.

Zander was left with only the howling wind for company. He had set out with a royal escort, the size of a small army, and his best friend amongst other companions; now, he was alone on the side of a mountain. As he started to trudge through the snow, Zander came across his first signs of civilisation—two crooked pillars covered in a language he had never seen before. Feet met stone as he sensed steps beneath the snow. The stairs twisted up a steep ridge. A rockslide had forced the path to loop dangerously over the edge. Each step forward dangled in the air. Testing his weight on the first step, his foot almost slipped straight off. Trying to cling to a boulder, he gingerly made his way up.

The wind shot past, threatening to drag him away. Taking a moment to steady himself, Zander felt a flare of anger. All his newfound strength was being taken away by a wobbly step; fear had returned so quickly. Letting go of the wall, the prince used the momentum to race up the steps. Between the wind above him and the ice below his boots, the mountain seemed to use everything in its power to banish him. Zander raced up; with the last stone falling away, he catapulted himself to the top of the ridge.

Turning around to watch the path evaporate to nothing, he smiled, wondering if anything could stop him. Immediately, that question was answered; the steps rose up again and then disappeared, all that was left was a shear drop. Zander was confused; it was as if a chunk of the mountain had been ripped out. He glanced over the edge. As he did, the wind rocketed upward, throwing him backwards. Picking himself up from the snow, Zander walked back to the same spot, more cautious this time. Another gale howled around the mountain.

Looking around, there was one pillar much wider than the others. Cleaning off the layer of snow, it was covered in an inscription. Zander ran his hand over the surface of its wooden top and felt a catch. Inside there was a single roll of tattered thick paper; the prince unrolled the scroll.

There was only one illustration. It was a basic drawing of a figure holding onto a square, appearing to ride a wave.

Zander looked back into the pillar and saw something else stashed at the bottom. Reaching down he pulled out a dusty old rug, the red now faded with most of the golden tassels now missing. Another strong gust of wind blew past, Zander then smiled to himself. Was he about to do this? The loose steps moments earlier were nothing in comparison to this. Still, if he was truly to accept his new sense of invisibility, these are the tests he would have to pass.

Zander took a deep breath and jumped off the mountain. The leap of faith quickly turned into a disaster; a lone body plummeted towards the emptiness. His ears heard it first, before the roaring wind came at him, the air catching under the huge rug he clung onto. Like a leaf floating on the surface of a river, Zander was carried up with the power of nature.

Almost enjoying the sensation, Zander remembered he had one shot and leaned forward. The movement changed his direction. With the wind fast evaporating, he did his best to throw himself towards safety. He began to fall again; the rug was now gone. Desperate hands searched for anything that could save him. Fingertips touched rock then his hand grasped on. Slamming into the side, with newfound strength, Zander pulled himself up, into a hidden world.

Built into the cove of the mountain, grey wooden huts dangled off the cliff faces. Attached with rusty, golden chains, the small cabins were battered by the elements. What surprised Zander the most was the amount of vegetation. The way the stones were formed around the summit meant there was some protection from the snow, giving the plants a chance at life. It had a magical feel; the aura shone through the smoke of the small bonfires. It was not clear how the huts were connected; they all stood alone with breaks in the mountain accompanied by massive drops. There were no bridges or ropes to help across; only birds could thrive here.

Unsure what to expect, Zander headed to the closest cabin he could reach. As he approached, he realised how much smaller they were in comparison. There was no guarantee that he would be able to even fit inside. Sensing his presence, out walked a tiny figure covered in golden brown fur. Its face was more mouse than man. It had long ears and a tuft of hair under the nose, mixed with whiskers which twitched at the presence of Zander.

Both waited for the first one to speak. The small figure began to circle Zander, looking him up and down.

"You're not one of us, are you? A Buzra." Zander was not sure if the Buzra expected a response. "No, of course you're not. I thought you could be one of Jackal's offspring; he has strange looking ones, but I guess you're not. It was more hope for me really. What I meant to say is that we stopped having visitors a long time ago. Leaving with it both the ability to cater and welcome. I have become a bit rusty it appears."

"It's fine," Zander replied.

"So you have come to worship? Most people do. That's how we guard everything that eats, sleeps, and continues the circle. I don't have the authority to let you do that though; I am just thinking about how to get you to the one who can."

A claw pointed to the highest building. It was in a much better condition than the grey huts. The care and craftsmanship which had gone into its creation were vibrant in its design. With curved doorways and spiralling staircases, the roof had been layered until it pointed into the clouds.

"Only it's my problem to get you there. What am I thinking then? When did you last have dinner?" Zander could not remember the last time he ate, or had the urge to. "Let's hope you're light enough then to travel by other means."

"You want me to jump off again?"

"How else do you think we travel? The sky is all giving; we merely are here for the ride."

Rox began to walk off, stopped, then gestured to Zander to follow.

"Okay, the winds are soft today but no bother, still reckon you should make it. Would have been a lot easier with the rug, but you lost that, so we are in need of a volunteer."

Out of thin air, a crowd appeared. All the other Buzra wore colourful, bright clothing and were surrounding Zander.

"Rox, you forget how to welcome a guest of the mountain. He may have lost the rug but still. The council will be happy to see him."

"Who then is willing to make the fall?"

One of the Buzra stepped forward, somehow ever smaller than Rox.

"One hand joins the other."

Zander gingerly locked hands with the pair. They smiled as they attempted to run off the edge of a cliff; Zander pulled back.

"There must be another way?" Zander stuttered.

Rox dragged Zander over the cliff's edge. All were in instant free fall. Zander flapped his arms in some desperate attempt to change their fate. Both Buzra still had a tight grip of the prince. In perfect timing, they both threw open their bodies. The three started to glide upwards. With all fours spread out, the air had caught in between their webbed skin. The winds which had once battered them, now were gently carrying them towards their goal.

Rox lost their grip and let go. The other could not keep Zander afloat and was dragged down with him. Rox brought in his limbs tight and aimed himself at the pair. Trying to play his part, Zander held out his arms. It was not long before the claws made contact with his wrist.

Gently, they drifted back towards their destination. The Buzra pulled their arms together, gracefully landing on the ground just outside the impressive structure. Zander's knees begged permission to turn to jelly, but he resisted as he was led up the stone path. Rox and the other Buzra hesitated outside the triangle entrance, Zander went to enter but Rox stopped him. Both the Buzra bowed and then walked in.

The huge wood beams overhead were forcing Zander to duck. Carved endlessly into the walls of the corridors were tiny triangles. They came across two more Buzra; both were sitting with a long spear propped up next to them. Each wore a helmet pulled low across their face. Rox cleared his throat.

"Wake up."

Rox kicked one of them. He jumped out of his skin and straight onto the lap of the other. Their spears slowly dropped to the floor. Another Buzra appeared; she had grey whiskers and tiny spectacles. Looking down her nose at Zander, she took off her glasses and then put them straight back on.

"Is it one of Jackal's boys?"

There were no walls in the next room; they had all been taken out to remove any barriers between them and the elements. The magnificent view was of the peak of the mountain; its mist circling the top would occasionally creep into Scarlet's chambers. In the centre of the room was a half-finished painting board; it was a picture of a turquoise teapot without a lid.

Scarlet poured out four cups of tea. All the Buzra sat around a table; Zander awkwardly positioned himself onto one of the child size chairs. Scarlet said nothing as she just stared into Zander's eyes. Steam lightly tickled the whiskers under her nose. The others just sipped their tea.

Slowly, Zander removed the rags from his face. As he peeled them away, it revealed dark, broken skin, bulging lines spread around his face like the branches of an autumn tree. There was a deafening noise; it was so powerful that it threatened to break the very skull of Zander. He curled up on the floor; the Buzra stood over him, except for Scarlet.

Still drinking her tea, she said, "It will only get worse."

The words revived Zander. Rox and the others helped as best they could to put him back in the chair.

"Can you hear it? Nobody else could," Zander asked in a weak voice.

"Not like you," Scarlet replied.

"Please, help me. Why can't I stop myself from getting closer to it?"

Scarlet moved away from the table to face the mountain. The wind had picked up; clouds were circling the peek at a rapid speed. Through the mist, there was a faint light.

"Rox, gather the council."

He did not move and started to rub his hands over his whiskers.

"What's the holdup?" Scarlet asked, looking down her nose at him.

"Well I can go get them, that's no bother. But should I, what with our guest and all," Rox said gingerly, glancing at Zander.

"It does not even matter now. Either we all will die or we do not," Scarlet replied.

"As always, you're right. I will go get them all now. Off I go." He bowed then slowly walked away; the other Buzra went with him.

Scarlet picked up the teapot.

"Another cup? Yours must be cold by now."

"Have I endangered you somehow?" Zander asked.

"Not you exactly, but also yes you have. The curse is in no way your fault, but bringing it back to us, it puts us all in jeopardy. Do you like my painting?"

Zander started to stutter. "It is fine, I take it then there are no other infected here?"

"Correct."

"Then I have brought it back," Scarlet repeated herself. "I did not think. How did you stop it before?"

"It stops itself; our little bodies cannot hold it. We just die out."

Zander looked horrified and started to stutter again. Before he could get a hold of his words, the council started to arrive. A mixture of old and young Buzra started to come straight in. They murmured and bumped into each other as they all argued over the lack of tea.

"It has been some time since we have all gathered to the council," Scarlet announced.

"Not since we decided on what flowers for Tam's wedding ceremony," Billin said, one of the older members of the council,

"Yes, I was referring to more important matters," Scarlet prompted.

"Tell me what is more important than a wedding?" Billin replied.

There was a wave of the noise of agreement.

"We have a traveller with the mark of the curse across him."

With that, the talking stopped. All the Buzra turned to Zander as if only seeing him for the first time. One of them leaned across the table and looked him up and down.

"Should we start planning some funerals then instead?" Billin asked.

There was an eruption of laughter, all except for Zander.

"Lighten up; you're not the one who might perish," Rox said.

"I still do not understand," Zander stuttered again.

Scarlet stood up.

"The reason why we have no infection here is that we cannot sustain it. Simply, we shall drop down to never rise again. It might be one or all of us. We made this choice after our previous form could not be controlled."

"How can you all be so calm?" Zander asked.

"It is simple to us. To fear death is like being scared of a storm cloud or a bird's song. It will come regardless. Why spend energy on something you have no control over? You may be able to bend your own fate, but at the end of it all, it's still fate that decides. Your presence here might cause some of us to become sick and die. The mountain however has called you here, and we believe in its choices. If our time must end to help continue the fate, then we do so with a smile," Scarlet explained.

"Plus, funerals are a lot easier to plan for than weddings" Billin added.

The laughter returned.

"How do I answer the call of the mountain?" Zander said bluntly.

Each of the Buzra looked at each.

"Without being rude, do not think you are special. The mountain has called out before. Many have turned up, even when it has been silent. Everyone is after something. There is a very good chance you do not have the answer, especially if you do not even admit why you are here," Scarlet said meeting Zander's gaze.

"Take me there. I need to see it."

Outside, the clearing on the mountain top was soon full of hairy, excited faces. Cheers followed the reveal of the device carried above their head. It would guarantee Zander's delivery, so he had been told. In their enthusiasm, the Buzra dropped the carrier; it almost split in half. There was little to it, a square basket with thin paper wings hanging down at each side. Scarlet gestured for Zander to get inside, but he just looked at her.

"This is the way we have always made the journey."

Begrudgingly, Zander forced himself in. His knees were pressed up by his ears. One of the Buzra demonstrated, as above Zander's head was a series of strings attached to a pole. By pulling one down, the wing would rise up or change direction.

"Use the winds to take you there. If it does not work, remember what I told you about death," Scarlet said followed by a wink.

The Buzra moved the carrier towards the edge of the cliff face, Zander could not quite believe he was about to commit to this. As he was slowly moved over, Scarlet made her speech.

"Again we help to serve the call of the mountain. For our fate or the travellers drawn to it, there will always be great value in serving its demand. We bid you the best of luck, and that your hands may help construct a better future for us all, even if now we cannot see it. Do not fret if it is not what you imagined, fate can be a funny old thing."

Zander was now a mere few feet from the edge.

"Wait, how do I get back down?"

"Oh, we hadn't thought of that," Scarlet said before pushing him off.

The basket only fell for a moment until the air caught the sails; slowly, Zander began to rise. Everyone on Shaddai Mountain held up their hands and cheered. Zander wished he had just an ounce of the enthusiasm they had in their mouse like faces. As he drifted upwards, higher and higher, there was a strong gale from the side. He was blown into a narrow tunnel. In the patches of light, he could see jagged rocks ready to rip apart the flimsy device. Pulling frantically, he tried his best to keep a straight course.

Its wings could not be tamed and already seemed to be on course for self-destruction. Zander was cursing himself for getting into the stupid basket. He yanked hard at another string, so hard it came off in his hand. There was another blistering gust; the wind howled in Zander's ears, driving him upwards at a searing pace. Around him, the rocks were closing in. As one of the wings came off, the whole basket started swinging in a circle. There was nothing to stop the device from crashing head first into the rock wall. Instinctively,

Zander held the sides, trying to hold the device together as it crumbled to nothing.

Scrambling at thin air, Zander started to fall into the darkness. The wind was whistling past him, but it was not enough to stop the free fall. Somehow, Zander still had a hold of the remainder of the basket, connected to the wooden slate. He twisted in the air and dragged the slate in front of him. As the wind pushed against the slate, Zander had seconds left before he hit the ground. Putting both feet on the wood and tensing his core strength, Zander prayed for another blast. The tunnel heard the request; it seemed to take a deep breath and unleashed a roar of air. It was enough to build resistance under the slate, until he was lifted upwards.

Zander frantically moved his body from side to side, trying to keep himself upright. Spiralling through the tunnel, the wind now came from different directions. Twisting his knees, he used the slate to ride the wave of air. A heavy mist had descended on the direction Zander was heading. There was no way of knowing if he was about to be slammed into a stone wall.

The force closed Zander's eyes; his mind went black. All of his senses crashed as the sound absorbed the inside of his skull. The slate was gone, but he was being carried towards the light beaming out through the mist. A range of snow-covered mountain tops all acted as an audience. Zander could see the entrance, but he was nowhere near it. Still soaring into the sky, he threw himself towards the goal. He moved through the air like a shooting star. It was exhilarating; as he raced toward the peak, Zander felt like he was unstoppable. With the ground now fast approaching, Zander now realised that he really could not stop himself. Slamming face first into the snow, he hit the rock buried underneath. There was a loud crack; it was not bone, but rather the rock splitting in two. As he dusted himself off, there was nothing but a minor scratch.

Alone on the peak of Shaddai, Zander started to wade through the snow. The entrance to the cave was small and easily missed. As he walked in, the light from outside soon started to fade. Zander wondered how much further he could go into the darkness. The cave answered; a torch became a light on the wall next to him. Zander jumped back, the clearing he just walked through was now just a rock wall.

He had no other choice but to wander down the tunnel into the unknown. As he did, the walls began to disappear and the floor beneath him melted away. He was standing on a signal step in a cavern of emptiness; the torch in his hand went out.

"Step forward," a voice passed him like the wind.

It repeated itself, and Zander felt an urge to obey. He did as instructed, falling instantly. Zander tried to cry out, but the breath from his lungs conjured up nothing. He opened his eyes, and he was face down in the grass. Wet dew brushed against his cheeks; there was an early morning mist across the field. A shudder went through Zander's body. In the distance, he could see a figure. Dressed only in grey, they were looking straight at him. It sensed Zander's gaze and disappeared behind a tree. The bony hands with fingernails as long as claws were still visible, digging deep into the bark.

Zander had to get away; the field offered little cover. Rubbing his eyes, he recognised the long red cloak of his father and the black dress of his mother. Both had their backs to him. Zander called out, but they did not answer, so he started to sprint toward them. As he did, he tripped over a small young fox. It howled in pain and curled up into a ball. It had been carrying a rabbit. Looking up with pain in its eyes, Zander decided not to see it. Reaching his parents, he yelled out as loud as he could, before pulling at the back of both of them. In one motion, they turned to face him; Zander jumped back. Their faces had been replaced with a doorway.

The shock caused Zander to tumble over. Back in the grass, the fox climbed back on top of him. Zander could smell the rich, damp fur of the orange creature. He pushed it away and continued to stare up at his parents. Both of the doorways in their faces opened up. A loud thumping could be heard in Zander's chest. He tried to take deep breaths to calm himself down. The more he did, Zander noticed how easy it was now for him to inhale. Looking down to his chest, there was no blackness clawing away at the muscle.

There was a rustling in the long grass; Zander spun round to see the orange tail disappear into the foliage. The sweeping panic returned; the parents were offering nothing as Zander pleaded with them. In their hollow faces, there was a glint at the endless doorways. The hairs on Zander's neck stood up; there was a hot heavy panting on the back of his shoulders. The grey voice whispered into the ear of Zander, who began to cry. Trembling hands arose; slowly Zander reached into the faces of each of his parents.

Out of his father's, Zander now held an apple. Juicy and tender, the piece of fruit was mouth-watering. His other arm was trapped inside his mother's face. Zander wildly tried to pull himself away; throwing his whole body back, he dropped the apple. The grey fingers wrapped themselves around Zander's arm. As soon as they touched the skin, he went numb— first at the limb then the whole body. The life from him was being drained; he no longer had the energy to stand.

Both doorway and the grey figure simultaneously released their grip. Face down in the grass, Zander watched as the fox was now nibbling at the discarded apple. The animal paused, then almost with a grin, stretched out the once injured leg. It took another bite, and then with its nose pushed the fruit in the direction of the rabbit.

A twinge of pain ran through the side of Zander's body. His arm was caked in black tar, eating away at the flesh. With wide eyes, he snatched at the fruit. The two animals jumped up, with drool hanging off their chins. Zander bit into the apple and heaved. It tasted like decay and rot. Pausing to gag, Zander then took another mouthful of the shiny apple. The flavour had become more toxic; it was overpowering to the senses and caused Zander to pass out.

After what seemed like an age, Zander's body could no longer resist the temperature. His eyes slowly started to focus; there was still a foul taste in his mouth. Zander was back in the cave, with walls and the wind around him. Illuminated by an invisible light was a small wooden door, slightly ajar. Zander ran his hand across the rough surface, before pushing it open. He froze, waiting for another trick to jump out at him. There was nothing but stairs, which lead up to another possible illusion.

At the top, he was greeted by high pitched shouts of alarm. A bundle of colour flapped up and down as Zander entered the cavern. Perched on every available rock face or chunk of wood, the birds yelled their distaste at the intruder. The further Zander explored, he mostly only discovered droppings. Most of the birds continued their protest, but the disturbance was not enough to move them. Soon, they got bored, as did Zander. He was still struggling to find why the Buzra had decided to build their way of life around a dingy cove. Without warning, from the shadows, the call of the mountain roared to life.

# Chapter 33

The crashing ocean split between the rocks, spraying water onto the cliffs. The constant sound of the waves was meant to be therapeutic, people said. For Hector, it only sent his thoughts into overdrive.

"*Pathetic and now alone, it was all there for the taking.*" The voice in his head had gotten louder, drowning out nearly every other thought.

"I only got caught because I was trying to keep you quiet."

Hector was not sure anymore if he was talking out loud.

"*The only way to make them want you again is to do this. No one will remember the failures of the past if you rule the future.*"

Looking back over the ledge, Hector thought he was going to leap off it. The rocks would break his bones and the water would fill his lungs. Eventually, the fish would come to eat the flesh of his body. Hector took another step towards the drop.

*"Don't even pretend."*

Hector sighed.

"Looks like there is little other choice."

Night was setting in, but the bay was alight and glowing. Each ship was illuminated with candles and long rows of lanterns; the floating kingdom was alive on the water. Protected by rock, the circular bay was jam packed with any type of floating vessel which could be squeezed in. Nearly all of them were tethered together; planks and rope bridges connected the floating city of Neptulus into a thriving hub. Smaller boats would navigate themselves through the tangle of huge vessels.

In the centre of the bay was a spiralling rock formation, rising high like a mast. At the top, a crow's nest had been formed, to keep watch of the entire fleet. Mainly though, the watchmen's time was spent yelling at the fishermen, warning them to stay clear of the whirlpools.

The only beings not charging around were the seals. Lined up across the small patch of beach, they laughed to each other, as the rest of the world around them never stopped. With all the blue surrounding the bay, there was only one way to walk in. A bridge from the valley's edge connected to various walkways down to the ships below. It was heavily guarded. Every trader and a new face was patted down and interrogated. Hector did not have the time or the patience.

Stepping off the edge, Hector started to clamber down the rock face. Over the years, the water had eroded the valley wall, giving an opportunity to find a route down. There was no hesitation as he leapt from one ledge to the next. He was not in a mood to be halted by such an issue as safety. If one of the rocks was loose or he slipped, then he would fall to his death; what would be would be.

No such luck, Hector made it to the bottom. Standing on the wet stone, the sound was deafening. Next to him was the bottom of the Infinitros waterfall, an endless source of immense power. Running his hand through the liquid, Hector struggled to keep his arm up. The freshwater had the strength to flatten boulders, and to keep a whole city living. Wedged amongst the rocks, there were dozens of little baskets, put out to collect the silver and yellow Funnel fish caught in the current. During the day, the rays of the sun would catch off the scales, causing the waterfall to sparkle.

Finding a gap, Hector slipped into the cave hidden behind the great barrier of water. It was a vast space, full of dislodged rocks and the deafening noise of the waterfall. Hector reckoned if he could make it out the other side and climb further, he would be able to slip under the walkways into the floating city.

Hector froze at the sign of approaching light. He recognised the navy-coloured uniforms, the studs and over polished armour of the Tulus soldiers. The other group he had never seen before; they were the form of men but of a different race. Orange skin covered in leather straps, they held red cloaks and white masks in their hands.

The outsiders shook the masks, but the soldiers stood firm. They pointed to the exit; the head of the outsiders threw his outfit to the floor. Slowly, they lent in to whisper something in the ear of the Tulus. The soldier sighed then gestured for the others to make a path. Smirking as they left, they headed for the edge of the waterfall and out into the city. After they left, all Tulus started to wave their hands. Weapons were drawn as they charged out of the cave.

Neptulus kingdom never slept. Small Pin, the spiralling island in the middle of the bay, acted as the anchor for all the largest ships. All of the fish, crabs, and shrimp that had been caught the night before, were dropped off to be sorted and sold. The haul however from each ship was growing smaller each time. Slowly, the bay was drying out, married with the outbreak of whirlpools. Nearly every day, another floating home was sucked to oblivion. In spite of this, there was still the daily catch to work with; the fishermen dragged back cages and rods. Engineers on the smaller ships travelled out on the emergency calls. Tulus soldiers walked the endless beams and bridges, connecting nearly every ship together.

It would be difficult for Hector to slip through unnoticed; he knew the people of Neptulus lived in each other's pockets. A habit derived from having the boats practically built on top of each other. Although banished, he was still the son of General Balder, leader of the Eldertude army. There would be those who would recognise him. Still, he had not diverted to the mask just yet, pocketed from the waterfall. The cloak too was under wrap; he had tried to hide it under his jacket, but it was so long, it trailed out. The red fabric was drawing in looks from those he passed; many said nothing until one of the fishermen almost jumped out of his skin.

"I know that colour," he said with a look of horror on his face. "The colour which comes after black, once the mark is upon the skin. They say the black will be the last thing you see but it's not, it's the red of the snatcher."

"Quiet old man, you are deluded," Hector replied.

The two of them stood on one of the higher walkways. Underneath was a tangle of smaller platforms, over where the boats would often cross. The old sailor's eyes narrowed; he stroked the grizzle on his face, causing beads of salt to flick off.

"It is cloth and nothing more," Hector dismissed.

"No of course, I don't know what I was thinking. The long working days mean the mind becomes stretched," the sailor nodded and walked on.

*"He is lying to you," the voice whispered, "being played like a symbol."*

Hector lashed out with the speed of a viper. He plunged the knife deep into the back of the old man and pushed him off the path. The body hit one of the walkways on its way down, before landing onto on a rowing boat. Those driving it looked up to see the smiling white crooked mask looking down at them. The red cloaks trailed behind as he sprinted away from the scene. The wood bellowed under his feet, creaking from the pressure.

Tulus soldiers had been alerted to the presence, "a rouge snatcher" he could hear them shouting. There were so many twists and turns, bridges and boats to leap from and climb under. Hector had now entered the infirmary for the Bow-riders, endless rows of the boats which needed love and care. Stacked on top of each other, Hector rolled himself into one of the boats and laid flat.

As he did so, the soldiers rushed past, all except for one. Now out of breath, the large Tulus decided to catch a break. Hector slid out from his spot in between the carcasses of the broken vessels. Silently, he struck the knife deep between the shoulder blades of the unsuspecting. Rather than crumble to nothing, the soldier twisted his body and lunged toward his attacker. Taken by surprise, Hector stepped back and tripped over a piece of rope. Both of them went overboard.

Plunging into the cold water, the pair was immediately in trouble. It was as if a long hand had reached out from the seabed. The whirlpool was unforgiving; it had trapped both of them in a spiral, dragging them downwards. It was clear the soldier was done for; the blow to his back had drained any strength left. Hector flapped in the water, the mask and cloak gone. His efforts were in vain as the relentless current kept pushing him aside. As his head bobbed up and down below the surface, it would not be long before he would be sucked down to the bottom.

"Swim to the middle," he could just make out the words. They were repeated again, and he had no other choice but to follow. Gasping for air, there were a few moments of relief in the centre, the water breaking on itself and the pull, until he dipped again. Hector threw open his hands in a last futile attempt to escape; his prayers were answered as his hand wrapped around a rope. At the other end, it was more of a floating home than a boat, round and built upwards rather than out. Different floors had been added in a makeshift pattern; the colourful sails had been mixed in with flags. All around the vessel were handpicked flowers. Hector crawled inside and lay on the floor, soaking wet and shaking.

"I knew this place was filth," he stuttered.

"We cleared up the other day."

Standing over him was a middle-aged woman with a young girl; both had matching thick platted hair.

"I did not mean this place," he looked around. There was not much room in between the stacks of books, beds, dozens of candles, and more plants. Most had been positioned to block out the windows.

"Maybe I did," Hector muttered.

"We could not save your friend," the mother said.

"No bother; he was a bit of a drip anyway." Hector laughed at his own poor joke; the others just looked confused. He went to the window and lifted up the curtain, the pair both jumped.

"It stays shut" the girl shouted and waved up a hand in protest. Her palm was a thick oozing black mess. The mother quickly pulled it back down.

"Please do not say anything. We beg of you."

"The treatment that bad here, is it?" Hector said looking uninterested.

"There is none, but we know in Eldertude they use a flower. We are going to grow our own."

Hector looked back out of the window.

"Do not believe everything you hear."

"You're not going to tell on us, are you?" the child asked.

"What's that ship over there, the big one?"

"Who doesn't know that ship?" the women asked.

"I can start shouting for the guards," Hector replied.

"It is the Sarago Wanderer, owned by Captain Holsten, the head of Neptulus. He is in; you can tell from the flag."

"Unlock the door," Hector ordered.

"Please don't let the soldiers know about us."

Both the mother and child had the same begging look upon their faces.

"If you're secret is so important, then why risk its exposure to save me?"

"Life is precious; we could not just sit back and watch you drown."

"When caught with those marks on your body, then you will learn not everybody shares that view."

Surrounded by a ring of warships, the Sarago Wanderer

rose up out of the water and towered over the bay. It stretched nearly the length of half the city. Made from Blackwood only found deep in the Circle Forest, bright cream streaks had been painted across the endless portholes. Three masts stood tall, blue sails flowed in the wind. The bowsprit was turned up so high; the nose of the ship was permanently stuck up.

Hector watched as boats full of guards sailed closely to the walkways. The direct route was out of the question. Only one much less preferred option. Back in the water, it now felt freezing and dirty to his skin. He cursed himself for having to risk the whirlpools again.

Finding refuge on a ledge hidden from view, the darkness was finally starting to set in. It would be a much-needed blanket. There was little cover in the wide stretch between the city and the Wanderer. Other military ships had positioned themselves to create a monitored channel.

The only boats which seemed to go relatively unnoticed were the night fishermen. Gliding through the water on long slim canoes, the men all started out into oblivion. Amongst the grunting, the only other sound was the cages trailing behind them. Hector waited for his opportunity. One of the smaller boats had only space for two. Moving into their regular spot, the first of the fishermen pushed down the anchor, whilst the other poured out the bait. As the maggots sunk down to the water around the cages, there was now nothing to do but wait.

Both knew the drill; one pulled up a chair and propped his legs on the side. Pulling down his tattered woolly hat, it was not long before he was snoring away. It was followed by a grunt, for as soon as he had started to sleep, it was interrupted. A strong light beamed down on them; the other fishermen waved it away as the warship moved on. The snoring quickly returned. Tying a string to his boot, the other fisher-men looked to get their own nap. There was an abrupt tug to his foot, the long rope entangled with the cages dipped under the surface.

Peering into the sea, the fishermen saw nothing. Waiting for another pull, he let his mind drift away. All that could be heard was the sound of the gentle waves, lapping at the side of the boat. The moonlight danced across the water, causing the blue to sparkle. Bubbles then offered the promise of a catch, enticing the fishermen in further. Leaning in, there was no protection from the knife into the belly. In a state of pure shock, the fishermen did nothing. Hector bound one of the cages around his neck before he was cast away.

"Fallen overboard again, bloody idiot?"

The other fisherman was now on his feet. Calling out for his colleague, all he discovered was blood on the decking. Walking over to investigate, his attention turned to the rope, quickly disappearing from view. Taking a hold, the fishermen had never had to use such strength to pull it back up, but he quickly found out why. Looking back at him was the grey, distraught face of his shipmate. His head locked within the cage.

Opening his mouth, the fishermen went to scream, but there was a blistering pain crushing his lungs and entire body. A spearhead was sticking out of his chest; it had ripped through his innards as bits of flesh hung on the tip. Hector gave out a boot and the woolly hat came flying off. The fish-ermen fell forward, causing a loud splash as he sunk to his death. Within almost an instant, the spotlight returned. One of the warships changed its path towards the small canoe. Hector lay still, only inches out of sight as the commands from the Tulus soldiers boomed out over the water.

"Show yourself. This is your last chance, or we will take action."

Hector stood up, facing the ship. He had the woolly hat pulled down low.

"Identify yourself."

One of the cages went overboard and then another until there was none left to throw. In the end, he gave a slow wave to the warship. The light eventually disappeared and Hector was left alone. There was now nothing between him and the Sarago Wanderer. Now all he had to do was come up for breath as he glided towards his goal. The closer he got to the Wanderer, the more glorious it became. Even with the moss and seashells stuck to the bottom, the world's finest ship was true to its name. Blackwood used to make the ship had been measured and crafted to the nearest inch. The result was that the huge bow flowed with the elegance of a dancer. It curved so high up that it looked to have joined the clouds of the sky.

No time to ponder, as there were still many soldiers and workmen marching the port. Sticking as closely as Hector could to the side, he eyed up a fishing net hanging near the end of the ship. It would provide an easy route to the deck. Hector was still hesitant; one turn of a head and he was in danger. As he drifted further backwards, Hector was now at the stern. The entire back of the ship was made from glass. Designed in a mosque, there were rich colourful patterns around the edges. In the centre, the glass, depicted the Wanderer facing an almighty sea creature. The mouth of Cycultra was open. One of the many widows had been pushed out wide, a steady stream of smoke drifting out of it.

Moving back to the net, Hector continued the debate of his next move. Then the answer hit him. A large bucketful of food scraps was now entangled in his hair. Cursing under his breath, Hector could see a hole directly above, almost inviting him in. Using the bolts running up the ship as a foothold, he dug his fingertips into the gaps of the wood and clambered up. Eventually, he reached the hole and squeezed through into the ship.

Hector found himself surrounded by large rice sacks and a variety of cold meats. The wooden floors echoed a warning. Ducking behind a crate of spices, there was a trail of water leading right to his spot. In strolled one of the younger kitchen porters. With a yawn, he chucked another bucket of waste out of the hole. Most of the content spilt out onto the floor; the boy did not look at all concerned as he left. Much like the city, even in the dead of night, most were awake on the Sarago Wanderer. Each time it rocked, the creaking of the boat hid the sounds of footsteps. There were little places to hide in the narrow walkways. Hector was constantly forced to change his path. Each new room offered a collection of items lying in wait. Storage rooms full of edibles, armouries without any signs of dust, or bags and bags of gold.

Hector winced; the next living quarters were a long room lined with sleeping beds. There were no separations between the rows of men and women, all snoring. They had been sent into a deep sleep by the gentle rocking of the boat. With the other option blocked, Hector tip toed forward. It was not long until one of the floorboards howled out underneath him. One of the men closest to him snorted, the air almost blowing out the only candle. The flame dithered but no such luck. Continuing on, Hector was now almost out the other side, when one of the sailors sat up. Hector froze and watched the women rub the sleep from her eyes; she had her back to him.

*"Do it, do it now."*

The knife was ready; Hector's body coiled itself, ready to spring upon the victim. She stood up and headed back down the hallway. Letting out a deep breath, Hector slithered out of the quarters. Now there was an impressive rug running off into the direction of the stern of the ship. It was as if the red carpet had been rolled out for Hector. Creeping around each corner, he was surprised to find the entrance to the office unguarded.

*"Time to make a name for yourself."*

The office was dark and still. Hector cursed; he had taken too much time. In the corner, there was a huge globe of the world, with a knife in the centre of Eldertude. A long oak desk was covered in maps with a telescope acting as a paperweight. There was a bookcase crammed with memorabilia from a lifetime at sea. None of it was of interest to Hector as he considered his next move.

There was a loud crackle. A puff of smoke appeared at the back of the room. A single leather chair faced the sea. The moonlight revealed more vapers clouding the air. There was a heavy stench of tobacco to follow. Drool dripped onto the shaking blade in Hector's hand. The captain's hat was in sight; the legendary kill was so close.

All of the lights came on; bodies burst into the office. Hector spun around the chair and stabbed out. A potato rolled out of the sack, followed by another half dozen. Looking back was a smiling face stitched into the bag, now missing an eye. Nearly all of the guards of the Wanderer were now positioned around Hector. In strolled Captain Holsten; he took one look at the scene and laughed.

"How fitting, the boy who put his victims in a sack is now caught by one."

Hector pulled at the bag as if it was some type of illusion.

"In all seriousness though, I am not sure if I should be insulted or relieved. Such a simple trap that you wondered into. We are in disbelief that Vidal would entrust such a naive assassin. If you were not the son of the general, I would not believe it," Holsten said, looking down on Hector with a hint of disappointment in his eyes.

Transfixed in a state of confusion mixed with sheer anger, Hector could not move. The captain took a long drag on his pipe.

"Keep the bag if you want, although the fleet might miss its chief commander— Stitchface."

There was a ripple of laughter through the guards. The leather chair was launched through the mosaic window. Before the glass had hit the water, Hector was restrained.

"Bring him here," Holsten howled.

"Do you have any idea how long that artwork has been a part of that ship, the battles it has survived?"

The face of the captain was bright red, as were most of the soldiers.

"I had always heard that you were a brat. For such a legend your so called father is meant to be, you're nothing in more than a dirty stain."

"So we end up at this, is there no end to this cavern of travesty? Now we are close enough, I want to taste it. Something to saviour from the drowning failure," Hector's voice was high pitched, full of venom. "You owe me, you weed."

"Boy, stop talking nonsense. If this is some type of play to try and distract from the fact you have been caught, it's pathetic. There are serious questions to be asked. Why has Vidal tried to have me killed now? I take it the spies know about the rot plaguing our ships, as well as the people. Well, if you try to take the head of serpent, miss and you get a fist full of poison," Holsten said defiantly.

"There is still time to take a chance; make a name and get in line for the crown again," Hector muttered looking up at the ceiling.

"Is that what the green king promised if you could murder me?"

The head of Hector dropped. Captain Holsten yelled the question again. "Look at me."

There was a signal to the nearest guard who went to put the captive in a headlock. Hector bit hard into the hand of the guard. Blood squirted out as the man pulled back in shrieks of pain. In a flash, Hector seized a loose sword and dug into the chest of its owner. As he turned, he ploughed the blade into the neck of a guard, then the next in line. There were already enough bodies to fill half a graveyard before the others reacted. A collective charge was the only way to withhold the fury. More guards perished as they wrested to finally retain Hector.

"Anymore for a punch of poison, you wretched worms?" There was red running down his chin. An order full of rage and spit was given to take him away from Captain Holston.

"If it's war they wanted to start, we will march on the Eldertude castle and rip the foundations from the very Borrowed Lands."

# Chapter 34

The Yellow Templar, Nyke, and the prisoners were all gathered around the dig sight. Fiddlers jumped from the scaffolding as the structures began to collapse. Cracks spread across the surface of the tomb like a strike of lighting. Decades of work were finally coming together. There was a thunderous crash as a dust cloud appeared like the eruption of a volcano.

Malum raised his staff; others shut their eyes. The endless tails and teachings of the immense power was about to reveal themselves. Leaders of the world were about to take a step down the ladder. All Templar dropped to the floor and started to hum. As the dust cleared, a figure could be seen in the centre of the four breaks of the tomb. The humming stop; some of the Yellow Templar stood up and looked at each other. There was a murmur throughout the Nyke.

"Our lord Thangrath, you are…" Malum stuttered "…not as it was written."

Dressed in a simple black rob, the small, bald man rolled up his sleeves and held out his arms.

"Still though, we welcome you back to the world. Our brothers and sisters have been pushed onto a knife's edge in order to insure they have the force to match. There is an army of Followers waiting at your feet," Malum glanced at the crowd, appearing nervous.

It was the first time the man opened his eyes and revealed two endless pits of black. Out of the back of his rope crept a dark oily tail, the end razor sharp.

"You must be in need of refreshments, some food may be. Let me get you away from this crowd, Lord Thangrath," Malum said with another sideways look.

"For this form, made of pink flesh, arms and feet, I am Draven. Only Draven. Take me to the highest balcony."

Malum nodded and made way for Draven, who started walking towards the cave. The Nyke were almost twice as tall and slowly moved out of the way, except for one. Trogon stood in the path of Draven, who did not hesitate to push into him. Trogon looked enraged but let Draven walk on. Instead, he held up the axe. More of the Nyke held up a weapon as the Templar started to retreat back to the cave.

Rexis was the only one on the balcony, unmoved from the spot where he had watched Terra fall to her death. There was a nauseating pain in his gut like he had been hit by a mallet. It was crippling and only getting worse as he crawled up into a ball. On the other side of the balcony, he watched as Draven headed up the stairs, with Malum following closely behind. A deal was struck inside Rexis' mind; the paralysing guilt loosened its grip just enough for him to stand up and walk.

"This is no time to be hiding."

Rave grabbed Rexis' wrist as he stood at the entrance to Malum's chambers.

"All Nyke are about to revolt; they think we have lied about the return, they wanted a powerful winged monster to conquer the battlefield. Instead we got a bald man. We must be ready to defend our leaders to a glorious death."

The slaughter had already begun as the Nyke had set upon the prisoners. Desperately defending themselves with spades and pickaxes, it only brought merely more seconds alive. The Yellow Templar had retreated.

"Journeymen." There was a crack of the whip. "Prepare yourselves," Pearlsa bellowed as the Yellow Templar spread out onto the balcony.

Rave went to bark more orders when there was an explosion from above. The cave shook as rocks fell from the ceiling. There was another eruption, this time in the form of the Nyke. They surged out of the tunnels, brandishing axes and machetes. There was a growl from Rave as he led the charge head on. The Templar did not hesitate in following as a fierce battle broke out. With twists and leaps, the short swords held by the Followers cut through orange skin. Chain spins ripped through the air as the Nyke crushed skulls.

Rave, wielding two swords, sliced away at the oncoming Nyke. There was a smirk on his face as he pinned the axe of one of the Nyke; leaning in he then bit into one of its ears. The Nyke yelled and tried to wrestle free; as it pulled away, Rave was left with a chunk of flesh in his mouth. Rexis then caught an axe inches away from his face; the Nyke went to pull away as the weapon was ripped away. Rexis then slammed the blade into the side of its head. He then threw the axe into the next oncoming Nkye.

There was another blast from above and more rocks came

crashing down. Rexis had to dive away right into the path of more Nyke. They set upon him, the first swing catching Rexis in the shoulder. More blows came as he tried to defend himself. One of the Nyke stepped forward and went for Rexis' neck with a powerful swing. Before it could land, rope diverted the machete. The whip then came thundering back as the spiked ends sliced open multiple Nykes.

There was an almighty roar throughout the cave. Trogon came charging in as more Nyke poured out onto the balcony. Rave ran to meet him; they became locked in a duel of sword versus axe. The Templar surged forward as Rexis slunk backwards; one of the Followers bounced into him. Rexis pushed them into the path of one of the Nyke, before disappearing up the stairs.

"Coward," the Follower screamed.

The word echoed after him as he made his accent. With each step, the sound of battle was fading away. As he reached the iron door to Malum's chambers, Rexis slowly turned the handle. It was a small space tucked away at the valley's peak. The chambers were basic, a single bed with a desk covered in books and scrolls. Malum's staff lay on the floor. Past it was Draven sat crossed legged with his back to Rexis. The black tail moved slowly from side to side. Taking a deep breath, Rexis crept toward the unsuspecting figure. The closer he got, there was now a weight across his body; Rexis had to battle with each muscle just to drag himself forward.

Draven had not moved as Rexis was now inches away. In his hand was one of the Follower's crooked swords. Looking to the clouds, he said a little prayer for forgiveness, and then struck as hard as he could into the back of Draven's skull. The sword went deep, cutting into the skin like butter until it disappeared along with part of Rexis' arm. He tried to pull away, but it was futile, as if his hand was stuck in a lock.

Rexis was flung across the floor into the wall behind him. Draven stood up and pointed his head upwards.

"So much of my time has been spent in the darkness." Rexis could not move; the intense pain was back in his stomach. "Ever since I was banished from the sky, the only benefit was finally enjoying the suns. There has already been one who made the mistake of disturbing me."

Hanging above them was the body of Malum. There was an invisible grip around his throat, as his eyes were bugging out of his head. For a second, the hold seemed to drop, letting him make a small, pathetic sound. Draven eyes flared up.

"That is the last strike."

The vice on the throat turned; panic like never before appeared across the leader's face. The skin around his neck turned red. As the veins burst out, tears ran down his cheeks. There was one last whimper before the body of Malum went limp, still hanging eerily in the air.

"I cannot say that he did not deserve it, but those that free you from captivity, who follow you, can be destroyed that easily. What are you?" Rexis asked, fearful of the answer.

"Do not insult me, trying to pretend that you all had only my best intentions at heart. Raising me from the tomb was simply a way to feed their selfishness. The only intention is to seek out more control, more power. What is the benefit for me? Their existence is as significant to me as the dust under my feet," Draven said.

"Is it not right that when you first fell to the land, you gathered an army of Followers? They talk about," Rexis stuttered.

Draven gave a deep, malevolent laugh.

"Is that the reason you have been collecting the coloured rocks, even swallowing them. The majority are simply from the coat I was wearing, when I first came to the land. Some though are different. I think you already know that though."

Rexis almost threw up.

"Normally, it is a toenail, a hair. I think though you owe me a finger. A grand prize I am sure you were highly respected for. I am however no longer in need of puppets; my power was spread too thin before trying to control these lands. Now I simply wish to clear it of the lesser beings around me, all of them," Draven said.

"How can your goal be to be the last one left alive?" Rexis asked.

"There is only the greedy and selfish left. Deep down, you only mourn your sibling because it is the choices you made that led to her death. Building up yourself to be the saviour when she was better off alone. Even now, you try and harm me to make yourself feel better; it will have no bearing on your sister's state. It is simply another way to exert the false feeling of authority my essence has given you. Being encircled by subordinates, watching them climb over each other to be top of the pile serves no purpose to me, not again. Total destruction makes absolute sense."

"That is not true," Rexis said with some defiance.

"I have already seen every corner of your mind," Draven replied looking directly at Rexis.

"My sister knew nothing but love."

There was a tremor in Rexis' voice. Draven's eyes flared.

"Do not ever question me. If the night's cold was too

much, you would let the world burn to keep yourself warm. I will prove it," Draven's face darkened.

"Lies," Rexis whimpered.

The pain in Rexis' stomach was gone; his body felt like it had rested for a week. He jumped up and with the sword still in hand, came at Draven. With all his might, Rexis swung the weapon as fast and powerful as he could. With ease, Draven sidestepped out of the way. The large swing caused Rexis to drag his entire body to the right. With one hand, Draven grabbed his throat and with the other sent his hand into Rexis' stomach. The pain caused Rexis to crumble; the glow was back as he could feel the retched fingers of Draven scrambling around inside of him. Draven finally grinned and went to pull away. As he tugged, the hand would not come free, Rexis then swung the sword a second time.

Seeing it head on, Draven smashed the blade in two with his forehead. The empty hand was released from Rexis' belly.

"It is hard to give up once it has been tasted. Some of you are less worthless than others. Now, witness the rebirth of absolute rule."

As Draven spoke, his eyes rolled into the back of his head. Steam began to bellow off his body as the skin started to bubble. Draven then pulled at his arms and shoulders. His skin was almost a liquid as it came stretched from his body until it ripped open. Outgrew a new form, expanding in size till it dwarfed Rexis and the chambers. Wings made of black, rotting flesh, claws as jagged as broken glass. It had oily black skin and burning sockets for eyes. As the demon rose into the sky, it loomed over the valley like a thundercloud. Below, the clash of steel came to a halt; there was a dark shadow as the suns became blocked.

The Yellow Templar dropped to their feet and started to

hum. Trogon held the axe above a Follower but hesitated. As he did, all the other Nyke paused. Looking back up to the sky, he let the weapon drop to his side. Rave pushed past him and stood on the edge of the balcony.

"Thangrath rises again."

"This is my rule; there would be none from these lands which have the right to walk with me. I banish you insects."

The demon let out a breath, hammering out like a tidal wave, a hot blue flame descending onto everything below. Those caught in it felt acidic solvent on the skin before the fire ripped off the flesh and bone. The burst decimated most of the valley below, leaving black stains across the yellow rocks. Those who had not been caught fled in retreat.

Rave fell to his knees as the demon came closer to the balcony. The power generated by its wings moved the bodies of the dead. It came closer to Rave, as he puffed out his chest and held out his hands screaming.

"Show me your power."

The blue fame washed over Rave's body like a starved plague. It pored through the cave tunnels and out of the entrance below, ripping through the foundations of the Templar and its members.

Crawled up into a ball, Rexis could hear the screams getting closer. He made no attempt to move as the air around started to boil over. There was the faintest of smiles across Rexis' face. He jumped as the demon landed in front of him. The spiked tail went into the stomach of Rexis; the stump of the broken horn central to the demon's head was glowing. As it pulled the tailback, Rexis was dragged across the floor. Still with the sword, he beat against it. There was no escape as the long rancid tongue circled Rexis.

"Time to witness the destruction first-hand."

The tail lifted up Rexis. He stared into the face of Thangrath; the burning revulsion looking back at him was causing his soul to decay. As the jaw opened, Rexis could see the blue flame ready to ignite. The tail moved again, and Rexis was swallowed whole.

## Chapter 35

The marvel which had arisen from the depths of the cave was mesmerising, so much so it had rooted Zander to the ground. It was as if every fairy tale and children's book had been sown together. The light crept through the breaks in the cave roof, glistening onto the scally red surface. Flesh mixed with gems and rare stones, which lay neatly over joints and knuckles connecting to black ivory claws. There was a long snout leading up to a deep complexion on the creature's face, made more so by the clear diamond sitting in the middle of its head, pushing its brow downwards.

It rose up on his hind legs and spread out its wings, revealing an opulent tapestry of golden coins. Rows upon rows, they chimed together in each movement. As the light hit it, it was blinding, like looking into a sun. It gave a roar; the cutthroat teeth looked as if they could bite through a kingdom. Zander took a step back.

"What is this? Why would one look to walk away?" The gem dragon's voice was low, like the rumble before the storm.

"I am not quite sure. Maybe I thought you were going to eat me."

The gem dragon tilted its head; out came a long red tong spilt at the middle like a serpent. It seemed to taste the air; Zander worried that he had now put the idea into its head.

"It would make little sense for me to grant you access, simply to eat you."

"Maybe you were hungry."

"If I were looking for a meal, do you think that your body would suffice?"

Zander felt as if he had to cover his mouth to stop the words from falling out. The gem dragon was engulfing his senses; he wanted to both run to it and flee. It rose up again and let out an almighty roar. Blood poured from Zander's nose and ears. Dropping to his knees, Zander's eyeballs almost popped out of the socket. The gem dragon grew bigger in size, looming over the victim before letting out a loud snort.

"The grey man is trying to get out."

Zander could just about hear the words, as if they were called out in the middle of a blizzard.

"Why do you think you are here?" the gem dragon roared.

Wiping away the blood, Zander started to blubber as he could not get control of his vocal cords. "Answer me."

The birds fled as the words rung out through the cave.

"I am drawn here; the sound, it has been calling me. You have been calling out to me."

"The voice of a friend is meant to rally those around them. Not to break its allies. So, tell me again why you are here."

Staring at his hands, Zander looked for the answer. "Start by telling me why you left."

"I am the prince of Eldertude. My kingdom is being consumed by the curse and on the brink of a civil war. There is no belief in me, but I left to change that. Supposedly, the Collector had a way to finally treat the disease, a way to end the conflict and make the kingdom whole again. It turned out to be a farce."

"A valid reason but it is not the real motivation."

The birds were returning to the cave, now over the initial fright of the intense power the gem dragon transmitted. They could be heard chirping away, discussing the break in routine.

"Many have ventured out into the world and have ended at the foot of this mountain. Even if they survive the climb, they do not always enter my cave. Both heroes and villains have appeared, full of stories of tragedy and joy. All noble in their own way, but their intentions mixed and debated to the point they had no real understanding of why they were here. You on the other hand are here for a simple reason, to poison me," hissed the gem dragon.

Zander almost wanted to laugh at the idea, a spec at the feet of a giant. The words however were causing a stir in the pits of his stomach.

"The grey man who lives inside of you, he is the reason you have answered the call. My voice is a melody to all the allies who are close enough to hear it. The only ear it disgusts is that which belongs to the grey man. He has much of you, but not yet your soul. That still belongs to your choices. So, tell me really why you are here?"

"I want to be cured."

The gem dragon's eyes narrowed.

"Say it again."

Zander screamed it over and over again.

"This is no life. My body has been in debt to this curse, eating away at it ever since I can remember. I deserve a clean slate. If I was healthy, I could then really take control and lead Eldertude."

"I take it you have not found the answer."

There was a nod from Zander who then looked to the floor. The gem dragon began to pace around the cave as much as it could. Old bones could be heard snapping under its weight. It stopped and turned to one of the small holes into the sky.

A brown hawk with its wings spread open sailed into the cave. It perched on a ledge next to the gem dragon's head and leaned into its ear. After a few moments, it took off again back out into the mountain range. The gem dragon watched it leave then turned to Zander.

"Your kingdom is about to fall."

## *Chapter 36*

The sails had a mind of their own; now with the full force of the wind behind them, they could not be tamed. As Luca wrestled with the rope, all around him, the Tulus sailors were watching. He chose not to meet their scowls but rather continue with the struggle. He and Erica had drifted out to the Everlast Ocean as quickly as they had been conquered by it. With little options available when trying to leave the Collector's remote palace, they had put their faith in the only remaining messenger boat not yet spent by rot. As soon as they had set sail down the ice river, they hit trouble.

A relentless current had taken them straight into the path of an iceberg. Hitting the ice head on, amazingly the boat had stayed together. The bow had bounced off, causing the entire vessel to spin. What little control Erica and Luca once had was gone. Quickly, they drifted out into the wide ocean and a new terror. The currents they had faced earlier seemed like a hot bath. As the open sea took a hold of them, they were in complete free fall. All they could do now was to curse their stupidity, whilst waiting to be consumed by the endless deep blue.

The horizon was littered with long lines of black shapes. As their messenger ship drifted towards it, the size of the swarm became clearer. Endless rows of the Tulus warships. Equally spread apart, their unique design meant they dominated the sea. Each bow of the ships had been split in two, curving inwards. The result was the front looked like the pincers of a crab; they were loaded with spikes and arrowheads. In the middle, platforms had been loaded onto selected ships. They held giant crossbows and catapults. Others had battering rams, with smirking faces carved into the wood. Frantically, Erica and Luca searched for any type of weapon. However, holding up a sword to the fleet of Neptulus seemed futile.

"There does not look to be a friendly in between all those spears and arrows," Luca said.

"Why are the Tulus army out this far? They look like they mean business," Erica replied.

"We are about to find out. Does Eldertude still have a treaty with them? Or have both the leaders finally decided to settle their differences."

"Raise the flag. There is less chance of them cutting down representatives of the Collector than our kingdom, hopefully," Erica prayed.

"I think I saw some spare uniforms earlier."

****

The symbol of the Collector still carried some weight in the world. A story of how their ship had become damaged in a storm had raised eyebrows but held, if only temporarily. Looking for assistance in the Collector's name, they had offered their skilled services as seamen. That they would work hard on any ship for their safe passage to shore. It was however too much of a risk for the Tulus to let them go early. Talk of an assault could easily reach the enemy. There was little room for negotiations as the Collector's ship was purposely sunk. Now Luca and Erica were sailing to wage a war on their very home, if they were not thrown overboard first.

Luca's disguise quickly wore thin. Grabbing the side each time a wave rocked the boat had not helped. His poor workmanship and lack of knowledge had become clear from the start. Luckily, Erica had picked up the slack, taking to most of the tasks like a natural fisherman. Where she lacked expertise, she made up with a relentless work ethic.

The pace though was worrying Luca. It would often be early dawn before Erica would lie down, only to stare at the ceiling. All around her, she was surrounded by swords and spears, designed to be stuck into the people of Eldertude. Worrying about her also gave him something to focus on, rather than his recent failings. Both the prince and the kingdom's heart were gone. Luca had failed miserably. So much so that he had considered throwing his badge into the ocean, as he no longer had the right to wear it. Still though, the diamond studded leaf remained hidden in his pocket.

In the berths, Erica and Luca were not the only ones struggling for sleep. Many of the Tulus soldiers would huddle in small corners and talk quietly. With each day they got closer to the destination, the tension would raise another level. There were few who were convinced the apparent resources were worth the inevitable lives it would cost. The scales had been tipped by the bundled assassination attempt. Most were still in disbelief that such a reckless move could be made. It was only the fact that King Vidal would have been the one making it which gave it validity. Personal grudges in hands of power meant destruction, for that they controlled. No doubt the Eldertude soldiers would be thinking the same. When the fleet arrived on the beaches, whatever the cause, it would be dog eat dog till the end.

## *Chapter 37*

Thick smog draped itself around the iron pipes, which stood out crooked from the factory roofs. The burning fuel leaked poisonous fumes into the already toxic city. No matter what time of the day it was, the gloom never lifted. All hope vanished in the dirty streets, not simply littered with rubbish.

Out stumbled a man with a wispy white beard and holes in his vest. Using the closest wall, he propped himself up, trying clumsily to do up his trousers. It proved too difficult, and gravity took him. Sprawled out in the mud, he laughed, watching the bottles roll away from his pockets. There was still a drop of liquid left in one. Out of the darkness, bodies appeared, snatching anything in sight. The man lashed out with a stifled cry. Catching a boot, the owner turned and smashed the sole into the man's face. Blood flooded from the wailing victims into the streets of Darnspur.

Kantra and Colton watched in silence before moving on. They moved like a gentle breeze, navigating their way through the twists and turns of the city. Much time had passed since the original six had narrowly escaped the Oko Gang. Colton was confident that the last thing they would have expected is for them to return.

"Here it is."

They stood in an alleyway between the back end of a factory and a grey wall. There was only a pile of scrap metal and the shadows for company.

"This does not look to be the hot spot for diamond sellers you promised. Are we to cower in the corner until some passer-by comes with a small fortune in their pockets? I have been away from the Eldertude too long to be wasting time," Kantra said, sounding more agitated than usual.

"I was under the impression that the more time away from the kingdom the better," Colten replied cheerfully.

"It's not the place; I have people relying on me to deliver, so you best do as well."

Kantra was well aware of how long she had been away. The money left with Harlow would be running out, even with her ability to save. Soon, she and the boy would be back on the hustle again, putting them in danger of being discovered. Let alone the dangers of the kingdom imploding on itself, being swallowed into the belly of Hellrous.

Colton rummaged through the scrap metal. At the bottom was a filthy sheet covered in dust. Pulling it away, Kantra scowled; underneath was a skeleton. All the bones were accounted for, despite the mess around it. Moving slowly across the ribs, a worm nibbled at the grime. In the jaw was a shell pipe. Colton broke off the only finger that had a plain gold ring. He tried to rub the bone across Kantra's face, who slapped it away.

"Hey, that's important."

Finding a tiny hold in the wall, he slipped in the ring finger. Nothing happened at first, until there was a creak of the jaw; the pipe slowly hummed to life. A puff of dust and then green mist slowly crept out. It circled in the air as if deciding where to go, before disappearing into a funnel in the grey wall.

"It is a skeleton key," Colton said with a grin.

There was a rumble as a shutter opened in the wall. Staring at them was a pair of long, piercing eyes, that sat on yellow pale skin. The face could barely fit the hole. Its eyes looked them up and down before a door in the wall opened. Bent down was a Butrins, an incredibly tall and gaunt creature, known for their mood swings and peculiar behaviour. They were dressed in a tuxedo far too small for them.

"Colton, using the dead man's entrance. Why I am not surprised?"

"Always good to see you, Grig. I do not suppose you have any space going? Maybe somewhere quiet in a back room?" Colton replied.

"The price will be high, very high. There is coin out for you already. I need to weigh up that loss of not turning you in. If you do not have anything, then leave," Grig said narrowing his eyes.

"Oh, do not worry; I have a proposal that should be most profitable for the both of us," Colton said with confidence.

Grig gave a greedy smile which summed up the city.

"Good, because you still owe for the state you left the last room in."

He stood back to reveal a narrow staircase. The pair were then led down a poorly lit hallway, with a dusty red carpet.

Portraits of morbid, dull faces seemed to watch each step. The rows of black doors only had a shape to distinguish the difference between them. Squares, circles, then a door with a star. Inside, the room was decorated as a mere extension of the hallway.

"Do you have another room for me?" Kantra tried to sound pleasant.

"You are not together?" Grig replied.

"Why else would I be asking."

Grig ruffled his greasy, messy green hair before adjusting a red bow tie.

"With the price on your heads, you are lucky I have not alerted the last of the Oko."

"But you haven't," Kantra said bluntly.

"I know there would only be one way you would turn up like this. I presume that is the stone?"

Grig looked at the satchel; Kantra held it to her chest. With a nod from Colton, she opened the bag, revealing the heart of Eldertude. Grig grabbed at it; Kantra pulled away.

"Forgive me; I get myself too excited sometimes."

"I can see that. We are here to sell, so unless you are buying, it stays with me."

"It is impossible to sell for the amount it's worth. So instead, you are going to give it to me."

"Try and take it and I will slice your fingers off."

Kantra put her hand on a sword; Grig made claws with each of his hands.

"Come on, I could not have caused that much damage to my last room," Colton stepped in.

"There was what you did in the bathroom as well."

The two of them looked at each other and began to laugh. Kantra did not join in.

"Since Lucid's mines had, let's call it an accident, and burnt down, there are not many with deep enough pockets to meet the price for a stone like that. However, I might be able to offer you something better. Darnspur has not always been a place run by outlaws. There was some authority a long time ago before it was driven out. Starvogue built a watchtower out on the outskirts of the city. There is a vault full to the brim of diamonds, gold, and silver. Designed to provide enough funds to keep the soldiers fed and watered long past their natural lives. The entrance to the vault is unbreakable, and when I say it, I mean it. The union was well aware of all the thieves lurking just down the road. There is only one way into the vault; the watchman's key," Grig explained.

"Which of course you have," Kantra said and on cue, Grig revealed the long, bronze key.

"The lady learns fast."

Kantra snatched the key from Grig's hand, including the smile from his face.

"Now we do not have to make a deal."

"Come on that is not how we do business here."

"He's right," Colton said. "We may be criminals but we have honour, sort of. Give him the rock and we will go collect our riches."

"I am still waiting for the catch though. Why have you not been up yourself to open that vault?" Kantra asked.

"It's full of Deathwalkers, and those things are not to be messed with. Hopefully, the new war between the last of the kingdoms might draw some of them out," Grig sniggered.

"Which two kingdoms?" Kantra said with a quiver in her voice.

"Eldertude verse the sailors, of course. It is going to be a blood bath."

Kantra's face went pale; she stared out of the dirty window. Colton went to comfort her. Twisting away, she screamed out and kicked over the bedside table.

"Don't touch me; I need to be back there but not empty handed."

"Well then, you best get ready for a break in."

****

Kantra paced up and down, only to stop to look at the clock. There was still no sign of Colton. He had insisted that she wait in the room, whilst he gathered the supplies needed for their raid. There would be less chance of them being spotted if he went alone. Kantra, in her blind state of concern, had agreed. It was very unlike her. Now trapped within these four walls, Kantra stared at the clock again, before breaking it in half. Turning the rest of the room upside down did nothing to change her mood. Colton would have expected this as Kantra marched down the stairs.

The dusty reception was empty; Kantra went behind the desk looking for some type of clue. As she ruffled through the ledgers and papers, Kantra started to cough. There was a faint light coming from underneath the sheet covering the doorway next to her. The closer she got, the more it reeked of the unnatural. What followed was a room full of skeletons and shadows. It was a collection of everything a mother would warn her child about. Sprawled out across the tables and floor, none turned to acknowledge Kantra. The smoke filled her lungs, but it was the sight that made her choke.

Nothing else mattered. Meals, appearance, or health, all sacrificed for another hit. The only sounds which could be heard were the occasional crackle and sparks, until a woman in the corner broke the silence. The strings of a harp rang out, a slow and hypnotic melody. Puff, puff, puff, the drags from the mixture of pipes danced through the air. Carved from shells and rock, they followed in with the rhythm, keeping everyone locked in a trance. On the walls were the shapes from the hotel doors, each intermittently glowing. The essence of the room was threatening to drain Kantra's soul. Desperate for air, she went for what seemed an escape. In her hurry, she stood on an unsuspecting arm; there was no reaction.

Kantra kicked out at the bony finger. Her name was shouted out; it was the voice she had been looking for. Swaying with the haze appeared Colton. Kantra looked him up and down as he was having trouble staying still.

"There's— these people are helping give information, gathering supplies," Colton spluttered.

"Just don't. If you came to rot away in this cesspit, fine, but do not drag me into it. I need people I can rely on; I am ashamed to have ever ridden alongside you."

Kantra pushed past him and charged out of the hotel.

"Wait, please."

Colton chased after her in the street.

"Point me in the right direction. Then get as far away from me as possible."

"Look, I am sorry; I brought us here because Grig really is the only one who could help us. I am short of friends in the city. It was stupid of me to think I could be here and not have to get lifted. It is a problem I have inside of me. When we were up in the mountains, the powder had gone; I had rid myself of it. The moment, I held that pipe, the itch at the back of my mind returned. It became so loud, that my own thoughts turned to one cohesive scream— commanding me to put my lips to the smoke again. Please, lead me from this place."

"You are going to be useless in your state."

"I will prove my worth; I promise."

****

The last of the sunlight was leaving. Colton and Kantra could just make out the winding steep path ahead of them. In the distance, the watchtower waited like a sleeping giant.

"So, not a word since we left Darnspur. It is not like you to go that long without telling me off," Colton joked. "We will get back to your family as soon as possible. I am sure the war Grig speaks off is not as bad as he makes out. I would not be surprised if they just come to some agreement anyway."

Still no response.

"You have not even asked why they are called Deathwalkers."

"I am getting into that vault," Kantra said without looking at Colton.

They had reached the foot of the watchtower; a once powerful and authoritative building, it had melted away over time. Nature had taken it back, the vines growing in between the stone, plants had flourished, and animals had made nests. The watchtower now squeezed itself around the vegetation as if it had truly submitted.

"We are really going to do this?" Colton said.

"Normally, you are not one for being scared," Kantra replied and pushed back a branch to climb into the tower. Inside, it was much the same; the once wooden floor was now soft grass. Vines still ventured inside as they spread themselves over the walls. The union coat of arms was nestled on the green. Kantra picked it up; there were symbols which vaguely could be connected to Eldertude.

"That is the sign of the four pillars, the foundations of Starvogue city," Colton said, now next to Kantra, who just stared back.

"Do they teach nothing in the classes of Eldertude?"

"Most of us have never been in a school."

"Oh, well let me educate you. Before the region of the Borrowed Lands was founded, nearly all lived in the one city. The many faces of the world lived under one roof, sort of."

"Did it work?"

"I believe it did in its own sort of way."

"Then why did it stop?"

There was a deafening howl, sending both of them to their knees. It was as if the watchtower had taken a deep breath, then attempted to flush out the cancer living in every corner and knock off its insides. As soon as the sound stopped, it was followed by blistering heat. The air inside felt like it had caught alight.

"I'm guessing that is the curse," Kantra said, drawing a sword.

"That is a good sign in all respect. It means there is only one of them."

"Hollower Monkey?"

"A Deathwalker."

They crept up the spiralling staircase. Frequently, their progress was halted by huge cobwebs or branches. Both of them were thankful for the break as the heat had only risen. Eventually reaching the top level, they walked into an empty mess hall, both with their heads upwards. The long tables were all hanging from the ceiling, connected to a tree in the centre of the room. Its crooked branches span themselves across the floor and spread all across the watchtower. The bark was peeling and twisted, in the face of the tree, there was an ominous black rot.

The howl came again as the tree had its own gaping mouth. Its noise forced Kantra and Colton to crawl on their knees. Out of the mouth, a long and bony figure appeared. Grey skin and morbid face, it moved unnaturally. The joints of its body rubbed against each other, as the bone looked loose in each socket. The Deathwalker slithered out of the tree; it tried to stand but his knees kept giving way. It would rise up again but never make it much higher than a crawl.

The Deathwalker opened its mouth and a rotten tongue appeared. Its eyes then rolled back into the skull. Around it, the branches began to twitch, then they moved towards the ridged figure. Wrapping themselves around the legs and waist, the branches then lifted the Deathwalker upwards.

"How is that possible?" Kantra said.

"I know you did not want to know, but there is something about Deathwalkers I need to tell you," Colten began to yell.

Before he could finish, Kantra tackled him, just in time to avoid the falling tables. The Deathwalker screamed again but this time they had to fight through it, as the roots now came for them. Kantra repelled the attacks from all angles. Her two swords sliced through the wood. Colton was spending more time being covered in splinters rather than fighting back.

The temperature rose again; the Deathwalker was blasting out more heat as it howled. Although Kantra had started in a high tempo, it was already dropping. Her senses were being strangled; the pressure on her body was weighing down on her movements. Colton had already succumbed to the bombardment; his arms and legs had become entangled with the roots pulling him to the ground. Kantra cut through some to try and save him, but as she did, the vines glided around her body in numbers. Both of them were tied to the floor, the roots of the tree acting like a padlock across their bodies.

"Kantra, I have to tell you about the Deathwalkers; they are fallout from the time of Thangrath. In the army which was built, some got more of a share of the powers than bargained for. They might have been able to adapt when the demon was active. Once the entrapment happened, their minds started to rot away, but the powers remained. I never fancied our chances going toe to toe with it."

"Then why would you agree to bring us here?" Kantra yelled.

"I did not think I would have much better odds convincing you not to come," Colton replied.

The abnormal body of the Deathwalker dragged itself towards them, a rancid bag of limbs rolled on top of each other. Its grey skin stretched as its jaw almost hanged off. Both eyes had the intensity of a starving prisoner fighting for the last scraps. It reached Kantra's feet. The stench of the Deathwalker was nauseating. It suffocated the senses so much she wanted to turn away but could not; the Deathwalker was forcing her to face it.

On its hind legs, it hauled itself onto her, the arms coming down on Kantra's chest. It was pulling itself up to go face to face with Kantra. Colton next to her was screaming at the top of his voice. The Deathwalker was inches away from Kantra's face; still she could not look away. Their eyes were locked together, balls of chaotic orange fixated on Kantra's swirling purple. The longer she looked, she could hear a voice in the back of her mind; it made no sense to her at first, just a rant of pain and frustration. It soon though made sense. The anger justified, the misery spread through Kantra as her eyes began to roll back in her head. The roots around her neck began to tighten.

*"Starlight, starlight, guide us back to the city.*

*For the days at rest, the union on our crest.*

*We must drink the gold; it cannot be sold.*

*Those to the west, who mourn the shadows.*

*Take us back to the city."*

Kantra was not sure where the song was coming from.

*"A home for all, the rings shall not fall.*

*In meadows we dance, for we shall wander."*

She was singing it now; the words felt warm and comforting. It was as if Kantra remembered walking down the streets of Starvogue herself. The Deathwalker too was signing, the voice soft like a child. The more it did, the vines began to loosen over Kantra's body.

*"Stars are hidden in the tower, the unsung power."*

Colton was still singing as loud as he could. The Deathwalker leaned back and closed its eyes. As it did, the voice from her head was gone. Kantra was able to wrestle an arm free.

*"United we stand, hand in hand to face..."*

Colton stopped signing, and as he paused, so did the Deathwalker. It howled and slammed its arms into the chest of Kantra.

"Keep bloody singing," Kantra said gasping for breath.

"I cannot remember the next line," Colton replied.

The Deathwalker rose up and screamed, making a fist in each hand. As it did, the ceiling started to collapse, causing huge chunks of rock to come crashing down. Colton was dragged up to the same height as the Deathwalker, still co-cooned in a vice by the roots of the tree. A slimy and bony hand went for the forehead of Colton. Now turning grey, he was desperately trying to muster the words together in be-tween drooling.

Kantra forced an arm out, then managed to cut herself free. In a fluid movement, she glided through the falling de-bris, cutting down any of the approaching branches. Using one of the fallen rocks, she pushed off it and leapt into the air. Before the Deathwalker could react, she sliced the two swords through its neck.

The vines from the tree dropped to the floor; so did Col-ton and the head of the Deathwalker. As its body went limp, the life from the tree faded almost instantly. The brown oak started to bleach, as the colour drained to nothing. Quickly, the entire room became a grey blizzard. The once powerful roots had turned to ash, which now circled in the air.

Colton had not moved; the grey flakes were settling upon his jacket. Kantra went to his side and turned him over. He had a morbid expression on his pale face. Kantra shook him but nothing changed; she sighed then tried to sing. The words, *"Take me back to the city"* came out of her mouth, but she could not get the tune right. Frustrated, she went for option B and slapped Colton as hard as she could.

"Wake up!" Kantra yelled.

"Wow, that hurt. I thought there might be another Deathwalker to deal with."

Kantra narrowed her eyes.

"Come on, we need to find the vault."

"I think I could give it a good guess."

The tree from which the Deathwalker had appeared had evaporated. It was now a huge pile of dust and ash, floating away to reveal the vault door. It was a solid, thick wall of bronze might. Across its surface was a huge array of cogs and mechanisms. Kantra brushed away the soot to find the hole; Colton slotted in the key. As he turned it, both of them stepped back. The vault rumbled to life; the cogs and wheels slowly began to turn. The vault groaned as the doors opened, kicking up more soot and ash, creating a smoke screen. As the dust settled, it revealed the vault's insides; it was empty.

"That piece of filth screwed us over."

"I really did not see that coming."

"This is as much your scam as the rat which gave us that key."

\*\*\*\*

On their way back into Darnspur, Kantra was still cursing. They turned a corner to the street on which Rat Bag normally sat on. There was now nothing but a smouldering building; the tavern was an empty shell ripped apart from a raging fire. Both stopped in the middle of the road as the angry carts drove around them.

"Charcoal and smoke are all we are left; Darnspur has short changed us again."

Kantra had not taken her eyes off the burning creator. Colton placed a hand on her shoulder, or tried to. A death grip followed as Kantra almost broke his hand.

"I have nothing to take back to Eldertude, nothing. This is all your fault. Why did I ever trust a pathetic worm? Go find a pit to die in."

## Chapter 38

Deep into the early morning fog, the fresh sea air was bliss. The hustle of the Pilpots created dust which muddied the air. With each breath, Jonah could taste the dirt of everyone around him. It was a blessing he was able to escape to the ocean. A handful of fishing boats remained in Eldertude. With no navy, there were few who knew how to swim, let alone handle a sail. Most residents still believed the age-old tails about the hidden monsters under the waves.

With the ocean vacant, it meant only the privileged had a taste for seafood. With little fish being brought into the market, the price was dear. A mix of vibrant coloured scales and an array of sizes had caught the eye of those with gold. Jonah lived amongst the starving but made sure indulgence was well fed. Knowing that he was a part of the problem, the hypocrisy of his role, was washed away when faced with the blue desert.

The sense of freedom was felt all across the long, cocoon shaped boat. There were cracks in between the joints, its paint had faded, and the small cabin looked as if it was about to blow away. None of that mattered to the fishermen. A crew of eight weaved in between the nets and buckets. Some wrestled with the sails as others argued about the best direction to steer the ship. For fishing spots, they were spoiled— another benefit of empty seas.

Absorbed in his labour, Jonah almost did not see the stern of the other ship. The rest of the vessel was concealed by the mist. All of the fishermen stopped; beaming into the distance, most of them smiled. They rarely came across other boats in the vast open sea. It was a reassurance that others existed within the blue planet, that they had not drifted into the forever unknown.

The boat was some distance away; slowly it was creeping out of the fog. It did not appear to be any type that Jonah recognised. The ship was circular for starters; oars helped push one massive sail. With smooth high curved sides, they acted as a protective shell for the whole ship. Jonah wondered how long their nets must be to reach the seabed.

"That's no ship for fishing; it's built to rule the ocean rather than farm it," one of the fishermen said next to Jonah.

The alien ship was getting closer, with no visible flag. Jonah waived his arm, and with it, the mist seemed to clear all around them. Slowly, his arm came to a stop as the fishermen could now see the vessel clearly. Spikes, spears and plates of steel to protect the two bows of the ship. An army of ships stood before them, armed to the teeth. The Eldertude fishing ship had nothing more than a harpoon.

Now, Jonah recognised some of the designs, the blue and gold war paint marked across each ship. It was not that far back to the kingdom's shores. There would only be one reason the Tulus would be this close in such force. Jonah's mind raced to that of his family, the devastation and loss of life they now faced.

"What are you doing?" The other fishermen were rooted to the spot, as Jonah had jumped up to the wheel of the ship. "We need to stay here and surrender. There is no chance we will outrun them in this," one of the fishermen yelled.

Jonah spun around the wheel. As the boat turned, the fishermen fell to the deck. Barrels of squid went spinning off into the sea. The wind picked up and they raced in the direction of the land. Jonah did not look back. His crew yelled and pleaded with him, waving back at the Neptulus fleet.

A shadow appeared on the bow of the ship; it started small and then rapidly picked up in size. The fishermen looked up and yelled, with one of them jumping overboard. Jonah started muttering under his breath, hoping that the words would be carried with the wind. A stone ripped through the ship, wood and fish launched into the air. Water rushed in; the crew which had not been killed in the blast cried out in desperation.

Captain Holsten and first officer Alden both stood on deck with a telescope. Slowly, the fishing ship sank and its crew made its descent to the bottom of the ocean.

"We have officially broken the peace treaty, which has been in place since the union disbanded."

"We are at war; may the light shine upon us for a clear and everlasting victory," Holsten announced loud enough for his entire crew to hear. "No matter what the cost, the pain which follows, the Neptulus will rule the day. Eldertude will be crushed, and a new kingdom will rise from the ashes."

## *Chapter 39*

It was now the height of summer; the evening light was so strong it illuminated the room. Sanctuary Chamber was bubbling; every possible head of the council was crammed around the table.

The men and women, dressed mainly in white robes, began their discussion.

"The soldiers have been watching day and night. Hellrous still remains impossible to enter."

"From the suns to the moon, the monstrous statues but wait. They wait for the next footstep of that who dares to face them. It is as if the Demon's Disciples have risen once again."

"Soldiers of the Infamous."

"Does this mean he is back?"

"It is not possible. It may be the reason they wait with no direction."

"Many have been ripped apart by the SIDD."

For a moment, every man and woman looked to the floor.

"So the zone is clear of all military?" Vidal asked to a repercussion of nods.

"There are, however, still sightings of civilians."

All faces turned to Vidal.

"The SIDD dismantled the entire of Hellrous, slaughtering men, women, and children with no hesitation. By the time the soldiers had arrived, it was too late. That's what happened."

The king banged his hand on the table.

"So we have no more infected, at least," Vidal said, in an attempt to change the tone.

"Not quite," the head of health shifted as Vidal glared at him.

"The bloodshed has massively reduced numbers, but some still remain, in a camp just outside the zone."

"We had to open gates and let those still alive escape; their screams were too loud to be ignored. Also, some were already outside Hellrous. How exactly is yet to be confirmed."

"So we still need a plan to get rid of these born again freaks."

The king stood up and turned his back to the council, hands in pocket.

"That's the reason why we are here, is it not? We look for your advice, your plans, from our great leader."

The attention of the room turned. Hunched over the fireplace was General Balder. He had not taken his eyes off the fireplace. One hand propped him up, the other held onto a flask.

Vidal crossed his arms. "Something to add, general?"

The shadows flickered across his gloomy face; it was the only sign of life. Vidal called out again.

"Why is your focus not on your son?" General Balder asked.

"There are more pressing matters" King Vidal replied, a sullen look upon his face.

"You just sent him out there into the world, knowing how brutal that it can be. He is missing, presumed dead. Still, you sit there giving orders with no thought to your own flesh and blood," General Balder cried.

The room naturally cleared a path for the king to march over.

"How dare you! We have search parties looking for him day and night. He could still be somewhere deep in the jungle. I suggest you get a hold of your loose tongue immediately," King Vidal ordered.

"My first family was consumed by flames, either they perished or were left with scars which would never heal. I tried again but only to have my second son taken right under my nose. He may have been destined to be a Hammer, but still I could have watched him grow. Now, I only have ghosts." The general took a long hit of the flask. "I just want to know how to forget, how to stop caring."

"As the ruler of this kingdom, I have no time to drag my heels. Nor do you. Pull yourself together or our army will be looking for a new voice."

The men were now face to face.

"It took the last of my spirit to leave Hector; you sent yours away without hesitation. No true father could do that,"

General Balder muttered, his breath thick with wine.

The doors to Sanctuary Chamber burst open, followed by a soldier who could not get his words out fast enough. King, council, and general all rushed to the top of the castle walls. As they made their way, there was a huge presence of soldiers all dotted along the walkways and stairs. Each was watching and waiting for the king's reaction. It took all his courage not to yell out when he looked to the distance. The blue horizon of the ocean was lost, covered in a deadly swarm of the Tulus warships. They covered every inch of the water, a plague descending on Eldertude.

Balder appeared next to Vidal.

"There is only one nation left with a fleet at that disposal."

Vidal crushed the leaves on the top of the wall.

"Why now? It has been more than a decade since they have ventured out of their corner," Vidal spat.

"They stripped their bay clean of resources. There is no one more to trade with; it makes sense they have become desperate. We have the castle and jungle around us; they can strip the bark to repair their ships. If I were them, I would have invaded here a long time ago," Balder concluded.

"We have been negotiating a deal; war benefits neither of us."

"Maybe Holsten has come to collect the queen."

The king shot him a look which the general absorbed.

"No, something has pushed them over the edge. Arrange a messenger; let us see if we can come to some sort of deal."

"We cannot surrender," Balder warned.

"My bloodline has resided within these castles since the

birth of the Eldertude. It has driven out tyrants and beasts far worse, entire nations have been crushed who dared to challenge before. I will be dammed if I am the one to give the castle away."

"That is the response I was looking for. I will ready our forces for the approaching battle."

****

"Don't pack too much; Otto won't be able to carry it all," Dace instructed Mills as they emptied all the draws and the cupboards. Otto was at the table, fiddling with his pencils as more soldiers charged past the window.

"We need to leave as soon as possible. Once the Tulus make it to the beach, the Pilpots will be the first to go. Otto, we won't have room for all your drawings," Dace warned.

"I am almost done; it's a note for Erica, in case she comes back," the young boy said. Mills and her mother both gave each other a look.

"We do not know if Erica is ever coming back from the jungle." Mills said in a soft voice.

Otto looked up from his note, eyes wide and lip trembling. Before he could speak, there was a face at the window; it was their neighbour Ymo.

"Dace, just to let you know, the whole street's on foot heading towards the hill. If you don't want to be left behind, the three of you best get moving."

Ymo was right; the Pilpots were abandoned, with their residents dragging as much of their belongings as they could. Mills looked out to the Everlast Ocean. Eldertude had next to no coastal defences; anyone could walk straight up into their streets. There was only one place anyone could be protected in the kingdom.

"Ouch," Dace said; she grabbed her shoulder as a bag clipped her. The woman carrying the bag glanced back and then pushed on. Everyone was heading in one direction. Mills picked up Otto as they let themselves get washed away with the crowd. It was not long before they met their first road-block, one of the outer walls. The Eldertude soldiers stood firm in front of the wooden gate.

"The castle is readying itself for the battle. You cannot move up the hill yet; turn around."

The voice was lost over the mumbles of the crowd. Numbers were increasing by the second. People pushed forward to argue the same point. Anger was masking the underlying panic seeping out of one person into the other.

"We are under strict orders not to let you pass. You all will be evacuated to safety at the right time," a soldier yelled over the noise of the crowd.

"Look up there."

Pointing towards the base of the castle, Elm Grove was being evacuated. Soldiers helped with bags as the owners were led up into the castle. The injustice ignited a spark in the crowd. A surge of rage propelled the group into the soldiers; they were pushed back into the gate.

"Draw shields; drive them back."

From the back came huge steal shields passed to the front of the line. In one motion, the soldiers pushed back.

"Drive, drive."

The steel smashed into the crowd. Mills and Dace tried their best to shield Otto; as they did, he collided with another boy. An elderly lady tried to steady the fallen child but was struggling herself against the crowd.

"Send them to the others outside Hellrous," the soldiers cried.

****

The prince's room was the highest in the main castle tower. From the window, it could see almost every inch of Eldertude. The figures below swarmed over the castle. Boulders, arrows, and panthers were all being organised for the oncoming siege. Even being so far up, the underlying fear could be felt. It crawled up the branches and leaves to the top of the tower. Hermenize wondered how many of those below would turn and surge towards her, if they knew the truth. Hellrous was burning; Soldiers of the Infamous had been unleased when it had been under her control. Now they stood plotting with no way to stop them. To add to the debt, her past had brought another enemy to the kingdom. Hermenize walked away from the window and collapsed onto Zander's bed.

"My queen."

Puros had appeared, in his hands a tray with smoked meats and cheeses.

"It has been days since you last ate."

Hermenize stared at the ceiling.

"Did you still want any more updates on the zone; things are changing rapidly."

There was no reply. Hermenize rolled over and buried her head into Zander's blankets. Puros sighed and placed the food on the floor. As he turned to leave, he almost jumped out of his skin. Vidal's glare spurred the retreat; Hermenize dragged herself up and pushed back the hair from her face.

"I am surprised to see you with an invasion on your hands; you must have a lot to do. Or have you just come here to hide?"

"The Tulus may have caught us off guard, but we will prevail. The trees that make the castle walls cannot be breached. I would have left you to it were not for your request."

The king took out a small pouch from his pocket.

"Have you not tried talking to Holsten, to come to some type of deal?"

"I thought you already had."

Hermenize just looked at the king.

"For years, I have stood by your side and still to this day you cannot trust me," Hermenize said this time with sorrow in her voice.

"There are some betrayals that time cannot forgive," Vidal replied coldly.

"I was pushed into it by your treatment. A single mistake followed by a lifetime of punishment. For me and my son."

"He had an opportunity to prove himself and it failed; I cannot take the blame for that," Vidal dismissed.

"Nothing is ever your fault; you are blind to the monster you have become."

Vidal placed the pouch on the table.

"It seems that I am not the only one with a guilty conscience."

He opened the bag and poured out the content. Hermenize watched as each Damdread petal drifted onto the bed.

"Normally, these are only given to sick animals," Vidal muttered.

"So it is not enough for you to end your son, but now your wife as well?"

"The plant would have gotten into this room another way. Once we have fought off the Tulus, there will be a rebuilding of the royal family. I will find a new queen, one that can give me an heir worthy of the throne."

"We both know I was never the problem when it came to having children."

The king went bright red.

"Enjoy your poison," Vidal said with as much venom in the words to match the plant.

\*\*\*\*

A lone ship sailed towards the fleet of the Neptulus. The warships lined up in formation only a short distance away from the shore.

"Not too fast; we don't want to spook them," one of the crew said.

The others gave a slight nod but stayed as still as possible.

Captain Holsten lowered his telescope and stroked his beard.

"It looks like they want to talk," Alden said.

"Yes, I can see that," Holsten snapped. "No Vidal though."

"Then they cannot be surrendering."

"Why would you send an assassin then be afraid for a war?"

"It could be a way to try and lure you out, or some other type of a trap. Either way, the king has made himself look weak," the first mate concluded.

Captain Holsten gripped the wheel of the ship, whilst staring out to the castle on the hilltop. The lone Eldertude vessel had now ventured deep into the enemy lair. It had become engulfed in shadows of the Tulus ships. The most senior of the crew held an envelope, sealed with a red, wax stamp. Tapping it against his leg, he closed his eyes and focused on the waves. They lapped against the side of their boat as it gently rocked their vessel.

"Look, they are signalling us aboard."

The crew member was right; the closest ship was letting down a rope. Another one of the Tulus soldiers gave a slow wave.

"Right, this is really happening. Start steering us towards them; the rest of you stand where they can see you," the messenger ordered.

The other part of the crew did as instructed, and made their way to the starboard bow. Slowly, they drifted towards the warship. As they did, the Tulus ships also began to move, closing around them.

"Just keep focused."

There was a crash as the lone ship hit the side.

"Idiot, you overshot it."

The messenger yelled at the crew member behind the wheel. Looking up, the soldier with a slow wave was still there, now grinning at them.

"Get the rope."

One of the crew went to dock. As they did, the rope disappeared back up towards the deck of the warship. The crew looked up, but the waving soldier was gone. Rather, there were now dozens of bowmen all fully loaded. Before any of the crew could react, the bowmen unleased a thunderstorm of arrows. The power the bows could produce was enough to puncture holes in the ship. Its crew had been turned into blood-stained porcupines, sharp mental and wood now deep inside of them.

As there was no one left to steer, the lone ship crashed back into the side of the warship again. Mixed in with the damage inflicted by the arrows, the vessel started to take on water. The mast came down as the whole boat started to col-lapse.

"Do not let it sink; we need something to send back to Eldertude," Holsten ordered.

Tulus soldiers started to jump onto the lone ship. As each one landed, there was a loud splash.

"Can you get any of the bodies?" Alden shouted.

Most of the crew were now underwater, drifting off to sea. The symbol of Eldertude stitched into the white sail was now covered in blood. As one of the Tulus soldiers held it up, Hol-sten smiled.

"That will do."

## *Chapter 40*

"Sharpen the points of your blades, polish the steel of your chest plates, and do not let your eyes deceive you. Those shores are not full of fathers and sons, mothers and daughters. Serpents of death are waiting, wriggling in the sand. They may take many forms, but each is ready to make your blood curdle. There must be no hesitation when facing these green savages."

Deep in the hull of the ship, rows of Tulus soldiers were crammed together. The quartermaster walked down the aisle banging his club. Huge chunks of metal were being loaded onto the tallest of the soldiers. They spread out their arms, to complete their transformation into juggernauts. Lastly, the full-face helmet was placed on. Each member of the Rams now looked like a walking castle.

The beaches of Eldertude were fast approaching. No smoke drifted out of the Pilpots as the kingdom looked to be holding its breath. Even the castle was still, watching from the hilltop as the fleet of the Neptulus invaded the horizon.

All launch ships were picking up speed as the wind seemed to side with them. On the deck, archers held to the side as each wave sprayed up. Below, there were no more words of inspiration, fight, or desire. Only chunks of steel and sweat forming in the heavy suits of armour. As they waited, the soldiers started to hum; as more picked up the rhythm, the whole ship started to vibrate. The energy was rising; it coursed through the bodies till those ready for combat struck their chests and head.

Splitting the water in two, the landing boat crashed into the sand. The drawbridge came down and the soldiers charged out, roaring as they created hefty footprints.

"Make it over the ridge, before the archers rain an almighty agony upon you."

Quickly, the sand turned into clay. The first wave charged across the open ground, making it over the ridge into the Pilpots. Taking a breather, the helmets swung side to side. There was not an archer or wall in sight. The streets of the Pilpots were empty. Confusion rippled through the Rams.

Slowly, they spread out deeper into the clay caverns, into the blind spot from the waters. The Pilpots closest to the boats exploded. Huge balls of flames engrossed the soldier's closet. Whole units had been lying in wait in the evacuated Pilpots. The Eldertude soldiers surrounded the Tulus Rams. Armed with spears, they looked for chinks in the armour. The Rams kicked up sand as they tried to stop the onslaught. Spearheads overwhelmed the sluggish swings of the long swords.

Quickly, it became too much; the remaining Rams tried to make their retreat but were hunted down. The Eldertude soldiers were relentless in their chase; spears plunged into the back of those not fast enough. More appeared with an added danger. Taking aim, they stepped forward and put all their might into launching the spears. The spikes had been soaked in petrol; they came like a hail of thunderbolts.

Now desperate, the Rams ran into the sea. Others crawled on their arms and knees as fire rained down upon them. It was not long before they drowned in the sand and blood. The Eldertude soldiers cheered as they watched their enemy burn.

\*\*\*\*

"Word is the plan was successful," the Eldertude soldier reported.

"That was only the first wave. The Tulus have made it to our shores; in a sense we have already failed" the commander replied.

The news had spread to the Eldertude soldiers outside the walls of Hellrous. Many had already taken it as a personal insult that they had been selected to watch the refugees. The sick had made do by making their own tents and surviving off the little supplies the kingdom had spared them. Vats of the treatment had been placed in the centre but stood mostly untouched. Each survivor of the massacre sat mostly alone, subdued with sorrow. Slotted in between them were the evicted residents of the Pilpots. They stood as far away from those with the mark as the soldiers would let them.

"Stay close to me, Maxen. There are many grieving mothers who might snatch you." Harlow said.

"I will, Grandma, but we have been here for so long."

"Go play with the other boys and girls but keep your hood up. If anyone talks to you, scream."

Maxen nodded enthusiastically and dashed off. There were a small number of children gathered in a circle. In a blind rush, Maxen almost collided with them. It was soon apparent why they were gathered. Slumped over on a rock was a young boy. His arms were rotten, the skin was peeling. Each breath looked like agony as his lungs wheezed.

"Otto," cried out Maxen in a burst of excitement.

There was the faintest of smiles as the boy tried to straighten himself up.

"You have not been to class for ages," Maxen said.

"I'm not allowed to go anymore since I got sick," Otto replied.

"I stopped going as well."

"Did you stop wearing the hat?" Otto asked.

"It was stupid," Maxen said.

"School is stupid anyway."

The two boys laughed; some of the children joined in agreement. A sound of joy was rare in the makeshift camp.

"What is going on here?"

Dace arrived, with Mills shortly after.

"This is my friend from when I used to go to school," Otto replied with some cheer in his voice.

Harlow now joined them, placing two hands on the shoulders of Maxen. The two families stared at each other.

"It's okay; you do not have to stand with us. Our young boy is sick beyond words," Dace announced, sensing Harlow's gaze.

"He was my best friend," Maxen said

"With all the violence brewing, the last worry I should have is being around those less fortunate," Harlow said then held out a hand. Mills awkwardly shook it.

"Sorry also for our frosty greeting. We haven't been used to anyone showing kindness for a while," Mills said giving a half smile.

"Horror has risen again behind these black walls."

"People have spoken about the slaughter, the things of a nightmare," Dace said with a cold look on her face.

"Were you not witness to it?" Harlow asked.

"Luckily, we had not yet been relocated to Hellrous," Dace said quickly.

There was a smirk from Harlow "Do you have any food?"

Dace started to stutter; Harlow did not blink.

"We have a little; I suppose we could spare some."

Mills brought out a loaf of bread.

"Not too much," Dace hissed as a good chunk was broken off. As Mills held out her hand, there was a black mark running around her wrist. Quickly, the sleeve was pulled down.

"Your boy looks like he is struggling. How have you been coping whilst looking after him? I'd imagine he has to be carried a lot," Harlow said as Otto gave a dry cough,

Both of the older women then stared at each other. The standoff was broken by ear biting scream. A body landed in amongst the crowd of people. Everyone went to gather around. The bones had broken through the skin as the young soldier was coiled up on the ground. All heads now turned upwards. Stood upon the walls of Hellrous were the Soldiers of the Infamous. Monstrous in size, the former people they had been was gone. Eroded away by disease, the curse had blacked their skin to the colour of the midnight sky. No longer was it peeling and broken. Each had hardened to a thick coat over their bulging muscles. The curse had taken the life from their eyes. Male or female, it was hard to distinguish between the faceless army.

The SIDD hit like a tidal wave. Eldertude soldiers were still in a state of shock as darkness now swept over their defences. They tried their best, fighting with swords, but furious punches broke steel and armour as the soldiers were pushed aside. It was not long before the soldiers ran up the stairs to the attackers only to be beaten back. SIDD were jumping off into the crowd of residents. An outcry of screams and panic followed. More soldiers poured into the bedlam. People fled in all directions as the Soldiers of the Infamous kept taking victims.

"Take my hand!" Harlow yelled as the two of them made their way through the chaos. Trailing behind them, Mills and Dace each had an arm around Otto. They were following the only person who moved with any type of direction.

"Watch out."

It was too late; a soldier came crashing down on Dace and Otto. Mills only just managed to roll away. Such an impact had crushed most of their fragile bodies. The sister screamed as she tried to pull them to their feet.

"Leave them," Harlow cried.

Mills did not respond, tears rolling down her cheeks. More people fell on top of them. The crowd was relentless; primal instincts meant that anyone else was expendable in the route to safety.

"If you want to live, you need to move."

Out of the sea of terror, a SIDD loomed over them. Fresh blood dripped off their knuckles. Mills screamed but kept pulling at her mother. Dace reached into her pocket and pulled out a knife. Using the last of her strength, she drove the blade into the shin of SIDD. The tip broke on its leather skin. Another SIDD arrived, heading straight towards Harlow. Mills was pushed from behind into their path. Dace struck out again and this time the SIDD reacted.

**\*\*\*\***

"The landing parties failed on the first attempt. We were caught off guard; the Eldertude soldiers were waiting for us," Alden reported.

"It was a foolish move, not to suspect these slippery tricks. Vidal is forever a rat. Arm the catapults," Holsten ordered.

Captain Holsten was on the observations deck with Alden. Both now wore the full military uniform.

"Already, we planned to use those as a last resort. There are now barricades put up the hill towards the castle. Many of the residents of Eldertude are caught in between them. If we unleash these, we cannot guarantee there will not be a mass loss of non-military life. It will be harder to accept their new leader if their family was slaughtered by them," Alden said, well aware the crew were watching the conversation.

"Entire units of ours lay dead on that beach. How many more would be lost trying to bait them out of those chimneys? I don't want to spill unnecessary blood, but I must put our people first," Holsten replied with a wave of the arms.

Sling ships were brought to the front line. The circular boats had curved launching arms and deep loading docks. Iron balls, broken glass, and chunks of stone were piled into the heads of the catapults. Ropes were attached to the vessels on either side. Each was then wound up until the rope was screeching, before being released. Death rained down upon the Pilpots. Stone and iron ripped through the clay shelters. As the Eldertude soldiers retreated for shelter, glass ripped into their flesh.

"They're backing off; we could stop now," Alden pleaded again.

"Keep firing; we need the beaches completely clear. No mercy was shown to our sailors," Holsten replied, not taking his eyes away from the shore.

More catapults unleased havoc on those caught in the crossfire. The Eldertude spearmen had dropped their weapons, and were sprinting up the long trail back to the castle. Various roadblocks and defences had been created in the path up the hill. In between the checkpoints, Eldertude residents had been caught in between. As they had watched their homes being flattened, they now had to fend for their lives from the missiles.

"What do we do? There are children down there" one of the Eldertude soldiers cried.

Peering over the wall of the wooden barrier, residents desperately banged at the door of the closed gates.

"We have been instructed to keep it closed. Otherwise, we have everyone flooding into the castle at once, which weakens the overall defences," the commander responded, not meeting the look from his soldiers.

The sling ships kept on firing; soldiers and residents sprinted towards the bulk of the crowd. This though was not what the attention was focused on. A far greater danger was rushing towards them, Soldiers of the Infamous covered in blood. None blinked as the stone and iron came crashing down around them. An overwhelming thirst for murder surged through their legs.

"The monsters are coming," a young resident cried.

"Unlock the gates and prepare the archers. We cannot let them die in front of us; blast to the orders," the commander ordered.

The doors opened and the crowd emptied in. As quickly as they had been unlocked, it was closed again, in preparation for the oncoming attack. All the fleeing soldiers were rearmed as the residents headed towards the castle. The SIDD were in full sprint. No armour or weapons, only the shared desire to cause pain. Now, the Eldertude soldiers were ready to deal out some of their own.

A shadow appeared over the SIDD; the sky became black with arrows. Then the heads dipped and hurled towards their targets. A blanket of deadly punctures covered the bodies of the SIDD. The skin was shredded as the legs were ripped apart. There was the will to keep moving but the body could not fight against the velocity of arrows. Most broke down, either dead or unable to run away towards the gate. There were trails of silver behind them.

Those not caught in the volley of arrows smashed into the gates. Immediately, they were set upon by the Eldertude soldiers. Spears and swords dug into the rotting faces. As the corpses piled up at the gate, those still able to move climbed over the bodies to the top. The bowmen reloaded and let another barrage of arrows; it pushed back the force of attackers momentarily. Even with the death toll rising, there were more coming from Hellrous.

"Soon, we will be out of arrows."

"Where is the fear of death? They sacrifice themselves just to get another inch closer."

There were already over a hundred bodies twitching in the pile. Soon, there would be enough corpses to reach the barrier's summit. Archers were slowly swapping bows for swords. Spearmen searched for any life in between the cursed hands and feet. Across the barrier were silver stains from the Improx treatment. Each of the SIDD paused and then started to retreat back over the ridge.

"We have done it; they are backing off," one of the soldiers yelled.

"I am not too sure. There isn't a reason for them to back away now; they were right on top of us," the commander said, shutting down any hint of a smile.

"Maybe they got scared."

Those of the SIDD still able to crawl slowly dragged themselves towards the gate.

"You think those creatures have feelings? No, I'm sure that they are planning something else. We have already lost the Pilpots. It looks like the Tulus are already taking advantage. Hopefully, they will run into these monsters," the commander said looking out to the sea.

"To make matters worse, there is a storm coming," replied the soldier next to him.

The beach below was covered in huge transport ships. There was an endless chain of soldiers and war machines. Some searched through the wreckage of the Pilpots for any survivors. Amongst the blood stained clay, there was little life.

****

"Let's try and slip away now while everyone is busy," Erica whispered.

"If they catch us, we will be executed. They are killing any of the Eldertude casualties they find," Luca whispered back.

"We will not get a better chance."

Erica and Luca both picked a crate each and made their way down the plank. In an attempt to escape the Neptulus warship which had found them stranded, whilst trying to sail back from the Collectors palace.

One of the Tulus soldiers watched as they fumbled their way down, "Stop, both of you. Where are you going?"

"You were kind enough to aid the Collector's servicemen in their time of need. We are just trying to repay the favour," Erica announced. The Tulus soldier looked down his nose; as if on cue, the bottom of the crate Luca was holding gave way. Dozens of metal gloves dropped out over the plank and into the sea. The soldier cursed at him as he desperately tried to stop the flow of loss. There was another loud crash; the wooden crane next to them had given way. One of the siege weapons had collided into the side of the ship.

"Get as many of those gloves you can find," the Tulus soldier demanded, before yelling at those trying to deal with the crane.

Quickly, the pair made their way to the beach and dumped the crates. With all the hustle of the army preparing for war, it was easy for them to blend into the commotion. Making their way over the ridge, Luca stopped. The neighbourhood he had grown up in now lay flattened in dust and stone. As he walked through the destruction amongst the shattered clay, eventually he found the remains of his home. Iron blocks had pounded the roof. He peered in through one of the holes. The collection of trinkets had been shattered with glass.

"They're only things," Erica said as she placed a hand on his shoulder. He kept looking into the ruins.

"We need to find your family," Luca said.

The Pilpot where Otto had been hidden was not far. It was in a much better condition than Luca's. Erica rushed inside and stepped into a pool of blood. It was leaking out of an outstretched hand; a Tulus soldier had stab marks all over their body. Others who had tried to hide lay next to her.

"It's a massacre," Erica said, as she pushed aside the broken spears and smashed furniture. "Our troops are unforgiving."

"I fear for what will happen when the two sides finally meet in force. The only good news is that your family is not here," Luca tried to sound cheerful.

"Where to though?"

The drawers of bedrooms had been cleared out.

"Maybe Otto got discovered. We should start with Hellrous; they should have had it under control by now. I'm sure I can find a healer who knows about the new arrivals," Erica concluded.

It was not long before they encountered more death. The remains of soldiers, men, women, and children were sprawled out in front of the black gates. Not a soul was stirring. Blood stains and desperate signs of resistance painted the picture of a nightmare. The people had been beaten to death. In silence, Erica and Luca walked through the butchery. Many of the victims had blows to the back of their heads. Above them, the skies had opened; rain thundered down on Eldertude.

Erica started sprinting up the hill. Luca went pale as he watched her dive to her knees. A lifelong friend in the shape of Mills lay broken in the mud. Next to her were the mother and the boy. Rain continued to fall; the water mixed in with the tears streaming down Erica's face. The thumping storm however could not hide the screams. Otto rocked in Erica's arms as she thrashed around in the dirt. It was not exactly clear what had ended the child's life. There were signs of puncture marks, but with the infection raging across his fragile body, it could have been the wind which killed him.

"I don't know what to say, Erica."

It was a while before she managed to get any type of control over her weeping. Luca just sat in the mud rubbing her back.

"We must bury them," Erica whimpered.

"Of course," Luca said gently.

"Then it is time for answers. Those who have caused this must pay for the bloodshed."

**** 

The SIDD still had not appeared after the attack on the outer barrier. There was a rotting stench from the remains of the first assault. While the Eldertude soldiers reinforced the wooden gate, more arrows and swords had arrived. All of the residents had now made their way up to the next checkpoint towards the castle. Each one of the soldiers was itching to follow. The Neptulus army was growing in force on the beach with each passing ship. To make things worse, the rain continued to pour; it cleared some of the blood, but the Improx had stained the wood.

"Contact, contact."

All of the soldiers spun around. In the middle of the path stood one of the tallest SIDD, a deadly look on its face. In one hand, it had a large vial of the treatment. The soldiers watched it pour the Improx over its head.

"What's it doing? It must be a signal or something."

A wooden torch burned bright in the other hand. The flame was strong enough to fight against the heavy rain. Arrows were loaded into bows, as the lone SIDD began its charge towards the gate. The soldiers reacted but even with the concentrated bombardment, the lone SIDD kept on coming. It ducked and dogged the spears. Every arrow which landed sunk into the skin but did nothing to slow down its target. The lone SIDD was almost at the gate until one of the spears went through the thigh. Finally, it paused, as did the soldiers.

A line of the SIDD had appeared over the ridge, in numbers that had never been seen before. The spear in the top of the leg of the lone SIDD could not be removed. In response, the lone SIDD twisted and ripped off the whole limb. Each watched in disbelief as the enemy seemed to know no pain. Still holding the torch, it threw itself into the pile of SIDD bodies gathered by the defences, each covered in Improx. A spark could be heard, quickly followed by smoke. A huge explosion erupted and ripped through the gate. Limbs and pieces of wood were thrown into the air. The blast was so strong; that the flames could be seen across the kingdom. All that was left was a clear path up the valley, straight to castle walls.

## Chapter 41

The news of the impending battle had crippled Zander. His newfound strength was now irrelevant, when stuck inside a mountain on the other side of the Borrowed Lands. All his thoughts were now focused on trying to understand the reality of war, and what it meant for his mother.

"I need to get off this mountain," Zander announced.

"How do you plan to do that?" the gem dragon replied, its voice echoing around the cave.

Zander looked at the gem dragon with a blank expression.

"Can you not take me there?"

"That is not my purpose. My fight is with the grey man, or whatever form he returns in. Until then, I wait, like I always have waited."

There was a protest from Zander, but the gem dragon stood firm. Only the taste of frustration was left in Zander's mouth as he stormed off. Another heavy mist swept over the mountain, filling the cave with grey smog. Zander was desperately searching for any source of help within the haze. Taking time to kick out at another bird's nest, he tripped over one of the hidden rocks. It was a skeleton which broke Zander's fall. Face to face with the skull, bugs crawled out the nose. On top was a simply designed helmet, covered in a tangle of cobwebs. The only stand out feature was the large gem in the centre.

Bony fingers were locked around the handle of a sword. Zander went to grab it and now felt a presence. The gem dragon had appeared behind him, the long neck almost coiling itself around Zander. He hesitated; the gem dragon's eyes watched each subtitle movement with deep intent. Then the head gestured back towards the sword.

Zander picked it up; the weapon was rusty and felt awkward in his hand.

"That belonged to father; he used to call me Garnet. Father always said that sword was only complete with the helmet."

He did as instructed, shaking out the cockroaches before putting it on. As he did, it was as if an avalanche had landed upon him. Endless images rippled in his mind like the surface of a lake. The snow was coming in hard. He was inside the cave but there were no birds; their perches were frozen over. A loud clunk could be heard, over and over again. With a collection of sticks and wood in front of him, a man was striking the sword against a rock.

Next to him was Garnet, now only days old, the dragon was wrapped in a tattered blanket. Garnet winced each time the metal struck. The diamond on the forehead of the dragon started to glimmer. Father waved his arms and then pointed at the sticks. Garnet sunk back into the blanket, before the man tapped his helmet. There was a begging look by both parties. Eventually, Garnet crawled out from his bed, opened its mouth, and roared. Nothing came out except a cloud of breath. There was a tilt of the head, the man sighed and then cradled the dragon.

"Never have I been able to produce fire."

Zander was conscious again, back with the skeleton and the birds.

"I had not long been in existence and could not keep myself warm. Father had tried his best to gather wood, but it was soaked through. He used his own body to save mine."

The words were echoing in Zander's ears, but the gem dragon's mouth was still.

"Father taught me a lot about sacrifice. That one day it would come for me, when I left this cave."

"You have never left?" Zander asked.

"I must only take to the skies once there is someone to meet me."

A bomb fire had been set alight in the chest of Zander. His sweaty palms clawed at his chest as he frantically tried to put it out. The smoke was filling his lung and creeping into his stomach. He was about to be sick or worse. Zander ripped off the helmet and took a deep, sensual breath.

The gem dragon lashed itself against the wall. Rocks fell from the ceiling. There was another ripple through the body of the gem dragon. Its tail was causing destruction to the cave. As abruptly as it had started, the gem dragon then froze. Its pupils began to dilate; there was a low rumble which echoed around the cave.

Pinning back its ears, the gem dragon charged, but

Zander was already on the move. The snarling jaws came within inches as he dived for safety, pinning himself under a rock. Black ivory claws frantically tried to rip away the small barrier between them. Zander put the helmet back on.

"I am not the grey man," Zander pleaded.

"It is here, from the opposite side. Truly, I did not think there was more than me," Garnet cried.

The gem dragon pulled away, then turned again and almost head butted the wall. Jumping up and down, it was sending shockwaves through the cave. Zander held up his hand, the gem dragon swung its neck and almost wiped him out. There was no sign of the dragon slowing down. It started to bite at any of the birds still senseless enough to be close. Abruptly, it stopped and lowered its whole body to the ground. High above the head of Zander was the rusty sword of its father. With each turn of the blade, the gem dragon crawled in the same direction.

"Come closer," Zander commanded.

Slowly, the gem dragon did as instructed. Tucking the sword under his belt, he started to climb up the back. Gems ran up the spine, infused into each point with liquid gold. The vibrant red scales were hot to touch as Zander made his way up to the neck. Taking up position, Zander then waited.

"Fly." Nothing happened. "It is time, we need to leave."

There was another almighty roar from the gem dragon. The wings spread open to reveal a blanket of gold. Rows upon rows of vibrant gold coins, they danced with each movement. As the strokes became more powerful, the coins rang out. With only one option, both braced as they drove themselves into the roof cave. They hit rock and dirt acting as the walls to their prison. The harder they pushed, the stronger the resistance. Trying to hold on, Zander punched at the dirt.

The ice cold winds which cut through the skin were a welcoming embrace. Dragon and prince had taken to the skies. Below, the mountain was fading into the backdrop as the pair split the clouds. Sunlight danced off the gold, the scales began to glow. Like a bird which had tasted air for the first time, the gem dragon soared higher and faster into the sky. The smile on Zander's face was disappearing. He took another handful of breaths but his lungs screamed back. Every second that passed, the world was closer to disappearing. He shouted out, but the words were as useful as trying to hold up that waterfall with a leaf. Fighting the urge to close his eyes, Zander kicked into the gem dragon. He summoned every thought and did it again. Finally, the gem dragon started to dip back down.

The mountain range was racing underneath them. It was both exhilarating and empowering as the pair moved with incredible speed. For all the splendour, Zander remembered the cause of their journey.

"Hatred has descended on your people. We are going to meet it."

## Chapter 42

"The last time we were in a space like this we almost died," Erica muffled.

"Well, it is ancient, so it could collapse," Luca replied.

"Thanks for that. How do you know about this place anyway?"

Erica and Luca were crawling through a long and stuffy tunnel. The faint light up ahead gave just enough guidance to navigate around the tangle of roots.

"Are you kidding? Zander and I know every inch of this castle. So much of our time growing up was spent skipping our lessons. We would then go hunting for new places to hide. When they were trying to carve out the kitchen, they made various runways. One of them led straight into a home in Elm Grove. Both of us slipped and we when came tumbling out through the family portrait. They had put up the picture to cover the hole. You should have seen their faces."

A rumble from above shifted the dust around them.

"I cannot believe this is happening. Why would the Tulus decide to attack now?" Luca said.

"It was inevitable, the last of the kingdoms to sallow each other up. I just hope there were some in Eldertude who were prepared. Unlike my family," Erica said through tears. Luca wished he could turn round to hug her.

"Here we are."

Running his hands across the light, Luca squeezed his fingers into the few holes he could find. Leaning forward, the hatch slowly opened. A shelf full of spices and cans came crashing down. Covered in dust and wood shavings, the pair crawled out into the royal kitchen. Half cut vegetables lay sprawled out on the counters. Meat lay in pans of cold water. There was a pile of aprons chucked on the floor. Erica started to cry again. Luca went to console her, opening up his arms. There was no embrace.

"Just take me there. You know that is where she will be. It is time the truth came out," Erica's voice was cold, the tears were now gone.

For all the uncertainty, violence, and pain that came with the return, on their way to the tower, Luca quickly buried his head into a wall of leaves for a moment of tranquillity. The flowers and trees which morphed themselves into a castle had always been his true home. Outside was an army ready to crush that life into a cloud of bleeding dust. He started to run. The oncoming siege had emptied most of the inner hallways. Luca's feet pounded the wood as he climbed the familiar stairs to the room he grew up in. The two guards standing outside immediately drew their weapons. Demanding they halt, one held up a hand bigger than Erica's head.

"No one should be up here," the guard boomed.

Luca stuttered; no longer did he have the freedom of the hallways he once had with Zander.

"We are here on official business," Erica announced. Both of them were still dressed in the Collector's uniform. One of the guards was eyeballing Luca.

"Where do I recognise you from?" the guard asked. Searching in his pocket, Luca then drew out the leaf embedded in glass.

"That is the badge of Maple. Please, we must see Queen Hermenize."

"The queen gave strict orders not to be disturbed."

"It is about her son."

The windows had been covered with bed covers and cloths. Empty plates lay stacked on the floor, as the air inside Zander's chambers tasted stale. From behind one of the sofas, a lone foot could be seen. Luca rushed to the body of the queen. As he picked her up, Hermenize was cold to touch. In her sleek black hair were chucks of sick.

"Looks like she took the coward's way out," Erica said, inspecting the half full bag of Damdread petals. Luca leaned into Hermenize's chest.

"She is still breathing."

Calling out her name as loudly as he could, Luca shook the queen. With each thrust, there seemed to be more life creeping back in. Eventually, her eyes rolled back in the direction of Luca.

"My boy, I cannot believe it is you."

Erica watched as the queen was helped into a chair. Luca

found the last of the water and waited patiently whilst Hermenize took sip after sip.

"Tell me, where is my son?"

The question burst out of trembling lips. Queen Hermenize looked a shell of her former, glamourous self. Luca was worried that the answer might finish her off.

"First, you need to answer for your crimes against the kingdom!" Erica shouted.

"Please, I need to know about Zander. Then do what you must; I do not care what happens to me."

Luca gave a pleading look; Erica gave a sign and then turned away.

"He has remained at the Collector's palace to receive treatment."

"So he is alive."

Luca gave a timid nod; Erica went to correct him but then stopped. Some of the colour returned to Hermenize's face. She leaned back in the chair as her face remembered how to smile.

"There, you have your answers, now I want mine. The treatment we have been giving to those in the zone, which I have been giving to them. Why is it that they never get better? Is it death I have been administering? Is the kingdom killing its own people?" Erica almost threw herself at the queen. Luca stood in between them.

"It may not seem like it now, but I never wanted to hurt anyone— none of us did. It got out of hand so quickly. Once the infection first appeared in Eldertude, we exhausted every method to try and stop it. By the time most were in place, almost half the population was sick. The Red Drops seemed to bring relief to the people. We hoped it would lead to a cure, but after time, it ended up reacting with the disease. With no other answers, it seemed humane to let the people simply slip away. But those whose bodies resisted then changed into something far worse. The centre was about as much protecting the kingdom, as ending their transformation into monsters. I took over the zone because I wanted to try and control it. I hoped to give those who were dying some dignity before the end."

"Dignity? Have you ever even stepped foot inside Hellrous?" Erica was bright red. "How many have looked to their kingdom for a chance of life, only to have a dagger in the back. Worst still, you made us do it. The only monsters here are sitting in the ivory towers. You even gave the poison to your own flesh and blood."

"My son never got the same treatment. There is no way to stop it, but it can be slowed down. Unfortunately, the plant does not grow enough to go to the masses. We saved it for our loved ones. It is unfair, but such is life," Hermenize looked to the floor.

"The centre is a thing of nightmares," Erica said, the painful memories flashing across her face.

"People rarely stay blind for long. As soon as Hellrous was created, suspicion skyrocketed. There was anger and disorder from the offset. Also, even with the treatment we were giving them, everyone is affected by the curse differently. We needed not only a mask for what was happening, but also a way to get a hold of it. Fear is one of the greatest weapons of control. Keeping the centre a mystery let the mind build far bigger horrors than we could construct."

"It was not far off."

"The centre was necessary. Those whose lives are not ended by the curse are changed by it. The infection makes their bodies stronger, their minds become twisted. For years, the masked healers had it under control, putting them down before they could not be stopped. Things though have changed. Never have these monsters been organised like they are now. I do not know if the soldiers of Eldertude and Tulus combined will be able to stop them."

"Me and the others were asked to volunteer to go back into the centre," Erica said through gritted teeth.

Hermenize gave an apologetic look. "We had to be sure."

"More sent to the slaughter like we are nothing, just pawns to those who rule."

A dagger appeared in a shaky hand.

"Erica what are you doing?" Luca cried,

"The young lady is right; I deserve to die," Hermenize said, accepting her fate.

Luca's eyes grew as he was transfixed on the blade. Erica could see the look of revulsion growing inside of him; it pained her that she was the cause.

"I have been a part of your mechanism of death. One which has taken the lives of people I have tried to save. You gave false hope which ends up lifeless in the mud, or worst still— to be slaughtered like cattle. The rulers of this kingdom have destroyed it, but you do not get to drift away. Face your sins and watch people like me and Luca rebuild it, if it is not too late already."

Hermenize gave a smile and nodded, before leaning back to stare at the ceiling. Sick ran down her chin; the body followed suit by seizing up and shaking. Luca leapt to her side; Erica just stood and watched. The poison was taking a hold of the body; each vein was on fire as it tried to flush it out of the system. After what seemed like an age, it stopped; Luca cried out. To his amazement, Hermenize tilted her head towards him; her voice was no higher than a whisper.

"The queen wants to speak to you."

Leaning in, the delicate tongue moved softly; Erica bit her lip. As soon as the words ended, there was an almighty crash outside. The impact sent a shockwave through the prince's towers and the entire castle. Sanctuary Chamber's doors burst open.

"The war has broken out. My queen, we must get you to a more safe location."

The guards stopped and stared at the lifeless Hermenize. Erica still had the dagger in her hand.

"My word, the queen has been attacked by assassins."

Any attempt at an explanation was futile.

"Surrender or be killed."

"It is not what it seems," Luca said, looking to Hermenize, who could barely keep her tongue still.

"Take them to the dungeons. Kill them at the first sign of resistance."

## Chapter 43

Kantra turned her face from the guard, the hinge of her swords poked above the waistline. War was almost upon the castle of Eldertude. The Elm Grove residents and any stragglers remained locked in one of the castle halls. Pushing her way past the well dressed, Kantra searched for a pair of hoods, trying to stick to a corner. With Neptulus knocking at the gate, the Eldertude soldiers had become paranoid. Anyone out of the ordinary was subject to integration, with extreme force at the first sign of resistance.

The path between Darnspur and Red Claw Jungle had been full of shadows. Once inside the jungle, dangers had been lurking around every tree. The Waro that had not been washed away patrolled the pathways. A feast of animals stalked anything that moved. Kantra had spent so much time pinned to the grass or diving into bushes. The drive to resolve one of the many injustices she had faced had kept her breathing.

Aiming for the valley of the Pilpots, her directions had been off and Kantra had strolled into Elm Grove. In the blind panic to reach some type of safety, she had been carried away with the evacuations. Amongst the fear for her family, Kantra could see the irony. Now surrounded by thick bushes with a coat of wood around them, snacks and drinks circulated the room on silver trays. Out of sight really was out of mind; conversation picked up and there was even the sound of laughter.

There was strong vibration through the hall. Leaves started to fall from the ceiling. Loud banging could be heard echoing toward them. Everyone watched as one of the guards marched down the spiral staircase. He headed straight toward the commander and leaned in his ear. After a quick conversation, both soldiers then checked the wooden beams across the doors.

"Tell us, what is that ghastly sound?" a well-dressed resident asked.

"Ladies, gentlemen, it is nothing. Only the sound of us consolidating our defences, as a precaution to keep you all safe," the commander announced.

Murmurs of satisfaction followed as the commander sent the other soldier away. One of the silver platters came past Kantra; she slapped it out of the young man's hands. Immediately, there were shouts of disapproval.

"I am suffocating." Kantra cried.

The guards were making their way through the residents. Seeing a gap, Kantra charged up the stairs to the castle walls. Now with a view overlooking the kingdom, it was only then that Kantra realised how much danger Eldertude truly was in. The Tulus had a well-established camp on the beach; the boots of the soldiers now covered nearly every grain of sand. All of the siege weapons had been unloaded and were being dragged up the hill. The checkpoint was left in tatters. It was now nothing more than a smouldering crater. Wisps of smoke still drifted from the bodies.

Any of the other blockades had been abandoned. Eldertude residents and soldiers alike were now at the castle gates. The towering timber guardians remained firmly shut. Other smaller entrances had been let open; there was a steady stream of those looking for protection. Kantra made her way to the main courtyard and started pushing past the residents. A father collided with her, dropping clothes and a bag of potatoes. Others pounced on the lost sack, grabbing as many of the loose vegetables as they could find.

The mob all stopped at once; a black and rotting hand was gripped around the largest of the potato. Its owner picked up the clothes and pulled his children away.

"You came back." Kantra spun round just in time for Maxen to come running into her.

"Of course, I did. Do you really believe I would break a promise like that?"

"Yes, maybe."

The little boy giggled as Kantra squeezed him.

"Harlow not able to keep up with you then?"

Maxen pulled away; there was a grave look on his young face.

"Tell me where she is."

From the castle walls, the soldiers started to shout. More of them rushed up the stairs. To the right of the castle, the Soldiers of the Infamous could be seen. They gathered in a long, endless line.

"We are leaving."

Kantra grabbed the hand of Maxen and headed for one of the doorways. An Eldertude soldier stood in their way.

"All the exits have been blocked; nobody leaves. The castle is at war. Make yourself useful and pick up a sword."

****

Another type of conflict was brewing in the Sanctuary Chambers.

"Our defence's barely held out for a day. It is bad enough we have got to deal with those scabs from the sea. Now the vermin from Hellrous are organising themselves. There are not many kings in history that have had to deal with this kind of mess."

"My king, there has been an explosion."

The soldier had to duck to avoid the goblet Vidal threw. Spinning back round to the window, Vidal's trailing red cape matched his face. General Balder watched from the corner, the shiny buttons on his uniform were almost popping off. Trumpets and drums could be heard in the distance; banners of Neptulus rose up the hill. Groups of Tulus soldiers struggled to drag up cages. Each time they hit a snag, the cage shook veraciously, almost throwing off their covers. Others were laboured with moving up the battering rams or carrying ladders. As the storm had passed, both suns had returned in full force. Armour glistened in the warm rays.

"They have been allowed to walk right up to our doorstep unchallenged. We should rush them now whilst they still have not fully organised," Balder jeered, waving an arm.

"So we can be caught out in the open with nowhere to seek cover? The will to break bones with your bare hands has always brought a sense of blindness to your decisions. No, this kingdom's best form of attack lies with the strength of this castle. It has never been breached. The captain will know this," Vidal spat back.

"Why do you think they have chosen now to attack?" Balder asked.

"Does it really matter? Holsten has wanted to get back at me for years. I banished him and this is his revenge."

"Maybe they are after supplies; their city has been on the water for years. Most likely they want the castle to strip down. There is no finer wood than those which make these walls."

"If that was the case, he would have just asked. Deals with the dirty are normally the most profitable. No, this is about me and unfinished business."

"How is the queen?" Balder said coldly.

"About as well as your boy," Vidal replied, meeting Balder's gaze.

All the advisors and guards in the room stopped.

"Go sort out my army. Make sure this place is a fortress."

Archers lined every crevasse of the castle walls. Each armed with longbows, piles of splinter head arrows were stacked up around them. Boulders, rocks, and jugs of fuel with rags poked in the top were being strategically placed. Huge crossbows were being wheeled out, loaded with missiles longer than the soldiers who carried them. There were shouts as the soldiers ran up and down the stairs. Most of the Eldertude soldiers had never seen real combat before, certainly not on this scale.

Another horn was sounded out in the castle. It was one long, powerful note. In sync, two long lines of glistening armour and refined weapons marched out. The stone-faced warriors of the Hammer units filled up the courtyard, pushing the residents back. Each held up a hammer or axe to the sky; the horn stopped. It was then followed by three consecutive clashes of the weapons with shields. All of the soldiers spread across the castle walls then cheered and got back to work.

Amongst the horde of the Tulus soldiers, a parade of titanic sentinels pushed their way past. Refined and sleek armour was hidden under blue cloaks. Stern faces were protected by the helmets' side guards, connected to mesh visors. Resting on their shoulders were long poles with sharp blades on each end. Tied round one of the handles was a razor-edged tooth. It was taken from a shark every High Sea Roller must catch with their bare hands.

Walking between the warriors was Captain Holsten. Banners of Neptulus flowed in the wind around him. Making his way to the front of the line, the drums rattled in anticipation. High above in the castle walls, the Eldertude soldiers watched his approach.

"The people of Eldertude, I am the commander of the Neptulus fleet. We already own the seas and now we have conquered your beaches. You awoke the sleeping giant; it will crush any resistance. I offer you one opportunity to avoid any more unnecessary bloodshed. Throw down your weapons and end this war. I promise there will be a place for you in the new order."

Holsten made his announcement. There was activity high up on the walls. The High Sea Rollers threw themselves in front of their commander. A single arrow landed in the mud only feet away. The arrow had been lodged in the body of a fish. Upon the castle walls now appeared King Vidal, supported by General Balder.

"A well-rehearsed speech but it only shows your desperation. All the armies of the world could wage an endless siege at these gates but not break them. In your faraway lands, balancing on driftwood, it must be hard to imagine the almighty sight of the castle. To see is to believe. Now do not embarrass yourself by asking us to surrender," Vidal shouted.

"So the king comes out of hiding, well almost. Standing behind the trees after his assassin has failed. Did you really think I would not return the favour? The kingdom of Neptulus is the last true power of the world. You have baited us; now, we are to take the final throne," Holston shouted back.

The king and the general seemed to converse. Together they whispered while thousands on both sides waited for orders.

"An assassination order was never given by me, the general, or any of the council. Do not hide behind lies. The once great sailor has directed his ships into the rocks. Now he must come begging for repairs. I know you are after the great wood, from the trees which make these walls."

"Maybe I am here to see the queen then. Why not arrange for a place for me and you to exchange fists?"

Laughter rippled through the Tulus soldiers.

"More lies from a man infected with mistruths. It is that retched tongue, which feeds the stories about what the leadership does with its sick. Grubby deals which have enslaved its most vulnerable. Is that why you have sailed to our shores, to abandon more of your people?"

Holsten's face dropped as did the smirks around him. Vidal just stared from the balcony, waiting for the next move. A message was given to the Tulus soldier closest to the captain. Up came the broken, lifeless body. Tied to a flagpole, they had been stripped of their clothes. The chest was covered in wounds with dried blood smeared across the face. Faded eyes had been pinned open, the pink handkerchief stuffed into the mouth. It took a moment for the people of Eldertude to recognise the dead icon, except for one. Balder was on his knees, pulling out chunks of leaves from the wall. Then he let out a roar like he had been punched in the gut. Almost jumping over the balcony in a blind rage, it took several of the soldiers to restrain him.

"Attack now with everything we have. Get my son back. Prepare all those ready to take revenge, for Hector."

The Eldertude soldiers started to make their way to the stairs.

"Halt."

Everyone paused and looked at the king.

"What did you say?" Balder was shaking.

"Use your head; open the gates now and lose the main advantage of this castle. Fighting back a siege from inside the walls will put us all in danger."

"Lost your heart or has it turned as black as the infection itself. If it were your son, you would ride out. Except you have never had a proper son. I am the director of the castle arms, and they will on my order."

"And I am the ruler of the Eldertude, who is telling you to stand down."

"Blast to you."

The general turned his back and marched down the stairs.

"Arrest that man." Vidal pointed. "A violation of a direct order from the king is punishable by imprisonment."

Nobody dared make eye contact; the rest of the soldiers on the balcony were still. Others on the castle walls were screaming orders. The siege had already begun.

## *Chapter 44*

The tension erupted in the valley of Eldertude. Energy and emotion surged through every soul of the men and women who gripped a weapon. Whichever flag they would battle under, the weight of their entire people would be felt in each swing. Both kingdoms now had all their cards on the table. Lose and their families would be enslaved before the beaming suns had set. In the heat, the Tulus army had implemented nearly all their siege methods at once. A move which had confused the castle, as it struggled on where to concentrate its defences.

Arrows, catapults, and battering rams all launched. Tulu soldiers held wide shields above their heads, and they were sardined together. They shuffled forward towards the castle walls. Loud clanks could be heard as rocks and missiles battered steel. Tied to their backs were the parts of a ladder. Screams broke out as one of the giant arrows ripped through entire units. Moving much slower as if hoping not to be noticed, three lumbering huge iron ships appeared to be upside down. The spearmen tried their best to break the soldiers underneath as they lumped their way forward.

"For all their noise, so far we have barely a scratch on us," one of the Eldertude commanders said as he stepped back, letting a huge bolder fly past him.

"Their archers are so weak, they cannot even reach us."

The tails of arrows were visible all the way up the castle walls. Fired high up into the air, they would dip and eventually land into the thick wood. Drums sounded out as the banners started to sway. Each of the cages was still rocking as they were lined up. In one motion, the covers came off and the doors unlocked. Out charged the Raging Squid, racing towards the castle as Tulus soldiers dived out the way. Dozens of tentacles frantically scurried across the mud; each one then bound themselves around the arrows and started to climb the wall.

Eldertude soldiers responded by launching spears and arrows. Many of the Raging Squid leapt out of the way, ripping off bark as they clambered higher. Those that could not move fast enough were struck by the metal tips. Spearheads entered the large sack of their body. Once past the jelly, most of the missiles broke off when they reached the tough underlying skin. Only a few of the sea creatures fell, as the others reached the summit and propelled themselves onto the walkways.

Nearly every bow was replaced with swords. The Eldertude soldiers surrounded the Raging Squid, looking for a weak spot. There were no visible eyes but only two gaping holes, lined with teeth. Attached to the end of every tentacle, was pincers filled with venom. From every angle the soldiers came from, the Raging Squid would respond by slicing open anyone caught in the tentacles. Some made it through with a well-timed run, sticking a blade deep into the sack. Purple jelly spilt out with the slimy organs dripping to the floor.

As the duel continued at the top of the castle, below, the Tulus were taking advantage. Once they had arrived at the foot of the wall, the real work began. One soldier would cover the other as they started to put together all the individual parts. Quickly, the ladders were increasing in size; others threw up hooks to any branches which could connect it all together.

"Get ready to be face to face with those sea dogs," the Eldertude commander bellowed.

"There are too many of the Raging Squid to clear all the ladders."

"Stop wasting time with the rocks then."

All of the boulders were released at once. They plummeted from the side of the castle walls crashing down the valley. Most rocked went towards the three iron walkers. The lead took nearly the full force of the stones. As the Tulus soldiers crouched down and lifted, eventually shells of the iron walkers were flipped over. Underneath revealed a number of horses, almost bolted to the floor. One of the many sacks they carried tumbled and then detonated.

The explosion caused nearly everyone in the kingdom to jump, including the iron walker behind. It charged over the smoking corpses; the soldiers threw away the iron case but the horses kept running. Colliding with the walls, there was another huge eruption. A shockwave ripped a hole in the deep chambers of the bark. Millions of circles that had formed over centuries disintegrated in a flash. Vines caught the fire like a fuse; the heat seared up to bushes with the emerald leaves catching alight.

"The castle is burning!" one of the Eldertude soldiers

yelled. Others charged through the flames to challenge the Raging Squid. More Tulus were mounting the ladders. Spears and arrows would send some plummeting to their death. Others would push on, holding a shield in one hand.

From the tower, King Vidal watched the smoke rise up from the castle walls. On the walkways, soldiers on both sides clashed whilst the Raging Squid were rampant.

"Release the panthers."

"My king, we never let them free inside the castle. It's the rule as we cannot truly control them in a confined space. Why not direct the Hammers to the tops?"

"No the Hammers are not to be wasted on those vile squids. The instincts of the panthers will drive them to fight the other beasts. Then they will mop up any of the Tulus stupid enough to walk on my walls. Concentrate our soldiers on bringing down the ladders and putting out the fires. These are my orders."

The barriers to windowless buildings were dropped. Out came a swarm of black fur in all directions. Handlers ran with them, gloves pointed at the Raging Squid. Blood, flames, and chaos rained down upon the animals' senses. The Raging Squid leapt off the walls towards the pack. Their tentacles wrapped around as many of the panthers as they could; this time though it was met with superior strength. Twisting their bodies and dinging their fangs, they cut through the thick skin. Chucks of the jelly ran down the chins as the Raging Squid failed to shake them off.

Vibrations could be felt across the castle, as horns sounded the gates were opening. Vidal screamed at the soldiers around him. Hammers on horseback stampeded towards the blue line, spearheaded by the general. Hector's limp body still hung in the air. The legs of the horses barely touched the ground as they moved with such speed.

Smoke quickly filled the main courtyard; through the grey blankets came a rapid test. Tulus soldiers started to appear, flying towards Kantra. Pushing Maxen back, she used both swords to fend off strikes. Quickly surrounded, the only option was to dart in between them. Spinning round, Kantra met each swordsman, one after another, until she was dictating the tempo. Jumping back, one of the Tulus soldiers missed and was punished for his mistake. Kantra dragged both swords across the face, causing the soldier's jaw to drop.

There was no let up for the other swordsmen. With an immense furry, Kantra beat the swords out of their hands. No mercy was shown to the defenceless Tulus soldiers. Small victories meant nothing with the numbers still pouring in. Kantra was yet again outnumbered and was trying her best not to be sliced open. A long sword came crashing down towards her face. Ducking at the last second, Kantra then sprung back up, pushing both swords into the chest plate. The action sent the Tulus soldier spinning into the others. One that had been more patient picked her moment and struck onto the arm of Kantra.

Ignoring the pain, Kantra remembered a move Latch had taught her, only to be used as a last resort. After a powerful block, Kantra lunged forward, shifting her whole body in a corkscrew motion. With both arms outstretched, the swords spun in a deadly circle. The theatrical and acrobatic move caught the Tulus soldiers by surprise, as did the deadly tips of both swords. As if inspired by the lone duellers' display, the Eldertude soldiers had rallied.

Kantra backed off and looked up. There seemed to be more Tulus coming over the top of the castle walls, despite the panthers running wild. More had entered the courtyard and with the Hammers riding out, the defences were bare. Kantra made a split decision; grabbing Maxen, both of them slipped out the castle gates just before they closed.

From the rear of the Tulus army, Captain Holsten stared down the barrel of his telescope. The plans to topple the unbreakable castle were working. For all the vast amount of gold spent on spies, the information had been spot on. Married with his own memory, the few weak spots had been exposed, if not for a stroke of good fortune. Still though, there was much work to be done, starting with dealing with the fury racing towards them. It was in the form of General Balder and the Hammers racing towards them.

"As the king watches, the general marches on. We have managed to separate the heart and brain." Holsten closed his telescope.

"The strategy seems to be working," Alden said.

"It appears that way; although, I will not be celebrating until we are dining in the royal halls."

"Any thought on what we will do with the king, if we catch him alive?"

"Every man, woman, and child will be sacrificed before that happens. We will have him breathing. He will be questioned first before I sentence him to death."

A single cry came from the near flank of the Tulus army. The soldiers closest to the source of all turned at once. Around the captain, the High Sea Rollers held their ground. The SIDD were descending on them like a black cloud, the valley was a swarm of the cursed. As the SIDD met the Rollers, they swung their swords in one motion, collectively cutting through the first charge with razor sharp precision. A new line of High Sea Rollers would step in and deliver the same blow. It did not however stop the flow of the SIDD. Some broke the line and immediately created bedlam within the ranks.

Stallions hit the front of the Tulus. Outnumbered by an overwhelming majority, the Hammers showed no fear as they pushed into the centre of the blue army. Bread for one purpose, they were now being given the chance to fulfil their destiny. Hammers, broad swords, and axes sliced down on their enemy. Representing their resilience was General Balder, his spiked hammer now red with blood and flesh hanging from the tips.

"On me, Hammers!" Balder yelled out, turning his horse. The bladed hooves had already left a trail of dead. With the captain in danger, the High Sea Rollers had been so focused on moving him away from the SIDD, that it had come almost as a shock as the horses came crashing towards them. Remembering their training, the Rollers composed themselves as the ground vibrated. Reflexes like a butterfly, the guard's side stepped at the last moment, leaving only their swords in the path of the animals' legs. Crying out in pain, the great stallions came crashing down.

The general hit the ground hard and let go of his hammer. There was no time to recover as the Tulus soldiers were upon him. Drawing out a knife the size of a small sword, he blocked one attack from the ground and pushed back. Balder was now on his feet and cursing. With the blade pointing towards his wrist, he went on the assault. Punching straight into the face, the general would follow through with the knife. One soldier swung an axe straight for the head but was stopped with his free hand—only to have their guts ripped open. Quickly enough, the Hammers arrived, making a circle around their general, giving him time to retrieve his own hammer.

A High Sea Roller tore off their cloak, revealing sleek gold and blue armour. Holding up a sword, they waited for the duel to begin. General Balder swung his weapon with such speed, that it crashed into the shoulder. The might of the hammer could not be blocked. Staggering backwards, the Roller then was set upon by an axe. Those from Eldertude were using brute force to batter their way toward the captain.

"I thought your guards were meant to be elite," the general shouted, spitting in the direction of Holsten. Two of the Rollers came forward; a Hammer pushed past Balder to meet them. The Hammer missed, one of the blades sliced through the Hammer's outstretched wrist. Leaning down, the other Roller put its sword right into his gut. Using the Hammer as a shield, Balder pushed the soldier onto the Roller. As they were pinned under the weight, spikes were crushed into the Roller's skull.

"Be a man and fight me, Holsten. You owe me your life for my son."

"Do not try and pretend to have honour, sending a silent dagger in the night like a coward."

"I would have never sent my boy to kill you. He was picked up in the open plains and murdered by savage seamen. You wanted a fight hanging him to that flag, well you have one now."

The general held a hammer in one hand, the knife in the other. More High Sea Rollers circled the captain but were met with the Eldertude Hammers. It left a clear path for the two figureheads to meet. Balder started by trying to break his opponent in two. Thunderous aggression rained down on Holsten, who was ducking and rolling for his life. Even with the sword drawn the captain could not get any sort of counterattack.

He did have one advantage; being more agile and fit, the general would surely burn out faster. Although there were no signs so far, the determination in the general's eyes had not faltered. Giving a swing of the hammer, Holsten dropped to his knees and dug his sword into Balder's belly. He did not get far as the general replied with the knife, snapping the steel inside of him. The large man grunted as Holsten backed off holding half a sword.

"I did not ride out into the centre of an army to survive."

Blood was steaming from the wound; the captain picked up a loose sword and went for the kill. He had misjudged how the drive for revenge could affect the body. The general came bounding towards him and drove the back of the hammer into Holsten's chest. Landing on his back, the general took another swing, the spikes coming straight for him.

A force crushed Holsten; he was struggling to breathe. There were however no punctures to his skin. A Roller had thrown himself into the path of the hammer, taking the full force of the blow. The dead soldier lay on top of him; the captain tried to push off the dead body but Balder loomed over. A thick black boot with all the weight behind kept Holsten pinned.

"Been practising with those slippery fish, have we? Well, there is nowhere to hide now."

Holsten could not reply as he dug around in the dirt gasping for air.

"This is for Hector."

Balder lifted the hammer high into the air. Raindrops were running down his arms. Storm clouds were now circling ahead, partnered with a ferocious crack of thunder. The general looked up; there were flashes of light all across the land. One was coming straight for him. A blue and black flame hit, blowing away all in its path. Screams could be heard as the hot, acidic cloud ate through skin and metal. All that was left were scorching trails zigzagging across the mud.

Delivering the bursts of the deadly flames, with the storm circling behind, was Thangrath. Black wings spread wide as they soared over Eldertude. It was like a nightmare that had burst into reality. The entire kingdom watched as the legend came to life. All the fighting had stopped. The SIDD inches away from blades and spears just stood with their hands to the sky. Thangrath gave another roar of destruction; it hit the castle like a meteor, causing the ground to shake. The tremors snapped the battlefield out of its haze.

Soldiers on both sides did not know whether to flee for cover or continue the battle. Archers aimed upwards and fired as the demon cut through the gales. More blue flames took chunks out of the Tulus army. With their captain smouldering in the dirt, any military organisation went out of the window. Some started heading for the boats. Through the flames and smoke, Eldertude soldiers cheered at the signs of retreat. Thangrath horns turned in the direction of their voices. Swooping down into the eye line of the castle gates, it took a deep breath. A huge cloud of definitive power was launched head on.

The gates had been split open; the unthinkable was happening. Tulus rushed inside, gripping onto their helmets. Eldertude soldiers held back as everyone searched for some type of sanctuary. Vidal watched as the kingdom descended into madness. So many voices on the balcony begged for orders, some type of direction. The king had inherited his responsibilities thanks to his bloodline, nothing more. Now, a tyrant had come to rip down that legacy, one which had taken the collective world powers to stop before.

"The castle is lost," Vidal said almost to himself. One of the soldiers asked him to repeat the words. "Nothing can be done to defend against that winged demon. It will consume us all. Let the Tulus be the cover we need to get as far away from this place."

Quickly, the king shuffled past his speechless soldiers and disappeared down the stairwell. Only one decided to follow. Outside, men and women continued to lay down their lives in a vain attempt to challenge Thangrath. As it glided close to walls, two stone arrows launched at once. Both hit the same wing, causing the demon to spin round. More black clouds were released, spiralling in all directions. Acid flames came bursting down the walkways of the castle. One of the younger soldiers dived onto the king, pushing him into an empty corridor. As the flames passed, the two got to their feet.

"My king, are you okay?"

Vidal brushed himself off.

"The demon, I have only ever heard stories about it. As soon as I saw the castle in flames, I left my unit, in order to protect you, my king."

Despite the raging battle outside, the young man's uniform was spotless. Vidal looked him up and down. Jet black eyes stared back at him.

"Why is your uniform so clean, there are no marks of the battle?

The soldier kept the king's gaze.

"As I said, my purpose has always been to protect my king. Even when all the king's allies burn around him."

Vidal said nothing for what seemed an age. There was no one else coming.

"Very well follow me."

"Are we really leaving the castle?"

"Look around you. Think we can defend against this? I have a better plan; one that will benefit the kingdom in the long run. This is not the end by any means."

"So what is the next move?"

"First, get me a cloak, one with a hood. Then I need a horse. If you want to come with me and help save Eldertude, no more questions. Otherwise, stay here and burn with it."

"Yes, my king. My name is Jocks."

"I did not ask."

Sticking out of sight, the pair weaved in amongst the anarchy. Soldiers and residents ran past them. Eventually, they found the last untouched stables. Each horse was teaming with energy; the tension from the battle had filtered its way in. The king chose the black steed which tried to throw him off straight away.

"Get your own horse then let them all out at once."

Jocks did as instructed. Out bolted a stampede of white and black stallions and mares. The parade flew past the courtyard and out the burning gates. Bursting onto the battlefield, there was free rein for the horses. Thangrath swooped down and went to take to a bite out of the lead. Catching the hip of the horse, it then collapsed. Those following so closely behind could not jump out of the way in time. Vidal and Jocks' horses went crashing down with them.

A young gardener rushed through the gates; he could not remember the last time he had been inside the castle. It was far from the pictures in his memories. Flowers and trees were inflamed, the colour and life drained out of the plants. In the air was the stench of death. Panthers ran wild soaked in blood.

"The monsters; they are coming."

More residents pushed into the gardener, who clung onto

a small bundle of cloth. Without realising, he now was face to face with Tulus soldiers. Pulling back a blanket, he revealed a wisp of blonde hair. The soldiers said nothing but let him pass. He then ran into one of the main chambers for shelter; straight away his eyes were burning. Thick grey clouds surrounded him. As he pushed forward, he started to drown in the smoke. Turning around, the entrance was now hidden. The lack of air was pushing him to his knees. Coughs could be heard from the bundle close to his chest.

Out of the darkness, an arm grabbed the young gardener. It gave him the strength to carry himself out of the pool of smoke. It led him into a small courtyard, littered with a number of other evacuees. Luca was helping the man find a seat, whilst Erica tended to the baby.

"We will not be able to stay here much longer. The fire is relentless, even if it did stop us from being thrown into the dungeons. We will not get the chance to slip away twice," Erica said.

"I never thought I would see the castle like this."

"Plants can be grown again, not lives though, Luca. We need to get these people out."

"There might be a way, but we must hurry."

All along the tops of the walls, a black shadow had emerged. Soldiers of the Infamous lined the walkways. On the ground level, they surrounded the exits as the castle was boxed in. Helplessly, the courtyard braced as the demon soared again, straight into the royal tower. Using its claws to rip the roots which held it in place, the tower collapsed on itself. Landing on the remains of the prince's room, Thangrath seemed to be enjoying being the centre of attention.

"So, the last castle was simple enough to crush as twigs

and leaves. How very helpful that so many of you have slaughtered each other. Many seem surprised by the return of my presence. Did you really believe I could be contained forever? No longer does the grey man direct me. This is my world, and I will do with it what I see fit. For now, I have an army truly fit to follow me."

Thangrath leaned forward and opened its jaws. Rather than unleash a ball of flames, the demon gagged. Out dropped Rexis into the centre of the courtyard. Covered in slime, he had the look of a newborn baby. Both sets of soldiers watched in disbelief as he gingerly stood up. A Tulus soldier then charged sword in hand; Rexis dodged with ease. Other soldiers joined the assault, but they seemed to be moving in slow motion. Rexis hit out, sending a body flying across the courtyard. Quickly, the others backed off; horror consumed their gaze. SIDD slowly gathered around Rexis. He held up both his black hands as the cursed army waited for orders.

Still wobbling, Holsten was also back on his feet. Tying a cloth around the burns to his arm, he could still move his fingers. Taking a deep breath, he then poured water over the side of his steaming face. Next to the captain was the crisp body of the Roller, which had shielded him from death. Firstly, it had been in the form of the general's hammer, then the fire of Thangrath. Others lay in smouldering craters as the landscape was scarred by the black streaks. Most of the Tulus had fallen back to shores, as the captain already assumed he was missing in action.

Amongst the bodies were also the remains of horses. One was still kicking out from the floor. Picking up a sword, Holsten went to end the suffering. Before he could reach it, the black stallion cried out. A cloaked figure wormed its way from under the beast.

"It is true then; you really are a coward."

Vidal reacted by spinning round to face Holsten. As he saw the captain, he sighed.

"How could you leave your castle, your post? That's your people back there, crying out for leadership."

"Give it a rest, Holsten; there is no crowd to hear you now."

"You are pathetic."

"So says the leader who has been hiding under his dead soldiers. This would not be the first time you have chucked bodies into the path of destruction. Look around you. Think there is any chance of stopping that demon? You started this war, but it has gotten away from both of us. It is time to re-build then conquer again."

"No wonder the queen wanted a real man."

Vidal picked up a sword. Turning around, he threw himself into the path of a loose horse. Managing to slow the animal down, he then jumped onto the back.

"Do not run from me; we need to finish this."

The numbers of the SIDD kept on growing as Thangrath blew more flames into the castle. Eldertude and Tulus soldiers now stood shoulder to shoulder. Both fatigued and bleeding, they now faced the common enemy. Erica and Luca waited with other residents. One of the soldiers rushed past and put a weapon in both their hands.

"Do not expect any mercy from those monsters."

Turning around, Erica watched as the elderly and children were handed weapons.

"It cannot end like this; there has to be more than this misery."

Luca kissed Erica, only once delicately on the lips.

"We are about to be obliterated; let's not make it any more awkward," Erica responded.

The SIDD made their move, tearing into the soldiers. Thangrath had not moved from his perch, occasionally sending down clouds of death. Those caught in it would have the flesh torn from their bones; the others could only wait to be next. Erica and Luca stood close together, holding hands, ready for the end.

A burst of light ripped through the storm, splitting the sky in two. Moving at incredible speed a force, it hit Thangrath, sending it crashing through more parts of the castle. The rain then abruptly stopped. As the clouds started to clear, rays of sunlight found their way through the darkness.

Light was glistening off the gold and emerald gems of the dragon. Hanging from the neck was Prince Zander, pointing his sword at the Soldiers of the Infamous. Only a few had heard tails of the gem dragon; none had seen it before. Now with this majestic being transmitting its power, there was a new balance of good and evil. In the face of an unstoppable enemy, there was a beacon of hope. Soldiers shook off their injuries as the residents picked up weapons. Rising out of the debris, Thangrath roared.

"So this is what I have been sensing, a cast off from the world above. It does not matter what rock you crawled out from under. Paraforce or not, I cannot be stopped."

In one motion, the SIDD charged toward the crowd. Soldiers and residents alike met them head on. The remaining panthers joined them, leaping onto the cursed enemy. Driven by a new sense of hope, the wave of resistance had transformed into an energy never seen before. The fighting was furious; the SIDD were charged up like crazed animals. Swords went deep into the cursed skin as the black fists shattered bones. Thangrath charged full force into the gem dragon, sending both of them twisting upwards. Fangs were locked onto the gem dragon; it replied by clawing into the wings. As they became entangled, both started to plummet to the ground.

At the last moment, they broke away to glide across the battlefield. Each had a fist full of flesh of their opponent. Now a fair distance apart, they picked up speed, before they came crashing together again. Such the velocity of the two powers colliding sent them flying into the castle walls; soldiers and SIDD alike were thrown from the walkways.

Erica was melted to the floor; the horrors of the centre now charged toward her. Amongst the monstrosities she could see the faces of Mills, Dace, and Otto. More innocent were being beaten to death. Taking a deep breath, she pushed past the fear and lashed out at the SIDD— almost on top of them. The blade bounced off the tough black skin. Luca tried again by pushing the tip of his sword into the chest. He was rewarded with a firm fist to the gut, sending him to his knees. Erica went to shield him as the SIDD lined up another strike. The tip of a sword then burst out of the throat; another then sliced off the head.

"This is no time for a nap," Kantra said, pushing the body away.

Erica winced "My ribs feel broken."

"Would you prefer it if it was your skull."

"Did you ever find the heart?" Erica almost whispered.

"No, it is gone for good, along with Colton."

"Then why are you here?" Erica asked. Maxen stepped out from behind Kantra. "I meant still here then; I'd thought you'd have left."

"We tried but it's too dangerous outside the walls. I had to kill one of those stupid panthers just to get back. Also, we are still missing one more," Kantra replied.

The battle of the sky continued. Thangrath fired off a ball of black flame so close to the gem dragon, it was forced to shield itself. Blocking with its gold wings, the flames left black stains.

The next wave would burn through. Thangrath took a deep breath. Sensing the danger the dragon roared. With it the gems studded down its spine began to glow. Thangrath unloaded again but this time it was met with its own contest. Hot roaring orange flowed out of the jaws of the gem dragon. Meeting in the air, the flames exploded with contact. As the titans circled each other, both were landing hits but no deadly blows.

"This is a waste of my time. I will not tire, and my slaves will not stop. It only ends once I have torn this world to dust," Thangrath roared.

"That cannot be allowed to happen. Eldertude will not be allowed to burn. There is no more a sign than the fire now unleashed from my heart, it has never happened before," Garnet boomed back.

"Why care about such a selfish race which is beneath you? One which causes more headaches than they solve. Ruling them does not work, they must be destroyed if I am to have peace."

"When I was born, I needed protection; now it is my turn to offer it. Unity will help rebuild lands once evil has been eradicated."

"Such a fool; I tried to side with them once and it caused the same result. They only end up turning on themselves.

This war had started before I had even arrived. It will end for all of them today. At least this way it is over quicker.

"I am not the only one fighting."

The gem dragon landed in the castle and lowered its neck. Dressed in a full suit of armour appeared Prince Zander. Head held high, he marched across the courtyard, the helmet catching the sun.

"The prince is alive!" Luca cried, running into the courtyard. Their eyes met and a smile crossed Zander's face.

Quickly, the SIDD surrounded Zander; they clicked their knuckles and spat out blood. At once, they attacked, punches coming from all angles. Ducking and twisting, Zander replied with the sword taken from the cave. It ripped straight through the torso, leaving the SIDD in half. One grabbed Zander's shoulder, digging its fingers through the steel. Zander took hold of the wrist and twisted the whole arm. The sword then came into its stomach. Keeping a grip on the SIDD, Zander then used it to shield off the others.

More Soldiers of the Infamous arrived, trying to overpower the prince. As he carved through more punches, one eventually landed. Zander turned and ran up to the castle walkways, the horde tight on his heels. Waiting for him was a panther, an orange streak across its face. It roared at his presence, spit and blood hanging from the fangs. Zander held up a hand and then pointed it in the direction of the SIDD. Immediately, the beast launched itself, Zander going with it. The two of them cut through the pack. As the panther clasp its jaws on the cursed army, it threw SIDD from the walkways. Even with the blows to his body, Zander kept fighting back.

SIDD grabbed at Zander's back, dragging him to the floor. Cutting through the shins and ankles, there was no end to the kicks and punches. Quickly, he was in danger of being crushed to red dust. Then, like a tidal wave, the panther stampeded into the mass, sending the SIDD flying. It stood over Zander, the hot breath leaving dampness on his face.

The moment was short lived, as the animal was lifted into the air and flung from the walkway. Zander sized up the monster in front of him. Unlike the others, there were still hints of the former person. Readying his sword, the SIDD stared into Zander's eyes. Amongst the darkness was the same look of underline fear, masked by a newfound sense of power.

"What am I?"

Zander did not reply; somehow he recognised the voice. The SIDD roared the words again. More were gathering behind him, but the other SIDD stopped their advance.

"You can feel it too, the grey man."

Rexis' stomach lit up. Instinctively, Zander lashed out with the sword, straight into the torso. The blade cut deep into the flesh. Still with their eyes locked, Rexis grabbed the prince's wrist. Steam appeared as the grip burnt through the armour. Zander pulled away, leaving Rexis to fall to his knees, the sword still in him.

Above, the sky was darkening; blue flames engulfed the walkways. The SIDD now blocked all the exits. Zander felt weak and defences. As the SIDD charged, there was only one option left. Taking a deep breath, Zander leapt from the wall. As he plummeted to the ground, only one thought went through his mind; the stone on his helmet lit up. Swooping underneath, the gem dragon timed it perfectly.

"Good catch; I was worried the bond had been broken," Zander thought, as the helmet flashed again.

"We cannot keep up this fight. I am almost out of energy. It does not matter how many of the SIDD you defeat, there will always be more. This needs to end now" Garnet replied.

"It came from the sky; maybe that is where we should send it."

"If we do that, there will be no return."

The gem dragon turned and directed its flight path, beating its wings at an incredible speed. Flames were launched but the dragon sailed straight through into the chest of Thangrath. The three of them soared upwards. Chucks of flesh and blood flowed with them. Thangrath was digging in its fangs, but the gem dragon did not flinch. One of the claws was then jammed into its eye. The gem dragon howled out in pain; they twisted and stalled in the air. Zander held on for dear life.

"Keep flying."

Holsten gripped the fur; it had been years since he had ridden a horse. Somehow, he still had the king in his sights. As they raced down the valley, they were heading towards the shore. It would not be long before he lost Vidal. Turning a blind corner, an abandoned cart blocked the road. With hesitation from the pole position, Holsten took his opportunity. Digging in his heels, he pushed his horse to leap off the closest ridge, landing right in front of Vidal.

"Get out of the way," Vidal hissed.

"Can you even feel shame?" Holston cried.

"Did you seriously ride all the way here to ask me that?"

"No, you must answer for your crimes. You kept the cursed here; now, they have turned against you," Holsten said, moving his horse to block Vidal's path.

"So it would have been better to cast them out into oblivion. At least we tried a practical solution of containment, rather than sending them out into the world. That's not why you are here though, is it?"

"I am here as an act of war was declared on Neptulus. You sent an assassin after me."

"So because someone tried to kill you, the entire kingdom set sail to face certain death. So they could die in the name of their captain's honour. Even now, when his army needs him most, the captain leaves the battlefield to settle a personal vendetta. We are the same, Holsten. No wonder Hermenize decided to stay with me. At least that way she got to live in a castle rather than a rotting ship."

Both of the men drew their swords. The horses reared up and then charged. Colliding with each other, there was a loud crash of steel. Each man picked their moment to swing and catch the other with a deadly blow. The two horses passed and slowed right down. Holsten looked down to his chest plate; there was a long scratch down the centre. Laughing to himself, he gloated at the miss. Vidal just smiled back. An arrow came thundering past. As Holsten fell, another missile hit him. Jocks rode down from the ridge.

"Give me the bow."

Holsten's wide eyes stared up at Vidal. His chest kept gasping for air which would not come. The king grinned and dropped the weapon.

"The leader of Neptulus is no more. You did well; that was not an easy shot. Now ends one of the bloodlines from the days of the union. His people are bound to seek revenge, no matter how many generations it may take. Looks like we both now need to lie low. Take me to the boats."

The battle in the castle was almost over. With the soldiers almost depleted, the SIDD continued their relentless slaughter. Erica's head was bleeding; she waved her sword in a desperate attempt to keep the semi-conscious Luca safe.

Maxen was crying as he watched the curse figures surround their small group. Kantra's arms were covered in wounds. Breathing heavily, she took her stance yet again with a sword in each hand. Dozens of bodies of the SIDD twitched around her. Another came swinging for the head. Kantra ducked underneath the punch and then spun round to the back. Jumping up, she plunged both the swords into the shoulders. The SIDD stumbled forward and then fell from the walkway.

Up above, dragon and demon still rocketed into the sky. The castle was quickly disappearing. As the air thinned Zander could feel his grip loosening. Thangrath let out a large ball of black flames; the heat raged through scales and skin. Zander caught fire and let go. Falling from the dragon's back, he grasped at nothing. A diamond studded tail caught him. Hanging on by one hand, the gem dragon pushed to the furthest point of the horizon. Thangrath roared as there was an enormous burst of light.

Everyone within the castle covered their eyes. Light engulfed every corner of Eldertude. As the red giant crashed into the small blue sun, the eternal partnership ended with an explosion. Darkness then followed with no stars to support the blackness.

A SIDD gripped the throat of Kantra; the power of the hold felt like a boulder had landed on her windpipe. It pulled her off the ground; she kicked back with no effect as the life was draining out of her. It pulled her face close, not flinching at the balls of saliva coming its way. Kantra could do nothing but stare back at the cursed, dead pupils. Around the eyes, the black rotting skin was starting to burn. Small puffs of smoke started to appear across the SIDD's face.

Rays of violet light were beaming down on them. One huge ball of the purple sun now dominated the sky. Kantra could feel the grip on her throat loosening. The SIDD dropped to its knees. Others followed suit; falling to the ground, they started to shake. Each of the cursed bodies seemed a magnet for the sunlight. Shrivelling up to nothing, the SIDD burst into ash. Nobody in the kingdom could believe what was happening; the cursed army had crumbled in front of them. In the burning wreck of the castle, cheers rang out.

"Luca, we are safe."

Erica cradled him on the floor; he beckoned for her to come closer. Leaning in, Erica then smiled.

"We are, honestly. And yes, you still do have your stupid badge."

There was a thud right next to them. More followed as bright and shiny objects hit the ground. The sky was raining diamonds and gold.

## Author's Note

Thank you so much for taking the time to read this book. I hoped you enjoyed it.

I initially started this book in 2013, before my wife broke my laptop and I had to start again. It has been roughly 7 years in the making.

The next book in the series is already being written 'Making of Elements: The Fall of Starvogue City'.

It focuses on when Thangrath first fell from the sky, leading up to the release of the deadly curse which changed the world forever.

Joseph Doliczny

Twitter: @NeverStopMOE

Facebook: /Making of Elements